TIME OUT FOR TEA?

"Shh," Jens said to his cousin Faral. "Here's the food now." The cook was coming out of the kitchen with a loaded tray which held a steaming pot of ruddy liquid and a porcelain platter with a pile of small round things under a napkin.

Then, without warning, the cook's posture shifted and she heaved the tray full of hot tea and pastries straight at their table. Faral threw himself sideways off his chair as the heavy crystal pot flew towards him. He thought he saw Jens ducking in the other direction, but he didn't have a chance to look. Immer-leaf tea splashed in all directions as the pot flew past where his head had been, and parchant buns pattered down like hailstones.

The cook was still moving, bringing up one foot in a kick that knocked the table over completely. He recognized the move—it was a common one in the hand-to-hand he'd learned growing up back home—but where did a sweet little old gentlelady pastry-cook learn something like that?

Porcelain crashed and broke into splinters, silverware crashed and slid and clattered, and somewhere close behind him a man shouted in surprise and pain. Faral took a chance on glancing up from the floor, and saw a man in tea-soaked blue and white livery clawing at his scalded face. In the next moment, a heavy blaster fired close by. Then another blaster fired near at hand—once, twice, three times—the crimson energy bolts taking the scalded man in the chest and head as he fell.

"Get on your feet, boys," said the cook, who had somehow acquired a blaster.

THE
LONG HUNT

**DEBRA DOYLE AND
JAMES D. MACDONALD**

A TOM DOHERTY ASSOCIATES BOOK
NEW YORK

This is a work of fiction. All the characters and events portrayed in this book are fictitious, and any resemblance to real people or events is purely coincidental.

THE LONG HUNT

Copyright © 1996 by Debra Doyle and James D. Macdonald

Cover art by Romas

A Tor Book
Published by Tom Doherty Associates, Inc.
175 Fifth Avenue
New York, NY 10010

Tor Books on the World Wide Web:
http://www.tor.com

Tor® is a registered trademark of Tom Doherty Associates, Inc.

ISBN: 0-812-53496-4

First edition: August 1996

Printed in the United States of America

0 9 8 7 6 5 4 3 2 1

For Nancy Hanger and Andrew Phillips

Prologue
Maraghai

THE LAST part of the journey he had to make on foot.

He'd come a long way, beginning in the Eraasi Sector and finishing with a suborbital hop to the long-range hoverbus that ran upcountry from Ernalghan—or South Landing, as the speakers of Galcenian Standard would have it. Not even the locals bothered to call the loose collection of warehouses and transport terminals a city, even though it was the second-largest built-up area on Maraghai. As far as Mael could determine, nobody actually lived in Ernalghan. They lived outside of it, strung out along the dozens of obscure roads and narrow footpaths that led away from the hoverbus route into the deep wilderness that covered so much of this planet. The house he was looking for was a half-day of steady walking beyond the last stop on the route.

He could have hired an aircar at South Landing—most people did—but he lacked the skill to fly one. The Eraasi of his childhood had lost the means of making such vehicles in the aftermath of the First Magewar. Mael could drive a ground-hugging flivver, and he could take a combat-equipped scoutship into hyperspace and out again, but he'd never picked up the knack of handling the nullgrav-assisted atmospheric craft that were commonplace on this side of the Gap Between.

He'd come to the opportunity too late, he supposed. He'd been a man full-grown when the Second War ended and the barriers between the homeworlds and the rest of the galaxy came down at last. He was more than happy to let the young people—the ones who remembered neither war nor deprivation—enjoy the new technologies without him.

The walk was long, but not difficult for anyone who had grown up on Eraasi in the days of the Republic's occupation. Mael wasn't young—his straight black hair had long since gone mostly to iron grey—but he came of hardy stock, and kept a steady pace on the uphill path. This wasn't the first time he'd made the journey from Eraasi to the house in the high reaches of Maraghai's southern continent, but it was the first time in almost twenty years.

The passage had given him less trouble in those earlier days. Twenty years ago—the recent war notwithstanding—most people on the Republic's side of the Gap Between had never met a genuine Eraasian. More and more, however, prosperity and ease of travel were giving people the chance, and not all of them had forgotten the war. Life spans were long on the Adept-worlds; some of the men and women Mael encountered had memories that went back farther than his own, to the Sack of Ilarna and the destruction of Entibor.

He might have experienced less trouble, he thought, if he had left behind the short ebony staff that marked him out as not merely a Mageworlder, but a Mage in truth. But that would have felt disloyal, to abandon the training of a lifetime—and the legacy of a friend and teacher—just to avoid hostile stares and bureaucratic entanglements.

And Mael Taleion was, above all things, a loyal man.

I. Maraghai; Galcen

Up on Graksha's Bluff the air was cool, but by late afternoon the sun had warmed the bare rock to basking temperature. The wind that sighed and rustled through the trees on the slope below brought with it a smell of conifers, sharp and resinous, underlaid with the dry granite smell of the mountain itself. Jens Metadi-Jessan lay on his back half-dozing, his eyes closed against the brightness of the sky overhead, and heard the faint scrape of boot leather on stone as his cousin Faral shifted position a few feet away.

"Noisy, coz," he said without opening his eyes. "Too noisy by half."

"Be grateful I decided to wake you up gently, thin-skin."

"Your skin's no thicker than mine . . . what's up?"

"Company at dinner, I think," said Faral. "I spotted somebody down on the valley trail."

"Let's have a look."

Jens sat up and joined Faral near the edge of the bluff. The cousins were much of an age, but otherwise resembled each other very little. Faral Hyfid-Metadi was dark-skinned, stocky, and heavily muscled, with sleek, close-trimmed black hair. A polished animal claw almost a handspan long hung from a leather cord around his neck. Jens, by contrast, was lean and fair-skinned, gone a pale biscuit golden from the sun. His yellow hair, tied back with a scrap of rough twine, hung in a loose tail between his shoulder blades. Like Faral, he wore boots and trousers, but—on this day in mid-summer—no shirt.

From up on Graksha's Bluff, the valley trail looked like a darker line drawn against a background of green. Now and again, a flash of sunlight reflecting off clear water marked where the stream at the bottom of the valley ran parallel to the trail for a short distance before diverging again into the trees. A group of black specks swirled upward from the tree-tops far away.

"Let me have a look," Jens said, and Faral passed him a pair of binoculars.

He watched the trail below for some time. "You're right," he said finally. "Something sure disturbed all the rattlewings along that stretch."

"Something on the ground," Faral said, "and coming this way at a walking pace. Offworlder, maybe."

"Maybe," agreed Jens. The local fauna wouldn't disturb the noisy fliers, and none of the neighbors—in the generous High Ridges sense of the word—would bother walking the valley trail. Most of them lived far enough away to make taking an aircar more practical; the few who lived closer came and went by hidden deep-woods tracks. Even somebody from elsewhere on planet would have known to rent a tree-skimmer in Ernalghan. "I wonder who it is."

"Somebody who didn't send word ahead, that's who." Faral sounded disapproving.

"That lets out most of the people we know." Jens considered the possibilities for a moment. "Maybe it's somebody who doesn't like talking on the public links."

"What kind of person is that?"

"A private one, at a guess. One of Father's relatives, maybe, if they wanted to be rude."

"What for?" Faral asked. "Mamma never notices—and Aunt Bee would give them hell if she ever found out. Not even a Khesatan would go through all that trouble for nothing."

"You don't know 'em, coz. There's one or two in the crowd who'd slit their own noses if they thought they could get at Father that way." Jens looked down again at the solitary figure on the trail below. "But you've got a point. I can't imagine any of them going so far as to hoof it all the way uphill from Ernalghan."

If it's a blood feud, cut in a third voice, *do I get to help out?*

The speaker was a young Selvauran female whose scaly hide was decorated in whorls of red and blue body enamel. She scrambled up onto the bluff and unslung a bulging backpack from her shoulders. Chakallakak *ngha*-Chakallakak—known as Chaka for short—stood over a head taller than Jens, which put her at medium height for one of the Forest Lords, and her scales under the body paint were a mottled bluish green. She set down the backpack and joined the two young men at the edge of the bluff.

"If I ever get in a blood feud," Jens promised her, "you'll be the first to know."

Faral, meanwhile, was eyeing the patterns in Chaka's body paint. *You get thrown out?*

Chaka grinned—courteously, with no teeth showing—and said, *Finally. I thought they'd never get around to it.*

"We know how you feel," said Jens. "The elders haven't decided what they're going to do with Faral yet, and it's been almost a year."

Do like I did, Chaka advised. *Pack your bag yourself and leave it sitting in the middle of the floor until they get tired of walking around it and take the hint.*

Faral scowled. *I might . . . I've tried everything else. Any idea where you're going to go?*

Away somewhere. There's no good fighting anyplace, worse luck.

"Don't let Aunt Llann hear you talking like that," said Jens. "She already thinks you're a bad influence."

Chaka laughed, a breathy *hoo-hoo* noise. *No, she doesn't. She just thinks that I make your cousin act more like a Forest Lord than he already is.*

"Comes to the same thing."

"Not really," said Faral. "If Mamma didn't like Chaka, she'd have fixed it so that the wrinkleskins threw her off-planet as soon as she was blooded."

Privately, Jens doubted that his aunt would ever make a tactical error of that magnitude—but Faral and Chaka weren't likely to be convinced by his arguments. Older, wiser people than the two of them had made the mistake of thinking that just because Llannat Hyfid was quiet and kindhearted, she didn't have a firmness of purpose that the rocks themselves would envy.

When Aunt Llann decides that she wants Faral to go off-planet, he thought, *the wrinkleskins will trip over themselves to send him there. But not before.*

Mael Taleion reached the top of the valley trail shortly before sunset. The path that led away from it into the deeper forest was little more than a narrow track marked by white blazes cut into the trees on either side.

He quickened his pace—the woods of Maraghai were no place for an off-worlder to linger at night. The predators on this planet came in sizes to match the towering vegetation that covered the mountain slopes all around him, and local custom held that none of them should be slain with any weapon besides the hunter's own strength. Humans, being weak and thin-skinned compared to the dominant Selvauran population, were allowed the use of knives and clubs in cases of dire emergency.

Mael didn't want to find out the hard way how dire the emergency had to be before a Magelord's staff counted as a permissible weapon. *Simpler by far,* he thought, *to avoid catching anything's attention, and let the question go unanswered.*

The sinking sun brought a rapid darkness under the great trees. The gloom made the trail harder and harder to pick out, and the ground was by turns rocky and boggy underfoot. It would not do, Mael reflected, for him to get lost. He took his staff from his belt and called the pale green witchfire to cling around it. The blazes on the tree trunks glimmered with its reflected light, but the shadows it cast between the stones and roots below were inky black, so dark that he couldn't tell whether they were truly shadows or ankle-twisting potholes. The going got slower.

Then, off to the left, Mael saw another light flickering among the trees.

Is that the place? he wondered. *Have I been going in the wrong direction all this time?*

It was possible, he knew. He'd never followed this trail by night before. If he'd mistaken the way in the dark, or missed a branching side path, then he might keep on walking far into the high country until weariness or disaster overcame him. At the best, he'd have to backtrack, shamefaced, in the morning; and at the worst . . .

The temptation to leave the path and strike out across country was almost stronger than he could resist. He told himself that it was folly. He was no countryman, though his first teacher had been, but he knew that anywhere off the trail he risked becoming stuck in a bog, or walking across the lip of a cliff. He wished now that he'd waited overnight at the transit hub before starting, or that his legs had been younger to carry him faster over the ground.

He walked onward. The night was deep; the wind made little whispering noises under the trees, and Mael fancied he heard footsteps behind him that matched his own, and far-off voices calling out his name. Anywhere else, he would have rejected such fantasies out of hand—but not here, and not when the night had grown so thick with Power that a man need no more than half-close his eyes to see the threads and colors of it like a tapestry against the dark.

The light off to the left was bobbing like a lantern or a hand torch. Mael halted and turned toward it.

"Hello!" he called out.

The light stopped moving for a few seconds, then changed its course to intercept him. Mael wished that he had dared to walk abroad in the Adept-worlds in his proper garments, and not with his staff alone. He would have felt safer wearing the enveloping robe that blurred all question of rank or person outside the Circle, and the mask that narrowed the outside vision and made the threads of the universe easier to find and grasp. He could see them now, the *eiran*—the silver cords of life and luck—tangled and leading off in all directions.

And tarnished, some of them, which is a thing that should not be.

Which is a thing that the First must know.

The light drew closer. Mael saw now that it was coming from a man, a cloaked and hooded man—but not from any light or lantern. Instead, the entire figure was glowing, and the tarnished cords seemed to draw closer to the apparition and knot themselves around it. The man halted an arm's length away at the edge of the trail, his face a shadow underneath the hood. Only his eyes glittered in the pale green light.

The man spoke in the language of Eraasi. "What you seek to do, I will prevent."

He raised his hands and cast back his hood, and Mael saw that the face within was nothing but an empty skull. Rotting shreds of flesh and patches of matted hair stretched across the bony cranium, and the hands were skeletal and thin. But the eye sockets burned with their own lurid light.

Mael brought his staff to the guard before him. "Homeless one," he said. "Nightwalker. Go away from here and trouble me no longer."

The ghost-man laughed and brought up his right hand to strike at Mael's face. Mael swept his staff up and inward, blocking the attack. The polished ironwood of the staff passed through the man's arm as if through fog, and the blow kept on coming.

At that moment, a scream sounded from the woods behind Mael. He half-turned, distracted from the specter by the urgency of the cry—and saw, by the flickering light of his staff, a tall, fur-covered beast rearing up, its gaping mouth lined with fangs, and in front of the beast a young, fair-haired man with one hand buried deep in the creature's belly.

Man and beast stood together for an instant like a tableau. Then the youth pulled back his hand, all black with blood in the pale green witchlight, and Mael saw that he had a heavy-bladed knife a double hands-breadth long gripped in his fist.

The furry creature, man-tall, crumpled to the ground. "Rufstaffa," the young man said, wiping his blade on the animal's fur before sheathing it. "They aren't all that dangerous, but the only way to kill one is to go in through the diaphragm up to the heart, and the only time you can get there is when it's attacking."

He stuck out his blood-covered hand to Mael.

"I'm Jens, by the way," he said. "Aunt Llann asked me to come see if you'd gotten lost."

Mael returned the handclasp, feeling somewhat bemused. "You didn't happen to see another man, standing over about there . . .?" He gestured. As he had expected, the apparition was gone.

Jens shook his head. "Just you. And we'd better get moving—that rufstaffa was trailing you for the last three miles. Rufstaffas travel alone, but there's usually a slam of rockhogs following after."

"Rockhogs?"

"Scavengers. They aren't really dangerous either, but you don't want to be around them when they get into a feeding frenzy."

He pulled a hand torch from his belt and flicked it on. In the clear white light, the path seemed more open, and Mael could see his footing. The two set off together at an easy pace.

Mael followed his guide along the uphill path, sorting out the young man's names and lineage in his mind as he did so: *Jens Metadi-Jessan* in the short form common among the Adept-worlders; by Eraasian reckoning, *syn-Metadi* and *sus-Rosselin* both in his mother's line. He carried the weight of all that lineage lightly enough. In his plain trousers and his leather soft-boots, he could have been a backcountry youth from Mael's own homeworld—if somewhat taller and fairer than most.

"Mistress Hyfid knew I was coming?" Mael asked after a bit.

"So did everyone in the valley," Jens said. "The trail is easy to spot from up on the bluffs. Watch it now, the path gets a little tricky here."

"Thank you," said Mael gravely. "It's discourteous enough of me to arrive on your doorstep unannounced. To show up injured and in need of tending would be even worse."

In the mountain peaks of Galcen's northern continent, the air smelled of snowmelt and the first hints of new growth.

Mistress Klea Santreny drew a deep breath, relishing the change in the atmosphere. Even after more than two decades away from the warmth of equatorial Nammerin, she still wasn't wholly reconciled to the winters here at the Retreat. Let others think that her preference for the high collar and the close-buttoned sleeves of an Adept's formal blacks signaled an ingrained commitment to distance and rigidity. Klea knew better. If she had an ingrained commitment to anything, it was to keeping warm during the two-thirds of the year when the centuries-old stone-built citadel was—for everyone but the natives of this windy and isolated district—damned near uninhabitable.

The Master of the Guild, she supposed, counted as a native. He'd come to the Retreat for apprenticeship when he was still a boy, and had grown to manhood inside its walls. Klea knew before she opened the door to his private office that he would have celebrated today's foretaste of spring by abandoning formal garb for a lightweight coverall in dusty black . . . *and never mind that it's going to be snowing again by the end of the week, he's not going to switch back until next autumn.*

She palmed the lockplate.

"You're right," she said as the door slid open, before he could make the remark she knew he would; "it's a beautiful morning, and positively balmy outside as long as the wind isn't blowing. Of course, the wind hasn't stopped blowing since the day I first came here, and that was back in '05, but what's a minor detail like that among friends?"

Owen Rosselin-Metadi laughed under his breath. "What, indeed?"

The Master was working at his desk, a massive, domineering piece of furniture that only grudgingly shared office space with three chairs and a Standard calendar. An overhead light panel, its crude metal brackets dating back to the first time the citadel had undergone a conversion to more recent technology, supplied the room with most of its illumination. The single window was a narrow vertical opening that might at one point have been an arrow slit. These days, treble-thickness armor-glass covered the gap.

Owen gestured at the more comfortable of the room's two empty chairs—the other was reserved for unwelcome guests and errant apprentices—and went back to contemplating whichever piece of business was currently occupying his desktop. Klea sat.

"So what's today's headache?" she asked.

There was always a headache, of one kind or another. Directing—however gently—the affairs of the galaxy's Adepts took more comm time and comp time and paperwork than any one job ought, especially for a man who would have been happy to spend his days teaching the apprentices and the junior masters. In Klea's opinion, it was all Errec Ransome's fault, for selling out the Guild and betraying the Republic and then handing everything over to Owen without bothering to clean up what he had done.

Dead over twenty years, she thought, *and still screwing up everybody's lives for them. Bastard.*

If Klea Santreny hated anybody these days, it was the former Master of the Guild. But she was careful to keep those thoughts well below the surface of her mind. Owen had loved his teacher—had willingly done whatever tasks the Guild Master had set for him—and the knowledge of Ransome's treachery had been hard for him to bear.

"The galaxy is behaving itself at the moment," he said in reply to her question. "It does that, sometimes. Mostly so I can worry about my family, I think."

Klea pressed her lips together. The members of Owen's far-distant family were more than capable, in her opinion, of handling their own problems without looking to the Master of the Guild for assistance. But she'd made that argument, and lost it, too many times already. These days, she tried to cultivate patience instead.

"What about your family?" she asked.

"That's a good question." Owen touched a spot on the surface of his desktop. "All I know so far is that this showed up in the morning message traffic."

A display panel lit up the desktop where Owen had touched it: letters and numbers, routing codes of some kind or another. Klea didn't recognize them. They weren't for the Retreat, she could tell that much, or for any other place on Galcen that she knew of.

"Transmission glitch?" she asked.

"That's what I thought. But this was riding the wave along with it—don't ask me how, I don't do that sort of work anymore."

He pressed another spot on the desktop. The routing codes vanished, and a voice—tense and hurried; it could have belonged to either a man or a woman from the pitch—came on over the desk's onboard speaker.

"I'm going to keep this short. I think this is a safe line, but you never know. Listen, Owen—there's something nasty going on with the Khesatan succession, and I want you to keep Jens the hell out of it. I can handle everything else, no problem, as long as the kid stays clear."

The audio clicked off and the desktop went dim. Klea let out her breath. "Your sister, right?"

"Who else? Jens is her boy."

"I thought he was on Maraghai with your brother's family."

"He is," Owen said. "But that doesn't mean he's going to stay there. The law on Maraghai says that once you're grown, you leave the homeworld—and Jens has been grown for a year now, by Maraghite reckoning."

"Your sister thinks he'll head for Khesat when they kick him out?"

"She's afraid he will, anyway." Owen looked thoughtful. "I don't know what's happening on Khesat . . . we haven't heard any rumblings from the local Guildhouses, so whatever's going on there hasn't spread outside the nobility . . . but I expect we'll be getting word on the situation before long, if it's so bad that Bee wants to steer Jens away from it."

Klea didn't need to ask whether Owen would fall in with the mysterious request. Beka was his sister, and he had been schooled since earliest boyhood to follow her whimsies and keep her out of trouble. Whatever she wanted, he would bend the universe itself, if necessary, to deliver.

"So what are we supposed to do?" Klea asked. "Fend him off from Khesat ourselves?"

"Fend him off or lure him elsewhere. As appropriate."

"Mmh." Klea gazed out the narrow window at a vertical strip of scenic vista: a shoulder of mountain, a scrap of sky, a ragged wisp of cloud. Troublesome and high-spirited young men were a problem she no longer had to deal with, thank fortune; the ones who came to the Retreat for training or apprenticeship had invariably been through a few chastening experiences along the way. "So what are you going to do with him?"

"Them," said Owen. "Jens has a cousin. Several, actually . . . but Faral is his agemate and foster-sib. If one of them leaves the planet, so will the other."

Klea suppressed a grimace of distaste. At that age, they were even worse when they traveled in pairs. . . . "All right—so what are you going to do with them?"

"*I* can't do anything." He gestured at the desktop, and the dark surface lit up with an eyestrain-inducing display of glyphs and icons and blinking response-requested message buttons. "And that's just the ordinary stuff. It doesn't count whatever's brewing on Khesat—we're going to have to watch that situation, in case the local Guildhouses are keeping quiet out of something besides ignorance or sheer Khesatan perversity. . . ."

He was sounding tired again. And she knew that more than anything else he feared the possibility of local Adepts involving themselves in political conspiracies. In the old days before the Republic, the Guild had earned a bad name for that sort of thing in some places—and the temptation hadn't gone away in the decades since. Klea sighed.

"All right," she said. "You watch Khesat. I'll watch the boys."

Some twenty minutes after meeting with Jens, Mael saw the lights of the house shining out in welcome through the trees. The house hadn't changed much over the years. The pillars that held up the long veranda were as tall as ordinary trees back on Eraasi. Other parts of the house *were* trees, more of the immense sky-tickling giants that made up the local forests. Warm yellow lantern-glow made the veranda pleasant and welcoming, although the faint haze-effect of a force field let Mael know that casual intruders—rockhogs and rufstaffas, perhaps—would not find an easy entrance.

Llannat Hyfid was waiting for them on the steps outside the force field. She hadn't changed much either, as far as Mael could tell. She was still a small, dark-skinned woman, with features closer at first look to plain than to pretty, although they had worn better over the years than some. Her black hair had the streaks of early grey that came to so many of those who worked with Power, but her face was almost as unlined as when Mael had first met her.

"Mistress," he began.

"Dinner first," she said. "Talk afterward. Jens, you go help Faral feed his sibs and send them off to bed; I'll be in to say goodnight to 'Rada later."

The young man nodded amiably and vanished through the force field into the depths of the great house. Mistress Hyfid called out, "And wash that blood off your hand before you go anywhere! I don't want Kei or Dortan getting any ideas about going out hunting with the table knives!"

Mael suppressed a smile, and followed her up the steps. She led the way to a dining table set up on an open porch illuminated by more of the lanterns. Her husband was waiting there for her, looming almost as tall among the shadows as one of the Selvaurs themselves.

"Flybynights are running," Ari Rosselin-Metadi said as they approached. He gestured at the steep slope out beyond the veranda, where shadows dipped and flitted in the clear air above the treetops. "Shall I send the boys out to get some for dessert?"

"No," Mistress Hyfid said. "There's no need. Let's pour a drink to absent friends, then have our dinner and get to business."

Ari nodded, and moved to a side table that held three tiny crystal glasses and a cut-glass decanter of something purple. Ceremoniously, he filled the glasses and passed them round. Mael took one, and breathed in a cautious sniff of the liquid's fumes. The scent was sharp and medicinal, and he wondered what the Adept-worlders made it from.

"Absent friends," Mistress Hyfid said. She tossed back her drink, and Ari and Mael did the same. The purple liquid had a sour, almost electric feel in the mouth. It was an acquired taste, Mael supposed, though he didn't plan on working to acquire it.

The meal itself was plain but satisfying: a great deal of roast meat and steamed grain, accompanied by thick slices of sweet, yellow-fleshed fruit. Mael found that his long walk upcountry from the last pubtrans stop had left him famished. He ate heartily, finding the textures and flavors sufficiently alien to be interesting but not—he felt certain the choice was deliberate—so strange as to be disquieting.

When they were all finished, Mistress Hyfid wiped the fruit juice off of her fingers with her napkin and laid the crumpled white fabric aside.

"I'm glad you could make it this far," she said. "I'm sorry I couldn't give you much of a reason in my invitation, but it wasn't something I—"

"Mistress—" Mael experienced a sudden sting of anxiety.

"—you *didn't* call me here. I came on my own to ask for your advice."

She looked distressed. Her husband rumbled something in the Selvauran language; Mael supposed he meant it for comfort and reassurance, but if so the effect was lost on a neutral observer.

"I sent messages," she said. "I even called in some old favors for the last one, and it went out by personal post on a Space Force courier."

Mael shook his head. "No messages from you came to Eraasi while I was there."

"And when did you leave?"

"A month ago, planetary reckoning."

"Then at least one of the messages should have reached you," said Mistress Hyfid. "But if it wasn't my summoning that brought you, why did you come?"

Mael paused a moment to gather his thoughts before presenting them. Llannat Hyfid was the First of all the Mage-Circles, but she had been born on Maraghai and schooled in Power with the Adepts on Galcen ... much about the homeworlds would always be alien to her.

"Let me tell you," he said, "about what happened to me on the way this evening."

"The rufstaffa?"

"In part. I should have sensed it following me ... a hunting-beast is a powerful disturber of patterns ... but I was caught up in watching the *eiran*. The cords are tarnished my lady, and decaying."

Mistress Hyfid's eyes were dark and sober. "I know. I've seen them more and more often of late. That's why I wanted to talk to you."

"The *eiran* aren't the worst of it." Mael looked from the First to her husband. "Back in the homeworlds, an *ekkannikh* has risen up to disrupt the Circles."

"*Ekkan—?*" Mistress Hyfid stumbled on the unfamiliar word.

"In the old stories," said Mael, "a hungry ghost. But among those who work with Power, it is the word for someone among us who has too much strength and too much will—or too much anger—to let himself die completely."

"I don't like the sound of that," said Ari Rosselin-Metadi. He stood up and fetched the decanter of purple liquor from the side table, then refilled all their glasses to within a hair of the brim. "Because the only dead man I can think of with that much of that kind of power is Errec Ransome."

Errec Ransome. Master, once, of the Adepts' Guild, and teacher of Mistress Hyfid when she first came to learn the ways of Power. *The Breaker of Circles*, they had called him in the homeworlds, for what he had done at the end of the First War. *Traitor*, they called him now, on both sides of the old border zone, and schoolchildren from one side of the civilized galaxy to the other made an insult of his name.

Mael tipped a splash of the purple liquor onto the smooth-planed boards of the veranda—a ritual gesture, of little worth against a determined adversary, but the habit of a lifetime could not be shed that easily. "You said the words, not I."

"I'm right, then."

"Yes," said Mael. "So far, the creature has not killed—it hasn't yet recovered enough identity to be that powerful. But the Circles on Cracanth have felt its touch these five months and more, and someday soon it—he—will cross the threshold."

Mistress Hyfid frowned. "Why Cracanth, of all places?"

Mael fell silent for a moment, the better to choose his words before he spoke. Not all the history of the First War was common knowledge in the Adept-worlds—especially history from the Eraasian point of view—but some matters were more ticklish to deal with than others.

"The story is obscure," he said finally, "and all those with direct knowledge of it are long since dead . . . but it was told to me when I was young that Errec Ransome had once been a prisoner among us, and that Cracanth was the world on which they held him."

"Now that," said Rosselin-Metadi, after another silence, "is something nobody mentioned when I was growing up." He took a long drink of the purple liquid in his glass. "I wonder if they even knew."

"It makes sense, though," Mistress Hyfid said. "The way he hated the Magelords . . ."

Mael said, "Yes. The stronger the *ekkannikh* grows, the more he will remember. When he remembers enough, he will know that it was not the Circles who defeated him in the end. And Errec Ransome was a man who devoted his whole life to crushing the ones who had injured him."

II. Galcen; Maraghai; Khesat

KLEA SPENT the rest of the day worrying about how to handle her latest commission from Owen Rosselin-Metadi.

She thought about it while she talked in the practice yard with Mistress Yarro, deciding on the quarterly schedule of instruction for the senior apprentices. She thought about it while she was closeted in the lesser pantry with Master Enolt, planning the Retreat's long-term food purchases. And she thought about it in half a dozen other corners of the ancient citadel, in between dealing with a host of smaller matters that would otherwise have claimed too much of the Guild Master's attention.

The basic problem remained intractable. She was somehow supposed to shadow and protect—and at all costs to keep away from Khesat—a pair of young men well past the age when they would tolerate such protection.

How to begin? She rubbed her forehead, where the beginnings of a headache had begun to gather. *I can't see calling up Maraghai and asking Owen's brother if his boys are still*

*at home . . . what am I supposed to tell him if they are?
"Don't let them go to Khesat"? As soon as the kids get wind
of that—and they will, they always do!—Khesat's going to be
the first place they'll want to go.*

And that's if they're home. If they've left . . .

Definitely, a headache. The only person she'd ever heard
of who'd successfully tracked a lost object outside of local
planetary space was Llannat Hyfid, the First of all the Mage-
Circles. Rumor had it that Errec Ransome had done something similar in his youth—but the subsequent careers of both
those individuals gave her pause.

One of them a turncoat, she thought, *and the other a traitor and a madman.* And both of them more powerful by a
long way than Klea Santreny.

She went to bed early that night, nursing her headache.
Sleep eluded her in spite of all her efforts. She was still
awake when a messenger found her several hours later, with
the news that the Second of the Mage-Circles had crossed the
old border zone, and appeared to be headed for Maraghai. In
theory, the border was now open, and Mageworlders could
come and go as they pleased. Klea didn't care much for the
idea. She'd killed Mages with her own hands, back during
the Second War, while other Mages had tried to kill her, and
she didn't have a forgiving nature about such things.

She pushed herself to her feet and addressed the messenger. "Tell Master Rosselin-Metadi that I've departed on
business."

"Will you need a car down to the field?"

"No," she said. "I'll walk. I need to think."

She pulled down her heavy black cloak from its peg beside
the door and started out for the landing field.

The walk, a long half-day of hard going in mountainous
terrain, took her even longer in the dark. She opened herself
to the universe on the way down the mountain, letting the
currents of Power guide her feet while her mind chewed over
the problem. Two problems, now—keep the boys safe, and
keep an eye on the Mages.

As if we didn't have more trouble than we needed already.

She reached the landing field at dawn, and found an aircar ready for her. Apparently Owen had approved of her action enough to call ahead and facilitate it. She realized then that her decision to walk had come from a hope that the Guild Master would forbid her to go.

A flight over the glistening fields of morning took her to the spaceport complex at Galcen Prime, where she scanned the listings for a link to Maraghai. The next ship heading out toward Selvauran space wasn't scheduled to depart for some days yet. Rather than going back to the Retreat, she decided, she would take up lodging in the city's Guildhouse and wait—but as she was turning away from the reservations kiosk, a flash of light on the message board caught her eye. Something had changed in the display.

She looked again at the listings, but found no updates on ships for Maraghai—nothing but a last call for the Tikún Linkship *Atli's Darling*, making transit to Ophel.

She walked to the Tikún Packet Line's reservation point and presented her papers. Before she had a chance to think why, she had tickets and a visa for Ophel in her possession and was on her way, with hardly time to inform the local Guildhouse that she wouldn't be needing a bed there after all.

Not until the pressure of the shuttle's lift to orbit eased did self-doubt assail her. Was this, then, the way such tracking and finding was done—following half-understood promptings and faint glimpses out of the corner of the mind's eye, with no reason to do so that she could in honesty give?

Propelled forward as much by the fact that she'd already paid for her tickets as by any deep conviction that what she did was likely to bear fruit, she went on through with the transfer. Once on board the packet ship, she checked into her small cabin, strapped in, and went to sleep.

We'll see what happens, she thought as the dreams claimed her. *If Ophel isn't where the universe wants me to be, I can always try again for Maraghai from there.*

Jens Metadi-Jessan D'Rosselin hummed the Fifth Mixolydian Etude under his breath as he left the unroofed summer porch behind the house in the woods. Getting his younger cousins—Kei, Dortan, and 'Rada-the-brat—to finish their dinner and clean up after the meal hadn't been particularly difficult.

"If you don't eat what's put out here for you and let Aunt Llann have her talk with Gentlesir Taleion without being interrupted," he'd told them, "then I won't show you the right way to kill a rufstaffa with a table knife."

That had calmed them in a heartbeat, and Faral had obligingly played the role of the rufstaffa when the time came for Jens to fulfill his part of the bargain. After that, with the dishes and the leftovers cleared away, the back-porch dinner had ended with wrestling and horseplay until all the parties concerned were exhausted enough to retire quietly to bed—even 'Rada-the-brat, whom Jens suspected on occasion of not sleeping at all, but merely withdrawing to plot mischief in private.

"And now," Faral said after his younger sibs had departed, "you can tell me what's going on with our visitor."

"*I* can? Why me?"

"You're the one who met him down on the trail." Faral leaned against the porch railing. "And whatever he's here for, I'll bet we're mixed up in it somehow . . . Mamma wouldn't have sent us off to have our dinner with the sibs if she wasn't worried."

"She isn't worried," Jens said. "She wants us out of the way so that she and this Taleion person can talk about Circle business at the dinner table without warping our young and impressionable minds in the process."

His cousin laughed. "Too late for that. You've been warped ever since Aunt Bee took you to Khesat to meet the relatives and the relatives sent you back here in disgrace."

"That," said Jens, "was because I wasn't warped enough."

"Sure, it was . . . I wish I'd been there to see it."

Faral sounded a bit wistful. He'd never been off Maraghai, since Jens's Khesatan relatives had made it plain that the extended family didn't extend to foster-siblings.

Jens had thought at first that the Jessani were trying to cast a slur on Llannat Hyfid and Ari Rosselin-Metadi—as if any-body could!—but then he'd figured out that his own parents were the actual target of their spite. It was his reaction to that insight, as much as anything else, that had finally disgraced him enough to succeed in making them send him home.

"Someday," said Jens, "I'll have to see if anyone on Khesat took pictures. As for Gentlesir Taleion—if his errand has anything to do with us, we'll hear about it in the morning." He yawned. "In the meantime, I'm for bed. Your sibs are an exhausting lot."

"Night, then."

"Night."

Jens yawned again and padded off to his room—and, he hoped, a good night's sleep. The back hallways of the house were dimly lit by low-power glows, and untroubled by any but the usual nighttime noises. Elsewhere, he knew, his aunt and uncle were still conferring with their visitor from the other side of the Gap Between.

Mael Taleion. A Mage, surely—he carried the short staff, just as Llannat Hyfid did. And Aunt Llann was a Mage; she admitted as much to anyone who asked, and that included the Master of the Adepts' Guild, whose one long-ago visit to Maraghai had left a strong impression on the younger Jens.

Uncle Ari had saved him that time, telling Master Rosselin-Metadi that he could hold off on trolling for Adepts as long as he was visiting family. Mael Taleion wasn't, as far as Jens could tell, hunting for future Mages on this visit. He looked like a man with other problems on his mind.

Jens pushed open the door to his room. Like all the other doors in the house, it had old-fashioned mechanical hinges, made out of iron to support a slab of native wood. Any number of Jens's Khesatan acquaintances would have heaped extravagant praise upon its quaint rusticity. The room inside had a bed and a desk and several closets, and a freestanding heat-bar for use in the wintertime. It had belonged to Jens since he first came to Maraghai for fostering; and it said "home" to him in a way that nothing on Khesat ever had.

The desk was blinking at him: a bright orange alert signal on the comp keyboard.

That's new, he thought. He went over to the desk and sat, bringing up the comp display as he did so.

PRIVATE TEXT MESSAGE, it said. SOURCE: KJ103X. TYPE: EN-CRYPTED. MANUAL KEY ENTRY REQUIRED.

Out on the dining porch, the talk continued. Mael finished the purple liquor in his glass, and did not refuse when Ari Rosselin-Metadi filled it again. Somewhere beyond the force field, a forest creature gave a cry of distress that cut off, sharply, in midnote.

"How long," said Mistress Hyfid, "do you think we have before this *ekkannikh* of yours starts causing serious trouble? I'll be honest with you—it's not an aspect of Power that I'm familiar with."

Mael hesitated a moment before answering. He'd known when he set out that he was coming to Maraghai with bad news; he hadn't anticipated that the news would become worse even before he arrived.

"Not so long, perhaps, as I had hoped," he said. "Something has happened I did not anticipate."

She took his meaning at once, or part of it. "The rufstaffa?"

"There's nothing odd about running into one of those," protested her husband. "They're dirt-common in this district, and not even good hunting."

"Nevertheless," said Mael, "that one might have killed me, if young Jens had not intervened."

Mistress Hyfid looked disbelieving. "Surely not."

"My attention, at the time, was elsewhere . . . I fear that the *ekkannikh* has already begun to try its strength beyond the Circles on Cracanth."

"You saw it here?" she asked. She didn't go pale; her skin was too dark for that. Only the sudden stillness of her features betrayed her apprehension.

"And spoke with it," Mael said. "The *eiran* weave around it like netting; it's already strong enough to pull them in and work with them. It succeeded in blinding me to the rufstaffa's attack—without your fosterling's aid, I would have been dead by now. But I fear the consequences."

"What kind of consequences?" Ari Rosselin-Metadi's voice was a dangerous rumble, and Mael chose his next words carefully.

"I turned aside," he said, "at the moment the beast attacked, and I saw the *eiran* wrap themselves around the neck of the boy Jens like a strangler's cord."

Faral couldn't get to sleep. The customary routine of the household had been broken, and the night disturbed by too many unaccustomed noises—the courteous, accented speech of the visitor; his parents' equally courteous but worried tones; the clicking of compkeys from Jens's room down the hall. After a while Faral gave up staring at the roof beams and got back out of bed. If he was going to stay awake, he might as well use the time to advantage.

He left the glowcube on his bedside table inactivated. His night vision had always been good, and a light coming on in his room when he was usually a sound and regular sleeper—would draw unwanted attention.

An empty carrybag waited in the back of his closet. Moving quietly, he took it out and began to pack.

As Chaka had said that afternoon, it was high time he went out wandering. He'd already stayed here longer than most younglings; Chaka was almost the last of his agemates to leave. Except for Jens, of course, but Jens was only an off-world fosterling. Off-worlders didn't count—they weren't sent away when they came of age, because nobody expected them to live on Maraghai permanently anyhow.

Faral, however, was the born-son of a full clan member, which meant that he was a Selvaur himself in all the ways that counted. He'd even made the Long Hunt that brought a youngling into the clan, killing a massive cliffdragon with no weapon other than his own hands and body—an incident that had caused almost as much fuss as Jens's own abrupt return from Khesat. Faral hadn't been supposed to make the Hunt at all; not when the luck of the genetic draw had given him a height and mass closer to his mother's than to his father's, and nothing at all like that of the Forest Lords.

Most thin-skin fosterlings skipped the Long Hunt anyway, and contented themselves with adjunct status in the clan. But Faral had slipped out of the house when the season came, going up into the mountains without bothering to ask for the permission he probably wouldn't have got. He'd come back a month later with the cliffdragon's hide slung over his shoulder.

That had been a year ago. It was time, by Selvauran standards, for Faral to leave the home planet and not come back until the elders said he was worthy.

Past time, he thought, *and the time is now.*

Clothes weren't a problem. A plain shirt and trousers would do the trick anyplace in the civilized galaxy where formality wasn't an issue. He'd seen free-spacers wearing much the same style in holovid newscasts, and if it worked for them it should work for anybody.

He added his good boots and a warm jacket to the stuff in the carrybag. For a moment he thought about packing a weapon—off-worlders did sometimes, free-spacers especially—then discarded the idea. He was one of the Forest Lords, the second generation in his line, and he could take care of himself without need for such things. He sealed the carrybag and stood looking at it for a moment while he wondered what to do, now that all his packing was done and he was still awake.

His thoughts were interrupted by a low whistle, like the sound of somebody blowing across the top of a pottery jug. A few seconds later, the sound came again. He grinned and whistled back a couple of octaves higher. Clawed fingers and toes scrabbled for purchase in the heavy logs of the outer wall, and a shadowy figure loomed up head and shoulders against the moonlit rectangle of window high under the eaves.

Are you going to take down the field, said Chaka, *or am I going to have to hang here all night by my foreclaws?*

Faral laughed and shut off the security. The window's force field was supposed to be switched on and off from the central console like all the others in this wing, but he'd figured out how to cheat the connection a long time ago. After a few seconds of squirming, Chaka fit herself through the unshielded opening and dropped to the floor.

What's up? Faral asked as soon as she regained her balance. He spoke in the Forest Speech; even with his thin-skin accent, the sounds of it blended with the noises of Maraghai's night better than would any human tongue. *I thought you were heading for the spaceport.*

I was. But I thought I'd come by here and check one more time to see if you were going, too. Looks like I had the right idea.

Faral picked up the packed carrybag. *I'm ready as I'll ever be. But first I have to tell Jens I'm leaving.*

"You don't need to do that," said his cousin.

The doorway had opened so silently that neither Faral nor Chaka had noticed its motion. Jens stood there, dressed like Faral in plain-style traveler's gear, and he had a carrybag in his hand.

"It's time, coz," he said. "I'm going with you."

Mael Taleion went to bed feeling easier in his mind than he had since leaving the homeworlds. The talk after dinner had not settled anything—best to look at the problem again in the morning, Mistress Hyfid had said, now that it had been properly broached—but he felt better for knowing that his concerns were shared by someone on this side of the Gap Between. Even if the First of all the Mage-Circles no longer had any formal ties to the Adepts who had trained her, her husband was own brother to the Master of their Guild. The warning would be passed on.

Jens Metadi-Jessan D'Rosselin was a different problem, and one that would bear thinking on in daylight. *Does the boy merely stand at a gathering-point for the cords of life and luck,* Mael wondered, *or does he draw them to him?*

No answer came to him from the darkness, but he had

expected none. He pulled the blanket over his shoulders and went to sleep.

Morning arrived sooner than he'd anticipated. The windows in his room faced the rising sun, and it was not yet full dawn when the first light shone down across his pillow and struck him in the face. Outside, a new set of birds and animals—diurnal ones, this time—practiced their characteristic noises at full volume. Mael groaned and got out of bed.

He'd been an early riser himself once, in the days when he was a young man determined to free the homeworlds and subdue the galaxy. These days, he'd learned to savor the smaller pleasures of life, and rising when he chose to and not when the planet's rotation decreed it was one of them.

Not this morning, though, he thought with resignation, as he pulled on his clothes and his boots. *Today we work.*

Ari Rosselin-Metadi had said something the night before about a come-when-you're-ready breakfast on the dining porch. Mael retraced his steps to the veranda, but found no table of food and drink waiting when he got there—only Mistress Hyfid, her husband, and a pot of cha'a.

He knew at once that something was wrong. Ari Rosselin-Metadi filled him a mug of lukewarm cha'a and he drank it, in spite of the fact that he had never learned to like the bitter infusion so popular in the Adept-worlds.

"What happened?" he asked, when the mug was empty.

"Faral's gone off wandering," Mistress Hyfid said. She poured herself another mug of cha'a and gazed into its murky brown depths while her husband took up the tale.

"It's not something we'd normally worry about," Ari said. "It would have been his time soon anyway. But he took Jens with him."

"Ah." Mael thought about the *eiran*, and how they had snaked across the darkness to entangle the young man he had so briefly met. "Took him where?"

"That's the problem. Faral didn't say. The younglings don't, most of the time, when they leave."

"*I* joined the Space Force," Mistress Hyfid said. "And so

did Ari. But that was thirty years ago, and things were different then. Faral could have decided to go anywhere."

Mael tried to remember what little he knew about the customs of Maraghai—which were known to be odd even by the standards of the Adept-worlds. "I thought that your sister's son was a fosterling, and not bound by the clan law."

"You know as well as I do that the chains are in the mind, not the law."

He bowed his head in acknowledgment of her point. "If young Jens feels himself bound, then bound he is. But the danger that entangles him is not going to grow any less just because he is off your planet."

"Taking care of it's going to be harder, though," said Ari. "For one thing, young ones out wandering are on their own— clan law is firm on that."

Jens isn't the only one bound by chains in the mind, Mael decided. *Not that anybody from the homeworlds is fit to point a finger on that account.*

"And what is the other difficulty?" he asked aloud.

"The other difficulty," Ari said, "is finding them in the first place. Unless they send a message home—and how often did you do that, when you were young?"

"Not often enough," admitted Mael. "Though my reasons seemed good to me at the time."

"I'm sure they did," said Mistress Hyfid. "And so will· theirs."

The spaceport at Ernalghan was a large, and mostly empty, building. No ships except the ground-to-orbit shuttles touched down in its docking bays, and those not more than once or twice a day—most of Maraghai's traffic with other worlds went through the nearspace station and the in-system planetary habitats. A single office window, tucked out of sight between two of the massive pillars that held up the building's vaulted roof, sufficed to handle any business that might pass through.

This morning, the work at hand included Faral Hyfid-Metadi and his cousin Jens, purchasing lift-and-transit tickets for the passenger liner *Bright-Wind-Rising*, out of Ruisi in the Eraasian sector and currently bound for Ophel. Chaka hooted at them as they paid down their money at the counter and fed their passports into the reader for the "No Return Until Permitted" stamp.

You're going to make us look more like tourists than wanderers, she said. *First-class tickets? I ask you.*

"Hey," Jens protested. "The trust fund wasn't my idea, and I have the right to draw on the line of credit just by existing. So I'm going to do it. They'll probably succumb to apoplexy back on Khesat when they find out what for."

He thought about it for a moment and added, "I hope Mamma gets to watch."

They left the counter and made their way to the outbound shuttle lock. One other passenger waited there, a stout and prosperous-looking man in Galcenian-style clothing.

Jens recognized Terrel Bruhn—a distant acquaintance of his foster-parents, a trader in rarities and luxury goods who made his home in one of the domed cities on Maraghai's moon, and visited the planetary surface from time to time. Bruhn wasn't a full-member of any clan that Jens knew of, and if he had the "Permanent Return Allowed" stamp on his passport, he'd never bothered to claim the privilege.

"Good morning to you," Bruhn said. "Off chasing fame like all the other youngsters?"

"We're headed for Eraasi," Faral said. "Everybody says that's where the interesting stuff is happening these days. But if we trip over some fame along the way—"

"Better to leave it lying where you found it," Bruhn said, "if you get the chance." The trader looked serious for a moment. "I fought in the war, you know, and I found out something about fame, and what it'll buy."

Thin-skins, Chaka muttered.

"It's different for Selvaurs," Bruhn told her. "But most of the famous people I knew were famous for the way they got killed, and two weeks later, no one remembered their names."

"We'll bear that in mind," Jens promised. "Because I, for one, intend to live a long time and be truly memorable."

Bruhn chuckled. "Watch it when you say things like that, boy. You never can tell what might be listening."

Then the door to the shuttle lock cycled open, and the conversation ended.

On the far side of the sector, a chittering info-rat noted an atypical transaction in the account of one of the Worthy Lineages, and went off to report its findings. Soon the news had come to the Guildhouse on Khesat that the youngest member of the Jessani line was drawing on the family account, and that the draw-down had been enough to cover a spaceship passage for three.

Noted, read the corresponding entry in the Guildhouse's Private intelligence log. *Under advisement.*

III. Ophel

THE OLD Quarter in Sombrelír lay on the opposite side of the city from the spaceport. Tourists desirous of exploring the Quarter's narrow, brick-paved streets and handkerchief-sized parks had to abandon their flivvers and hovercars for more archaic modes of transportation at the edge of the modern business district.

A surprising number of them made the effort. Ophel—falling as it did between the Mageworlds and the rest of the civilized galaxy—presented an exotic face to travelers from both sides of the Gap. The First Magewar had seen the isolated world prosper as a trading and transshipment point for raiding ships from the Eraasian hegemony. Later, in the decades leading up to the Second War, Ophel had provided the blockaded worlds with access—however restricted—to galactic technology and culture. Through it all, the Ophelans had grown wealthy by keeping neutral.

Twenty years of genuine, if sometimes unsettled, peace had increased Ophel's importance as a trade and communications nexus. Merchants and bankers from all parts of the civilized galaxy met to make their trades and cut their deals in Sombrelír. Between negotiations, they refreshed themselves in the enjoyment of those unique art forms—musical, culinary, and others even more exotic—that had grown up in the tension and isolation of earlier times.

Bindweed & Blossom's was a tea shop near the center of the Old Quarter. The shop occupied the bottom front of one of the Quarter's handsome stucco houses, and the proprietors occupied the rest.

The pair of elderly but still handsome women who ran the shop had been serving tisanes and pastries to discerning guests ever since the end of the First War. Business folk from central Sombrelír came to Bindweed & Blossom's every afternoon to drink sweetgrass tea and discuss politics. Shoppers from the smaller towns paused in midday to rest their feet and nibble on filled finger buns before heading back into the press. Even galactic travelers up from the port ventured inside to sample the local delicacies. A brass plaque beside the front door indicated that a number of languages were spoken within, and all varieties of cash accepted.

This morning the shop opened its doors on time as usual. The Sombrelír/Port-Antipode suborbital shuttle rumbled skyward on the other side of the city, the front door of the tea shop opened, and Gentlelady Bindweed came striding down the walk to hang out the NOW SERVING sign on the wrought-iron gate.

Something of a mystery, was Bindweed. The lean, elegant woman with the mop of iron-grey curls had answered to what was clearly an alias for as long as the inhabitants of the Old Quarter had known her. Where she had come from, and what she had done with her life before settling down, "in retirement," as she put it, to sell penny nutcakes and other dainty nibble-bits, she had never bothered to say.

In point of fact, Bindweed was Ophelan born and bred—although the same couldn't be said of her partner, whose voice carried traces of Lost Entibor. The two were nearly inseparable, however, and were well known to the merchants in the fresh-goods markets of the Quarter, who supplied the tea shop with all of its perishable supplies.

This morning, with the sign duly put in place, Bindweed returned to the interior of the shop. The main room was bright and fresh, with white tablecloths and crisp starched curtains, and the odors of yeast and spices added piquancy to the air. She straightened the tablecloth on the nearest table, more out of habit than actual need, and repositioned the bowl of flowers in the center. Then she continued into the tea shop's kitchen, a homey place half-visible through the arched doorway from the tables outside. Blossom—a small, thin woman whose efficient bearing contrasted oddly with her chosen by-name—was already taking the first tray of sweet biscuits out of the big stove.

Bindweed went over to the gleaming steel urn on the counter and poured herself a first-of-the-morning ration of strong black cha'a in a delicate bone cup. The shop had a menu of teas and tisanes longer than the wine lists of some local restaurants, but no one had ever seen Bindweed drink any of them.

"What's the news?" she asked her partner.

Blossom glanced over at the readout screen set into the kitchen wall, where it couldn't be seen from the main dining room. The display showed a list of portside shipping schedules. "*Liberty's End* is due in this morning. Do we have anything on her?"

"A five-percenter. Nothing that's going to make us rich."

"Enough of them, and they'll add up," Blossom said. "There's three other merchantmen due in, too, and a passenger liner making connections for Eraasi. A good day for travelers, maybe."

"We'll put on an extra tray of buns," Bindweed decided. "Something sweet. Parchants, do you think?"

"Only if we serve them with sugared berry-root. Shall I start a bit going?"

Before Bindweed could answer, the chimes above the front door rang to announce an arrival: Gentlesir Thalban, most likely, stopping by on the way to his shop across the square.

He liked to arrive before any of his employees, and he liked a steamed fouma to eat beforehand. Bindweed picked one up from its warmer on the stove and hastened out into the main room to meet their first customer of the morning.

Faral Hyfid-Metadi stood with his cousin Jens on the observation deck of the passenger liner *Bright-Wind-Rising*, watching the world of Ophel swing beneath them. The huge blue and green planet filled the viewport, its glittering, cloud-streaked surface brilliant in the light of the local sun, and dark like black velvet on the side of the globe beyond the sunset line.

So this is where Granda's privateers caught the Mage-worlds treasure-fleet.

He almost said as much aloud, but thought better of the idea. Simply because the Ophelan run had made Jos Metadi's name ring out from Galcen to Maraghai didn't mean the folks down below at the time had approved of it. The data files in main ship's memory—or, at any rate, in those parts of ship's memory available to the text readers in the passenger cabins—didn't say whether the subject was one to avoid or not.

Faral had checked, just in case. He knew that he couldn't help being an off-worlder, but he didn't want to make things worse by acting like a boor. If he couldn't match Jens at High Khesatan elegance, he could at least put forward the impression of being an experienced traveler. The data files had helped some, but not enough.

"Are you and your cousin planning to go dirtside while the *Wind* is in port?"

The speaker was another of the passengers on the observation deck, a youngish, dark-haired man in dusty black. Faral didn't remember seeing the man before today, but the *Wind* carried so many people on board that he wasn't surprised he hadn't yet encountered them all. The phrase "planning to go dirtside" marked him out as a spacer—Aunt Bee talked that way, too, using the same word no matter whether the world in question was a barely civilized outplanet or Galcen

itself—so Faral thought the man in black might not be a passenger at all, but part of the ship's crew.

"We haven't decided," he said. It didn't take reading the
cautions in the data files to know that volunteering one's itin-
erary in public was a bad idea.

"Ah," said the stranger. "If you like sightseeing, there's always the Old Quarter. Beautiful architecture there, and nice
shops if you want to pick up something besides the usual
cheap souvenirs."

Jens turned away from the viewport to join the conversation. For a moment, Faral thought that his cousin had already
met the man in black—recognition or something like it flickered briefly in his eyes—but he only asked, with the same
well-bred blandness he always used around strangers, "Is
there some place in particular that you'd recommend?"

The stranger considered for a moment. "Almost any place
in the Quarter is good . . . but if you're after small objects of
artistic value, Thalban's is probably the best."

Before Faral or Jens could say anything in reply, a bell
sounded throughout *Bright-Wind-Rising*, and a soft alto voice
came over the observation deck's comm system.

"All passengers are required to return to their cabins for atmospheric entry," the voice said. It spoke Standard Galcenian
with a faint Eraasian lilt. "All passengers are required to return to their cabins for atmospheric entry."

The voice switched languages—to Ophelan, Faral supposed, or one of the languages from beyond the Gap—and
kept on speaking. At the same time, the SIT DOWN AND STRAP
IN glyph began to flash above the viewport, and there was no
more time to talk.

Faral and Jens made their way back to the triple suite they
shared with Chaka. The Selvaur was already there and
strapped down onto her deceleration couch.

About time you showed up.

Faral took one of the two remaining couches and began
fastening the safety webbing. A sharp jolt ran through the
ship as he hurried to get the last of the buckles snapped.
Chaka gave a rumbling laugh.

*Like I was saying . . . *

"It's a reminder," said Jens—though Faral noted that his cousin hadn't delayed getting his own webbing into place. "To hurry along the stragglers."

Another jolt shook the cabin, and the deckplates beneath the couches began to vibrate.

"I don't know," said Faral. "That feels like the real thing to me."

Chaka hooted in agreement. *Read your tickets. These guys don't guarantee *anything*—not even that there'll always be air for us to breathe. And not a word about holding up landing waiting for everyone to get webbed.*

The back room at Huool Galleries in Sombrelír was windowless, dim, and climate-controlled. Shelves and cabinets and stasis boxes lined the walls and occupied most of the floor space. Gentlesir Huool specialized in the acquisition and disposition of precious objects, and not all of his stock in trade could risk public display. Some of the cloistered items, like the woven gemgrass funerary ornaments from Miosa Mainworld, depended upon preservation technology for their continued existence; others, more simply, had no legal business being in the gallery at all.

Mizady Lyftingil, Huool's work-study intern, had grown accustomed to spending most of her time surrounded by the rare, the valuable, and the highly sought-after. Miza found the back room a good place to work in if the weather was bad outside, though somewhat confining on pleasant days. Today was hot and humid enough that she hadn't even gone out for lunch, but had eaten her bread and cheese and fruit without leaving her worktable.

She crumpled up her empty lunch bag and tossed it into the mouth of the recycling chute, then turned back to the status display glowing on the table's surface. The Atelier Provéc, one of Huool's closest competitors, was having an auction today, and there was something about the bidding patterns . . .

On the far side of the room, a door slid open and snicked shut again. Miza glanced up, saw that it was only Huool coming back from his own, more private, lunch hour, and kept on working. Huool was a Roti, and sensitive to giving offense; he couldn't do anything about the fact that his digestive system demanded live—or at any rate fresh-killed—meat, but he did make a practice of eating his noontime ration of locally bred foodmice in a side room where his human assistant didn't have to watch.

The display on Miza's worktable shifted and shifted again, as bidding continued across town in the Atelier Provéc. She frowned. Something was going on, she knew it . . . she could see the ripples of it on the surface, in the changing patterns of the bids.

She heard a faint rustle of body feathers as Huool drew closer and looked at the display over her shoulder.

"You see something, young one?" he asked. His Standard Galcenian had the distinctive Rotish accent, all breath and clicking beak, but the words were kind.

She gestured at the display. "Look here."

Huool's eyes were bright yellow and perfectly round, with tufted, astonished-looking brows. But Miza had learned by now not to judge the Roti's state of mind by his expression, which never changed much anyway. The soft clatter of his beak as he looked at the table display told her that he'd spotted the same anomalies that she had.

"The patterns," he said. "What do you make of them?"

She wanted to ask what Huool made of them, since his experience in the field surpassed hers, but she knew better. The Roti wasn't a hard taskmaster—he was, if anything, softhearted to a fault—but neither was he one to let misplaced benevolence interfere with the proper training of those students whom the Arthan Technological Institute gave into his charge.

"Somebody's looking for something," she said.

"Yes. That much is plain. But does Provéc have it?"

"I don't think so." She frowned at the patterns again. "I'm not even sure the big fish is bidding. But all the other fish are nervous . . . you can see it, the way they scatter and regroup, as if something hungry and large is swimming in the waters beneath them."

Huool gave a brief chitter of amusement. "You grow poetic ... but I believe you may be right. You have a gift for judging the flow of data, young one; perhaps the Guild should be training you, not I."

"Oh, no." Miza threw up her hand in the gesture her grandmother back on Artha had always used to avert an evil omen. Not that she believed in such things, but one couldn't be too careful. "I come from a respectable family. And I don't want anything to do with those people, thank you very much."

Huool chittered again. "Their loss, then, and not yours. But let us consider the data once more. What do you think this big fish of yours is seeking?"

"Hard to say. We're dealing with proxies, agents, that sort of thing; whoever's behind it isn't acting directly at all. Something of value—"

"Of course, young one. Whatever is wanted has value."

She gave an impatient snort. "I already know the basics, Huool. What I was going to say is, I don't think our hungry fish is looking for the sort of thing that gets displayed out in the front gallery. Either here *or* at Provéc."

"No," Huool agreed. "And this is your lesson for today. I believe that what is being sought is not an object that can be held in the hands at all. Rather, someone seeks to hire a surprising service. Watch and learn."

"Sombrelír at last," Jens said. "And in the morning on a business day, at that. I say we take the advice of our acquaintance from the observation deck and go sightseeing."

The two cousins stood in the Grand Concourse of the main spaceport complex. Faral was trying hard not to gawk at the crowds. The port building back home on Maraghai was almost the same size as the Ophelan Concourse, but much emptier. The civilized galaxy in general, he was close to deciding, had too many people in it. He should have stuck with Chaka—the Selvaur had stayed on board *Bright-Wind-Rising* to oversee the transfer of their luggage onto a ship for Eraasi.

"If you ask me," Faral said, "there's plenty of stuff to see right here in the Concourse. Look over there." He nodded toward a full-size holodisplay in a nearby window. " 'Personal Comforts for the Weary Traveler'—you sure can't find anything like *that* in Ernalghan."

Jens glanced over at the window and gave a dismissive shrug. *It's nothing compared to Khesat,* the gesture seemed to say—and for all Faral knew, he might be right. "Father says that sticking to the portside strip is a good way to lose your health and your money both. I've checked the maps. We can make it across town and back with plenty of time in the middle to look around."

Faral gave up the argument. He followed his cousin out through a high archway marked GROUND TRANSPORT: SOMBRELÍR, NANÁLI, DUVIZE. Outside, hoverbuses and wheeled jitneys waited in ranks under the great portico. Jens had already picked out one of the jitneys. It was painted bright green, for some reason, with darker-green vines and purple flowers twining all over it.

"You're joking, right?" Faral said.

Jens raised an eyebrow. "Of course not. We're appreciating the local art forms, and this is one of them."

Faral gave up. When his cousin started acting more Khesatan than the Khesatans, there was nothing to do but leave him alone until he got over it. Maybe he'd explain later what had put him on edge, and maybe not.

In the open-topped jitney, the ride from the spaceport through outer and central Sombrelír was breezy and pleasant. The warmth of the morning contrasted with the chilly atmosphere the cousins had grown used to on board the starliner, and the air was full of interesting smells.

At the edge of the Old Quarter, the driver stopped. "No further," he said. "Foot and carriage only from here."

Jens paid the fare—it came to more than Faral had expected, but not enough to cause distress—and the cousins got out of the jitney. One of the carriages the driver had referred to clattered by, drawn by two of some draft animal that Faral didn't recognize. The creatures had stubby horns and hooves the size of dinner plates, and he was glad when Jens ignored the carriage and set out into the Old Quarter on foot.

They walked for some time through a maze of narrow streets and little square parks with bronze statues in them. The stone-and-plaster buildings of the Quarter were painted in bright pastel colors, and strange flowers grew in boxes along the sidewalks. The walks themselves were paved with black and white tiles in mosaic patterns. A wide watercourse ran through the heart of the area, and floating bridges connected the streets on either side.

There were few enough people about that Faral felt less uncomfortable than he had in a long time. The crowding on the ship and in the spaceport had gotten on his nerves—he wondered if that was what had affected Jens, as well.

They wandered at random for a while, looking at the shops, the inhabitants, and the other tourists, until Jens exclaimed, "Ah, there it is!"

Faral looked where his cousin was pointing. Up ahead, in a shopwindow, a hand-lettered placard rested on a driftwood easel: THALBAN'S.

"That looks like the place," agreed Faral, and the two of them entered.

The lunchtime crush had ended at Bindweed & Blossom's. In a corner near the front, two country ladies in town from Duvize lingered over tisanes before resuming their shopping. Other than that, the shop was empty. Bindweed was changing the linen on the last of the vacant tables when the two boys came through the front door.

Tourists, she thought at once. *Up from the port. Old enough to be out loose on their own, but green as a pair of pressed-glass cuff links.*

One of the lads was tall and fair, with long yellow hair tied back in a neat queue; the other, darker one was stocky and muscular. In the old days, she could have pinpointed their world of origin at first glance—but the modern habit of dressing for travel in an abstract version of the basic Galcenian mode blurred most of the possible cues. A long way from home, that was for sure; they'd been souvenir-shopping in the Quarter already. The fair one carried a shopping bag emblazoned with Thalban's logo in flowing script.

Money, too, she added to herself. Thalban dealt in high-quality goods, and they didn't come cheap.

She picked up her datapad and went to take their order. It would be interesting to see what language they addressed her in. *Standard Galcenian,* she wagered with herself. *But not like a native.*

The fair one spoke first. "Good day, Gentlelady,"

Bindweed smiled to herself—Galcenian, indeed, but with a faint, musical intonation that spoke of someplace else besides the Mother of Worlds. "Good day, Gentlesirs. What would you desire this fine noontide?"

"A bit of food and drink, before we get back to our ship." His voice was light and pleasant, without the edges that came with time and hardship. "If you could recommend?"

"Of course," she said. "We have fresh-made parchants today, and sugared berry-root. Perhaps those, and a pot of immer-leaf tea?"

He inclined his head in a gesture of gracious acquiescence that almost succeeded in looking unstudied. "That would be delightful."

Khesatan, she decided, as she headed back into the kitchen with the order. *Maybe second-generation expatriate. He's got some of the body language for it, and about half the accent. Not his buddy, though—I don't know where that one's from. If he'd said something, maybe then I could have placed him . . .*

Blossom caught her eye as soon as she came through the door. "Something's up," her partner said, and beckoned her over to the readout screen. "Take a look at this."

"Look at that," Miza said.

She leaned forward and used her light wand to circle a glyph on the work surface. The pattern she'd been following crystallized briefly, then cycled color from warm amber to deep purple. Eraasian-style display technology had taken her some getting used to when she first came to study with Huool—Artha used the standard Republic interfaces—but now that she'd learned its peculiarities, she found it handy and expressive.

"Whatever our big fish was looking for," she said, "he just found himself a seller. In my opinion, of course."

Huool came to look over her shoulder, and clicked his beak in approbation. "Very perceptive, young one. And what is being sought, I think we will soon learn."

"I didn't spot that."

"See here," said the Roti. He tapped another of the changing glyphs with a taloned forefinger. "The magnitude of the ripples makes discovery nearly certain."

Miza looked at the glyph more closely. "Now I've got it. We're talking extreme volatility—what should I do?"

"Continue to watch," Huool said. "And if the ripples from this affair threaten to touch our establishment, pray inform me at once."

He left to take his place in the front gallery for the afternoon shopping trade.

Miza stayed at her desk and watched the fluid information-shapes come and go on its work surface. Drawing her finger across the desktop's input area, she engaged its "record" mode. She still had her final exams to worry about when she returned to Artha, and it made sense to preserve the transactions of the next few hours for study and review.

Then she checked the timeline again. Huool had been right: the crossing would be soon.

Faral wasn't sure why his cousin had picked an Old Quarter tea shop as the best place to have lunch before returning to *Bright-Wind-Rising*. True, Thalban's Handcrafted Arts and Musicks occupied quarters across the square, and Jens had been looking for that establishment since first hearing of it on board ship—and if he thought that a carved bone fipple-flute and a set of bluestone counting-beads would make perfect souvenirs for his aunt and uncle back on Maraghai, then Faral wasn't going to argue with him—but just the same . . .

"Parchants and berry-root—are you serious?" he asked Jens under his breath. "The plate probably comes with a doily under it, too."

"I certainly hope so," said Jens. "The experience wouldn't be complete otherwise."

Faral sighed. "Is there some reason you're being difficult, foster-brother, or is this only a ploy to keep from getting bored? Because I remember what happened the *last* time you decided you didn't want to get bored."

His cousin abandoned his Khesatan manner for a few seconds and grinned at him. "It worked, didn't it? We weren't bored."

"Yes, but—"

"Ssh. Here's the food now."

And, indeed, a second woman—this one in a cook's apron over a neat white shirt and plain black trousers—was coming out of the kitchen with a loaded tray as Jens spoke. The tray held a steaming crystal pot of ruddy liquid, a cut-glass dish full of greenish cubes dusted with coarse sugar, and a porcelain platter with a pile of small round things under a white napkin. Faral couldn't tell if there was a doily under the platter or not.

He wondered if the cook was Bindweed or Blossom. The other woman, the one who'd taken their order, was up at the other occupied table with her datapad—settling a bill, it looked like. The cook drew closer, smiling.

Then, without warning, her posture shifted and she heaved the tray full of hot tea and pastries straight at their table. Faral threw himself sideways off his chair as the heavy crystal pot flew toward him. He thought he saw Jens ducking in the other direction, but he didn't have a chance to look. Immer-leaf tea splashed in all directions as the pot flew past where his head had been, and parchant buns pattered down like hailstones.

The cook was still moving, bringing up one foot in a kick that knocked the table over completely. He recognized the move—it was a common one in the hand-to hand he'd learned growing up back home—but where did a sweet little old gentlelady pastry cook learn something like that? Porcelain crashed and broke into splinters, silverware crashed and slid and clattered, and somewhere close behind him a man shouted in surprise and pain.

Faral took a chance on glancing up from the floor, and saw a man in tea-soaked blue and white livery clawing at his scalded face. In the next moment, a heavy blaster fired close by, its distinctive zing echoing through the shop. Then another blaster fired near at hand—once, twice, three times—the crimson energy bolts taking the scalded man in the chest and head as he fell.

"Get on your feet, boys," said the cook, who had somehow acquired a blaster in the few seconds that had passed since she'd stopped needing to hold on to the tray. "We have to get the two of you out of here."

She snapped off a quick shot through the milk-glass of the right-hand front shop window, where a shadow had moved. The glass curled away, leaving a neat round hole, and the shadow dropped suddenly down. Then she shifted her grip on the blaster and drew back her arm to throw it.

"Bindweed!" she shouted. "Catch!"

Well, that settles the question of which one is which, Faral thought, as the cook tossed the blaster across the room to her partner. The other woman plucked it from midair as it whirled past her, fired a quick bolt at an unseen target outside the door, then dropped and rolled. She came up kneeling on the other side of the doorway, half-covered by the frame, with the blaster gripped two-handed before her.

"Got you covered!" she called back to Blossom. "Go!"

Faral scrambled to his feet—Jens was already up off the floor, he saw with relief—and let Blossom steer them both toward the back of the shop.

"They'll have the alley covered," she said. "But maybe . . . come on!"

They were in the kitchen now, and she was pushing a button underneath the counter. The stove swung aside, and Faral saw that there was a trapdoor set into the tiles beneath. Blossom grabbed the recessed handle and pulled the door upward, revealing a circular, brick-lined shaft. A vertical ladder of rusty iron extended downward into darkness along one side of the tunnel.

"Get inside," said Blossom. "Go."

From the front room the blaster sounded again—a group of two shots, then a burst of three. Blossom grabbed a hand torch from its charging bracket on the kitchen wall and started down the ladder herself without bothering to wait.

Faral went in after her, with Jens so close behind him that his cousin's boot soles were on the rung above his head. As soon as Jens's head was below the level of the kitchen floor, the trap fell. Except for the glow of Blossom's hand torch, down in the shaft below them, they were wrapped in darkness.

The ladder ended in a horizontal passage. A stream of water ran through the tunnel ankle-deep, and the air was thick and foul. Based on the smell, Faral was glad that in the limited light he couldn't see what the water looked like.

"Come on," said Blossom, stepping down into the malodorous stream. She began moving away from them, her feet splashing in the foul water as she went, and he had no choice but to follow her. "There's a chance they won't figure out right away where we're heading."

They waded on in silence for a while. The way was slippery underfoot, with half the stone covered by flowing water and the rest of it coated with mud and slime. When Faral put a hand on the tunnel wall to steady himself, his palm came away smeared with something viscous and unnameable. He had an uncomfortable feeling that his right boot had a leak in it—his sock was beginning to squish. The thought failed to cheer him.

He drew a deep breath—regretted it when the thick miasma in the tunnel made him cough and wheeze—and said, "Who exactly is 'they'?"

"The people who were shooting at you, of course."

"Ah." That was Jens, bringing up the rear. From the sound of his voice, he didn't like the stink of the tunnel either. "*Those* people. Tell me, Gentlelady Blossom, if you possibly can—what in the name of hell is going on?"

"Bindweed and I object in principle to customers getting killed in our shop," she said. "It's bad for business."

IV. Ophel

IN THE back room at Huool Galleries, Miza watched the info glyphs on her desktop shift and transform themselves as the situation changed. Bidding intensity at the Atelier Provéc had plummeted; at the same time, a disconcerting ripple of excitement and anxiety had begun to manifest itself nearby. She waited long enough to make sure that the ripple was genuine and not an artifact of the graphing process, then tapped the comm link to the outer office.

"Gentlesir Huool, I think you ought to see this."

Most people, Faral suspected, would have lost track by now of how long and how far they had been slogging through the tunnels of Sombrelír's waste-disposal system. Most people, on the other hand, hadn't been brought up in the unmarked forests of Maraghai. For his own part, he had a good idea of both the time and the distance—he could retrace the route later at street level if he had to—but he didn't think the knowledge was going to prove useful anytime soon.

Blossom halted, finally, at the point where another iron

ladder, identical to the one in the kitchen of the tea shop, led up toward the arched ceiling of the tunnel. She directed the beam of light from her hand torch upward at what looked to Faral like the bottom side of a trapdoor.

"There," she said. "We should be safe now."

Such an air of confidence, Jens muttered to Faral in Trade-talk—the Maraghaite pidgin of Galcenian and the Forest Speech. *I love it.*

Blossom paid no attention. She started up the ladder, climbing briskly for a woman of her years who had just spent half an hour wading through chilly, ankle-deep water. At the top, she knocked on the trapdoor with the butt of her hand torch, waited a few seconds, then knocked again. It wasn't long before Faral heard a heavy sliding sound, like a piece of furniture being shoved aside. A crack of bright yellow light appeared among the shadows overhead.

"Come on," said Blossom as the trapdoor opened the rest of the way. She climbed through the opening and vanished from sight. With a shrug, Faral started up after her.

The glyphs on the desktop had stabilized. Miza wasn't certain what they portended, and she suspected that Huool didn't know either.

The Roti clicked his beak and ruffed up his neck feathers. "Disturbing. If I did not know better, I would swear—"

A sharp rapping noise interrupted him. Miza stared about, trying to pinpoint the direction of the sound. Huool's hearing was keener than hers: by the time the rapping came a second time, he was shoving at a stack of crates in the far corner. Miza left her desk and went to help him.

Together they shifted the boxes away from a section of tiled flooring that appeared, at first glance, to be no different from all the rest. On closer inspection, Miza spotted the hairthin lines that marked off a hidden door. Huool bent and pressed a taloned finger against what looked like—but obviously wasn't—a flawed spot in the tiles, and the trapdoor lifted and turned.

A nasty, sewer-reek odor billowed out of the opening, followed by a reed-thin, grey-haired woman in white shirt, black trousers, and a proper Ophelan-style apron and cap. The shirt and apron were mud-stained and streaked with rust.

"Huool, you old pirate," the woman said. "Are you glad to see me?"

Huool chittered with amusement. "Speaking as one pirate to another, Gentlelady, I certainly am. What can I do for you today?"

"Got a couple of lads here with me that need to get off-planet fast."

As she spoke, a dark-haired young man stuck his head up above the flooring, paused for a moment, then clambered the rest of the way out. A moment later another youth followed, this one taller than the first and as fair as the other was dark, with long yellow hair tied back from a lean, intelligent face. Both of the young men, like the woman, were smeared with sewer muck and rust—though Miza suspected that given a chance to wash themselves and change their dirt-stained jackets and trousers for less bedraggled clothing, they would clean up to something entirely presentable.

Huool chittered again. "I see you won the bidding."

"We didn't even know there was an auction going on," the woman said. "Not until the bill collectors showed up, anyhow. Three, maybe more, from the Green Sun gang."

"Not cheap talent," Huool said. "But . . . it appears . . . not terribly *talented* talent. Or perhaps merely outclassed."

"It's good to learn we haven't lost our touch," said the woman modestly. She turned to the pair of young men. "Who knew that the two of you would be coming to the shop?"

The fair one shrugged. The gesture had a casual grace to it that Miza thought might be Khesatan; his voice, when he spoke, confirmed her suspicions. "Since we hadn't planned on it beforehand . . . no one, I suppose."

"No." The other youth shook his head, frowning. He had a solid look to him that Miza approved of, and his manner was free of airs and affectations. She couldn't place his accent at all as he said to his fellow, "We didn't plan on Gentlelady Blossom's tea shop, true enough. But you spent half the morning asking for directions to that music store right across the square. Thalban's, or whatever it was called. And *it* came recommended."

The woman called Blossom glanced at him sharply. "Recommended by whom?"

"A fellow on board *Bright-Wind-Rising*. We were talking about things to do while the ship was in port."

"Have you got a name on him?"

"No. He was an ordinary-looking guy—dark hair, plain clothes. A bit older than Jens and me."

"Where was he from?" Blossom demanded. "What kind of business? When did he board?"

The two youths looked at one another. Miza could see the suspicion—*a bit belated,* she commented to herself; *we've definitely got a pair of sheltered innocents here*—making itself visible in their eyes.

"He didn't happen to mention it," the fair-haired one said after a moment or two. Miza got the impression that he was choosing his words with considerable care. Maybe Blossom hadn't brought in a matched pair of innocents, after all. "And we didn't speak with him for all that long."

"You were a whole fortnight in transit," Blossom demanded, "and you didn't even get to know your shipmates?"

"We weren't traveling for the sake of the giddy social round." The young man paused. "Turnabout is fair play. What I want to know is how *you* knew how long we were in transit."

"Because I know who you are," Blossom said. "You're Jens Metadi-Jessan D'Rosselin and the short one over there with all the muscles is your cousin Faral Hyfid-Metadi. And you're both in a world of trouble."

"I'd never have noticed if you hadn't mentioned it." Jens Metadi-Jessan D'Rosselin took a step backward, set his shoulders against the storeroom wall, and pulled a blaster out of his front coat pocket. His fair skin had gone much paler, Miza noted, and his blue eyes were very bright.

"The gentlesir in the tea shop dropped this," he said. "And yes, I do know how to use it. So if you don't mind, my cousin and I will leave now. Thanks for the help and all, but we have a ship to catch."

Huool ruffled his feathers in agitation. "My dear boy!" he exclaimed. "You have no appreciation of the seriousness of the situation. You are, how shall I say this, hunted?"

"Think about it for a minute," Blossom added. "You need to make it to the port and get off-planet. We want you to make it to the port and get off-planet. There shouldn't be any problem working something out."

"My mother told me that I should be careful talking to strangers," Jens said. "And I'm afraid you know more of our names than we do of yours. Nobody is working out anything until we've had some proper introductions."

Blossom looked more amused than Miza thought quite proper for an elderly gentlelady being held at blaster-point. "When a young man with a blaster asks for my name," the tea shop owner said to Jens, "I believe in giving it to him. And as it happens, I owe a duty to your House."

She made a deep bow, after some style of etiquette that Miza didn't recognize; not the local Ophelan mode, nor yet the generalized manner of a seasoned traveler. But her next words explained much. "I'm Tillijen Chereeve, quondam Armsmaster to House Rosselin of Entibor."

The dark youth—Faral, it seemed his name was—growled a foreign-sounding phrase somewhere in the back of his throat. "For a planet that got blown up fifty-something years ago," he added, "there are entirely too many of you people running around."

"My sentiments exactly, coz," said Jens. He hadn't lowered the blaster, and the note of suspicion wasn't yet gone from his voice. "One question more, Gentlelady Tillijen—if you are indeed who you say you are. Who was the Number One gunner on *Warhammer* back when Granda was a privateer?"

"That was Nannla Rue," said Blossom promptly. "She and I worked the *'Hammer*'s guns together, with Ferrdacorr *ngha-*Rillikkik in the engine room and Errec Ransome in the co-pilot's chair."

Jens nodded. "Then, Gentlelady Tillijen—"

"Call me Blossom. It's what I go by these days."

"—Gentlelady Blossom, if what you say is true, and the attack in your shop was not merely an elaborate charade you've staged in order to gain our trust—then what would you have us do?"

"The first thing," Blossom told him, "is to get yourselves tidied up. You can't go wandering around town looking like you've been crawling through the sewers. People will talk."

"Easily handled," said Huool. "Miza, take our young guests upstairs and show them the washing facilities. Make them clean."

Miza stared at him in surprise. "Me?"

"Consider it part of your education, young one. I'll see that you get extra credit."

In the Old Quarter of Sombrelír, the metallic wail of sirens cut through the quiet afternoon, and a smell of wood smoke drifted on the wind. Mistress Klea Santreny, her polished staff of Nammerin *grrch* wood firmly held in hand, strode across the open square. Ophel was a civilized planet; an Adept's staff was sufficient to win passage for her through the barricades that local fire and security forces had put up to keep out gawkers.

Around her, the flashing lights of emergency vehicles made a disorienting jumble of garish color against a background of neatly trimmed trees and pastel shopfronts. A vertical-lift aircar with City MedServ insignia took off in a roar of heavy-duty nullgravs. The aircar hovered for an instant at rooftop level, then darted away toward where the hospitals, tall and sleek, raised their platforms above the crowded buildings of the modern city. On one side of the square, underneath a sign proclaiming the shop behind it to be the home of the finest shoes in the world, a team of medics worked over a prone body.

I haven't seen a mess like this since the war, Klea thought. She noted on the shoemaker's wall the distinctive blast patterns of an energy lance. *Looks like a near miss. A hit wouldn't have left enough for the medics to bother with.*

Across the plaza, people wearing the caps and armbands of Sombrelír's Civil Guard were talking into autoscribes and pointing hand recorders at the scene. The focus of their activity seemed to be Bindweed & Blossom's tea shop. The front of the building was stained with soot, and most of the downstairs windows were broken out. A line of scorch marks showed where somebody had swept a blaster set on "continuous fire" across the painted stucco wall.

Klea moved nearer to the iron fence that surrounded the tea shop's trampled garden. The Guild Master's wayward nephews were not, she hoped, in this place any longer, but if she wanted to pick up their trail, this was where she would have to do it. Unobtrusively, she opened her mind to the search—and felt the hairs rise on her neck as the presence of Magework came to her like a bad smell on the wind.

She looked about for the source of the unpleasant sensation, and saw a man approaching the shop from her left. Like her, he wore black and carried a staff; but his staff was the short, silver-bound rod of a Mage, and he wore a Mage's featureless black mask under the hood of his cloak.

This is Ophel, Klea reminded herself. *People here don't feel about Mages the way we do back home.*

The Mage in question strode purposefully forward, his goal apparently the same as her own—the blast-marked façade of Bindweed & Blossom's. Klea moved to intercept him, stepping up beside him and placing a hand on his sleeve.

"Hold, friend," she said.

He halted, and made a nodding acknowledgment of her presence. "Mistress Santreny." His accent was strong: harsh in the consonants and oddly pitched in the long, musical vowels. "I beg your pardon, but I am engaged."

"You have the advantage of me," she said, not letting go his arm. "I'm afraid that I don't know you at all."

The Mage swept back his hood with his free hand, and removed his mask in the same gesture. Klea saw that he was a man about a decade older than she was herself, with ordinary, unterrifying features. His thick black hair was streaked liberally with iron-grey. After a moment, Klea realized that she knew him.

"Mael Taleion," she said. "Second of the Circles."

"As you, too, are Second," he said. "After the Adepts' fashion. Now, please, let us go each to our own business."

A suspicion stirred in Klea's mind. "Your business wouldn't happen to concern a pair of young men from Maraghai, would it?"

"And if it does?"

"Mine does as well. The Master of the Guild wants to see them kept away from danger."

"If that's the case," Taleion said, "you appear to have had little success. But I dare not chide you for it—I have similar orders from the First of the Mage-Circles. And, like you, I tracked the young men from the spaceport to here. Where, trust me, they currently are not."

"This part of the trail is cold," Klea said. She nodded toward the tea shop, where two members of the Civil Guard were talking with a straight-backed, grey-haired woman. A smudge of soot marked the woman's forehead where she had wiped away the sweat, and blaster-fire had scorched the gold-embroidered fabric of her vest and skirt. "We need to talk to that one over there sometime soon. Maybe she knows where our birds have flown."

In the plush and paneled offices of the Green Sun Cooperative, a man stood at uneasy attention before the desk of Nilifer Jehavi—the son of the organization's founder, and currently in charge of its day-to-day operations.

"Well?" Jehavi said.

"There were . . . complications," the man said. His name badge, clipped to his left breast pocket, said that his name was Kolpag Garbazon, that his serial number was 13tq4908y, that he was an Operative First Class, and that he was cleared for Upmost-level secrets. He had over a dozen years of experience in the service of the Cooperative.

"I know there were complications," Jehavi said. "If there

hadn't been complications, we wouldn't have had to refund the deposit. You don't know how we hate doing that."

In fact, Kolpag had a fairly good idea how much the head man—and his son—hated to give back a customer's money. Not to mention how much they hated seeing any lowering of the firm's reputation. Now, however, was not the time for a prudent man to talk about such things.

"I know there were complications," Jehavi repeated, more quietly, and in a kinder tone. "You had orders that the packages were not to be damaged in any way, and you walked into an ambush."

He paused a moment. Then: "Please, sit down."

Kolpag sat, and tried not to show his relief. The young boss wasn't as dangerous or as unpredictable as his father had been, but he still wasn't a man whose wrath anyone could take lightly.

Jehavi leaned back in his chair and looked at Kolpag. "Well, then," he said. "You are still my best field operative, regardless of what our recent contractors expressed to me in some exceedingly colorful language just now. Leaving all that aside—you lost your partner. Will you be able to work?"

"Yes," Kolpag said. For a simple snatch-and-go on a couple of tourists, this afternoon had turned into a complete disaster. He knew intellectually that Freppys wouldn't be waiting in the employees' lounge cracking jokes when he walked out of Jehavi's office, but the emotional reality hadn't yet sunk in.

"Good. These are your new orders. You are still to pick up the packages. Previous rules of engagement remain in effect: the packages are not to be harmed in any way. The difference is that this time, instead of delivering the packages anywhere else, you are to bring them here to me. Clear?"

"Clear." Kolpag allowed himself to wonder, briefly, what new enterprise Jehavi had in mind. Then he laid the question aside: he was an employee, not an executive, and the Green Sun did not pay him to think about such things.

"Excellent," said Jehavi. "And if, in the course of your efforts, you learn who set up the ambush this afternoon—and why—I would be delighted to learn of it. Where *that* matter is concerned, survivors among the opposition are neither necessary nor desired. Clear?"

Kolpag nodded. "Clear," he said again. He didn't add, because it was not a matter for the boss's concern, that with the death of Freppys, finding out who'd arranged the ambush in the Old Quarter had ceased to be merely a business obligation.

"Excellent. Let us move on to the next item."

One thing, at least, Jehavi had in common with his more notorious father: whenever he was in a room, he commanded the attention of everyone else present through the sheer force of his personality. When he gestured at a chair over against the wall to his right, Kolpag noticed for the first time that another man had been sitting there all along.

"This is Ruhn," Jehavi said. "He's your new partner."

Ruhn was a short man with close-cropped red hair. He nodded once, politely, at Kolpag, and Kolpag returned the nod without enthusiasm. He didn't need to waste time right now settling into a new partnership ... but it was against Green Sun policy for operatives to work alone.

Both men turned back to Jehavi. "Right," the boss said. "My gut tells me that the packages are on-planet, but not for long. The two of you know your jobs. Do them."

Kolpag pushed back his chair and stood up. "Expenses?"

"Draw them from the accounting office," Jehavi said.

He turned back to his desk. "That's all, gentlesirs. You can go."

Faral glanced over at his cousin. Jens hadn't yet put down the blaster, and everybody else in the crowded storeroom—Gentlelady Tillijen, the Roti named Huool who apparently owned the place, and the girl Miza who worked there—was waiting to see what he would do with it.

"Come on," Faral said. "I think we can trust these people." In Trade-talk, he added, *If it turns out we can't, you can always shoot them later anyhow.*

The girl stepped out from behind her worktable and gestured at a door on the far side of the room. "This way," she said. "Upstairs."

The staircase was narrow and steep, as well as being heavily soundproofed. Red glowdots set at intervals into the paneling gave a murky crimson light.

Miza led the way up the carpeted steps. She wore snug green trousers—Faral had an excellent view from the stairs behind her—and she had a thick brush of bright red hair that bobbed against her shoulder blades as she walked. If Jens's blaster frightened her, she was doing a good job of not showing it.

Faral moved a bit closer to his cousin. "What exactly are you planning to do with that thing?"

"Protect us from snakes and strange men," Jens said. "I think we've fallen into a den of thieves. Right now I just want to get to the port and get out of here."

"So do I. Chaka's going to laugh her head off, though." He switched back to Trade-talk. *Is there something else going on that you know about and I don't?*

Maybe, Jens said. *We'll talk about it later.*

They reached the top of the stairs and followed Miza down a narrow passage. The walls, paneled in dark wood like the stairway, hemmed them in on either side. Light panels overhead provided enough illumination to show that the carpet underfoot was dark green, patterned with a convoluted design of golden serpents. The deep nap muffled the sound of their footsteps. No outsider in the rooms below would know if someone came or went on the upper level.

Miza stopped at a door on the right-hand side of the passage. It slid open, not swinging on hinges the way most of the doors in the Old Quarter had done, and revealed a small, windowless room lined with shelves and cabinets. A bank of comps and repro units filled most of the remaining space.

"All right," Miza said. Her Galcenian sounded as idiomatic as Faral's own—maybe more so, without the Forest accent to get in the way. "Hand over your identification plates. I'll need them to create new personas for you. And take off your clothes."

Faral blinked. "What?"

He was grateful that his skin didn't show a blush easily. Jens might have heard stranger requests every day while he was living on Khesat, but life under the Big Trees was more sedate. Miza didn't seem to notice his reaction, however, except as a request to explain further.

"Dump your old things in the recycler and put on clean outfits from the stuff over there." She pointed at the far wall, where piles of folded cloth in assorted colors and textures lay on shelves next to racks of boots and shoes.

"With you in the room?" Faral asked.

She looked at him impatiently. "Where else am I supposed to be? I've got to get your documents ready, and this is where I do it."

Faral looked at Jens. His cousin still held the blaster at the ready, but he'd already removed his ID case from his jacket with his left hand. If Miza's request had startled him, it wasn't showing. Faral shrugged—*Mamma always said things were different out here in the big galaxy*—and pulled out his own ID case.

The girl took both sets of ID without comment and carried them over to the comp setup. Turning her back on the rest of the room, she began feeding their datacards and flatpix into the reader. She ignored Jens's blaster completely, as if it had been a younger brother's water toy.

"Now what?" Faral muttered to his cousin. "Am I supposed to go first, or you?"

Jens looked at Miza's back. She was hunched over the comp, her hands busy on its input panel. The repro unit next to her hummed and blinked and spat out hard copy.

"Here, take this," he said, handing Faral the blaster. "Essence of Sewage isn't my favorite perfume, and there's no point in walking around Sombreír in this condition if we can reasonably avoid it."

The weapon felt heavier than Faral had expected. "How am I supposed to—"

"The safety's off. If you need to shoot, the firing stud is that red button there by your thumb."

Faral held the blaster gingerly, keeping his grip well clear of the firing stud. "I'll try to remember. Foster-brother . . . if it isn't too much to ask, what do you think you're doing?"

"Changing clothes." Jens already had his boots off and was peeling away his socks.

There were times, Faral reflected, when his cousin became almost too Khesatan to put up with. "I *know* that. But why pull a blaster on someone who's helping us out of trouble? Are you expecting—?"

"—treachery? No." Jens pulled a clean white shirt off the nearest shelf and held it up for a critical inspection. "But it doesn't hurt to be careful."

"You were never this suspicious before you went off to visit Khesat," Faral complained. "What did they *do* to you back there, anyway?"

"They told me to think of it as a learning experience," Jens said. "I learned a lot."

As soon as he'd finished changing, he stuffed his old clothes into the recycling bin and held out his hand for the blaster. Faral handed the weapon over with relief. It didn't take him long to shuck out of his mud-stained garments and put on new ones—as long as the size was approximately correct, he didn't care about the finer points of style and color. He'd just gotten the shirt over his head and had started tugging on the collar laces to tighten them when the repro unit beeped.

Miza gathered up the stacks of items from the unit's various output trays and sorted the lot into a pair of leather credit cases. She turned around and held the cases out to Faral and Jens.

"Here," she said. "Take these. The best fake ID that money can buy. And it's yours for free."

Was the timing on that just good luck, Faral wondered, *or did she keep her back turned in order to spare our feelings?*

He took the case she offered him, uncertain whether having his feelings spared was a good thing or not. A quick glance inside the case showed him that he was Ilwyn Fane, of Therabek, and that he had a more-than-respectable line of credit with the banking firm of Dahl&Dahl on Suivi Point. He slid the case into his pocket.

"Thanks," he said. "But what about our real IDs? And what about our tickets? We can't get on board ship without them."

Jens was inspecting his own credit case—a bit awkwardly, because of the blaster in his right hand. "With the stuff they've set up for us in these, coz, we could buy a ship outright if we had to."

"Nothing but the finest merchandise from Huool Galleries," said Miza. She gave the blaster a dubious glance. "Are you planning to lug that thing around in plain view all the way to the port?"

"Yes, I am," Jens said. "And I hope you remembered to include a permit-to-carry along with all the rest of the fake paperwork."

"It's in the back with the insurance papers," Miza said. "But I wouldn't take it out yet, if I were you. The ink may not be all the way dry."

V. Ophel; Cracanth

CHAKALLAKAK *ngha*-CHAKALLAKAK had slept
late that morning. Let Faral and Jens tire themselves out with rushing about in downtown Sombrelír; some
people had more sense than to bother. She'd gotten out of bed
in her own good time, and had spent a pleasant day lazing
amid the trove-stores in the spaceport concourse, before making her way over to RSS *Lav'rok*—the ship that would carry
them all to Eraasi and who-knew-what adventure.

As she'd expected, Faral and Jens weren't aboard yet. If
the pair of them ran true to form, they'd arrive breathless and
flushed with exertion moments before the ship's main passenger lock snapped shut for lift-off. Chaka looked forward to
watching the two thin-skins try to strap in while the nullgravs
were tilting *Lav'rok* to launch position.

Already the luggage was strapped in place in the middle of
their travel compartment for their use during the trip. Rather
than unship it and have to put it back again before launch,
Chaka left the cabin and headed for the *Lav'rok*'s common
compartments. Now was as good a time as any to look over

their shipmates for the coming transit. From Ophel to the Mageworlds was a long haul no matter how you sliced it.

Lav'rok's common passenger space had room for a gaming area, an industrial-size refreshment dispenser, and a holovid lounge. Chaka stopped first at the dispenser to get a tall frosty mug of Khesatan *sulg*. She'd never tasted it before, but starting off your wandering-time with a new experience was supposed to be good luck. Besides, Jens claimed that the bright blue liquid didn't taste half-bad.

Jens was wrong. It did taste half-bad, and then some. No point in wasting it, though, or the luck. She pulled the membranes across her nostrils and swallowed anyway. Mug in hand, she walked across to the holovid lounge, where a dozen local broadcast stations were displayed on as many monitors.

The main holovid tank was showing an ancient *Spaceways Patrol* episode with voices dubbed into the local lingo. A glowing line of unfamiliar script ran around the base of the tank, translating the dialogue into a second language that Chaka didn't understand either.

A flatvid screen set into a nearby bulkhead was showing what looked like a newscast from downtown Sombrelír. A thin-skin wearing what Chaka had learned was their sober-and-serious expression gazed earnestly out over his audience and spoke in rapid Ophelan. Behind him, a long shot of the city showed a plume of smoke rising from among the buildings.

Chaka sipped at her mug of *sulg* and gave the newscast half an eye. Some kind of disaster in the city, apparently—thin-skins in medical and emergency uniforms rushed about while the announcer kept talking in front of them. Suddenly two pictures flashed on the screen, side by side: Jens and Faral, in their entry-visa flatpix.

Wait a minute! Chaka shouted as she slewed around toward the screen fast enough to slosh her drink. *What's going on? Does anybody in here speak that forsaken lingo?*

Settle down, young one, came a low growl from the table beside her.

Chaka turned in that direction. The speaker was a big male

Selvaur, his grey-green hide starting to go coarse and wrinkly with age. A ripple of scar tissue ran down his left arm, and his left eye was filmed over. He had a mug of redbriar ale in one hand, and his demeanor was considerably calmer than her own.

Did you understand what the announcer said? Chaka asked him—adding the honorific, *Known One,* almost as an afterthought at the end.

Maybe I did . . . what's your interest?

I believe I'm acquainted with those two thin skins.

Then this could be your lucky day, said the older Selvaur. *There's a reward out for both of them—for them personally, or for knowledge of their whereabouts.*

Never mind the reward, Chaka said, tossing back the *sulg* regardless of the taste. *They're my friends.*

No good ever came of consorting with their kind, the old one said. *Take it from me.*

Thanks, said Chaka. She stood up and slapped the empty mug down on the table as she spoke, then headed for the door. *I'll try to keep that in mind.*

The secret way out of Huool's back rooms opened onto a brick-paved street in another block, beneath a green-painted arch of metal sculpted to look like a flowering vine. An open-air café stood on one side of the arch, a millinery shop on the other; the arch itself bore only a house number worked into the metal. This was the section of the Old Quarter where the more conservative members of Sombrelír's business community were in the habit of keeping their established paramours, in jewel-box apartments with just such unmarked entrances. Anybody who happened to see three young people leaving together in the middle of the afternoon would think, with a bit of amusement, that some paragon of wealth and respectability was not getting all the fidelity that he or she had paid for.

Miza led the way, setting a brisk pace—but not, she hoped, one so brisk that the two young men behind her would think she was trying to outrun the blaster that Jens Metadi-Jessan D'Rosselin had inside his jacket pocket. Huool had made it clear, by his words and his manner, that the safety of Jens and his cousin was a matter of paramount importance, and that responsibility had fallen upon her to get them to the port and away.

Huool wanted somebody who'd never done escort duty before, she thought. She knew what that meant, too. On all the civilized worlds, a package in the hands of a recognized and neutral courier was, by tradition, safe from attack. So if Huool was taking pains not to let a known courier like himself be connected with the two young men, then he wasn't counting on people being civilized.

Miza wondered what had made the pair such a hot item on everybody's requisition list. She'd probably never find out.

Get them safe to their ship and that's an end to it, she thought. *Maybe I'll hear about them someday on the holovid news.*

"All right, guys," she said, turning back toward them. "We go left at the next corner."

The words were all the way out of her mouth before she noticed that neither of the two young men was there anymore. They were, in fact, gone. And they'd been right behind her—she could have sworn it—not a second before.

"Oh, damn," she muttered. She could see the failing grade on her work-study transcript already. She hopped up onto the plinth of a bronze statue of the city's first Lord Mayor, the better to look back at the street behind her, but her wayward charges were nowhere visible. They were well and truly gone.

"Oh, damn," she repeated, with deep feeling.

"The problem with letters of credit," Jens said, "is that they're traceable."

Faral made a noncommittal noise. He was fairly certain that his cousin's knowledge was a secondhand acquisition, much as the blaster had been. So far, their escape from pursuit hadn't been difficult—giving Miza the slip had required nothing more than an exchange of glances, a nod, and a quick fade at the nearest corner; easy work for anyone brought up under the Big Trees—but the hard part was yet to come. If

Jens knew something useful, it didn't matter to Faral how and where his cousin had picked it up.

Jens was still explaining, or remembering aloud as the case might be. "Once you draw on the credit you leave a record of your exact whereabouts for at least the person or entity who issued the letter. Cash, on the other hand—"

"—doesn't have anybody's name on it," said Faral. A shopwindow beckoned ahead on the left, with the word EX-CHANGE glowing inside a sheet of what looked like solid armor-glass. The display technique—the effects of depth and movement embedded in a solid substance rather than pro-jected outward—was one that he'd already learned to associ-ate with the Mageworlds, and half of the languages in the display looked to be from the other side of the Gap Between. He pointed at the sign. "Is that what you're looking for?"

"It is," Jens said. "Let's see how much of the local coin we can draw on these instruments, and then drop Gentlesir Huool's generous gifts down the nearest recycling tube."

The little shop had an armor-glass wall against the back, thick enough to slow almost any portable energy or projectile weapon. A single clerk, a wizened little man wearing a green apron, sat behind the glass reading a datapad. He looked up when Faral and Jens walked in.

The clerk's mouth moved, but the security screen blocked whatever sound came out of it. Instead, an amplified voice spoke from the upper right corner of the outer room.

"Can I help you?"

The speaker's accent was local, but the words were Galcenian. Faral wondered if he and Jens had that obvious an off-planet look, even in borrowed clothes from the upstairs room at Huool's establishment.

Probably, he thought. *Nothing we can do about it right now, except hope that this guy doesn't care as long as our money is good.*

Jens had apparently reached the same conclusion. "We find ourselves in need of ready funds," he said. He drew forth the credit voucher—using, Faral noted, his left hand, which meant that his right was free for the blaster now tucked out of sight in his coat pocket—and slid it toward the exchange slot. "How much can you advance us on this paper?"

The letter of credit vanished with a gentle sigh of air as the security screen's vacuum system pulled it under the armorglass. The purple glow of an active scanner flashed from the narrow aperture a second before the slip of paper appeared on the other side. At a nod from Jens, Faral extracted his own letter of credit and slid it through the scanner after the first one.

"A fairish amount," the clerk said a moment later. "On both of them combined, considerably more than a fairish." It was disconcerting to see the man's mouth move while his words came from a disembodied source in the outer room. "Assuming that you are the persons to whom these letters apply."

"We have identification," Faral said.

"Assuredly," said the clerk. "Such fine gentlemen as yourselves. Please put your identity chit in the slot, then place your hand in the receptacle."

The panel below the security screen lit up, revealing a row of narrow slots paired with open bays. Faral regarded the setup dubiously. Back among the woods and rocks of Maraghai, only foolhardy off-worlders reached barehanded into shadowy recesses—and some of them came away with fewer fingers than they'd started with. But Jens was already feeding his ID card into one of the slots with a studied nonchalance; Faral supposed that he had no choice but to do likewise.

The reader swallowed his card. An amber light flashed on the panel, and he fitted his right hand into the bay underneath. A tight band closed around his wrist, trapping his hand in the reader.

Foolhardy off-worlder, he thought. *That's me, all right.*

He supposed that if anything awkward showed up in the data scan, the cuff wouldn't let go until local peace officers arrived and escorted him to someplace where he could assist them in their inquiries.

It wouldn't be a problem, he reassured himself. *Even if they did show up. We were attacked, and that wasn't our fault, and nothing that happened afterward was our fault either. A few words with local security might be the fastest way to get back to our ship, and maybe the safest, too.*

He was almost hoping that the papers would ring up false—that Dahl&Dahl had never heard of him, or that his fingerprints and his protein scans didn't match. But instead, he heard a buzzing sound from somewhere inside the panel, and the pressure of the restraining cuff diminished. He pulled his hand away as the clerk spoke again.

"And how would the noble sirs prefer their cash?"

"In large tokens," said Jens. "Though not so large as to be unusable. I have obligations to meet."

The clerk began pulling out stacks of orange chits and sliding them through the inner door of the exchange lock.

"How are we going to carry all those?" Faral asked.

"Silence, coz," Jens said. "We'll purchase a carrybag at the first convenient opportunity. In the meantime, I'm positive we can stow them about our persons somehow."

Miza carefully traced her way back from the corner where she'd noticed that Faral and Jens had gone missing. *They can't have made it too far,* she told herself. *They're strangers here, they have no friends, they're being hunted. Where would they go?*

Where would I go?

Their first stop, she decided after a few seconds of panicky deliberation, would be to get cash. That meant visiting a cambio, since the pair of them couldn't have been in town long enough to set up a local account. And with neither hard money nor transit tokens in the packets she'd handed them, they couldn't hop into a jitney and tell the driver to take them somewhere.

On foot, then. And close by.

Faral and Jens would have spotted a cambio in Fracini Square, if they'd been alert—it was the only such place in the neighborhood with a visible sign. That gave her a logical place to start looking.

She was right, too. When she arrived opposite the cambio, she saw two figures inside the shop, dimly visible through the armor-glass of the front window.

Miza frowned. Tourists who got more than a double fifty-chit from Barapan's establishment would meet a mugger later in the day, all but guaranteed. If the sum advanced to the off-worlders was sufficient—and Miza, who had made out the letters of credit herself, felt certain that it would be—Barapan might even have sent for the strongarms already.

She changed position to another spot, this one not so advantageous for watching Barapan's cambio, but somewhat better for watching watchers. Then she waited.

Yes . . . there they were, halfway up the street in either direction: a man in a grey hat, window-shopping, and a woman carrying a bouquet of flowers, pausing to arrange her bustier. Miza couldn't see the backup team, but she knew that the strongarms would have one lurking a block away, ready to swing onto whatever path Faral and Jens took when they left the cambio. In only a couple of minutes, half of Barapan's money would be heading back into his personal accounts, with the other half going to the robbers.

Now what do I do? she wondered. She wasn't a physical operative, and she didn't want to be. She was an analyst, and knew that someday she'd be a damned good one, but violence had never been part of her training. If the two off-worlders were depending on her . . . *There they come now.*

Faral and Jens came out of the shop, their pockets bulging with what must have been every decimal-bit the letters of credit would allow, and took a right-hand turn onto the street. Miza followed, walking fast but trying not to be conspicuous in her hurry. Over on the other side of the street, and a little bit ahead of them, the gentlelady with the armful of fresh flowers and the embroidered bustier was drifting in the same direction at a deceptively easy pace.

The two young off-worlders didn't seem to notice. They ought to have had "tourist" written on their shirts in three different alphabets and five different languages, Miza reflected, the way they were gazing at shopwindows and ambling along as if they hadn't a care in the world.

The lady with the flowers was still following them. So was Miza—far enough behind to watch, but not close enough to appear part of the group. With any luck, when the inevitable happened, no one would be hurt. Then she could get back to taking the two young men down to the port, perhaps a little chastened and easier to handle for their misadventure.

The blaster, she thought suddenly. *You're forgetting about that blaster. If Jens is foolish enough to go for it in the scuffle . . .*

He won't have time to get it out.

Up ahead, in another of the Old Quarter's little. parks, a tree-lined bower opened its shadowed mouth onto the street. *That's where it'll all happen,* Miza thought. She strove to observe everything and remember it clearly. If she made a good report to Huool afterward, maybe her grades wouldn't suffer too much.

The woman with the flowers crossed the street and headed back in the direction of the young off-worlders. Their paths converged at the opening of the bower. The woman, feigning surprise and clumsiness, lost her grip on the bouquet, scattering white and yellow josquiths all over the pavement. At the same time, a pair of muscular gentlemen stepped from the shadows and reached out to lay violent hands on the two young men.

And then—Jens spun and kicked high, his yellow hair flying as he moved, and the point of his boot struck the nearer of the two muggers on the jaw. The man fell. At the same time, Faral grabbed the woman by her upper arms and dropped, using the momentum thus created to throw her against the second mugger. Thief and decoy collapsed together onto the grass inside the bower, entangled as if caught in the midst of some bizarre assignation.

Miza hurried forward, but before she could reach the spot, she felt herself caught, spun, and thrown against the trunk of a tree, with Jens Metadi-Jessan D'Rosselin pressing the business end of a blaster into the flesh of her throat.

I was wrong, she thought. *He did have enough time to get it out.*

"Are you with these people?" he asked. His blue eyes had a dangerous brightness to them. "Is there a good reason why I shouldn't stun you now and leave you here while my cousin and I make our complaint to local security?"

Miza drew a deep breath. It wouldn't do to have her voice squeak with fright like a Roti's breakfast. A few feet away, she could see Faral going through the pockets of the fallen men. Both the strongarms were lying quite still, though their chests were moving. The woman had, apparently, recovered herself and fled, leaving her flowers scattered broadcast across the pavement.

"Well?" said Jens.

"Don't be an idiot," she said. "I'm on your side."

Faral made a noise of satisfaction and straightened up from his search of the unconscious men. "ID," he said, brandishing their personal card cases triumphantly. "We were wondering where we'd find some new stuff."

"Good," said Jens, without looking away from Miza. "If you're on our side—name a city within an hour's travel of Sombrelír."

"Nanáli. Duvize is closer, but more links go to Nanáli."

He made the blaster vanish. "Great. Let's go to Nanáli. You lead, we follow. Just don't try to get to a public comm booth—I don't want to lose you again."

Miza gave him what she hoped was a scornful glance. "I wasn't the one who decided to break away from the guided tour, remember?"

"Foster-brother," Faral said to Jens in an undertone. "I think we need to leave here in a hurry. People are starting to talk."

Miza saw that he was right. Passersby were already gathering in a knot a discreet distance away from the altercation. *These two,* she thought, *desperately need a good courier.*

"This way," she said, and stepped over the pair of recumbent strongarms toward the back of the bower, not looking to see if Jens and Faral came after her. The front steps and doorway a private house lay on the other side of the shadowed arch of greenery. Over to one side, and conveniently invisible from the street, a wrought-iron fence marked the edge of another bower, this one cleverly planted to look like a patch of untamed woodland.

Jens looked at the fence with approval. "Very nice design."

"We don't admire it," Miza said. "We climb over it. Quickly."

"You heard the gentlelady," Faral said. "Let's go."

"They're right about off-worlders on Khesat," Jens said, vaulting lightly over the fence. "No taste for the finer things in life. None at all."

"This place you want me to go into," said Mael Taleion. "I cannot."

Klea pressed her lips together for a moment before answering. Of all the problems she had anticipated from this unwelcome alliance, she hadn't expected to encounter a Magelord with philosophical scruples.

"Then you'll have to camp on the street," she said finally. "And in this district, I don't think that would be a good idea."

She knew intellectually that Mages were only human. Just the same, she'd never liked dealing with them. All the time she'd been growing up on Nammerin, in between the first war and the second, the Magelords had been bogeys to scare small children—stock villains of a thousand holovids, requiring no motivation for the basest crimes other than the fact of their Magery.

Nothing in her childhood, or in what came afterward, had prepared her for this: a quiet, unassuming man whose calm demeanor failed to disguise the fact that he was as dubious about their situation as she was. In spite of what she had told Mael Taleion, she knew that staying outside was not an option. The Sombrelír Guildhouse occupied an otherwise empty block in a neighborhood that had once been fashionable. Now the area was an industrial slum. The Guildhouse, with its grounds and garden, stood like a lonely sentinel amid the encroaching sterility of prefab warehouses and manufacturing bays.

"Come on," she said. "If I can work with you, you can go in there with me. Not that this place is anything special, as Guildhouses go. I suppose Ophel is lucky to have one at all."

Mael sighed. "For the sake of the greater good," he said, and made a hand gesture that Klea supposed was meant to avert evil. Not only did Mages have an unconscionable belief in luck, but they were superstitious as well. Since Mael was technically Klea's guest, she tried hard to suppress the discourteous thought.

The Magelord drew his cloak around him and settled his mask over his face. Then, with a defiant air, he took his staff and attached it to a belt clip. "Let us go in."

"Are you sure you want to wear—"

"I will not pretend to be other than what I am."

Even under the distorting effect of the featureless plastic mask, Klea could hear the stubborn voice of a man who has made all the concessions he has it in him to make. She abandoned the subject and pushed open the Guild-yard gate. It squeaked on its hinges. She frowned at the noise—*if these people neglect the upkeep of house and grounds, what else do they neglect?*—and side by side with Mael Taleion she strode up the gravel walkway to the high doors of the main house.

They hadn't gone a dozen steps before an apprentice emerged from inside the Guildhouse and held out his hand in a minatory gesture.

"*Guira dán!*" he said in Ophelan—a warning of some sort, Klea supposed, from his tone and his expression.

"And good afternoon to you, too," she replied in Galcenian. She took another step forward.

"Mistress!" the apprentice said. "You don't want to—you can't—he's a *Mage!*" The apprentice's voice went up about an octave, and he flung out a hand to point at Mael's chest.

"The fact has not escaped my notice," Klea said. "Now, either call your Masters or let me pass, but don't just stand there gabbling."

The door opened again, and more hurrying footsteps

crunched in the gravel ahead of them. A man in the garments of an Adept was running toward them, his fat cheeks bouncing in his haste. He was trying to seal his tunic and fasten his belt at the same time, and making little progress with either.

"Are all Guildhouses thus?" Mael asked in a quiet voice. Klea couldn't be sure, but she thought that he sounded amused.

She ignored his comment and turned to face the newcomer, now coming to a panting halt before her. "Master Evanh," she said. "I know you, and you know me. Now, enough nonsense. I have a great need of secure communications and information banks, and this Guildhouse has both. And while you're taking us to them, you can explain why you've let your guard down here. And where's your staff?"

"Mistress," Master Evanh said, taking a deep breath, "that man—he's a Mage!"

"Yes," Klea said patiently, "he's a Mage. He is the Second of all their Circles, and he is under my protection. When he speaks you hear my voice. Do you understand?"

"Under *your* protection?" Mael said, while at the same time Master Evanh said, "Mistress, you forget yourself. This is my Guildhouse and I am the Master here."

Klea shook her head. "That may not last much longer. Be aware that two of the Guild Master's nephews are on this world, and that I am sent to guard them. If you had been at your meditations rather than asleep in the middle of the day, you would have felt the currents of Power shifting at the very moment they were lost."

Evanh stared at her, eyes round and fishlike with incomprehension. "Lost?"

"You heard me. Reach out and test the currents yourself if you don't believe it. And while you're doing that, give me leave to use your communications setup. Master Owen must be kept apprised. Stand aside."

On the southern hemisphere of Cracanth, deep in the night sector, candles flickered around the perimeter of a circle. Two had burned all the way down and guttered out. The room was painted black, with black hangings to muffle any sounds made within, and a white circle glimmered against the black-painted floor. Around the circle lay bundles of dark cloth, tossed here and there like dirty laundry. But inside each bundle was what remained of a man or a woman. Dead.

Eiadon sus-Gefael, First of the Circle of Bareiath Ai, looked down on them. He had seen the twisting of the cords, and had come as quickly as he could. Other members of his Circle, roused from their beds to accompany him, were searching the rest of the house. Outside, the domestic security forces waited until he had declared the house fit for them to enter, in case this turned out to be a material crime. He rather doubted that it was.

"There's one alive!"

Eiadon turned toward the voice. It was Jairen, Third of the Bareiath Ai Circle, recognizable by her slight frame even under mask and robe.

"Where?" Not in this room. All here had flown. Eiadon had checked for himself.

"On the third level. A boy."

"Lead me."

Together they made their way upward to the room where the boy—too young to be a member of the Circle—lay in a narrow bed. He twitched and thrashed about in his sleep, and drops of sweat beaded his forehead. Two more members of Eiadon's Circle stood nearby, mechanical lamps in their hands.

Eiadon lifted his staff, and let it blaze as power entered him. The red glow illuminated the object of his curiosity: Lord syn-Hacaeth's son and student in the ways of Power. Did he know that his father lay dead below? Workings requiring a death had always been rare, and now in time of peace they were rarer still.

If such a thing had been called for, Eiadon reflected, he himself would surely have known of it before now. He turned to Jairen.

"Summon medical services," he said. "But warn them that this is a special case. No one is to touch this boy with flesh to flesh. No one."

VI. Khesat; Ophel

RHAL KASANDER, Exalted of Tanavral, and a man known for his ability to tell good wine from bad even when drunk, walked out into the city of Ilsefret, where the Highest of Khesat met with his council. The sun was rising, tinting the Golden Tower with light while the rest of the city lay in darkness. No law forbade the construction of buildings higher than the Tower, but a general agreement, unspoken for more than two thousand years, held that to do so would be ... unseemly.

Kasander's head was clear, even this early—or, from his point of view, this late—and the crisp air of autumn braced him nicely as he made his way on foot through the empty streets. Vehicular traffic was prohibited in central Ilsefret, lest the sleep of the householders be disturbed by uncouth noises. A servant paced along behind him, carrying his indoor slippers in one hand and a pair of caged orfiles in the other, to provide sweet music with their singing.

The Plaza of Hope opened up before them, the Golden Tower rising high above its western side. But Kasander's destination was on the side opposite, where a series of low buildings provided dwelling places for those fortunate enough to have inherited them. The balconies overlooking the square were enough to make the apartments valuable for the view they afforded once or twice in a generation. Perhaps even soon. Perhaps even now.

The Exalted of Tanavral walked in through one of the arches of whitewashed stone on the façade, then sat in a carved ocherwood change-chair while his servant stripped off his street shoes and replaced them with the slippers. The slippers were of red velvet sewn with rubies, accented with red carnelian to show the common touch.

"One hour," Rhal Kasander said, addressing the air—though the message was, in fact, for his slipper-bearer. Without waiting for a response, he rose and took the circular stair to the living compartments above. He reached the upper chamber, a study with its high windows flung open to give a view of the platform at the top of the Golden Tower, at the same moment as Caridal Fere, Master of Nalensey, entered from an inner room.

"Our joy is complete now that you have returned," Kasander said, bowing as he spoke.

"And ours," replied Fere, bowing in turn. "Will you break your fast here?"

"With greatest pleasure."

Fere picked up a glass bell from the table beside him and let it give forth a single sweet and piercing note. The last reverberation had not yet died when a young woman appeared on the threshold of the study, carrying a laden serving tray in both hands. She deposited the tray on the central table and withdrew, her eyes downcast the entire while.

Kasander looked over the dishes she had brought. Then he plucked a savorfruit from the glass bowl where they sat under their dusting of powdered sugar, dipped the fruit into its side dish of carent sauce, and raised it to his lips.

The sauce was cold.

He looked up sharply at his host. The time of his arrival had been arranged in advance, and he had been punctual.

Someone in the kitchen would answer for this disgraceful in-attention to detail. Unless—

"You failed."

The words hung in the air, shocking in their bluntness. Caridal Fere had plainly not expected so strong a response to his indirect admission. He reddened.

"You speak to me thus in my own house."

"I do," said Kasander. "The crisis is here. Two days ago, unknown brigands entered Gerre Hafelsan's house and changed all his carpets for grass matting."

The two men considered the implications of that anony-mous and wordless—but emphatic—statement.

"Hafelsan didn't say anything about it when we spoke yes-terday," Fere said after a moment or two had passed.

"Would you have, in his position?"

"Well," Fere admitted, "no."

"There you have it," said Kasander. "There are changes at work in the world, and not all for the good. For our own sakes, we must form a party, and our party must back a Worthy." He looked at Fere sharply. "And we don't *have* a Worthy."

Again, Fere reddened. "We have a Worthy," he said. "It is merely that he remains, as yet, unaware that we have him."

"What a day, foster-brother." Faral flung himself onto his bed in their newly acquired hotel room with a tired sigh. "What a day."

"No kidding." Jens tossed the carrybag full of money into one corner and collapsed onto the lounge chair. He extended his arms overhead in a bone-cracking stretch. "When Granda told us stories, he never once warned us about buying tea and parchants from sweet little old ladies."

"*Somebody* should have." Faral pulled off his boots, using nothing but his feet, and let them thump one at a time onto the floor at the foot of the bed. "Next time we stick with the sleazy bars and the cheap booze."

The room—two beds, a chair, a table, an entertainment wall, and a rudimentary comm setup—was one of many similar at a midclass hotel in Nanáli. The multicolored glowsign on the roof advertised "family rates," and the clerk at the front desk had accepted Faral's cash and his stolen ID. In return, Faral had pocketed the key wafer without bothering to mention that there were two more people planning to use the room, one of them female. Brisk, redheaded Miza-from-Huool's wasn't somebody whom he had felt, at that moment, capable of explaining.

She still wasn't. She stood, arms folded, inside the locked door of the hotel room, and regarded him and his cousin with a challenging air.

"What are you two planning on now?"

"A bath or a shower, I should think," Jens said. "The wash-rag in Huool's storeroom was better than nothing—but judging from the looks we got on the hoverbus, it wasn't good enough."

"Bathrooms are down the hall," Faral said, without moving from his place on the bed. "You go first."

"Thanks. Any idea how we're going to manage the sleeping arrangements?"

"There's a scratch pad over by the comm. We can draw slips to see who doubles up with our guest."

"Oh, no, you don't," Miza said promptly. "All three of us draw, and the loser takes the lounge chair."

"Some people," said Jens, "have no sense of adventure." He stood up and stretched again. "I'm off to make my ablutions. Keep an eye on the gentlelady while I'm gone."

"I'll do that. And you keep an eye out, too . . . I didn't want to mention it earlier, but I spotted a familiar face back on the bus."

"Oh?" Jen's voice didn't change, but his eyes brightened. "Who?"

"Remember the man on *Bright-Wind-Rising*?"

Plainly, Jens did. "The one who recommended we shop at Thalban's? Him?"

"Him. I think we lost him, but you never can tell."

"No, you never can . . . this puts a new complexion on things." Jens stepped past Miza and unlocked the door. "But nothing that's going to keep me away from a tub full of hot water. I'm going to be dreaming of raw sewage for the next week as it is."

Jens left, and the door snicked shut again behind him. Miza seemed to relax a little—perhaps, Faral reflected, she had taken Jen's threats concerning the blaster more seriously than the situation warranted. She walked across the room to the entertainment wall, where a tiny cold-unit held a selection of drinks and fruit juices.

"These things cost like a weekend of sin," she said, taking out a bottle of something bright red, "but I figure a big spender like you can spare the charges."

Faral propped himself up on his elbows and watched her drink. "You know, Gentlelady Miza, in all the excitement I don't think we ever got properly introduced."

She lowered the bottle and regarded him suspiciously over its rim. "I already know who you are. I had to read your old ID cards if I was going to fix you new ones."

"Then you have the advantage of us. Who are you?"

For a moment he thought she wasn't going to answer. Then she said, "I'm Mizady Lyftingil of the Podsen Lyftingils, from Artha, and I'm doing a work-study internship with Gentlesir Huool."

"Internship in what?"

"Information tracking and analysis," she said. Frowning, she added, "Desk work, mostly. And a few simple errands. Which is what this was supposed to be."

"Sorry," said Faral. He let his eyes close as he lay back on the pillow. "You're an analyst—"

"In training."

"—in training. So what do you make of our situation?"

"A formal analysis would need better gear than we've got in this room." Faral opened his eyes in time to see her gesture at the entertainment wall and the comm setup before she continued. "But for starters . . . your cousin is Khesatan, right?"

He thought about the question for a while. As far as the wrinkleskins back home on Maraghai were concerned, Jens counted as the thin-skin fosterling of a blooded-and-returned full-member of an old and famous clan. But it was barely possible that not everyone in the galaxy fully understood the implications of such a relationship.

"Sort of," Faral said. "He claims it's a boring place."

"I'm sure he does." Miza's voice was tart. "But let me tell you something that maybe he didn't mention. Any day now, Khesat is going to become the most exciting place to be in the entire civilized galaxy."

Chaka halted briefly at the entrance to the main concourse. If she left the spaceport now, with time so short, her luggage would go on to Eraasi without her. But if Jens and Faral had gotten themselves in trouble, then pulling the two of them out of whatever bramble-pit they'd fallen into would be an adventure in itself.

Where had they said they were going—the Old Quarter? That would be the first place to look.

Fortunately, most of the signs in the concourse were in Standard Galcenian as well as two or three of the local languages. Chaka could read Galcenian, though she couldn't get her throat and her vocal cords around the high piping noises that passed for the spoken version.

She followed the arrows to Ground Transport, and located a short-mover stop with connections to central Sombrelír and the Old Quarter. The mover had not yet arrived, so Chaka took her place in the queue and waited.

The late-afternoon sun was hot, and the wind was dry and dusty. The delay didn't help Chaka's nerves. The thin-skins sharing the stop with her took notice of her agitation and either moved away or remembered business elsewhere. After a longer while than she would have wanted, the short-mover arrived. It was a wide platform with grab bars, mounted on low-tech rollers—a much cheaper form of transportation than either the hoverbuses or the wheeled flivvers, but slower and more crowded than either one.

The short-mover eased away from the stop, and headed off toward the center of town at roughly double a walking pace. Chaka had plenty of time to gaze about and get herself oriented. Most of the public signage in Sombrelír was written in two or more languages—usually Galcenian, either above or below what Chaka assumed were the same words in Ophelan script—but the advertisements and most of the smaller signs used only the local scrawl.

The Old Quarter, fortunately, seemed to be a popular tourist destination. She took note when the smooth modern pavement changed to brick, and jumped down at the next stop. The short-mover rolled off toward the banking district, and Chaka stood sniffing the air for a hint at where to go next.

The news stories on the vids had shown something burning. The air here smelled abominably of chemical exhausts and too many thin-skins, but a sharpness in her nostrils told of a wood fire somewhere not too far distant. She headed in that direction. If it wasn't somebody's trash barrel . . .

It wasn't. A local security barricade stretched across the road ahead, guarded by a thin-skin in uniform, with a drawn weapon in hand.

Chaka scowled. *Oh, damn.*

What's the problem? The words were in Trade-talk, not the true Forest Speech, but either one was unexpected enough, here in the heart of the Old Quarter to make Chaka hoot with astonishment and turn toward the bystander who had spoken.

Who's asking?

"Me." The speaker had switched back to Galcenian now. "When a couple of lads from under the Great Trees run into trouble, and a Forest Lord shows up not long afterward . . . *somebody* has a problem whether they know it or not."

Chaka looked at the speaker curiously. She was a small woman, with the grey hair and lined features that marked the old ones among the thin-skins. She wore a plain shirt and dark trousers, and to Chaka's sensitive nostrils she smelled unmistakably of sewage.

"My partner's still in there," the woman said, nodding at the barrier. "But your two friends are well away. Now we have to figure out how best to help them—that *was* what you were thinking, wasn't it?"

Something like that.

"Then let me buy you a drink," said the woman, "and we'll think about what to do next."

* * *

"The most interesting place in the civilized galaxy," repeated Faral dubiously. He looked at Miza. "You wouldn't happen to want to explain that, would you?"

Before she could reply, the cardlock buzzed a warning and the door slid open. Jens came in, looking considerably cleaner than he had a few minutes before. He wore the pair of trousers he'd gotten from Huool's, and carried the rest of his garments slung over one arm. He had his boots in his hand, and his feet were bare.

"I took a shower," he said before Faral could say anything. "It was faster."

"That's a first," Faral said. Jens liked his hot baths; left alone, he could soak for hours. "Gentlelady Miza and I were just talking about you, by the way."

Jens dropped his boots and his clothing onto the floor beside the lounge chair and sat down. He leaned back against the upholstery. "Oh. And what conclusions did you come to?"

"We didn't. But she did say something about how pretty soon Khesat wasn't going to be dull anymore." ·

Jens sighed. "She's right."

"What's going on, then?"

"Let me see if I can explain . . . two months back, Standard reckoning, the Highest of Khesat decided that sixty years and two wars were more than enough. At the next Midwinter Festival, if all proceeds according to custom, he will retire to his country estates and take up lacemaking."

"Good for him," said Faral. "I don't suppose that's the whole story, though."

"No. After that, things get complicated."

"What do you mean, complicated?"

"Complicated as in, nobody knows where his replacement is going to come from."

"Why don't they just hold an election or put in his firstborn child or something?" Faral wondered. "It works for most places."

Miza snorted. "Catch the Khesatans doing anything so common as voting . . . and they don't go by strict succession, either. You'll never guess how they *do* go about it."

"They all put on silly hats and play scissors-paper-stone until there's only one of them left."

"Funny, coz." Jens didn't sound amused. "But no. The process starts with a pool of candidates from all the Worthy lineages. Legally, any one of us would be acceptable."

Faral looked at his cousin sharply. "You said 'us'—are you actually holding a ticket in this lottery?"

"I'm afraid so," Jens said. "My father managed to get himself declared ineligible—next time I see him I'll have to ask how—but I'm in the running."

"You and how many other people?"

"A few thousand. Now shut up and let me tell the rest of it. When the time comes round for the Highest to be replaced, the nobility select one from all the eligible candidates. He or she is taken at dawn to the top of the Golden Tower in Ilsefret. Down below, the plaza and the streets are filled with the populace in general. Two burly fellows present the new ruler and proclaim, 'Behold the Highest!' At which point the populace in general shouts either 'Huzzah!' or 'Bring him low!' If they shout 'Huzzah!' then the Highest is indeed the Highest, and the rest follows. But if they shout 'Bring him low!' then the two burly fellows toss the candidate from the top of the Golden Tower, and he falls down four hundred feet to his death."

"Didn't I tell you?" said Miza. "Elections would be a whole lot simpler."

"But not nearly so colorful," Jens said. "The mob is thoroughly bribed. And sometimes the guards are also bribed to be hard of hearing. You name it, and it's probably happened. And even the candidates who descend rapidly are, for those few seconds, Highest of Khesat, and are so inscribed in all the appropriate public places."

Faral looked up at the ceiling. It was painted blue, with glowdots set into the plaster to form patterns that he supposed were the local constellations. They didn't look anything at all like the stars back home.

"Gentlelady Miza is an analyst," he said. "She thinks the fact that you're from a crazy place like Khesat is important for some reason. But she hasn't said why."

"I don't *know* why," said Miza. "But if your cousin is from one of the Worthy Lineages, then I can hazard a guess."

"Please. Hazard away."

"You don't have to bother," Jens said. He sounded resigned. "Now that everything's gone to pieces anyway, I suppose I ought to admit the truth. The real reason I wanted to go shopping this morning was because I was planning to give you the slip on the way back to the port."

"And head off on your own for Khesat?" Miza asked.

"That's right."

Faral sat up, the better to glare at his cousin. "Did you really think that Chaka and I would take off and leave you behind?"

"The timing was going to be the crucial part," Jens said. "It had to be exactly right . . . but that plan's all blown sky-high anyway, so it doesn't matter."

"I guess not. But why in the name of everything would you want to go to Khesat?"

"Fame," Jens said promptly. "Khesat doesn't usually offer a lot of fame as the Selvaurs understand it—Khesatans don't really care about that sort of thing—but when the rule is about to change, everything is different."

Faral shook his head. There was something not quite right about Jens's explanation, and it bothered him. "So you were going to Khesat because you want to take a dive from the Golden Tower?"

"No. I'm not that crazy. Besides," Jens added, "the real fame goes to the backers of the winning candidate. All the Highest gets out of it is a lot of hard work."

Faral shook his head. "And here I thought the most exciting thing anybody ever did on Khesat was dress up and go to the opera."

"That too," said Jens. "But I don't like opera."

The Ophelan Guildhouse turned out to be as run-down and neglected on the inside as Klea had feared. It was a large building; in its best years, she reckoned that it might have held as many as twoscore Adepts and an equal number of apprentices. Such a figure was no match for the population of the Retreat, or even for a major Guildhouse in the Central Worlds, but it was nonetheless a healthy size for a house established on the fringes of civilized space.

Peace, and normal relations with the Mage-ruled planets on the other side of the border zone, had not brought good times to the Guild on Ophel. Nothing about the building's interior was any newer than the end of the last war, and everything, from curtains to furniture, spoke of lassitude and loss of purpose.

The Adepts here made a stand against the Mages, Klea thought, *while most of Ophel got rich trading with the enemy. And when the war ended, their reason for being ended right along with it.*

She could sympathize—the Adepts of those long-ago days deserved better of the universe than to have all their faithfulness made obsolete—but her sympathy didn't extend to condoning laxity in their successors. By the time Master Evanh had shown his two unexpected visitors the way to the House's comm room, her unspoken disapproval had the Ophelan sweating and visibly full of intention to reform. Which was, in Klea's opinion, only as it should be. The man himself was hopeless, but his apprentices at the Sombrelír Guildhouse were still in a position to be of some use to the galaxy.

The communications gear, fortunately, was working. She switched on the hi-comms rig and punched in the codes that would send her text message on its way through Ophel's orbiting links and the deep-space relay stations to the links that circled above far-distant Galcen. Owen wouldn't be happy to get the news of his nephews' unauthorized disappearance, but it was something that he needed to know about as soon as possible.

Let him figure out whether or not to pass the word on to that sister of his, Klea thought. *I've done my part.*

The comm unit beeped, letting her know that the message had reached its destination. Then, to her surprise, it beeped again— a three-tone sequence, this time, the signal that another message was coming back in reply. A strip of flimsy came curling out of a slot on the unit's main console; she tore it off, glanced at the first couple of lines, and handed it to Mael Taleion.

"It's for you."

She couldn't see his expression for the mask he wore, but she thought that Mael looked startled. "How——?"

"The Master of the Adepts' Guild sends his greetings," she said impatiently, "and passes along some news that came to him from someone on your side of the border. You're supposed to take it to the First when you go see her."

He shook his head. "I already have seen her."

"Whoever sent Master Rosselin-Metadi the message didn't know that. My guess is that your people sent this news out along as many different routes as they could, hoping that one of the messages would get to the right place. Read it and tell me what you think."

"A moment." Mael took of his mask and clipped it onto his belt next to the ebony staff. Then he smoothed out the flimsy and looked at it, frowning. His lips moved a little as he read—written Galcenian was not, it seemed, a language in which he was easily literate. His frown deepened, and she thought he grew paler.

"Well?" she said.

He folded the slip of flimsy into a square and tucked it into an inner pocket of his robe. Something about the careful deliberation of the gesture convinced her that whatever he had just read had shaken him deeply.

"There is a plague," he said, "on Cracanth. The First of one of the local circles is appealing to the First of all the Circles for aid."

"Plague is a medical problem," Klea said. "Not a problem for ... for whatever it is that Circles do. Your people on Cracanth would do better to talk to Health and Emergency Services on Galcen."

Mael was shaking his head again. "No. This is not a true plague, whatever they are saying aloud on Cracanth. This is the *ekkannikh* at work ... this is what I feared when I went to speak with the First on Maraghai."

"Ekkannikh." Klea rolled the unfamiliar word around on her tongue. Its consonants were harsh and rasping against the

back of her throat. "You're going to tell me what that means, aren't you? Because I haven't got the slightest idea."

"A homeless ghost," said Mael. "An unpropitiated spirit. Surely you have them on this side of the Gap Between?"

"No." She paused a moment, before honesty compelled her to add, "Not under that name, anyhow. And I've never seen one at all."

"Count yourself lucky," he said. "I suspect, from what I learned on Maraghai from my First, and from this communication just now, that a revenant of great power is loose—the one who in life was called by my people the Breaker of Circles."

She knew the epithet, of course. Errec Ransome had gloried in it while he was Master of the Guild.

"Bastard," she said. Mael blinked, and she added, "Not you—him. I have to admit, if there was ever a man likely to keep on making trouble even after he was dead . . ."

"You begin to understand the problem," Mael said. "The *ekkannikh* has already taken one body, and may take more. Further, I believe that it is well away from Cracanth, in the shape of a human it controls."

"Is that possible?"

"With such a one as Ransome, anything is possible. Even while he lived, he was not a man easily caught and confined. And now . . ." His voice trailed off. Then he straightened, and his resolve seemed to grow firmer. "I must find out where the *ekkannikh* is at this moment, and where it is going. I will need to meditate upon the problem."

He paused then, and looked directly at Klea. His eyes held hers. "It would be helpful," he continued, "if you would work with me."

Klea took a step backward. "Are you asking me to participate in Magecraft?"

"Only in the mildest sense of the word," he said, with a faint sigh. "But if I am expected to live and work among Adepts, surely I may expect a bit of assistance in return."

"I don't . . ." She let her voice trail away.

"Suit yourself. In the meantime—I shall carry out my needful meditations in the Guildhouse garden."

VII. Ophel; Cracanth

CHAKA LET the strange woman guide her away from the Security barrier and down a side street.

"We're not going that way anyway," the woman explained, with a nod toward the barrier. "Your friends are safe. They'll be heading off-planet before much longer."

*On the *Lav'rok*?*

"No, I don't think so. Besides, they won't be running under their own names." The woman paused at a street vendor's pushcart—a cold-and-hot wagon that could lift on light nullgravs—beneath a flickering holosign of a bottle pouring its liquid into a frosty glass. She pulled a handful of small change out of her belt pouch. "Do you want cha'a, or something different?"

Different, said Chaka. *What's the point in wandering if you don't take a chance?*

"That's the spirit. Hot *uffa*, then."

The woman purchased two steaming cups of bright red liquid and handed one to Chaka. The drink was sharp-flavored and faintly spicy. It didn't have as much kick as cha'a, but it had a pleasant, lingering aftertaste.

"We saw your names on the passenger list for *Bright-Wind-Rising*," the woman said to Chaka a few minutes later, as the two of them made their way through the Old Quarter. "Three young travelers from Maraghai ... when we saw who the others were, we were a bit surprised that you didn't show up in their company."

I don't like shopping, said Chaka. *Who's 'we'?*

"My partner and I—we run Bindweed and Blossom's. I'm Blossom, by the way."

*Chakallakak *ngha*-Chakallakak. Chaka for short.*

"Thanks for the short-name," Blossom said. "I'm honored. Ah, here we are."

They had reached a broad street lined with shade trees and elegant shops. One of the shops had a sign in florid Ophelan script—with HUOOL GALLERIES in small Galcenian letters underneath—on a brass plaque by the front door. The single shopwindow was a velvet-lined oval in which a jade bowl sat beside a mask woven out of feathers and sparkling multicolored grass.

Chaka stared. *What kind of place is this?*

"Expensive," said Blossom, as they passed through the winking lights and sonic barriers of the gallery's security system. "But that's all right; we're not buying anything."

She led the way through the hushed and carpeted front rooms, where precious objects stood on display in pools of carefully directed light. Chaka followed, keeping her distance from anything that looked breakable—which in practice meant almost everything—and felt a surge of relief when they reached the EMPLOYEES ONLY door in the far back. Blossom touched the lockplate and the door slid open.

You work here? Chaka asked.

Blossom shook her head. "No, no. Bindweed and I are independents. But we have a certain—relationship of courtesy—with Gentlesir Huool."

I see. Chaka wasn't sure if she saw or not. She let Blossom lead the way into the back room, where a feathered biped sat behind an Eraasian-style workdesk. He rotated his head to face them as they came in, a birdlike movement that didn't change the orientation of his shoulders, and looked at them out of staring yellow eyes.

"Ah, good, you found her," he said in heavily accented Galcenian. Then, to Chaka, he said, "I am Huool, and it is my pleasure to make your acquaintance."

Chaka bowed. Blossom nodded toward the glyphs on the surface of the workdesk and asked, "Confirmation that the boys are away?"

Huool made a clicking noise with his beak. Chaka couldn't tell whether it was meant to indicate agreement, dismay, or something else completely unreadable.

"Nothing," he said. "And this disturbs me. Miza is a very sweet girl, and if anything had gone wrong, I'm certain her first action would have been to contact me. And the same, if the young men were safe and her mission accomplished."

Blossom shrugged. "She's a good-looking girl, they're good-looking boys—maybe they're in a rental room right now having a party."

"The ways of your species," Huool said. He made a chittering noise that Chaka presumed was intended to convey amusement. "I suppose you know them best. But—there *is* another matter."

"Holding out on me, eh?"

"Never," said Huool. "See here." He pointed to the workdesk, and both Blossom and Chaka leaned forward to look. "They were supplied with much credit. I tracked the credit, and found that they had used it already—not for passage off-planet, mind you, but in a common exchange shop."

"Barapan's," Blossom said, in tones of disgust. "Whose bright idea was that, I want to know? Your guide—"

"You do my teaching injustice. Miza opposed it, I'm certain—she knows of Barapan's artifices." Huool tapped another glyph on the surface of the desk. The patterns shifted, and a text entry appeared. "But see here: only a few minutes after the transaction, we have a security report from Deládier Row. An assault in which two men and a woman were attacked. The two men were left behind unconscious while the woman fled."

"If Barapan's put our boys in the hospital, I'll—"

Huool made the clicking noise again. "No need, no need. The woman was unhurt, and if it had been Miza—"

"She would have contacted you by now."

"Just so. I think it much more likely that our three young people surprised Barapan's accomplices, much as the Green Sun was surprised earlier. But why they may have felt it needful to vanish afterward when help was so readily available here . . ." Huool didn't shrug—Chaka doubted he had the joints for it—but the flick of his feathery brow-tufts was clearly equivalent.

Blossom turned to Chaka. "You know the boys. What do you think?"

Chaka considered the problem for a minute. She thought about Faral, coming back blooded from a Long Hunt the elders had never planned on asking him to make; and Jens, sent home in disgrace from Khesat for doing something, nobody ever said what, that apparently even the Khesatan wrinkleskins had never thought of to do. Those two would have plans of their own right now, of that she was sure; and while Chaka could guess at their intentions, she didn't think it right to speculate aloud. Merely because the one called Blossom had spoken in Trade-talk did not prove she was a friend, and her interest in Chaka's agemates might not be benign.

I think they don't want to be found, she said after a moment, *and asking for help is not in their natures.*

Another possibility that had come to mind—that Faral and Jens had stuffed Huool's guide in a trash disposal and lost the pursuit completely—she decided not to mention. Let her friends keep their plans, and their lead, if they had one.

"So we wait," Blossom said. "Once Bindweed gets clear of Security paperwork, she'll join us and we can see what develops. Meanwhile—" She pulled a well-used deck of cards out of her hip pocket. "—I learned years ago that time passes quicker when you've got something else to think about. Do either of you know how to play kingnote?"

No.

"That's okay, I'll teach you. How about you, Huool?"

The gallery's proprietor gave his chittering laugh. "With your cards? I'd need to have run mad." He opened a drawer in the workdesk and withdrew an equally well-used deck. "Here, use mine."

The last of the afternoon sunlight filtered past the closed louvers in the dim room to make bars of light against the far wall. Kolpag Garbazon looked over at his newly assigned partner. Ruhn was taking off his gloves, a disgusted look on his face.

The man sitting in the chair in front of Kolpag and Ruhn remained upright only because he was tied there. His ankles were bound to the chair's legs, his chest to the chair's back. His arms were tied to his sides. The man's head lolled, and a trickle of blood ran from the corner of his mouth to stain the shirt below.

"I believe this one doesn't know anything about our packages," Ruhn said.

Kolpag nodded. "You're probably right. He's told us everything else."

He raised his blaster and shot the man once in the head. The man jerked convulsively in his bonds, then sagged and was still.

Kolpag and Ruhn left the cheap rented room and walked down the outside stairway to the street. Their hovercar waited for them by the sidewalk. Ruhn slid into the passenger side and Kolpag took the controls.

"We've still got too many questions," said Ruhn, as the hovercar's nullgravs lifted it above the cracked and potholed pavement. "The names they're using right now. Who helped them. Where they are."

Kolpag brought the hovercar out of the seedy downtown neighborhood and into the main traffic stream. "There's no report of anybody close to their description leaving the spaceport," he said. "Let's assume that they're a smart couple of lads—we know they were smart enough to spot Barapan's purse-lifters and take care of them without yelling for help. So. Where would a smart person be right now?"

"Holed up somewhere," Ruhn said at once. "Waiting for the surveillance to relax and go away."

"That's what I think too. Our boys won't make their move off-planet for a week, maybe longer."

"The boss won't like having to wait that long."

"Yeah. I know." Kolpag maneuvered the hovercar into a gap between a green-and-yellow jitney and a crowded short-mover coming up from the spaceport. "We'll have to work another angle. . . . What genders did our late friend say his partners were?"

"One male, one female."

"Right. And our two packages have apparently picked up a female escort, a special courier from Huool Galleries. So now they're also two males and a female." He turned onto the main traffic artery leading from downtown Sombrelír to the suburbs, pushed forward on the yoke to bring the hovercar up to speed, and continued, "Did you notice that our late acquaintance wasn't carrying any ID?"

"I did," said Ruhn. "Are you thinking that the boys may have lifted the papers of their assailants?"

"That's right."

"Definitely not your average tourists." Ruhn brought out his datapad, full of material from the active interrogation session, and punched in a link through the hovercar's comm rig. "Set out full data-group search on the following three names. Best fit, eliminate duplicates. Mauris Fant, Brix Gorlees, Keyíla Danít."

The grounds of the Sombrelír Guildhouse were as run-down and untended as the rooms within. The flowers and the ornamental shrubs had long since overgrown their beds, and the lawn had not been mowed for some weeks. Even the kitchen garden made a poor show, with straggling weeds mixed in among the rows of anemic herbs and vegetables.

I might have done better to remain inside, thought Mael Taleion. But generations of Adepts had imbued the wood and stone of the Guildhouse with the unmistakable stink of their workings. If he attempted anything, his efforts would be wrenched out of the true patterns by the malign influence. Outdoors was safer—the Great Magelord who had trained him, years ago now, had preferred the open sky for that reason among others, and Mael still honored his teacher's memory.

He found a clear area in the garden and scratched out a rough circle in the dirt with his staff. Then he settled his mask once more into place, knelt, and set his mind adrift on the currents of the universe. An Adept might have been content to float so, letting the surges and ripples of Power carry him where they would, but that was not the way of the Circles. Somewhere out beyond this untended bit of ground, the *eiran*—the silver cords of life and luck—waited to fall under Mael's hand.

At first the cords evaded his touch. The overwhelming feel of Adeptry distracted him and made him clumsy. He remained patient. The *eirän* drew closer, almost within reach, and he saw them as he had seen them before on Maraghai, their lines of bright silver all tarnished and broken, with a threat of darkness twisted in. Their intertwinings made no true pattern— only a botch, like the ruined garden around him.

Where a pattern has grown awry, the work of the Circle is to make it right.

Mael's teacher had died long ago, giving his life to the Great Working that had ended the last war, but his voice spoke clearly to his student now. Mael took hold of one of the tarnished threads.

Find where it comes from, find where it leads.

He began tracing the path of the darkened *eir.* Once he had found out its origin, he could untangle the clump of disorderly Adept-work that knotted around it and see what could be done.

The problem turned out to be worse than he had thought.

Wherever the tarnished thread lay across a clean one, the unblemished thread had also darkened. He laid his hands on the nearest of the *eiran* and pulled on it, trying to work it free of the tarnished strands. The effort did him no good. The cords were stuck together at the point where they touched, like a bundle of wires that had rusted into one.

Mael drew his hand through the threads like a comb, trying to break them apart by force. He failed. The silver cords were strong, and sharp as the edges of knives. When he took his hand away, the blood from his cut fingers ran down in red streaks across his palm.

Ignoring the pain, he wrapped the cords around his hand to gain leverage and tugged more sharply. His efforts brought a hint of order to the tangle—not so much that a casual observer could have found it, but enough that someone who knew what to look for could see the beginnings of the true design.

His hand was still bleeding when the stinging in his cut fingers was matched by a sudden, sharper pain in his left shoulder. He tried to grasp the dark cord that ran through the tangle and pull it out, but the *eiran* were fading before him, and the solid lines that wrapped his hands were turning into mist.

The pain in his shoulder stayed with him, matched by a pain in his knees that had not been there a few moments before. Mael opened his eyes to the world of physical reality. The sky had grown dark in the time since he had commenced his meditations, and he was no longer in the Guildhouse garden. He was in a narrow, trash-filled alley, with stone walls rising to either side and a dead end facing him. Close at hand lay the chunk of stone—half of a red clay brick—that had taken him on the shoulder and driven him to his knees.

"Look at what we've got," said a voice behind him—a young man's voice, speaking Standard Galcenian strongly flavored with the local dialect. They wouldn't speak their own patois, Mael thought, not when there was a chance their victim wouldn't understand them.

"What do you think he's doing here?" Another voice.

"Doesn't belong. Think he's got money?" A third.

Mael rose to his feet, and turned slowly. His staff had been in his hands when the meditation began. Where was it now? His hands were empty, and so was the clip on his belt. He was alone and unarmed, and a hot trickle under his robes told him that the half-brick had drawn blood—even as his fingers, cut on the *eiran*, also still bled.

When Faral Hyfid-Metadi left home to seek his fortune, he'd cherished—privately, of course—certain daydreams about the wild nightlife available to galactic travelers in exotic ports of call. His fantasies, though weak on specific detail, had glittered brightly in his imagination during the transit from Maraghai. Not a single one of them had involved watching zero-g cageball on the holovid sports channel in a family hotel.

He and his cousin and Gentlesir Huool's courier had made a skimpy dinner out of the canned drinks and highly salted snacks in the room's cold-unit. Given the chance that somebody's blaster-packing goons were on their trail, they hadn't dared leave the hotel to buy proper food. An economy-minded establishment like this one didn't provide room service; and even if it had, Faral wouldn't have felt safe opening the door to strangers.

Miza lay napping, stretched out fully clothed on one of the room's two beds. Faral and Jens sat on the other bed and the lounge chair, respectively, watching the cagers from Nanáli and Irique chase each other around the nullgrav playing cube. According to the running score at the bottom of the holovid tank, Nanáli was ahead twenty-three points to seventeen. Faral couldn't remember whether the local team wore the black jerseys or the yellow ones, and didn't particularly care.

Jens looked even less interested, if possible. Catching Faral's eye, he gestured in the direction of the tank. "Is there a reason we're watching this?"

"News clips," Faral said. "I want to see if our fight this morning made it into the evening edition. The announcers might give us some idea who it is we're up against."

"I certainly hope so," Jens said. "Once we know that, we can make plans. You have no idea, coz, how much I dislike sitting here and doing nothing."

"Considering that we almost weren't here to do anything, I feel lucky."

"I suppose." Jens finished his can of Varney's Pre-Sweetened *Uffa* and tossed the empty container into the waste recycler before nodding toward the other bed. Miza was snoring faintly. "What are we going to do about her when we leave here?"

"She's got the local knowledge," Faral pointed out. "And we don't."

"That's going to change as soon as we reach high orbit."

Faral considered the problem. "She's also pretty."

"Now we see what comes of being brought up on the South Continent a day's hard walking from anywhere," Jens said. "You've gone and fallen in love with the first human female you've ever met who wasn't also a blood relation."

"Only the fact that we're stranded together on a hostile world, surrounded by dozens, maybe hundreds, of possible foes, prevents me from pounding you into the carpet for that remark. I am *not* in love with her."

Jens gave him a skeptical glance. "If you say so."

"I say so. But we don't know how long we may need to keep her around—and we can't leave her behind for the rockhogs to pull down afterward."

"I suppose you're right. It would be ungracious."

"And we don't want that," Faral said. "What would the Worthies on Khesat say if they ever found out?"

"An octet in rhyming couplets," Jens said, "to the effect of 'Stuff a sock in your mouth, coz.' "

"You, too, foster-brother."

The conversation lapsed into silence. In the holovid tank, a cager in a black jersey slammed the ball against the target. The announcer interviewed somebody else in the arena who seemed excited by the feat—since neither the sports enthusiast nor the announcer spoke Galcenian, Faral never did learn why.

Eventually regular play commenced again in the cube. As it did so Faral said to his cousin, "So tell me. What *are* you planning to do once we get off-planet?"

"Go to Khesat," Jens said. "And continue my plan to become wealthy and famous by means of influence peddling."

"Isn't that dangerous?"

"Frightfully." Jens's blue eyes had the bright, sharp-edged expression that usually meant he was looking for trouble. "But it should be amusing."

"In that case, I'm going with you."

He had been running, running, most of the night. His side hurt, and his breath came in racking sobs. He wore the orange and grey of a Cracanthan peace enforcer, and knew when he looked at himself that such was what he was, but it all seemed so unimportant now. What was important was to find . . .

He didn't know what he wanted to find. He pushed his legs on, moving them through sheer force of will.

Just keep going, and I'll know what it is when I find it.

A light above the corner ahead threw a pool of blinding white down beneath it, making the rest of the night darker by contrast. His breath steamed a bit in the cool night air. In the light was a kiosk, which announced that this was a place of transportation. That one of the places served was a spaceport.

He was certain that he didn't know the language in which the writings were made, but equally certain that he understood them. His foot splashed in a puddle. He had run once before, and it was important to get to the spaceport: another hint of his task.

Yes, get to the spaceport, and then . . .

He would know what it was he had to do when the time came.

In the brick alley, Mael turned to face his attackers. He knew the type—city-bred troublemakers, all of them, resentful of outsiders and willing to commit assault to make their opinion clear. The streets of Ruisi Spaceport had been full of such people, back in the days of the Republic's occupation. Fear and poverty bred them, and helplessness nourished them. Mael remembered the feelings well.

He almost felt sorry for the bullies who confronted him. The street fighters of his youth had known that they could blame the Republic and its Adepts for their troubles. Some of them had been lucky enough to find the Resurgency—or the fellowship of the Circles—before their bitterness turned inward and they died in pointless battle over a fancied insult or a bit of illegal trade.

These three would not be so fortunate. His staff was gone, but those who had been trained in the Circles had other resources to aid them.

The street thugs had not spoken since he turned around. They had attacked him from behind, seeing only a cloaked and unfamiliar figure. Perhaps they had not expected to find a Mage. Still, they had not retreated.

"You wish me to fight you because I am in your territory?" Mael asked. "That is easily remedied. Come to mine."

He stepped . . . sideways . . . and drew the three along with him into the Void.

It was at once the simplest thing that the Mage-trained could do, and the hardest to learn. Not everyone who came to the Circles could attain the level of true sight that showed the path away from reality, into that place where Power was not, but where fact and illusion became one. But once seen, the road was an easy one—*garaeth sus-etazein*, the Circles called it, the Great Lords' Way.

The Void was as he remembered it. No sky, no horizon, only a grey mist-that-was-not-mist all around him, and a ground under his feet that had no reality but what his own mind gave to it. The three bullies huddled together and stared about wide-eyed with fear. They had grown up, perhaps, on grannies' tales of Mages and Adepts, and on what those who worked with Power could do to people who were reckless enough to anger them.

"Here, what I will becomes real," Mael said.

He gestured—an unnecessary flourish, but something the

three would remember later—and called forth a night-whip from the mist of the Void.

The creature was a thing out of legend on the homeworlds, all floating fog and long, ropy tentacles that sucked away a bit of a man's life every time they touched flesh. This was a young one, and not especially hungry. Mael had no desire to kill his assailants, only to escape from them and—if their minds were receptive—to educate them somewhat in the folly of throwing bricks at off-worlders.

"If what you will here becomes real," a voice whispered behind him, "does that mean you have willed me to exist?"

Mael turned. It was the *ekkannikh*, cloaked in black as he had seen it before on Maraghai. This time its pale skeleton hand gripped an Adept's staff.

It has remembered that much more of what it was, Mael thought. *If it remembers everything, we are lost.*

"I grow stronger," the revenant said, "and closer. The final victory has always been mine."

"If that is so, then I will delay it while I can."

"While you can." The *ekkannikh* laughed, a sound like seeds rattling inside a dry gourd. "Let me show you the future."

It lifted its free hand, and Mael saw that the bony fingers held a square piece of polished silver. His own face looked back at him from the mirror's surface: his own face, and the flesh rotting from off the bones, and the bare skull beneath.

"You see," said the *ekkannikh*. "We come to the same place in the end, you and I."

"Not while I have strength to will it otherwise," Mael said, and called up the shadow of his Mage-staff out of the all-enveloping mist.

He raised the staff in his right hand, guarding his chest and head, and stepped back with his left foot to take the proper stance. As he had expected, the *ekkannikh* let the silver mirror drop into the swirling fog, the better to lift up its longer staff in an Adept's two-handed grip.

A quick motion of the revenant's bony hands, and the staff—almost two meters of polished wood—spun and flashed downward. Mael brought his staff up in a block against it. The Void deadened the sound of the impact to a dull *thock*. He twisted away as the staves met and the blow slid off harmlessly to one side.

The revenant hissed in frustration.

Mael had learned long ago that the tall staves of the Adepts were best suited for distance work. Get inside of their length and they became a liability to the wielder. The difficulty lay in passing through the deadly arc of their strike. But now he *was* inside, and smashing his staff against his enemy's ribs in a move that should have broken bone.

The blow passed through the body of the *ekkannikh* with no more resistance than through the mist of the Void. Mael himself was out of position now. The *ekkannikh*'s long staff shot forward, end on, and Mael—unable to block, unable to sidestep—could do nothing but watch it come.

The staff took him in the midsection like a spear, and passed through him as his own staff had passed through the body of the revenant. It left a trail of ice in his guts, not painful, but cripplingly cold.

He tried to raise his staff, and failed

The *ekkannikh* spoke. "Look for me on Khesat," it said, and vanished.

VIII. Ophel

THE HOTEL room in Nanáli was dim and quiet. The holovid tank in the far corner had its sound turned off, so that the images inside it moved silently, without meaning. Faral and Miza were asleep, the gentle sound of their breathing a constant susurration in the background. Jens sat, wakeful, in the lounge chair and conversed, as was his habit, with the shadows around him.

He had slept for a while after the last of the news reports had ended, only to come awake again later. He was not surprised to find the far corner of the room occupied by a quiet, dark-haired man who was not, in the usual sense, present there at all.

"It's been a while," he said, as if speaking to an old friend. "Was that really you on board *Bright-Wind-Rising*?"

"After a fashion," said his visitor, with a faint smile. "I do what I can."

"Faral saw you. Then, and again later."

"Your cousin is not without his abilities," the man said. "Although he doesn't think of them as such."

"Then why don't you talk to him instead?"

The man smiled again. "Faral Hyfid-Metadi will get along in the world without my advice."

"And I won't?" Jens raised an eyebrow. "Should I be insulted, do you think?"

"If it pleases you. But you were wishing for advice not so long ago, or I would not have come."

Jens regarded his visitor thoughtfully. "It was a practical matter . . . not your sort of thing at all."

"I was a practical man once. A good while ago, I think, but not everything changes. Tell me."

"All right." Jens drew a deep breath. "Do you have any idea how to get from here to Khesat—safely, that is? People are chasing us for some reason, and I'd prefer not to draw their attention."

"You could walk past them, unseen—"

"Maybe *you* could. But I couldn't, and Faral certainly couldn't, and I don't think Gentlelady Lyftingil has any hidden talent in that direction either."

The visitor looked at him thoughtfully. "In that case . . . a long time ago, I worked on a ship moving Eraaslan goods across the border zone from Cracanth to Ophel. Smuggling them, to be precise. And unless everything in the known galaxy has become legal since then, such people—and their ships—must still exist, and their loyalty can be bought with coin."

"I've got coin," Jens said. "Huool made those letters of credit generous enough to handle almost anything. I don't know why."

The visitor shrugged. "Perhaps he felt an obligation."

"I'd like to know to whom," said Jens. "And something else I'd like to know: what do all those people have against Faral and me in the first place?"

"They don't have anything whatever against you, strictly speaking," the visitor said. "They have their own uses for you, that's all, which aren't necessarily in your interest."

"Not terribly ethical of them," Jens said.

"I suppose it isn't. Though you'll do worse than that before your life has ended, I assure you."

"Say something to cheer me up, why not?"

The other smiled again. Laugh lines formed around his dark eyes. "Very well. Convincing a smuggler to get you off-planet shouldn't take long. Money is the hard part, and as you say, you have the money. For the initial contact—" He nodded toward the sleeping Miza. "—She's your key. Ask her for help, if you aren't too proud."

"Proud? Me?" Jens's voice rose indignantly.

Across the room, Faral's steady breathing changed rhythm, and Jens heard a faint snort as his cousin awoke.

"Hey, Jens," Faral said. He palmed the lightplate beside him, and the reading light popped on. "Who're you talking to?"

"No one," Jens said. The room was empty again. "Myself, I guess."

"Okay. I've been thinking—"

"While you were asleep?"

"Doesn't everybody? I've been thinking—we've been here too long. Let's move."

"Is that a joke?"

"Not even a little," said Faral. "Thinking like prey instead of a hunter, that's all. We've frozen in place when we should be running."

"I'd pretty much reached the same conclusion myself," Jens said. "Wake up Miza and tell her it's time to pack her toothbrush and hit the road."

"She didn't bring a toothbrush," Faral pointed out.

"We'll pick one up at the transit station," Jens said. "And on the way we'll ask her if she knows where to find a nice, reliable pirate."

The yard outside the Guildhouse was dark. There had been a streetlight once, but the glowcube inside it had burnt out and no one—neither Sombrelír City Services nor the local Guild—had bothered to replace it. Klea called Power into her staff and let its blue-green glow light the way as she hastened down the deserted street. Master Evanh followed, panting.

Klea spared the Ophelan Guildmaster a disapproving glance. "Lord Taleion left the grounds, and you didn't follow him?"

"I granted him the privileges you asked."

She pressed her lips together for a moment before answering. "Use some initiative, Master Evanh. He is still a Mage. Haven't you got any idea where he might have gone?"

"None."

"Then we'll stop here for a moment," she said, "and search for him. Wherever he is, the currents of Power will make his presence felt. He can't help it, being what he is and working as he does."

The two Adepts stood quiet. At last Klea said, more in puzzlement than frustration, "He isn't here."

"You know the man better than I do," Master Evanh said. "How far could he have gotten in the time he had?"

"Quite far," said Klea. "Where some things are concerned, the Mages are much more . . . casual . . . than we are. If he has gone into the Void, we may spend more time looking for him than we really wanted."

"It isn't even safe to be out on the streets at this hour," said Master Evanh unhappily. "Never mind other places."

"Not safe? Don't the Ophelans have any respect for an Adepts' staff?"

Master Evanh shook his head. "I don't seek—I don't like confrontations. They make everyday business so difficult. . . ."

Klea pursed her lips again. Evanh was hopeless, or close to it. It was the Ophelan Guild's right to choose a spineless nonentity for the local Guildmaster, but there were ways to shake up that complacency.. . . . *Later,* she told herself. *After this affair is over we can deal with the Guild on Ophel.*

"We'll search for him one more time," she said. "Sooner or later he's bound to return to the universe that we know, and then—"

She stopped.

"What is it?" asked Evanh.

"He's here." She closed her eyes for a moment and let the currents wash over her. Then she opened her eyes again and pointed at the side street ahead. "Or, more precisely—over there. Follow me or not, whichever you please."

She set off at a fast walk, not looking to see if Evanh came after her. The staff in her hand made a pale green beacon against the darkness. The way was fronted on both sides with nameless industrial buildings, their doors of rolled steel closed against the night. Tall metal fences blocked access to weed-grown squares filled with rubble. She lifted her staff, and saw by its light the opening of a narrow alley, hardly more than a passageway walled in by high brick on either side.

Protruding from the opening, visible in the glow of her staff, were the legs of a prone and motionless man. His torso was hidden in the shadows of the alley.

Mael Taleion's ebony staff lay on the pavement near the man's feet. Klea slowed her pace long enough to stoop and pick up the staff with her free hand, but she didn't stop. The discovery made her even more alert. Master Evanh was far behind her now; if he caught up at all, it would be after everything was over. The air here tingled with power, making her skin prickle at its touch, and somewhere up ahead, Mael Taleion was deeply upset about something. Not about the man on the ground, she could tell that much, but *something*.

She entered the alley. The Magelord stood there, robed and masked, his empty hands ablaze with crimson light. Three motionless bodies, young men in shabby work clothes and heavy boots, lay on the pavement before him. Not dead—the one nearest the mouth of the alley was twitching slightly— but very thoroughly chastised.

Klea ignored them. She came forward into Mael's line of sight and offered him his staff.

For a few seconds more he remained unmoving: then he took the staff from her hand, and the red glow that surrounded him died. He clipped his staff onto his belt and took off the mask. His face was pale and streaked with sweat.

"Mistress," he said, "I believe that we have a problem."

"We knew that hours ago," Klea said. Her relief at finding Mael alive and on his feet, and his assailants still breathing, made her voice sharper than she had intended. "Will you come back with me to the Guildhouse?"

"Yes . . . but we can't stay there for much longer. Mistress, we have to talk."

"Later, in private," she said. Hesitant footsteps in the street beyond the alley signaled the tardy approach of Master Evanh. "Tell me one thing—were you in the Void?"

For a moment she thought he wasn't going to answer; then she realized that he was translating the concept from Galcenian into his own tongue. His everyday use of the common star-traveler's language was fluent, if accented; it had not occurred to her that there were some things he was accustomed to thinking of in Eraasian, when he thought of them at all.

"Yes," he said finally. "It was necessary."

Klea waved a hand at the unconscious bodies sprawled on the pavement. "These?"

He nodded. "But they aren't important, except that they pushed me into going where I could find out what I needed to know: the *ekkannikh* has slipped its bonds to Cracanth, and goes now to do mischief in a particular place."

Klea glanced over her shoulder. Master Evanh was just coming into sight, puffing from the unaccustomed exertion of a brisk walk. She lowered her voice. "Where?"

"If not to the worst possible place," said Mael, "then surely to the most inconvenient for our purposes." He paused. "Mistress Santreny—will you come with me to Khesat?"

Blossom's partner Bindweed didn't show up at the gallery until after sunset. She turned out to be a lean, grey-haired woman—old for a thin-skin, like her partner, but equally trim and vigorous. She wore dark trousers and an embroidered vest; and, like Blossom, she entered through the front of the shop.

Blossom looked up from the card game as she walked in. "What kept you?"

"I was involved in some troublesome legal matters," Bind-weed replied. "Depositions, and insurance, and entirely too many questions from people who weren't at all familiar with the ways of spacers. It was all I could do to explain how I came to have a blaster in my hand."

Huool chittered with amusement, and Blossom said, "I hope the explanations didn't get too expensive."

"Nothing we can't cover. But it did take a while. And then I had to change clothes and pack our bags."

"Time for us to move on?" Blossom looked regretful. "I've enjoyed it here."

"Nothing so permanent, I hope. I've put a 'Closed for Repairs' sign on the shop, but that's all. A little vacation will do both of us good." She sat down at the card table opposite Chaka. "Deal me in."

The game continued until past midnight. Chaka thought it just as well that nobody was playing for money, since neither Bindweed nor Blossom showed their opponents any mercy, and Huool—even with his attention divided between the cards and the glyphs on his workdesk—was dangerous enough to challenge them both. For herself, Chaka was outclassed all round, and she knew it.

Blossom had won yet another hand when her belt pouch chimed. She pulled out the still chiming comm link and keyed it on. It was an expensive model, no bigger than the deck of cards she'd brought out earlier, with a tiny built-in flatscreen. From her expression, the caller was a known, if unexpected, quantity.

"Captain Amaro," she said. "To what do I owe the pleasure?" She paused, and looked at Huool. "I trust this room has the usual privacy screens?"

Huool ruffled his neck-feathers indignantly. "Of course."

"Then I trust your honor." She turned back to the screen. "What brings you calling?"

"An offer of a cargo, Gentlelady. It might amuse me to carry it, but I thought I'd ask if you had other plans."

Blossom snorted. "You mean you've already accepted the offer and wanted to let me know."

Chaka couldn't see the caller's face, but she could hear the shrug in his voice. "We haven't yet talked price. Three passengers, destination to be stated after we reach high orbit."

"Young people—two male, one female?"

"You're magical. How did you know?"

Blossom turned to Huool. "Not your little Miza, surely?" Huool ruffled his feathers in reply, and Blossom said to the caller, "Tell me more."

"Little enough to tell. A fat profit, an easy job."

"Those are always the tricky ones. You're flying *Dust Devil* again?"

"As always."

"Not quite," Blossom told him. "My partner and I will be accompanying you, and we're bringing an engineer along. Explain to the passengers that for security's sake they aren't going to see the other crew members."

The caller laughed. "They'll be too busy dodging vermin in the cargo hold to even think about meeting the crew."

"Excellent notion. I'll see you when you have the cargo all packed. Blossom out." She shut down the link and turned to Chaka. "Is it true that all Selvaurs are natural engineers?"

Never been in an engine room in my life.

"There's nothing to it, really, and I'm sure Captain Amaro will have his own engineer show you whatever you need to do. You might as well start learning now."

The Freemarket Plaza in Sombrelír lay far enough outside the spaceport district to make it safe for tourists—in large groups, and in daylight. By night, it was another matter. At least, all the data files aboard *Bright-Wind-Rising* had implied as much, and as far as Faral could tell, the data files had told the truth. If anything, they had understated the situation.

Although the hour was past midnight, the Freemarket was thronged with buyers and sellers from port and city alike. Ophelans, Eraasians, Central Worlders, and a host of others all crowded into the market's baffling labyrinth of tables and tents and booths. Illumination from many different sources— flickering torches, yellow incandescent globes, and the steady blue-white of miniature glowcubes—filled the square with a wavery, disorienting blend of lights and shadows.

In the center of the plaza, a massive bronze statue identified in the *Wind*'s data files as the last ruler of independent Sombrelír brooded over the scene below. The vendors in the booths shouted their prices, and hoarse-voiced barkers outside of closed tents promised live entertainment and surpassing pleasure to be found within. A man spewed flames from his lips at one booth, two women wearing nothing but oil and glitter juggled frightening-looking knives in front of another, and in a third a short creature of indeterminate species offered to tell fortunes.

Faral was hard put to keep from staring—the jugglers in particular were like nothing he'd encountered on Maraghai— but he was unwilling to betray his lack of sophistication in front of Miza. Huool's student-courier was pushing through the jostling mass of people with an undiverted singleness of purpose.

Maybe they see this sort of thing all the time on Artha, Faral thought.

He glanced over at his cousin. Jens was looking bored, which was some consolation—Jens never looked bored, except when he was trying to cover up some other, and potentially more embarrassing, state of mind. Faral turned back to Miza.

"We're meeting our, um, freetrading captain here?" he asked. "In public?"

"Safety," Miza replied. "We meet if we both want to. Otherwise we don't bother to recognize each other."

They walked deeper into the maze of booths, twisting and dodging through a wild variety of goods being offered for sale. Tables loaded with farm produce stood beside racks of jewelry, while nearby an artisan turned a block of what looked like gold into a series of tiny naked figures linked together in unlikely but educational poses. High above the press, the massive central statue grew ever closer.

"You're seriously expecting to find one specific person in all of this—this collection of oddities?" Jens asked Miza.

She scowled at him. "Look, I know what I'm doing."

The pedestal of the statue came in sight past the booths. And there, leaning against the carved stone, was a man. He wore bright red and black garments cut in the free-spacers' style, and high, polished boots. At his waist he wore a pair of blasters, rigged with the grips forward for a cross draw.

"That's him," Miza whispered. "Stay here a moment."

Without looking to see if anyone was following her suggestion, she continued forward. The crowd was thinner here at the base of the statue, and the pathway wider. Faral had a good view as Miza first passed by the gaudily dressed fellow, then returned and leaned against the pedestal next to him. The two of them talked for a little while. When Miza came back to where Jens and Faral waited, the man came with her.

"I'm Captain Amaro," he said. "I won't ask for your names, so don't bother making any up. Now come with me."

The four of them walked away from the base of the statue, into the shadows among the tents and booths. After a few minutes, Amaro halted them with an upraised hand.

"Listen carefully," he said. "Here is a cargo carrier." He nodded toward a looming object that Faral recognized after a few seconds as a wheeled conveyance. Dark cloth stretched over arched poles made a screen to hide the contents. "On the carrier, inside where none may see, is a crate. Enter the crate, and make no sound until I myself open it. What luggage do you carry?"

Faral hefted the carrybag in his hand. "You're looking at it."

"Good," Amaro said. "Recall what you are buying: food, water, air, and a passage. No questions until high orbit, and no memory later. Agreed?"

"Agreed," said Jens, before Faral could say anything.

Amaro gave a curt nod. "Good," he said again. "One thing more. Once we hit high orbit, if I don't like where you're going, back you come. No questions, no refund."

"Wait a minute—" Faral began.

Miza touched his arm, silencing him. "It's a fair bargain,"

she said. "For him, the danger is in leaving port and in land-ing. The payment is for that."

"If it's customary," said Jens, "then we agree."

"Until high orbit, then," Amaro said. He made a florid bow, and turned away. A moment later he was lost in the crowd.

"I don't like it," Faral said. He regarded the carrier with suspicion. "No telling where that crate's going to be when it's opened, if it ever is opened."

"Amaro has a reputation for honesty," Miza said. "In his own business, at least. Trying a double-cross would ruin him."

"Trust her judgment, coz, and relax." Jens's eyes were once again very bright. "She's climbing into the crate right along with us, after all."

Miza didn't make any protest—possibly she realized that anyone who'd remained in their company for as long as she had been was now also a target for their enemies.

The three of them scrambled into the back of the cargo car-rier. Under the cloth covering, the vehicle's interior was as dark as the inside of a rockhog, and Faral located the solid metal crate by stumbling against it. After a few seconds of fumbling, he located a button near the top edge. He pressed it and a wave of stale air washed across his face as the lid of the crate groaned open.

"Here we are," he said. "Who goes first?"

"After you, coz."

"I was afraid you'd say that." He grasped the edge of the box and vaulted over. There was less room inside the crate than he'd expected—most of the space was taken up by what felt like pads and safety webbing. Captain Amaro had obvi-ously taken passengers into orbit this way before. "Give Gentlelady Lyftingil a boost, then."

"Here she comes."

"I don't need—" Miza's protest began on the other side of the crate from Faral, and finished when a warm and surpris-ingly solid body landed in his arms. "—any help!"

Jens followed her into the crate a few seconds later. The fit was tight for the three of them, but after a certain amount of fumbling they got all of the straps and webbing sorted out and began to buckle themselves into place.

"Do you need—" Faral began.

"No," Miza said. "I don't need any help with this part, thank you."

"We're crushed," said Jens. "Absolutely crushed. Who's nearest the button to close the lid?"

"You are, I think," Faral said.

"So I am. Here goes."

The lid groaned shut. Faral experienced a brief surge of panic—*I only thought it was dark in here before; now it's dark*— and nothing but the awareness of Jens and Miza listening inches away kept him from gasping for air in terrified mouthfuls. It was impossible to stay frightened forever, though. When nothing happened for some time, boredom supplanted fear and eventually he went to sleep.

In the hours after midnight, the outskirts of Nanáli were all but empty of traffic. The occasional delivery van bumped past the Nanáli Starlight Family Hotel on straining nullgravs to deliver fresh grain or vegetables into the city before morning. Now and again a night-laborer on his way home went by on foot, or an early shift worker coming in. But aside from those few, there was nobody awake to notice the hovercar with a Sombrelír traffic-control sticker parked behind a nearby building.

Kolpag and Ruhn stood in the upstairs hallway of the hotel. Kolpag had the master keycard in his hand. He'd obtained the card from the desk clerk through the persuasive efforts of a large wad of cash, and had already used it once to unlock the bathroom at the end of the hall. The bathroom had been empty.

Now, outside the room assigned to Brix Gorlees, Kolpag and Ruhn paused for a moment to draw their blasters and thumb the settings to Stun. Then Ruhn took up a position on the right side of the door, and Kolpag stood on the left.

Kolpag swiped the keycard through the door's built-in scanner, then touched the cycle button.

The door slid open.

As soon as the door had opened all the way, the two men fired their blasters—each man aiming for the corner of the room diagonally opposite, so that the fiery streamers crossed paths in midair. Then Kolpag threw himself onto the floor in the center of the doorway with his blaster in front of him. Ruhn stood behind him, shooting straight ahead at the center of the far wall.

. They had fired at least three shots before they noticed that there was nobody else in the room.

"Oh, damn," Kolpag said. He pulled himself to his feet and allowed the door to slide the rest of the way shut behind him. "Missed them again."

Ruhn was already searching the room. "No luggage, no personal articles. Our birds have already flown."

"Maybe they're out at a restaurant or something?" Kolpag made the suggestion mostly for form's sake.

Ruhn snorted. "At this hour? Hardly. Think they'll be coming back?"

"Not likely," said Kolpag. "But we'll have somebody from the local office put a watch on this room all the same. Not that they'll find anything you didn't."

Ruhn nodded. "The beds have been slept in, it looks like, but they've gone cold. I'd say our packages have about a two-hour lead on us by now."

Kolpag holstered his blaster and pulled a comm link from his jacket pocket. He keyed it on and said, "Message to watchers at spaceports, case five niner. Heads up, they're coming."

"What about us?" Ruhn asked. "Where do we go next?"

"Sombrelír," said Kolpag. "I want to pay a visit to Gentlesir Huool."

IX. Ophel; high orbit; hyperspace; Galcen

FARAL AWOKE in absolute darkness. Only the lessons he'd learned in the forests on Maraghai—*stay silent, don't move, no good comes of noise*—kept him from shouting and flailing about. Then he remembered that he was closed up with Jens and Miza inside a padded crate, being smuggled into high orbit like so much untaxed aqua vitae.

Before he could make inquiries about his companions' state of mind, however, the crate began to vibrate around him. A huge roaring filled his ears, and shortly afterward came the feeling of immense weight that meant a launch. A little while later, gravity first vanished, then reappeared in the opposite direction, so that he felt like he was hanging up instead of falling down, and the safety webbing began to pinch him in a number of awkward places.

More time passed, and the crate's lid groaned open. Faral blinked at the sudden light—there wasn't all that much of it, objectively speaking, but even a dim cargo hold was too bright after several hours spent in complete blackness. Miza exclaimed something in a language he didn't know—probably Arthan, though he supposed she could have picked up an Ophelan catchphrase or two during her internship—and put up a hand to shield her eyes. Jens yawned.

Captain Amaro waited outside the crate. "Welcome to *Dust Devil*," he said. "Now it's time to talk about where the three of you are planning to go."

"No," Jens said. "First my friends and I remove ourselves from this fascinating receptacle of yours. *Then* we talk."

"Of course," Amaro said. The smuggler waited without speaking while the three companions unbuckled themselves and clambered one at a time over the side of the padded box.

Except for perhaps half a dozen smaller crates griped down to the deckplates in the same manner as their larger one, *Dust Devil*'s cargo hold was empty. On top of one crate stood a hotpot of cha'a and a stack of interlocking mugs. Amaro unstacked the mugs and began pouring cha'a like a gracious host.

"All of my passengers," he said as he passed around the steaming mugs, "are going somewhere, even if it is merely 'away.' I will not lie to you—'away' is the simplest, because I get to choose the destination. But if you have a place in mind, this is the time when you say truthfully what it is."

Faral sipped at the bitter, reenergizing cha'a and didn't say anything. *Let Jens handle it,* he thought. *He's the one with all the plans.*

Jens waited a moment before answering—for effect, Faral was certain. "Where I want to go," he said finally, "is Khesat. Will that be a problem?"

"Khesat." Amaro looked thoughtful. "That's a sticky one. I don't run anything through there, as a general rule."

"Understood," said Jens. "But are you persuadable?"

"It all depends. Do you have a valid passport and a visa?"

"Ah . . . no. In the haste of our departure from Ophel, we didn't have time to observe the diplomatic niceties."

"In that case," Amaro said, "we've got a problem. Either pick another destination, or resign yourselves to going back dirtside."

Jens bit his lip and glanced at Faral and Miza.

Faral shrugged. Khesat had never been all that attractive to him as a place to look for fame. "There's always Eraasi, like we were planning."

"Like *you* were planning. I don't want—"

Miza said hastily, "How about Sapne?"

Both Faral and Jens turned to stare at her.

"Sapne?" Faral said, and Captain Amaro said, "That might work, yes."

"I don't see how," Faral said. "Everybody I've ever heard talk about it"—which was mostly his Aunt Bee, who claimed to have traded on Sapne during her free-spacing days—"says there hasn't been a real government on-planet since the Biochem Plagues."

"That's the whole point," Miza said. "I learned all about it while I was working for Huool. People use Sapne for a cargo transfer point a lot, because you don't need anything to do business there except a good autolander set. There's no inspace control on Sapne—there's no port at all, really—and there's definitely no customs office."

"We're not trying to smuggle salt," Jens said. "We're trying to get from Ophel to Khesat without a visa."

"Let the gentlelady finish," said Amaro. "She knows her business, I can see."

Miza looked flattered. "That's the other thing," she said. "From Sapne you can get a visa to anywhere."

"How?" Faral asked.

"Something Huool mentioned once. There's a passport office on Sapne that's got the validations and everything, right out where anyone who wants to can walk in and use them."

"There's a catch, right?" Jens said.

"It's at the old spaceport."

Memories of holovid adventure programs stirred in Faral's mind. "Isn't the old port on Sapne supposed to be haunted?"

"Supposedly," said Amaro. "But that's a useful reputation to have in some quarters."

"What fun," said Jens. "Sapne it is, then, if the good captain agrees."

"One-way to Sapne for three passengers," Amaro said. "After we make planetfall, either you're on your own or we can negotiate another deal. Done?"

Jens held out his hand. "Done."

Kolpag and Ruhn left the Nanáli Starlight Family Hotel and walked out onto the street. The two operatives nodded as they passed to the outside men sent over from the local branch. The locals would keep on watching the hotel in case the packages returned, but Kolpag didn't hold out much hope of that.

"Where to?" his partner asked as they unlocked their hovercar and strapped themselves into the seats.

Kolpag thought for a minute. "Let's see if we can touch the beaky-boy. His fingerprints are all over this."

"Do Rotis have fingerprints?" Ruhn asked curiously.

"I suppose they do . . . no, actually, I think I read somewhere that they've got distinctive quill patterns you can use to identify them by, as long as they've been considerate enough to shed a few feathers for you first."

"We could arrange that."

"Problem with Huool, though," Kolpag said as he started the hovercar. The vehicle rose on its nullgravs and hung there, humming softly, until Kolpag pulled on its control yoke and set it to moving slowly in reverse. "He's political. Can't touch him too hard."

"Politics," said Ruhn. He sounded disgusted. "Let me tell you, I hate politics. As of right now, we don't know if our packages were even here. Someone might have been fibbing to us, and if we can't twist an arm on the beaky-boy we'll never know."

"Maybe we were working on bad assumptions," Kolpag said. He backed the hovercar out into the deserted street and started off in the direction of Sombrelír. It was close to dawn, now, and the sky was faint pink along the distant horizon. "Before we risk messing with Huool and his patrons, let's try getting the information by technical means instead."

"Yeah," Ruhn agreed. "I'll get the division working on it, see what they come up with."

He brought out his datapad again, and used the comm link to put through a brief, coded request. A few seconds later, the datapad blinked and beeped to let him know that the information he'd asked for had come back through the link. Ruhn scrolled through the text, reading quickly and making notes as he went. After a few minutes, he looked up.

"Hey, check this out. You remember the fighting grannies?"

Kolpag tightened his grip on the hovercar's control yoke. "How could I forget those two? They got Freppys, and he was as good as they come."

"I've got a dossier on both of them. A *thorough* dossier, this time . . . and let me tell you, the intel people really screwed this one up. You guys didn't go into that tea shop anywhere close to heavy enough."

"Now the man tells me."

"No," said Ruhn. "What this means is that the whole organization got sold out this time. The big question is, who was it that did the selling?"

Captain Amaro left his three passengers in their quarters and made his way through the cramped passageways to *Dust Devil*'s bridge. So far, the current business deal had been nothing out of the ordinary—he'd smuggled people as often as material goods, if not oftener—but this would be the first time he'd made a freetrading run with the *Dusty*'s actual owners on board.

The Gentleladies Bindweed and Blossom were already on the bridge when he arrived, safety-webbed into the auxiliary seats behind the captain's command and control position. The *Dusty*'s navigator, Trav Esmet, occupied the number-two position on the captain's right.

Amaro glanced at the main console. The telltales shone a reassuring green. "Have all the crew reported in yet?"

"Yes," said Esmet. "All on station and correct."

"Very well." He turned to Blossom. "You were right,

gentlelady. They went for Sapne. Esmet—do we have the navicomp data for that one fed in?"

"Fed in and ready."

"Then let's make transit." Amaro picked up the handset for the *Dust Devil*'s external comm link and keyed it on. "Security, Security, Security," he said aloud. "This is Freetrader *Dust Devil* departing high orbit. Stand by, out."

He pointed at Esmet. "Stand by, run to jump."

Esmet was in training for his own pilot's papers, and the Ophelan system was a good place to get in the necessary practice. Ships had been coming and going out of Ophel for a long time, and the navicomps had lots of accumulated data to work with.

Amaro settled back in the command seat to watch the stars outside the *Dusty*'s viewscreens, all the while keeping a surreptitious eye on the comp data readout and the jump-point indicator. They lined up nicely as Esmet handled the controls. The stars shifted color, then blazed and vanished, replaced by the grey nonsubstance of hyperspace.

"Good run," Amaro said to Esmet. "One more just as good and I'll sign you off on that. Assuming, of course, that we arrive somewhere within shouting range of Sapne."

Mistress Klea Santreny stood at Loading Gate 2B in the Sombrelír Port Complex, waiting for a shuttle to take her and Mael Taleion to the low-orbit transfer station where the Magelord had left his ship. A small Eraasian-built craft, not designed for atmosphere work, Mael's *Arrow-through-the-Doorway* had range and speed that the cargo tubs and groundgrabbers of similar size didn't match . . . or so its owner claimed. It had been assembled in orbit, and would stay that way forever.

Klea had spent the rest of the previous night working the diplomatic problems presented by their departure. Taking a privately owned vessel out of Ophelan space and into the Khesatan sphere of influence—especially when the vessel was fast, was armed, and had a point of origin in the Mageworlds—required a number of passes and permissions. She had been given to understand, early on, that gratuities of sufficient size, distributed in the proper quarters, would make everything simple. Out of principle, she had declined to make any such payments. The officials concerned would do their work, and do it promptly, because that was what the law required.

It had taken a great deal of hard work and persistence on Klea's part, but in the end the officials had capitulated. *Arrow-through-the-Doorway* would be leaving Ophelan space before day's end Sombrelír time, as Mael Taleion had asked.

And I still don't know why the hell I agreed to help him do this, Klea thought. *Except that he's chasing shadows, and so am I.*

"Are there any Mages on Khesat?" she asked aloud. "Other than the ones on the Peace and Trade Commission, I mean."

"None on the Commission," Mael said. "At least, not if you're talking about Circle members. We would not be able to perform our devotions properly under such circumstances." He gave her a speculative glance. "Why? Do you Adepts have your own members on the Commission?"

"I'm not sure," Klea said vaguely. Inwardly she gave Mael points for his deflection of the unwelcome line of inquiry. The smoothness of his maneuver, however, argued that there might well be Mages active somewhere on Khesat.

Active in what? she thought. *That is a good question. And I wish I knew the answer.*

The passenger cabin on *Dust Devil* was a long way from the suite Faral and Jens had occupied with Chaka aboard *Bright-Wind-Rising*. The bunks were stacked three high along one bare metal wall—*bulkhead*, Faral reminded himself, *they call them bulkheads*—and a battery of storage lockers filled most of the available space on the side opposite. An airtight door led to the passageway outside, and at the other end of the narrow cabin a second door led to the refresher cubicle.

The bunks were fitted out with the pads and webbing to double as acceleration couches, and a red Strap Down light glowed over the main door on the inside. Once *Dust Devil* had made her straight-line run to the jump point and entered hyperspace, the red light went off.

Faral unbuckled his safety webbing and climbed down from the middle bunk of the tier. "If I ever have to get smuggled off-planet in a cargo crate again," he said, stretching out muscles still knotted and kinked from the experience, "I'm going to insist on getting the custom-fitted model."

"I'll make sure to put that in your file." Miza, on the bottom level, was short enough to sit on the edge of the pad without bumping her head on the rack above. "If Huool hasn't thrown me out of the program already for making a botch."

Jens didn't bother getting down from the top bunk at all; he unstrapped and propped himself up on one elbow to look at her. "We cruelly took you captive and forced you to accompany us against your will," he said. "Gentlesir Huool would never fault you for that."

"I'm supposed to be clever enough not to get caught," she said. Faral thought he heard a catch in her voice, and decided that he didn't blame her; it had been a long and trying day, and the hour or so of sleep at the Nanáli Starlight Family Hotel hadn't lasted nearly long enough.

"Don't worry," he told her. "You said you were training to be an analyst, not some kind of field person. Nobody expects their in-house people to be any good at this sort of thing."

She snorted. "Nobody expects a pair of tourists to be any good at that sort of thing either. Who taught you?"

"The wrinkleskins back on Maraghai," Faral said. "And my father. I don't know who taught my cousin how to snag blasters off of corpses, though."

Jens sketched a nod and a one-handed flourish. "One of the many skills I learned at my mother's knee and other low joints."

The chime of the door signal interrupted him. Faral went over to palm the lockplate and admit the newcomer—but the door was already sliding open.

So the cabin doors are keyed to external controls, he thought as the airtight seal broke and the metal leaves parted. *I wonder which side has the override.*

When the door had slid all the way open, Captain Amaro stepped into the cabin. He looked brisk and businesslike, as if he smuggled off-worlders every time he left port.

"I see that you made the translation to hyperspace without any trouble," he said. "Now that we're in, the three of you can take your meals with me if you like. I'm afraid, though, that you won't be able to meet the rest of the crew. Safer for them that way, and safer for you."

"You've carried nondocumented passengers before?" Jens asked.

Amaro glanced up at the top bunk. "You really expect an answer to such a question?"

Jens shrugged. "I was going to ask about the mechanics of changing names, and I thought you might know."

"A minor thing," Amaro said. He sounded flattered. "You have a name picked out that you like?"

"I have an alias that I want to get rid of," said Jens, "and a pressing need to arrive on Khesat under my own name."

"Sapne," Amaro said at once. "Everything you need is there. Mind you, a Sapnean ID is a hasty remedy, and not something to stand up under any kind of deep scan."

"All I need is the right name," Jens told him. "Sapne sounds like it will serve admirably."

"Then we're all set. The dinner gong goes off at fifteen-thirty ship's-time; I'll see you gentles then."

Amaro left. The airtight door slid closed behind him. After a few seconds, Faral went over to the door and thumbed the Open switch. The door didn't budge.

"So that's how it is," said Faral. He tried the switch a second time to make sure, then turned to look at Jens and Miza. "We'd better work hard on staying friendly . . . because otherwise we aren't going to enjoy this hyperspace transit at all."

In his private office at the Retreat, the Master of the Adepts' Guild regarded the day's schedule with resignation. In the morning, he had conferences with the senior masters about food and laundry for the new apprentices and about ongoing repairs to the Retreat's physical structures. In the afternoon, he had a meeting with the Guild's treasurer, Master Adan, to discuss whether the Guild's privately held funds should remain on Galcen or be transferred to one of the financial institutions on Suivi Point. And at a late-evening hour that was the only time even remotely convenient for half a dozen people on as many different planets, he had a hyperspace comm conference with the heads of the Guild branches in Khesatan and adjacent space.

Work and more work. And boring *work at that.*

Once, some years before, Owen Rosselin-Metadi had declared himself ready to defeat the invading Magelords and restore the Guild to its accustomed place in galactic affairs. He'd expected the task to be difficult and dangerous, but that prospect had never swayed him. He'd spent years as the previous Guild Master's personal apprentice and trusted right hand, and the work he'd done in those days had been by no means light and easy.

The civilized galaxy, he thought, *is damned lucky that nobody ever bothered to tell me the job of saving it came with two decades of ongoing administrative follow-up.*

The incoming-message light on his desktop blinked at him. Owen touched the sensor dot that activated the status display: coded compressed-text, keyed to his ID, point of origin Ophel. He allowed himself a moment of satisfaction. His own former apprentice and trusted right hand, that would be, with a report on the troublesome situation involving his two scapegrace nephews.

Another touch on the desktop, this time to feed in his ID scan and lock it into the message. The text poured into the display space.

Mistress Klea Santreny to Owen Rosselin-Metadi, Master of the Adepts' Guild, sends greeting.

Both of your nephews, I'm certain, are dutiful and well-brought-up young men. This leaves us with the question of exactly who taught them to shed pursuit like a pair of professionals. They are no longer on Ophel. Nor does anybody on Ophel seem to know where they have gone, though the members of at least one sublegal organization are apparently searching for them with great diligence.

If it's any consolation to you, your sister-in-law on

Maraghai also seems to be worried about possible developments. She has sent out her Second to look for Jens and Faral—and he, in his turn, believes that their voluntary disappearance is tied in somehow with events scheduled to occur on Khesat. He speaks also of a revenant, a "homeless one" in his language, coming out of the Mageworlds on a quest for some kind of vengeance; he references in particular the message forwarded by courtesy from the Circles on Cracanth.

I confess that I do not entirely follow, nor entirely trust, his line of reasoning. However, I'm forced to admit that if he is correct about the Cracanthan matter, we could all be in serious trouble. You most particularly—since the name he gives to the revenant is Errec Ransome.

We are preparing now to take ship for Khesat, on what may possibly be a fool's errand—but having found nothing but dead ends on Ophel, I am reduced to following a Magelord's intuitions.

If you could send me your best information on what is happening on Khesat these days, I would rest easier during the transit.

Her identification code followed the message, along with her name. Owen smiled a little as he closed the message, in spite of the gravity of its contents. Mistress Santreny had been one of the better things to happen to the Guild, back in the bad times during the Second Magewar.

Then the smile faded. If the Guild's former Master had reason to pursue his onetime apprentice even after death, then Klea herself, though she didn't say so, was equally a target.

She was there, out in the Void. All of us were, when we had to—

—when we killed him. This is what comes of doing a thing, and then not thinking of it for twenty years. The consequences of it rise up while our faces are turned away, and the dead come back to haunt us.

Owen was tempted to summon Mistress Santreny back to the Retreat and let Llannat Hyfid's tame Magelord keep up the chase alone. But Klea had asked him for information, not for protection—she appeared to have her work well in hand, in spite of her protestations of bafflement, and would not appreciate being called away from the pursuit.

The Green Sun's operations center in Sombrelír was brightly lit, although at this hour only one comptech was on duty. An open box of take-out sausage buns beside her elbow said that she wasn't leaving her console, but the smell of *hnann* in the air suggested that maybe she hadn't been concentrating solely on her job before the field ops arrived.

Kolpag and Ruhn weren't interested in either fact. They had transcripts and files called up all over the central worktable, and their cups of *uffa* had dwindled to red-ocher dregs as they looked through the files and ran the databases.

"Well, well, well," said Kolpag suddenly. "Look what we've got here. Comm conference, twenty-one thirty-one decimal five hours. Someone inbound to Huool's. Duration of contact under two minutes."

"Got a transcript?" asked Ruhn.

Kolpag indicated a screen's worth of gibberish on the worktable. "Scrambled. But let's look at this another way. Our boys must have had help. Huool is expensive. So who's paying the bills?"

"Got that one. Huool."

Kolpag felt like smacking his new partner. "No, no, not that letter-of-credit thing. Who paid Huool enough for him to provide it?"

Ruhn shrugged. "I can't think of anything smaller than planetary royalty who could come up with that kind of cash in a hurry."

"Let's not jump to conclusions." Kolpag turned to the comptech, who was finishing off the last of the sausage buns. "Time to earn your pay. A little traffic analysis. Calls from Nanáli to Sombrelír, no more specific origin, within one half-hour prior to twenty-one thirty. Cross-ref to call from same location to anywhere within Sombrelír, same time period. Go."

"Working." The comptech wiped her fingers, switched off

the deedle music from a local rover-channel, and swiveled her chair back to her console. Her hands danced over the comp keys to another, more insistent rhythm.

Kolpag looked up at the map of Ophel's western political zone on the ops room wall and pressed his fingers to the bridge of his nose. He was coming up now on a solid day with no sleep, and he could feel the case hedging him in, making him crazy. The loss of Freppys—he turned back to the file in front of him. After a moment, the data on the screen began to make sense again.

"I see something odd here," he said. "Freetrader *Dust Devil*, Amaro commanding. In port for a scheduled one-week layover, cargo beginning to arrive tomorrow morning, loading to continue through Sabinnight."

Ruhn looked bored. "So?"

"So she lifted at zero-two this morning."

"The hell." Ruhn turned to the comptech. "Any luck?"

"Still running."

"Halt run. Narrow the parameters: in and out within ten-minute walk of . . ." Ruhn leaned over and looked at the line Kolpag was pointing to. ". . . Docking Easement G-Nine Old Town."

"Meanwhile," Kolpag said, calling up yet more files onto the worktable, "let's see just who's associated with *Dust Devil*."

The answers came in quick succession.

"We have matches on twenty-seven comm calls, match criteria," the comptech said. A strip of printout flimsy scrolled out of the slot beside her. Ruhn snatched it free as soon as it cut, and ran his finger down the rows.

"Time, time," he muttered. Then— "Here." He starred two lines with his stylus and shoved the flimsy toward Kolpag. "What do you think?"

Kolpag looked at the starred items. "Call from Nanáli, Central Rail Depot, to Sombrelír. Eight minutes later, call from Sombrelír number to Sector seven, duration and time match the incoming call to Huool. I think we're in business."

"Closest point to the Sombrelír location is Easement G-Nine." Ruhn looked impressed. "How did you do that?"

"I'm good. Now let's track down the rest. Get me ops, and find a track on where *Dust Devil* went."

"Hang on," said Ruhn. "Background on Amaro coming in. Sworn man to Bindweed, the Old Town restaurateur. She and her partner are co-owners of his ship. And you remember what the intel files said about those two."

"Backtrack complete," the comptech said. She shook her head. "My, oh, my."

"What do you have?" Kolpag demanded.

"My, oh, my . . . those two boys you were tracking. I found out who paid for their tickets to get here."

"Going to tell us?"

"Yeah," she said. "Highest of Khesat."

"Planetary royalty," said Ruhn. "What did I tell you."

"Damn. Did the boss happen to mention who our original clients were supposed to be, back before everything went sour?"

"No, and I didn't ask, and neither would you. The boss is the client right now."

"Right you are." Kolpag pushed his green-painted metal stool a little back from the worktable. "I'm feeling good about this one. I think we've got the bastards. Bet me that the *Dusty* didn't make an arc for Khesat."

"That's where you're wrong," Ruhn said. "Got that track already. They're on the way to Sapne."

"Sapne's nothing but a customs dodge. Once they get what they came for, they'll be gone." Kolpag stood and addressed the comptech again. "I want tickets to Khesat for me and my partner. Next available ship."

The comptech punched the request in. "Got it. Standard drop."

"Thanks," Kolpag said. "Now I'm going to go to my room and get some sleep. See you in a few."

The midmorning sun was streaming in brightly through the windows as he left the ops center. But for the first time in hours, Kolpag Garbazon felt that he had the case in hand.

X. Hyperspace; Sapne

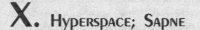

NAVIGATOR AND pilot-apprentice Trav Esmet had made over a dozen runs with Captain Amaro on the *Dust Devil*, three of them by way of an unlisted port call on Sapne. This was the first time he had set up the course and made the jump for Sapne himself, but he had confidence in his work. Amaro was a cautious man when it came to matters of piloting and navigation. He wouldn't have turned over the jump to his apprentice in the first place if he hadn't thought that Trav was ready.

The transit itself proved an uneventful one. Most of them were, Trav had learned by now, unless the ship or the crew had brought some kind of trouble into hyper along with them. In general, however, hyperspace was a good place to be if you were a spacer—you had plenty of time to work on internal repairs to the ship, or to catch up on your sleep, or to wait out whatever enemies you'd left behind.

The run-to-jump, now, was always dangerous. A pilot had to balance the ship's power between realspace engines running at extreme speed for a jump-point—falter even once, or deviate from your straight-line course, and you lost the point and had to make your run-up all over again—and hyperspace engines that had to be warmed up and ready to cut in at the moment of translation. If something mechanical was going to fail, it would fail then, and the result would be ugly.

Dropouts could be bad as well. If your navicomps had gone sick on you, or if you'd made a mess out of setting the course, you could find yourself drifting someplace off the charts, or burning up in the heart of a star. And not even good piloting and good comps would save you from piracy and ambush.

Trav knew that his piloting was good. And Captain Amaro kept the *Dusty*'s navicomps repaired and up-to-date—he'd put out good money for a data-file upgrade a couple of Standard months back, and that made the second time since Trav had apprenticed to him. If there was going to be any danger at the Sapne dropout, it would come from outside.

"What's the inspace situation like for Sapne?" Gentlelady Bindweed asked. She and Captain Amaro were playing kingnote in the *Dusty*'s common room while they talked over the possible hazards of transit. Her partner, Gentlelady Blossom, sat watching the card game from a chair nearby.

The ship's two owners confused Trav a great deal. It wasn't unheard of in the freetrading community for respectable dirtsiders to be silent partners in a ship's business, or even to own the vessel outright; but such people didn't invite themselves to come along on a less-than-legal run, and they didn't answer to names that even a still-green apprentice could recognize as aliases from half a room away. The fact that either one of the two women could have been Trav Esmet's grandmother only made the situation odder.

Captain Amaro played a card. "Sapne's been enough every time I've gone by there. No system fleet to worry about, and the Space Force doesn't patrol that sector very heavily most of the time either."

"I'm not worried about the Space Force." Gentlelady Bindweed considered her hand, then pulled out the three of trefoils and laid it down on the table. "I'm worried about the sort of people the Space Force would scare away."

Gentlelady Blossom nodded agreement. "*Dust Devil* has guns; we required them when we made the purchase. Does she have gunners ready to use them?"

"The purser and the supercargo are cross-trained."

The gentleladies glanced at each other. "Not cross-rated?" Bindweed asked.

Amaro played a four on top of the three. "I wouldn't put either of them up on the hiring board as a gunnery specialist, if that's what you mean. But they've both scored above qualifying in the sims."

"'Above qualifying.'" Bindweed's voice was rich with scorn. "That's what comes of having your minimum standard fixed by law ... pretty soon the minimum's all you're going to get."

Amaro looked skeptical. "If the minimum wasn't good enough it wouldn't be the minimum. I suppose things were better in the good old days."

"Oh, I don't know," said Blossom thoughtfully. "Nobody dirtside gave me a qualifying exam before the first time I hit the guns live. I'd been taking lessons from the ship's main gunner in my spare time—playing at it, mostly—and when she got killed and the number two got wounded, there wasn't anyone left to shoot back at the Mages but me. Our ship was still in one piece when the fighting stopped, and the other guy wasn't, so the captain said I was qualified and gave me my papers herself. But it was months and months after that before I was anything I'd call good at the job."

Bindweed smiled at her partner. "You were *always* good at the job," she said. "After a few months, though—by then, you weren't just good, you were excellent."

Blossom laughed. "Flatterer." She turned to Amaro. "What happened in the old days doesn't change the situation here. We've got two gunners with paper qualifications—how about your navigator, have you trained him?"

Esmet had been studying the Pilot III and II manual at the

flatscreen in the corner, and trying to stay invisible; now he blushed as the others all turned to look in his direction.

"Trav's working on getting his pilot papers," said Amaro. "That's a heavy load already on top of his regular job."

"This is hyperspace," Bindweed said. "The boy can take his turn at gunnery practice along with everybody else; it'll keep him from getting bored. But *Dust Devil* is going to have fully-trained gunners on duty when she drops out of hyper, even if it means that Gentlelady Blossom and I have to run make-up classes from now until the end of the transit."

Chakallakak *ngha*-Chakallakak had spoken the truth when she said that she had never been in a starship's engine room before in her life. She did, however, possess a thorough grounding in the general principles, thanks to diligent work back on Maraghai in the basic instructional sims.

"You could probably qualify for an apprentice's papers, no problem," said Bindweed. She and her partner were drinking hot *uffa* in the *Dusty*'s common room, and Chaka had encountered them when she came there on a similar mission. "You're doing an apprentice's work, that's for sure."

I don't think so, Chaka said. *There's no glory in running somebody else's engines for them.*

Blossom looked thoughtful. "Ferrdacorr *ngha*-Rillikkikk got all the fame he needed that way, and then some."

There was a war going on, Chaka said. *Ferrdacorr ran engines for Jos Metadi—and *he* had fame and to spare for anybody who ever met him.*

"She has a point," said Bindweed. "There aren't many like our Jos. So, Gentlelady Chakallakak . . . how were you planning to chase down your own fair share of fame?"

Before I started chasing down my thin-skin buddies instead? Chaka's mug was empty; she filled it with more *uffa* from the hotpot. *I was going to head for Eraasi and look for something there. Word on Maraghai is that things in the Mageworlds are still fairly loose and exciting, if you know where to look. Fame grows wild in places like that.*

The *Dusty*'s two owners glanced at each other. "You want

to be careful, if you try Eraasi," Bindweed said. "The Mageworlders aren't just another bunch of thin-skins who happen to talk funny. Things are different out there."

What do you mean . . . "different"?

"For one thing," said Bindweed, "you can get called out for a duel by a respectable citizen in the middle of downtown Port Eraasi, which is something you don't often see these days on our side of the Gap."

Chaka bared her teeth in a grin. *The Mageworlders sound like sensible people to me. Tell me what sort of thing starts a duel on Eraasi.*

"So you can make sure to get into a couple?" Blossom asked. She turned to her partner. "Tell me truly, Bindweed, was I ever that young and hotheaded?"

"You'd calmed down some by the time I ran into you," Bindweed said. "But considering what I heard about you from the friends of your childhood—you were probably worse."

"It was lies, all of it. But if that's the way that Chaka, here, wants to chase fame, it can be done." Blossom gazed thoughtfully at the bottom of her mug. "I don't know if it's a good idea, though. Another thing they believe in the Mageworlds is that fighting duels for no good reason dooms maybe the loser and certainly the winner to punishment after death."

Bindweed looked surprised. "You really believe in stuff like that?"

"I don't believe in betting against myself," Blossom replied. She circled the rim of her mug with her forefinger. "And I gave up fighting pointless duels a long time before I met you."

What form does this punishment take? Chaka asked. *Is there any fame in standing up to it?*

"You'd have to ask a Magelord about that aspect of the situation," Blossom told her. "But my feeling has always been that making yourself deliberately miserable was a rotten way of going about gaining anything."

* * *

Not much to Faral's surprise, the hyperspace transit from Ophel to Sapne turned out to be profoundly dull. The door to the passenger cabin stayed locked except when the gong rang and Captain Amaro came to escort them to their next meal. Faral supposed that dining with the captain gave them a status somewhat higher than that of ordinary cargo—"but I'd say we were prisoners," he said to Jens and Miza, "if we hadn't paid good money for all of this."

"At least we've got access to the entertainment library and the unlocked data files," Jens said. "If we were prisoners in here, they'd be making us pass the time by counting rivets in the deckplates."

"Fifty-four on a side," said Miza. "Twelve plates in the main cabin, two in the 'fresher. Since you asked."

The whooping sound of an alarm broke into their conversation, and the red Strap Down light started blinking over the cabin door.

"Time to quit worrying about how low we rank on the shipboard social roster," Jens said. "It sounds like we're about to drop out and make orbit."

Faral strapped himself back into the padded bunk. "The captain could have given us a bit more warning."

"The captain isn't going to give you anything that you haven't paid for," Miza said. "You bought a passage. Information costs extra."

"Next time I buy a ticket from the gentlesir," Jens commented from the top bunk, "I'll make sure to purchase the 'jolly camaraderie' upgrade. In the meanwhile, let's hope his piloting holds good."

"Worried, foster-brother?" Faral asked. The alarm was still whooping, and the Strap Down light had stopped blinking and gone to a steady glow. The illumination from the cabin's overhead panels grew slowly dimmer, until the red light over the cabin door glared out into the room like a bright red eye. "You never even broke a sweat when we left hyper on *Bright-Wind-Rising*."

"At the risk of stating the obvious, coz, this ship isn't the *Wind*, and Sapne most definitely isn't Ophel."

Before Faral could answer, he felt the faint shiver of dislocation that meant the *Dust Devil* had emerged from hyperspace. The overhead light panels came back up to full intensity, and the steady vibration of the ship changed in pitch and timbre as the realspace engines cut in and began to work. The alarm kept on sounding, though, and the Strap Down light didn't go out.

Faral experienced a moment of alarm, then forced himself to relax. The odds were that the continued Strap Down mean nothing more than that the *Dust Devil*'s captain had made his dropout close to atmosphere, and wasn't bothering to wait around in orbit before making a landing.

"This is no way to gain fame, either," he grumbled. "Paying people money and then sitting around in the dark while they do the work for you."

"So learn how to do your own piloting," Miza said. "That way, if there's a problem, you know exactly who to blame."

"That's easy for you to say. Do *you* know how to do your own piloting?"

"Pleasure craft, limited." Miza sounded smug. "Class B and up."

Faral heard Jens give a deep sigh from the upper bunk. "Had I but known ... this, coz, is what comes of underestimating one's travel companions."

Captain Amaro brought *Dust Devil* out of hyperspace himself, and Trav Esmet was glad to let him. After listening to the gentleladies tell their tales of privateers waiting at known drop points to pick off unsuspecting cargo ships, Trav didn't want to take the responsibility. The *Dusty* made the translation to Sapnean space with her guns fully crewed and ready for action, and Trav had enough to do monitoring the sensor boards for contracts. They'd never had any trouble making planetfall on Sapne before, but as Gentlelady Bindweed had said to the *Dusty*'s purser, it only needed to happen once.

"The boards are clear," Trav reported to the captain. "Nobody in orbit, nobody in realspace transit."

"Taking her down," Amaro replied. "I have a visual lock, the altitude bounce is set, we're in."

The *Dusty* bucked and shivered as she passed through Sapne's turbulent upper atmosphere. Soon the ground below became visible in the forward viewscreens—a wide expanse of many shades and textures of green, patched with irregular splotches of blackness. Here and there among the luxuriant green, light glittered as the sun reflected off some half-hidden surface of metal or glass.

A light blinked red on Trav's board. He checked out the signal. "I'm getting a transponder," he reported. "Tradeship *Set-Them-Up-Again*, out of Ninglin, on the dirt."

"Pick me a spot close enough that we can chat with 'em, but far enough away they don't get nervous," Amaro said.

"Landing data coming up on screen," Trav said. "All yours, Captain."

Almost as much as the run-to-jump, a clean landing was what made a pilot's reputation. Captain Amaro was known in the business as a good but not flashy shiphandler, and Trav Esmet had ambitions toward someday earning the same description. He watched closely Amaro brought the ship down—first slowing the vessel's descent with braking jets, then flipping to landing attitude and bringing up the nullgravs to stabilize the final touchdown.

The *Dusty*'s landing legs deployed at the last minute with heavy metallic clanks. The ship's nullgravs eased off a bit at a time, and the hydraulic systems sighed massively as they took over the strain of the *Dusty*'s weight. The vessel settled into place without a bump.

"And we're down," Amaro said, unstrapping and standing. "Stay close while I let our passengers off, then meet me back in the commonroom. Who wants to go visiting with the Mages?"

The Gentleladies Bindweed and Blossom had been observing the landing from the same seats as before. Bindweed glanced out at the expanse of trees and vines that filled the *Dusty*'s viewscreens.

"Not us, I think," she said to Captain Amaro. "But if it's

customary to pay a courtesy visit, you should by all means do so."

"It'd look odd if we didn't talk with them," Amaro said. "Maybe we can swap trade goods—they wouldn't have come by Sapne in the first place if their cargo didn't need its pedigree improved."

Faral, Miza, and Jens stood at the top of the *Dusty*'s main ramp, ready to go out into the forest that covered Sapne's old spaceport. Captain Amaro had escorted them up from the passenger cabin himself, and now stood in the open hatch to say good-bye and wish them luck.

"A word of advice," he said. "You might want to take a portable generator with you. You'll need to get into the filing system, and there's no guarantee that you'll find any power out there to do it with."

"Right," said Faral. "And where do we get a portable generator?"

Amaro glanced at Faral's carrybag. Its soft leather sides bulged with most of the Ophelan money they'd gotten at the cambio in Sombrelír. "I just happen to have one for rent."

Several minutes later, the carrybag was lighter by a pile of cash for a security deposit. Amaro, in return, produced a generator—a small one, built into a box not much bigger than the case Faral was carrying, and fitted with a backstrap.

"This should give you all the power you'll need," he said. "Once you've taken care of your business in the port, we can talk again about Khesat."

"Until later, then." Jens shouldered the portable generator. "Faral, Miza—let's go."

The three of them went down the *Dusty*'s ramp and out between the vessel's landing legs, onto the surface of Sapne. The ground wasn't as level as it had appeared from higher up. Though the area had been used lately as a landing zone, most of the tiny plants that would have been scoured away by the fires of a working spaceport still covered the rocky ground with sprawling patches of green and blue.

Faral took a deep lungful of the warm outdoor air. It carried the scents of fresh vegetation and recent rain.

"Smells good," he said to Jens. "I hope it's safe."

"If it wasn't, I don't think Captain Amaro would have opened the hatches. Besides, it's been a long time—two or three generations—since the plagues hit."

"People trade here all the time," said Miza impatiently. "And a lot of them bring stuff in to Huool's. If this were still a plague port, I'd have heard about it."

Faral looked around. The trees and the underbrush were full of life. Brightly feathered birds darted in and out among the trees, a garland of flowers uncoiled itself from a lower limb and became a snake with garish, many-colored scales, and the insects whirred and stridulated everywhere. "I don't see any people here right now."

"They stay clear of the port," said Miza. "The files at Huool's talked a lot about that."

"Then we're heading in the right direction," Jens said. "Presumably we'll find what we're here for when it's ready to let us find it."

Faral tried to work that statement out as they made their way across what had once been, from the look of things, a landing field. The stony surface underfoot might have been baked earth or concrete or tarmac; it was hard to tell. Tree roots thrusting upward from beneath the surface had heaved and broken the formerly level expanse.

"Does either one of you know which way to go?" Miza asked after a little while longer.

"Not the slightest," admitted Jens. He didn't sound particularly worried. "But if we follow a straight line we're sure to get somewhere."

"There was a map of the old port area in *Dust Devil's* files," Faral said. "I got a good look at it during transit."

"No fair doing research," Jens said. "Are we going in the right direction?"

"More or less."

* * *

"You understand," said Bindweed to Chaka, "what it is we want you to do."

The woman and the Selvaur stood in the shadows of the *Dusty*'s landing legs. Chaka glanced out at the forest into which Jens and Faral and the redheaded female had recently disappeared.

You don't trust my agemates out loose without a keeper, it sounds like to me.

"Not exactly," said Bindweed. "We have entirely too much confidence in those two. They've ditched the perfectly good plans older and wiser heads have made for them at least once already, and I've got a bet going with my partner that they're going to figure out some way to do it again."

Chaka grinned, taking care not to show her teeth—Bindweed was an elder, as thin-skins reckoned age, and deserved a semblance of respect no matter what she was asking. *I don't believe in messing with other people's wagers.*

"Neither do I, hothead." Bindweed laughed. "Our boys will do whatever they decide to do. But Blossom and I don't want to lose track of them, either. So . . ."

*So if they do something stupid like stow away for the Mageworlds on *Set-Them-Up-Again*, I don't have to stop them, I just have to watch.*

"Right," said Bindweed. "And bring us back the word." She handed Chaka a pocket comm link. "Save this for emergencies; there's no crypto on it, and in an unauthorized port like this one you never know who might be listening."

Faral and his two companions continued on beneath the vine-draped trees. Jagged slabs of stone poked up here and there among the bushes. A light wind rustled in the leaves, and the sunlight shone down in golden dots and speckles through the lace of greenery.

Ahead of them, a swirl of vines climbed up some half-hidden object. Through the gaps in the woody stems, Faral glimpsed the sheen of metal: beneath the broad leaves and delicate pink blooms a derelict spaceship waited for a launch command that would never come.

Jens looked at the ship with an expression that Faral couldn't interpret—not curiosity, and not the fake-Khesatan insouciance he sometimes put on as a cover for nerves or indecision. "Do you suppose the crew is still aboard her?"

"What makes you say that?" Miza asked. The words came out in a jittery rush—she was a city girl, Faral reminded himself, and liable to imagine all sorts of strange things.

"A feeling," Jens said. "Somebody is watching us here. And this place is full of ghosts."

They kept on going, but Miza remained edgy, starting at commonplace noises and glancing around with wide, uneasy eyes. Faral had also been put on his guard. He'd known his cousin to do any number of things purely for dramatic effect, but telling outright lies had never been one of them. If Jens said that he sensed ghosts, then ghosts—or things that moved just like them—were somewhere out there.

It's not the bodiless spirits we need to worry about, Faral told himself. *It's the living, breathing ones.*

Now that he looked closer he saw that the entire forest was made of abandoned hulks. Looming objects that he had taken at first for hills and boulders had mechanical structures beneath their coverings of green and brown, and what appeared at one point to be a cave turned out to be the darkness beneath a flattened ship-disk, supported like the *Dusty* on landing legs. Another vessel had not been so lucky. Its legs had rusted away, or had been knocked out by some natural force, so that the ship had fallen onto its side. The metal plates that made up its hull were pushed inward like the sides of a crumpled egg carton.

Faral glanced over at Miza. She'd lost some of her apprehension—maybe it was recognizing manufactured structures underneath the wildness that had done it—and was regarding the toppled freighter with an appraising eye.

"There's probably a fortune in treasure lying around out here," she said. "Sapne was a major transshipment point back before the First Magewar—stuff going from the Central Worlds out to the fringes, and raw materials coming back."

"We didn't come here to steal from the dead," Jens interrupted sharply. "Don't even think about it."

They kept on walking through the graveyard of lost ships, surrounded by trees and by tangled draperies of foliage, across ground cracked and mounded where broken slabs of stone protruded above red earth.

Captain Amaro settled the dagger he had taken out of *Dust Devil*'s armory into its tooled leather sheath, and double-checked the available charge in his cross-draw blasters. The Mageworlders he'd met in times past, and the old-stock Eraasians in particular, had tended to be impressed by good-looking weapons. Reassured that everything was in order, he left the *Dusty* behind and set out on his courtesy call.

The air of the morning smelled sweet, and a gentle breeze sighed past the looming bulk of his ship. Based on the transponder readings, the Eraasian vessel would lie a bit to sunward. Captain Amaro took his bearings and commenced hiking.

The Mages would be expecting him to show up fairly soon. As the newcomer in port it was his obligation to call on the senior arrival, unless he intended to be hostile. And a merchant and trader was never hostile without provocation; it tended to cut down on business opportunities thereafter. In any case, Amaro had moderate hopes for the visit. He hadn't taken on a full cargo at Sombrelír, but there were two or three things in the *Dusty*'s hold that might work as trade goods— and news and contacts were always valuable.

An hour of steady walking later, the other ship came into view: a Magebuilt trading craft, nowhere near as pretty a sight as the *Dusty*, but a good bit larger. Under its shadow the Eraasian free-spacers had set up tables and piled them high with trade goods of the cheap but glittering kind. Bolts of patterned cloth and cheap cast-in-one-piece hand axes lay on the tables beside holocubes of fractal landscapes and plastic boxes set with synthetic gems.

Even this early in the day a few locals had shown up, short and sullen-looking types dressed in crude handwoven fabrics, solemnly picking over the tables of trade materials. They carried woven baskets full of barter items of their own—beetle shells, bark, and small glittering stones.

Most of the local items would be medicinals, Amaro knew. The Mageworlders had a lively pharmaceutical industry going, and you couldn't leave your ship on a nonindustrial planet without tripping over a plant-and-earth prospector or two. Primitive artwork was another trade possibility, but a risky one. No telling in advance what the collectors in the Central Worlds would like, and if you guessed wrong you could wind up with a worthless cargo. It took a clever cargomaster to make a profit out of the Sapne run, and a good ship that didn't need refueling in order to enter the system and leave again.

The captain of the Eraasian ship was sitting in a folding chair behind the tables of trade goods. He rose and stepped forward as Amaro approached.

"Greeting," he said. "I am Haereith, captain of the Freetrader *Set-Them-Up-Again*." He spoke passable Galcenian—at least as good as Amaro's Eraasian. "We had not expected to see another merchant here on this voyage. Have you anything interesting by way of a swap?"

"One or two things, maybe," Amaro replied.

"Then let us drink to the one or two things." Haereith reached under the table and pulled out a stoppered flask and a pair of mugs. He filled both mugs with a deep red liquid—wine, from the sharp, rich smell of it—and offered one of them to Amaro before taking the other for himself.

The Mageworlder splashed a few drops of his wine onto the ground before taking a drink. "Ghosts about," he explained, sounding a little embarrassed by the action. "A place like this, you cannot be too careful."

"That's what I always say, myself," Amaro replied, and poured out a dollop of wine from his own mug.

"Then come aboard with me," Haereith said. He extended a hand to Amaro, who took it briskly in return. "And if it pleases you, tell all of us on the *Set-'em-Up* where you have come from, and what are—what *is*—the news."

XI. SAPNE; KHESAT

THE FOREST of derelict ships extended for several miles beyond the point where Faral and the others had begun walking. They were lucky, Faral supposed, that Amaro had set the *Dusty* down close to the edge of the old landing area, and not near its center. The maps in the shipboard data files had shown an extensive port complex at Sapne Market, with a landing field bigger than some small towns.

Now, if he'd been right in his guess about the building most likely to house a black-market passport-and-visa operation . . .

Sometime about noon they left the forest behind them. The terrain changed from woods to open ground overgrown with stands of tall grass. Here and there a trail appeared among the waving, head-high stems.

"Do we need to be following one of those?" Miza asked.

"Depends," said Faral. "Do we want to be ambushed?"

They continued in a straight line, guiding on the sun. At last a building appeared, looming tall and wide above the grasses, with blank walls that gave back the light in a fierce dazzle. They'd built well on Old Sapne, before the Biochem Plagues—neither time nor vandalism had made any change to the building's armor-glass sheath. Many paths converged in the open ground before it, and the grass there was trodden short.

Jens shifted the weight of the portable generator on his shoulders and squinted up at the building. "If this isn't the place where we get our passports validated, it certainly ought to be."

"Somebody uses it for something, at any rate," Faral said. "All those trails leading up to it—those are footpaths, not animal tracks."

Cautiously, they approached the building. Its main doors stood open, the dilation membrane that had once covered them jammed apart at the three-quarter point. Beyond, lit by high skylights, lay the entrance foyer. Once it might have been a grand atrium in the prewar style. Now it was dim, and decorated . . . oddly.

Carved images of human forms, larger than life, stood at intervals along the atrium walls. At first glance they seemed to have been crudely hacked out of tree trunks, then planed to smoothness. A closer look revealed that the distortions and the twisted, half-melted postures were deliberate, the results of careful hand-carving and polishing. Where light from above struck the images, their surfaces gleamed with oil.

In between the wooden statues, huge plates of hammered metal hung in pairs and threes from the interior balconies surrounding the atrium. The ropes that suspended them were wrist-thick cables of twisted wire. The panels hung closely enough together that the vibration of footsteps on the atrium floor caused them to shiver and strike against one another with a sound like flat, atonal bells.

The floor itself had once been a solid sheet of pure unmarked—and unmarkable—crystal, whose deep black luster would have given back reflections like an unmoving tarn. Now it was covered with spiraling, labyrinthine pathways drawn out in lines of pollen, petals, and colored stones.

"It's . . . different," Jens said, after contemplating it for a few moments. "The combination of decadence and primitive vigor—"

"Never mind the art criticism," said Faral. His ears had picked up the sound of movement somewhere in the vast atrium, faint noises that the constant chiming of the metal plates had for a while obscured. "I think we're about to get an escort."

"I think you're right," Miza said. "Look there."

Faral looked. On the far side of the atrium, a stairway curved down to the floor from the first-level balcony. A woman was coming down the staircase toward them.

She was dressed in shades of green and brown, as if to blend in with the forest that covered so much of the old spaceport. In one hand she carried a musical instrument of some kind—a wooden frame strung with wire, with metal and glass beads threaded on the wires. Its high, rattling chime echoed the lower notes of the heavy metal plates.

The combined notes, high and low, blurred the ambient sound even more than had the chiming of the plates alone. Faral was not surprised when the first unfamiliar voice came from behind him, where the outer doors stood open and anyone might have entered on their tracks.

"We expect you."

It was a man's voice, speaking Standard Galcenian with a stilted accent, as if he had learned the tongue in adulthood from one who did not speak it as a native. A quick glance toward the door revealed a young man of about Faral's own age, dressed in more greens and browns. Instead of a stringed rattle, he carried a spear.

The woman had reached the foot of the stairway. "Come." she said.

Faral looked at Miza and Jens. In response to his unspoken question, Miza shrugged and said, "Beats me. Huool's reports didn't say anything about what kind of people were running the passport office these days."

"Come," the woman said again. She turned and started

back up the stairs without waiting to see if anyone followed her.

"That kind of people, apparently," said Jens. "Let's take care of our business and be gone."

The woman led them up onto the balcony. Faral was aware of the young man following behind with his spear at the ready. Dark hallways going back farther into the building opened off the sides of the balcony. A three-legged table of wood lashed together with twine stood near the top of the staircase, and a woven grass basket stood on the table; the woman reached into the basket and pulled out a glowcube. She pressed the activation stud and the glowcube came on, filling the balcony with cold white light.

So much for the primitive bit, Faral thought, as the woman entered one of the hallways.

"You come," said the man with the spear. "We expect you."

"We come," agreed Jens. "Faral, Miza . . . ?"

"Right with you, foster-brother. Let's go."

They passed through the door after the woman. The blue-white light of her glowcube bobbed down the hallway ahead of them like a marshwight's lantern. Pairs of doors opened off on either side of the corridor. Offices once, Faral supposed. Now, each time the light of the woman's glowcube passed a door, another glowcube would come to life in response— illuminating as it did so the man or woman who held it. All of them were armed, some with spears like the man behind, others with knives, a few with blasters.

They didn't have to do all this just to impress me, Faral said to Jens in Trade-talk. *I was already impressed.*

Shut up, Jens replied.

They came at last to a round room at the far end of the passage. The room had a domed skylight above, and a spiral staircase leading down, but it was small compared to the great atrium. Aside from handwoven carpets and piles of large, gaudy pillows, the room had no furnishings save a metal brazier full of red coals. A heavy, sweetish smoke rose from the brazier in thick curls.

Another woman, this one far older than the first, sat on one of the pillows. She also wore brown and green, but over the homespun her gown was stiff and glittering with embroidery done in metallic threads. Her face was distorted and scarred, and her white hair was thin and patchy.

She must be one of the generation that survived the plagues, Faral realized. He wondered what she had been, back when Sapne was more than just the ghost of a living world. Had she been a portside dataworker, somebody who knew how to create the stamps and the certificates of passage? Or had she been something else?

"Sit now," said the man with the spear. He indicated the pillows strewn about the floor. "And wait."

They sat in silence for a while. The blue-grey smoke hung in the air in long, flat ribbons, and the light that angled down through the skylight slowly changed in quality as the sun moved farther past the zenith.

The building wasn't silent at all, Faral decided. He could hear the faint rustles of people changing positions, the fainter sounds of breathing, and the coming and going of distant footsteps. The brazier hissed as the younger woman sprinkled a handful of powder on the coals.

More smoke billowed up into the room, this time dark and with a smell like moldy leaves. As he breathed it, Faral could feel himself detaching slightly from reality. Time passed, but not in a way that seemed to have anything to do with him.

The light outside faded. Somewhere else in the building a drumbeat sounded, throbbing like the pulse in Faral's arteries. People in the room came and went beyond the edges of his vision, but the old woman and her younger attendants had not moved, except to replenish the brazier, since the interview began. Faral wasn't certain that the other people, the ones he didn't turn his head to see, were actually there. He was certain about the smoke, however—it had stuff in it that would make even an unbeliever see ghosts and visions.

And this is a place for seeing ghosts. With or without chemical aid.

A red glow suffused the room; high above, the clouds had gone rosy with the sunset. And in that moment, Jens

unsnapped the portable power source from its carrying straps
and shoved it across the carpet toward the old woman.

"A gift," he said in slow, careful Galcenian. "For you and
your people."

You know we won't get our deposit back, Faral said in
Trade-talk.

Jens kept his eyes on the old woman. *It doesn't matter. Be
quiet.*

The old woman said something in the local language. One
of the men in the room came forward and picked up the
power source, retreating with it into the shadows that gathered with the coming night. The younger woman sprinkled
more powder on the coals in the brazier. The black smoke
rolled forth again, its tendrils catching in Faral's lungs and
throat and reaching up into the back of his brain.

Nobody said anything. More people came and went in the
rotunda. Some of them sat and joined the circle around the
brazier; others remained for only a moment before leaving.

After a while, and dimly through the increasing shadows,
Faral became aware that one of the watchers in the circle was
different from his fellows. Where the others were dressed in
leather and homespun, this man wore a spacer's coverall in
plain unmarked black. He'd come into the room quietly—
Faral had never heard his footsteps—and had taken a place in
the circle next to Jens. Now he was watching the old woman
as intently as Jens was himself.

I saw this man on Bright-Wind-Rising, Faral thought muz-
zily, *and again on the transport to Nanáli from Sombrelír.
Unless he was one of Amaro's crew members . . . but what
was he doing on the* Wind, *if he's a free-spacer?*

*The smoke. It's making me see things that aren't here. Or
maybe it's making me think that things that* are *here, aren't
real. I can't decide. . . .*

The music of gongs and rattles continued in the distance.
Faral continued to watch and wait. The man in black, whoever
he was and wherever he came from, was still there, or maybe
he wasn't. Sometimes he seemed to fade into the shadows
around him. But that didn't prove anything—so did Jens.

Miza, sitting on Faral's other hand, stayed unchanged in spite of the shadows and the ghost-smoke, and Faral decided to fix his eyes on her instead. Having something true and solid to look at, like Miza's red hair and rounded form, would keep him anchored in reality when the incense fumes threatened to tease out his mind from his body and send it floating away.

As was common with Magebuilt ships, *Set-Them-Up-Again* was both like and disturbingly unlike its counterparts on the Adept side of the Gap Between. The technology for hyperspace transit was much the same regardless of what shipyard had produced the engines, but the vessel's layout and interior proportions responded to a different aesthetic than that to which Captain Amaro was accustomed.

He sat with Captain Haereith in one of the *Set-'em-Up*'s common areas, looking over cargo manifests. Amaro couldn't read Eraasian-style glyphic displays, and the comps aboard *Set-Them-Up-Again* weren't configured to accept a Standard date feed, so they had loose sheets of hardcopy spread out all over the tabletop.

The data incompatibilities were only a minor annoyance, however. The two captains had a flask of red Norgalian wine between them, and a pair of blue-glazed ceramic mugs. They passed the wine back and forth and talked—like freetraders everywhere—about long runs, clever trades, and other people's bad luck.

"I'm waiting for the time when we can trade with other galaxies," Amaro said. "There'll be plenty of luck for everybody then."

Haereith topped off the mugs. "The Masked Ones speak of galaxies," he said, "and say they have been to see. Nothing solid comes back with them, though . . . not by their road."

"When they have the nav posits, let me know." Amaro took another swallow of his wine and wondered how the Magelords got to places that not even starships were built to reach.

He didn't ask, though. That went against the unwritten rules of a conversation where nothing was said outright, and where both parties traded oblique hints in hopes that the other

person would say more than he'd intended. Haereith of the
Set-'em-Up, matching his guest drink for drink and pouring
from the same bottle, was already playing the game a good
deal fairer than many captains would have bothered to do.

A wavery musical note over the ship's comm system
turned out to be the call to dinner. Captain Haereith swept the
hardcopy manifests off the table in time for the first of the
crew to appear and be seated. Amaro was invited to join them
for a meal—more customary hospitality; the crew members
back on board the *Dusty* wouldn't be surprised that he had
stayed—and he accepted. The food was space rations, clearly,
but augmented with fresh fruits and a stew made out of some
variety of local animal flesh.

Over dinner, and more mugs of red wine, Amaro inquired
about parts of the Mageworlds sector where high profits
might currently be made. These things changed all the time,
and a good port on one run might go cold by the next.

"Tell Geise's Clearinghouse on Ruisi that you know me,"
Haereith said, "and they will give you good prices."

And a cut to Haereith, Amaro suspected, but that was the
way such things were often done, and not a matter for resent-
ment or suspicion. "What do they have?"

"Jade," said Haereith. "Raw stuff and polished both."

"Any artwork?"

Haereith shook his head. "That, the collectors already have
taken. But there *is* a demand for unworked jade on Cashel at
the Feltry Fair."

"I'll keep that in mind," Amaro said. "Now, if you're dealing in medicinals, Jaspar High Station is a good place to
make a trade. . . ."

And so the talk went on, until the hour for leavetaking approached and Amaro rose from the table.

"They'll be expecting me back on the *Dusty*," he said.
"Why don't you stop by my ship tomorrow? Show you a
good time, repay you for your hospitality."

"Assuredly," said Haereith, rising also. "Allow me, then, to
see you on your way."

The two men walked together through the *Set-'em-Up*'s

narrow, twisting passages to the main hatch. A crew member waited there—not doing anything that Amaro could see, except looking out at the darkening jungle through the blur of the entry force field. The crew member turned away from the jungle at their approach and seemed to focus his eyes with some difficulty on the two captains.

Haereith frowned. *"Naenemeis-de keth, Feashe?"*

Amaro didn't blame the Mageworlder for asking if Feashe should be working; he'd have asked the same question himself of an idler on board the *Dusty*, especially one he'd caught looking lazy in front of a visitor. The man's reply came in a rapid mumble of some dialect Amaro couldn't understand, and Haereith replied in the same dialect, more sharply this time.

The crew member muttered something under his breath and headed back into the interior of the ship. In passing Amaro, he stumbled, swaying, and seemed about to fall. The Ophelan captain reached out and steadied him.

"Easy . . . you don't look well," Amaro said. He switched to Eraasian; a common crew member like Feashe might not speak any languages beyond that and his local birth-tongue. *"Brive feraet—"*

Feashe shook his head. *"Ie-briyai,"* he said. He caught hold of Amaro's supporting hand and looked straight at him. *"Ie-briyai,"* he repeated, then let go and stumbled back into the ship.

Amaro stood motionless for a moment, then shook himself as if putting the incident aside.

"Until later," he said to Haereith, and walked down the ramp and out into the forest.

The Eraasian watched him safely out of sight, then turned to go back into the *Set'-em-Up*. He would pay a return call on the Ophelan captain tomorrow, Haereith decided. In the meantime, he would have to locate Feashe and find out whether the crew member was truly unwell, or merely dodging his rightful share of the dirtside labor.

He didn't have to look far. Feashe lay on the deck a few feet beyond the first turning of the corridor. The crew member's eyes were closed, his breath gasping and shallow.

Haereith raced to the nearest comm speaker and pushed the transmit button to call for medical assistance. But it was already too late. By the time the *Set-'em-Up*'s biotech came running to answer the summons, Feashe was dead.

Jens drew in another breath of the thick, mind-blurring smoke. The silent presence in the circle beside him of the man in black came as no surprise; he had been half-expecting such a thing ever since passing through the graveyard of lost ships. The man in black had been a potential presence, whatever Jens might be doing, for longer than Jens could remember—always there if Jens looked for him, a quiet observer somewhere at the edge of any gathering.

Jens did remember, quite clearly, the day that he and the stranger first spoke.

It had happened during midsummer in the High Ridges. Mamma and Dadda had come to visit, bringing with them a wealth of exciting stories and strange and wonderful presents. Then the whole family had left the house among the trees to spend a day and a night on what Uncle Ari said was "a little hunting party" and what Dadda had called an "al fresco entertainment."

"What's an al fresc—whatever he said?" Jens asked. "And what are we hunting?"

"I am about," his mother said, "to lose patience with both of them. It's an overnight camping trip."

His mother was tall and fair—as tall as Dadda, and with eyes as blue as Jens's own. Today she wore what she called her spacer's clothes, snug trousers and a ruffled shirt and high boots to the knee. She strode along under the great trees as if she owned the whole world, and Jens, who was not yet big enough even for regular schooling, had to half-run to stay on the path beside her.

They were alone together for the moment. Faral, usually his constant companion, was riding on Uncle Ari's shoulders up ahead, and Dadda was walking with Uncle Ari. Aunt Llann and Baby Kei had gone on before in the hovercar with the tents and the cooking gear; there was going to be another baby soon, and Aunt Llann hadn't wanted to travel such a long way on foot. Some years later, Jens realized that his mother had slowed her own pace to let him match her stride—but she never spoke of it, and all he felt at the time was a great pride at keeping up with her at all.

They walked on for a while in a companionable silence, until Jens ventured to ask a question that had been puzzling him for some time.

"Mamma—who's the man with the eye patch?"

She didn't say anything for a moment. Then she said, quietly, "What man?"

"The one who comes and goes inside your head."

"Oh." She was quiet again for a while. "Somebody I pretend to be sometimes," she said finally. "He's not very nice, I'm afraid."

"Dadda likes him."

She smiled a little. "Your dadda's funny that way. Do you see things like that often?"

"Uh-huh."

"Wonderful. And what does your aunt Llann have to say about all this?"

"She doesn't know."

"Maybe you ought to tell her."

Jens looked up at his mother. "You wouldn't have."

She snorted. "Good point. But I was a rotten little brat when I was your age, so don't go taking me for an example. How about your uncle Owen?"

"He doesn't come here. Uncle Ari gets letters sometimes, and Aunt Llann got a comm call once."

His mother frowned. "We'll have to fix that. I think you ought to talk to him when he shows up. He used to see inside people's heads, too, when both of us were young."

She hadn't spoken any more about it, and Jens had not thought about the question again until much later, by the firelight after dinner. Baby Kei was already asleep in the big tent, and Faral was nodding off with his head against Uncle Ari's knee. The grownups were talking—Mamma was telling a long story about a Mandeynan customs officer and a shipment of green glass paperweights—and Jens was trying his best to keep awake and listen.

After a while Jens became aware that the man in black was there and listening too. The man had a wooden staff as tall as he was, and stood leaning on it just outside the circle of the fire's yellow glow. Jens thought about the matter for a while and decided that the man looked lonely. In all the times so far that Jens had seen him, he had never spoken—

—but Jens had never spoken to him, either.

Carefully, Jens got up and moved away from the fire. Nobody saw him do it; his mother was approaching the climax of her tale, something to do with the customs official's identical twin brother and a comm link that had chosen that very moment to stop working, and she held everyone's attention but his.

Jens walked quietly, almost on tiptoe, over to where the man in black was standing. "Hello," he said. "I should have talked to you sooner."

The man looked at him and smiled. Jens saw that he was fair-skinned, almost pale, with straight black hair down past his collar. "It's all right," he said. "Until today you didn't have anything to talk with me about."

"I guess not."

Jens heard a burst of laughter from near the fire, and Aunt Llann's voice saying, "And he combed his hair with a *what*?" The man in black looked amused as well.

Jens plowed on. "I'm Jens Metadi-Jessan D'Rosselin," he said. "Who are you?"

A shadow of sadness passed over the man's face. "I don't know. I've forgotten a number of things, and that seems to be one of them. But it doesn't matter yet."

That meant it was going to matter someday, Jens thought. But the man said it was all right for now, and that was good. "Why can't anyone see you but me?"

"I'm not talking to anyone else right now."

"You're not someone from inside my head, like the man I saw inside Mamma?" This was a possibility that had not occurred to Jens before. Now that he'd thought of it, he found that it disturbed him a great deal more than the glimpse of his mother's internal companion had done in the first place.

"Definitely not. You are yourself, and not double-minded at all."

Double-minded. He'd never heard the term before, but it answered some questions all by itself. "Aunt Llann is double-minded too, I think. But the other person inside her head is still her. . . . Mamma thinks I ought to talk to her about what I see sometimes."

"Not to Llannat Hyfid"—the man in black spoke firmly—"and not to your uncle Owen, either. He belongs to the Guild, and she is a Magelord. And you are not meant to be either one of those things."

"Do you mean to tell me," said the Master of Nalensey, "that this time *you* have failed?"

Rhal Kasander, Exalted of Tanavral, lifted a slice of toast to his mouth and munched delicately, making sure that none of the jam touched his fingers. "As you yourself said on an earlier occasion, a setback rather than a failure."

His houseguest remained unmoved. "Our Worthy has utterly disappeared," said Caridal Fere, "and our former hirelings now openly oppose us. A delicate touch is always best with setbacks. Not this—"

"A setback," Kasander repeated. "Nothing more. Our hirelings remain unenlightened; they fight only against others of their own kind. And our Worthy is not dead; therefore in time he must emerge."

A peal of bells sounded in the distance, a broken, untuned chord like the notes of wind chimes in a light breeze. A servant appeared at the door of the balcony overlooking the forest glade that surrounded Kasander's country retreat. He carried a flatchip on a silver tray.

"Exalted," the servant said. "A message, with the highest of identifiers upon it." He placed the tray on a side table and departed, bowing.

The conversation between the two men turned to landscape

design and the next year's flower season. Half an hour later, Kasander picked up the flatchip, and inserted it into a shielded reader.

"Failure?" he said after a moment's study of the chip. "Here is our Worthy. See? He appears on Sapne, under his own name, requesting entrance visas. And see here, a vessel on Sapne projects a transit."

"Do we see a date of arrival?"

"Two weeks hence," said Kasander, "by the captain's estimate."

Fere looked pleased. "Then the time has come for us to declare."

"No," Kasander said firmly. "Not until the lad is safely here. If we had succumbed to temptation and declared already, these minor setbacks would have seen our names mentioned in the *Ilsefret Tattler*—in the section devoted to subscribers' attempts at humorous topical verse."

The voice of the old woman drew Jens back from his reverie. Again she was speaking in the local tongue—though he would have guessed that she understood some Galcenian—and the man with the spear acted as interpreter.

"What do you seek?"

"A name," said Jens. "We have heard that the old machines for talking between worlds are here. I wish to place our names into those machines, so that those on other worlds may know me."

"You do not need a name," the old woman said through the interpreter. "You need luck."

The man in black spoke for the first time. "There is no luck. Only what happens, and what we make to happen."

Jens heard a startled intake of breath from Miza. Huool's intern had apparently also seen the man in black—and hadn't expected a smoke-born illusion to open its mouth and begin arguing philosophy with the local oracle. The old woman, on the other hand, appeared unsurprised by the development. Maybe for her the illusions talked all the time.

"Then we will make luck to happen," she said.

She added something further that the interpreter didn't bother to translate, and a couple of the people at the outer edge of the circle moved off into the shadows. Time passed. The old woman remained silent, and everyone else in the circle followed her example. Then one of the attendants who had left came back, this time carrying a necklace of leather cord strung with odd-shaped bits of bone. At a word from the oracle, the attendant dropped the cord over Jens's head.

"This is luck for you, Jens Metadi-Jessan D'Rosselin," the oracle said. "Wear it."

Jens didn't ask how she had learned his full name and lineage. The old woman clearly did not live in reality as most people knew it—and in the place where she did live, anything could be possible. He wasn't especially startled when another of the women came back into the room holding thin plastic ID cards: one each for Jens Metadi-Jessan, Faral Hyfid-Metadi, and Mizady Lyftingil. Miza gasped a little in surprise; Faral said nothing, but his silence was eloquent.

"They have the visas and passports?" Jens said.

"They are complete," said the old woman.

There was another long pause. Something hissed and popped among the coals on the brazier—a seed pod, maybe, or a nodule of incense—and sent up a tiny spiral of red-orange sparks. The old woman spoke again, this time more urgently. "You must not leave this planet by the way you came."

"How are we supposed to manage that?" asked Faral. Jens's cousin was taking great care with his words, as if he distrusted his own voice under the influence of the pungent smoke. "We came in a spaceship. We're going to have to leave in a spaceship. There is no other way."

The man in black leaned forward into the circle of the firelight. "This is a spaceport. There will be more than one ship. If you let me, I can find one for you."

XII. Sapne

THE OLD woman rose. Two attendants came forward to support her, and with their aid she walked down the spiral stairs and away into the shadows below.

The man with the spear stepped forward from among those who had remained behind.

"You have your name," he said to Jens. "Now you go."

Jens tucked the ID card into his pocket and stood up. His head spun a little from all the smoke he had taken in over the past few hours.

"We go," he agreed. He looked at the others in his party: Faral, Miza, and the man in black. He felt somewhat resentful that the stranger—for so long his private, invisible companion—had chosen this occasion to make himself seen and heard by all comers. "Are we ready?"

"We're ready," said Faral.

He stood, and held out a hand to help Miza to her feet. She didn't need any help that Jens could see—she'd already proved herself to be quick and limber during their adventures on Ophel—but she took Faral's hand anyway. She blinked a little, as if trying to clear the smoke out of her eyes.

"Captain Amaro was right," she said somewhat fuzzily. "We really did need a portable power source to get our visas."

"Cheap at the price," said Faral. He turned to the man in black. "You said you could help us find passage to Khesat on a different ship. Are we talking about the one you came here in?"

"No. That wouldn't be a good idea."

Faral scowled. "Not a good—who *are* you, anyway?"

"One name is Guislen," the man said after a moment.

Guislen, said Faral in Trade-talk. *It sounds a lot like an alias to me. Jens—foster-brother—are you seriously proposing that we trust this guy? We don't even know who he really is.*

I'm pretty sure that Guislen isn't his name, but I've seen him around before.

Faral shrugged. "It's your decision—you're the one who's calling the dance. Miza and I are just here for the show."

Jens looked from his cousin to Gentlesir Huool's redheaded intern. "Then I say we trust him," he said.

He turned to the man whose real name was probably not Guislen. "You said you could find us a ship. Let's go."

Guislen led the way out of the rotunda and back down the hall to the main staircase. The great building was empty now; the men and women who had guarded the long corridor were gone, and only the lit glowcubes remained to show where they had stood.

The atrium was dark and full of shadows. The planet's small, fast-moving moon shone down through the skylight, making odd-shaped patches of illumination on the hanging metal slabs and the crystal floor. Jens wished that the sheets of metal wouldn't brush and slide against each other so much; their faint, musical sound was too much like voices whispering all around him in the dark.

He was glad when they passed through the atrium and out onto the grassy plain. The sky overhead was clear, and outside the building the moonlight cast sharper, blacker shadows than it had within. The forest was a deeper darkness ahead of them at the far edge of the plain.

"Which way is the ship?" Jens asked.

Guislen pointed at the forest. "That way."

"Are you talking about another trading ship like the *Dusty*?" Faral demanded. "Or one of those wrecks out there in the jungle?"

"Not a wreck," said Guislen. "An antique, in good condition. And one of you knows how to handle such things."

"Pleasure craft, limited," Miza said hastily. "That's not the same as knowing how to operate a commercial starship."

"It will be enough," Guislen told her. "I can help you with the hard parts."

Miza didn't look reassured, and Jens didn't blame her. She was still frowning when they reached the forest. After that, the darkness around them was too deep for her expression to matter. Only the occasional shaft of moonlight came down through the tangle of vines and tree branches to illuminate their way. The forest had a nighttime smell to it that was different from the scent it had by day—a sweeter, heavier smell, almost the sweetness of decay, as if some carrion-fed flower had opened its blossoms with the coming of night.

They had been walking for some time when Faral said, in a low tone, "Someone's following us."

"You're sure?" Miza's voice was commendably level, Jens thought, but she moved, almost involuntarily, a little closer to his cousin as she spoke.

"I wouldn't have said so if I wasn't," Faral said.

Jens pulled out the blaster he had tucked in his waistband. He'd carried the stolen weapon this far without incident—unless you counted target-firing it during the dull parts of the transit from Ophel—but now he felt better for having it ready.

"You can trust Faral," he said to Miza. "He's good at that sort of thing."

Guislen said only, "We have to hurry," and quickened his pace. "I fear . . ."

"Fear what?" asked Miza. She got no reply.

At last they came to a part of the forest where the moonlight filtered down through the leaves to reveal a single isolated spaceship. The vessel was small, and covered with a thick mat of vines and creepers, but it stood balanced on its landing legs with its nose pointed high. Its doors were sealed shut at the top of a roll away ramp.

"We won't need nullgravs to lift this one," Guislen said. "She's a Gyfferan Class Elevener—one of the old straight-up designs."

"Someone's standing beside the ramp," Jens said.

But the dim figure, glimpsed only for a moment, had vanished again into the shadows before he finished speaking.

Faral said, "I don't see anyone."

Jens shook his head to clear it. "I must be seeing things. It's not there now." He gave an unsteady laugh. "What do you suppose we were breathing, back there at the passport office?"

"Strong stuff," Miza said. "I'm not surprised that the Mages trade here for medicinals, if that's what a bunch of backslid primitives can do with the local resources."

"Not all that primitive," Faral said. "They've got a good racket going in the passport-and-ID business. All the imported technology they want, no questions asked . . . I think we got some kind of special treatment."

"We're wasting time," said Guislen. "It isn't safe to delay outside here much longer."

"All right, but how do we get in?" Faral eyed the grounded spacecraft. "Violence is out if we want the thing to be airtight afterward. Assuming that it's airtight now."

Jens became aware that the others were watching him expectantly—even Guislen, which disturbed him somewhat. For some reason, it had become his responsibility to take the next step, whatever it was. He looked at the ship. Nothing new came out of the dark between the trees to stand in the patchy moonlight beside the landing legs. One beam of pale silver-grey, coming down unbroken through the leaves overhead, touched the ramp like a pointer.

I don't want to do this, Jens thought. But he was already

walking up the ramp, breaking away a tangled net of vines and branches as he did so. His boots rang out on the slanted metal, sounding unnaturally loud and drumlike in the quiet of the forest.

There was a lockplate beside the sealed door at the top of the ramp—an old-fashioned model, square and bulky. He wondered if the standby power had trickled away in the years since the Biochem Plagues. *Nothing for it but to try,* he thought, and laid his hand against the scanner. Maybe it was the lingering residue of the Sapnish incense affecting his perceptions, but it seemed to him that he could feel the circuitry inside, waiting for the proper touch to open it.

But his touch wasn't the one that the silent circuits required. He was aware, without quite knowing how, that the door had tested him and found him wanting.

"Some things require practice," Guislen said. He was standing beside Jens, and so quiet had been his approach, or so intent had Jens been on the door, that Jens had been unaware that he was coming. "Let me see what I can do."

Guislen laid his hand beside Jens's on the scanner. Jens felt again the flow of electrons in their concealed ways—but this time they clicked the circuits over, accepting the new directions in which they had been sent.

"There's a trick to it," Guislen said, "and if you have the knack it's easy. I can show you later."

A red light glowed briefly within the depths of the scanner as the door came to life and began to cycle. Clinging tendrils of vine tore free as the door sighed open, its smooth, corrosionless metal withdrawing into slots on either side of the hatch.

"Permasteel construction throughout," said Guislen. "The Eleveners were tough little ships."

Jens didn't answer. A wave of foul air had come cascading out as the door opened, making his gorge rise and his head spin. Choking, he retreated down the ramp.

"Good job," Faral said as Jens staggered up to him. "If that works, maybe the rest of it—hey, what's the matter with you?"

"I feel wretched," Jens said. He sat down abruptly on the ground and let his head hang in between his knees while he willed his queasiness to subside.

"Don't feel wretched for any longer than you can help." That was Miza, sounding scared. "Because there's a light moving out in the woods. It's hanging away from us, but it's there. I've been catching it out of the side of my eye."

"Could be one of our friends from the port-control building," Faral said. "I think they were the ones who were following us."

"Maybe they just wanted us to open a ship so they could loot it," Miza said.

"No," Jens said. He pushed himself up onto his feet. "It isn't the locals. None of the ships we saw this morning had been touched."

He looked back at the ship. Guislen was waiting at the top of the ramp by the open door. Jens drew a deep breath of the forest air. Even heavy as it was with the cloying scent of the night-blooming flowers, it was better than what waited for him.

"I'm going aboard," he said to Miza and Faral. "See what's there ... maybe get the vent system running." He pulled the blaster out of his waistband and handed it to Faral. "Here. In case I'm wrong about the locals."

Miza was scrambling inside her belt pouch. After pulling out a coin purse, two flatchips, and a hairbrush, she came up with a small, rattling object—keycards strung on a loop of plastic cord, and along with the keys a miniature glowcube, no bigger than a thumbnail.

- "The light's not good for much except finding lockslots in the dark," she said. "But you'll need something to see by once you're inside."

"Thanks," Jens said. There didn't seem to be much else left to talk about, and there was no point in waiting. "Be careful," he added finally, and started back up the ramp into the derelict ship.

The worst of the foul air had dissipated by the time Jens made it back to the top of the ramp. Only a faint, persistent trace remained, an underlying staleness and corruption that was almost more a taste in the back of the mouth than a smell.

Guislen was waiting for him. "Come. Let's see what this ship has for us."

Together they went through the open door, with Guislen a little in the lead. Inside the ship, everything was black; the light from outside extended only a few feet beyond the threshold. Jens fumbled with Miza's key loop until he found the activation stud on the miniature glowcube, and pressed it with his fingernail. The cube flickered into a pallid life—it was an old one, and weak to boot—and the interior of the derelict Gyfferan Elevener saw light for the first time since the plague days.

Reflections danced back at him from deck and bulkheads. The Elevener was bright permasteel within as well as without, and whoever her masters had been they had kept her in good order.

"A trim little ship," said Guislen. "A bit short on cargo space for some people's taste, but that shouldn't matter."

Jens turned toward his companion. At first glance he thought that Guislen was holding up a glowcube like his own, only larger and brighter than Miza's key loop pendant. Then he saw that Guislen held nothing at all in his upraised hand except for the light itself, pure white and apparently sourceless.

"You're an Adept, aren't you?" Jens said finally.

"Yes," Guislen replied after a moment. "I was an Adept once. I suppose that I still am one, of a sort."

"If you're an Adept, what happened to your staff? I remember you having one before, when I was young."

"I gave it away," said Guislen, "to someone who needed it more than I did. And after that I followed other paths."

"Which led you here."

Guislen smiled. "Yes—and now that we *are* here, we should see what the rest of the ship holds for us."

He led the way forward and up into the body of the ship by interior ladders, taking the steep metal rungs nimbly like a man accustomed to shipboard life, with the brilliant immaterial light following him obediently all the while. They climbed past the realspace engines and the hyperdrives, and up into what Jens supposed would be the engine control room. Unlit monitors and blank readouts filled the gleaming steel walls, along with dials and gauges of antique design.

Guislen stopped before a covered control panel. The housing had words embossed on it in a script that Jens didn't recognize. Other objects in the room had similar labels.

"What language is that?" Jens asked, pointing.

"Ilarnan," Guislen replied. "It says this is the vent-control system. Open the cover and let's see what's what."

Jens pulled, and the cover came open on hinges, exposing an array of switches, knobs, and toggles.

"The captain took good care to shut the ship down in an orderly fashion," Guislen said. "Look there. The third switch from the top. That's external filter and vents. Rotate it to the right. The bottom switch is for the internal airways. Slide that one all the way to the right, too."

As Jens followed the instructions, the green telltale lights beneath each switch winked on. All around him, in the bulkheads and the deckplates, he could hear the distant sound of machinery coming to life. The air inside the ship began to move, stirring the fine hairs on his neck and arms, and the scent of foulness and decay came back full force.

He swallowed. "It's going to take a while for all the air to cycle through the exchangers. Why don't we go back outside while that's happening?"

"Can you find your own way out?" Guislen asked. "I want to explore things a bit further."

"It might not be a good idea to split up," Jens said. The bad air was worse when it was moving; it made his head ache and swim at the same time. On top of the disorientation caused by the Sapnish incense, the effect was distinctly unpleasant.

"I'll be fine," Guislen said. "Go join your friends, and I'll come for you when everything's ready."

Jens didn't feel like arguing. He turned and left the way he had come, going down the ladders to the outside. The air of the landing field, when he reached it, smelled even sweeter than before, and he could almost feel the oxygen reaching his blood again. He sagged against one of the ship's landing legs and closed his eyes.

"What a smell," Faral's voice said. "It's even better than the sewers."

"Get used to it, coz; we'll be living in it. When we reach Khesat, you can buy a whole new wardrobe."

"Considering that we left Ophel in the clothes we stood up in," said Miza, "we're going to have buy a new wardrobe anyway." She paused, and Jens could hear her breath catch as if something had startled her. When she spoke again, it was in a lower voice. "That light's moving around out there in the trees again, and this time it's coming closer."

Jens lifted his head. Miza was right: a bluish-white light was bobbing along the forest trail toward them.

Faral moved up beside him and lifted the blaster. In the weak illumination of Miza's tiny glowcube, his face looked set and determined. Miza stood close by him. Faral glanced down at her.

"Don't worry," he said. "I haven't seen anything truly dangerous around here yet."

Jens watched the light moving steadily among the trees. "Better switch off the safety on that blaster. Your experience may be about to change."

The light flickered and came closer. There was movement in the underbrush—movement but no sound that Jens could detect—and a man stepped forward into the open ground. He wore a black cloak, and a deep hood concealed his features. The light in the woods had come from the Adept's staff he carried. Power clung to the staff like a cold white flame, making the faint light of the miniature glowcube seem grey and pale.

"Hello!" Faral called out.

His cousin sounded relieved, Jens thought. Nobody had ever said there were Adepts working on Sapne, but members of the Guild could turn up anywhere. They had their own goals, and their own reasons for pursuing them.

But the newcomer didn't answer Faral's greeting, and made no further move. Miza edged closer and said in an undertone, "What do we do now?"

"Wait until we find out what he wants," Jens said. "This may not have anything to do with us at all."

"Do you really believe that?" said Faral. "I don't."

Miza gave a visible shiver. "You're scaring me."

"I'm scared myself. Getting involved in the private affairs of Adepts isn't healthy—I'd sooner fight a slam of rockhogs."

"And you the son and nephew of Adepts." Jens pushed himself off from the support of the Elevener's landing leg. "Ah, well. If you don't want to wait . . ."

He stepped away from the ship and toward the Adept, taking care not to block the clear line between the stranger and the energy weapon in Faral's hand. "Do you have business with us? Show us your face and we can talk."

As he walked forward, Jens noticed that in spite of the stillness of the night air, the folds of the Adept's cloak moved as if whipped by a silent but rising wind.

"Show us your face," Jens said again. He spoke in Standard Galcenian—most Adepts had it at least as a second or third language—but the man didn't answer.

Jens switched languages. "Do you speak Khesatan?" he asked in that tongue. "If you do, then let us know who you are."

He repeated the question in all the other languages he knew enough of to let him form the words: Maraghai Tradetalk, Old Court Entiboran, even Gyfferan.

No reply came to any of them, and the hooded Adept didn't move. The glow of power from the staff he carried cast a harsh white light onto his cloak, and onto his one visible arm in its long black sleeve. With an inward shudder, Jens saw that the pale hand gripping the staff was little more than dry skin stretched over bone. The flesh had cracked and split across the knuckles, but it didn't bleed. Sinews and tendons showed through the gaps like string.

This can't all be the fault of that smoke back at the passport office, Jens thought. He began to walk backward, keeping his eyes fixed on the mummified hand. He didn't want to look at the pale blur that was the stranger's face.

"Jens, what is it?" Faral called out.

Does he see something funny too? Jens wondered. *And is that better or worse than not having anyone see it but me?*

He took another step backward—not straight back toward the ship, but leading away at a slight angle. If Faral ever decided to use the blaster. Jens felt the vines and undergrowth behind him catching at his knees as he stepped back, but he didn't dare turn around to see where he was going.

The stranger moved to follow, narrowing the distance between them. Time seemed to slow. Now they were close enough for Jens to see a gleam of white underneath the deep hood of the stranger's cloak. He couldn't make out exactly what it was, but he didn't like it. The insects had stopped singing. In spite of the tropic night, Jens felt cold.

Then he felt even colder as he realized what had happened to make visible that flash of white. The Adept's glowing staff was in motion and swinging toward him.

XIII. Sapne; hyperspace; Khesat

Jens flung himself backward, barely avoiding the staff as it passed horizontally through the air where his head had been. He hit the ground hard and rolled away to one side—a second later, the other end of the staff smashed into the leafmould beside him. He kept on rolling. The rattle and sway of the underbrush around him would betray his passage, but to keep still would be death.

He heard a high-pitched sizzling noise, like water on hot metal, and a blaster bolt passed through the air above his head. Two more bolts, glowing a dark blue with ionizing energy, followed the first. All three of them hit the cloaked figure straight on. White smoke curled up in the darkness after each impact. But the stranger—surely no Adept, Jens thought—never staggered, and the glowing staff was swinging down again.

Jens didn't have time to stand up. He scrambled backward like an upside-down mudspider, pushing himself along with his hands and feet, shoving away from the blow as it descended.

Then another light appeared, white against the white light from the stranger's staff, shining from somewhere above and behind Jens's vantage point on the ground. He twisted his head back to look for the source.

Guislen stood at the top of the ship's ramp with a ball of dazzling light in his upraised hand.

"This is not the place," Guislen called to the intruder. "This is not the time. But if you want to fight me . . . do it here, and do it now!"

Jens looked back at the stranger. The brilliant light that Guislen had summoned illuminated what Jens had glimpsed briefly within the man's hood a few seconds before: a skeletal face with glittering deep-set eyes. What features that remained to it were contorted by loathing, and the stranger raised an arm to shield himself from Guislen's light.

At that moment, Jens kicked out and upward with both feet, supporting himself on his arms and shoulders. His heels smashed into the stranger's midsection.

But instead of the solid thud of boot leather on flesh, Jens felt his legs passing all the way through the other's body. A numbing cold spread through him at the contact, his legs went limp, and he collapsed onto his back in the leafmould of the forest floor. In the same instant, the stranger vanished.

A few seconds later, Faral arrived at the run, and Miza with him. "What the hell *was* that thing?" Miza asked, and Faral said, "I hit him; I *know* I hit him."

"I don't know what it was," said Jens. "Help me up, coz; when I touched it I went cold all over."

"Are you all right?" Faral asked as he reached down to give Jens a hand.

Jens's teeth were chattering. "I hope so."

His rescuer came up to them at a steadier pace. The glow in Guislen's hand was dimmer now, not the blazing white it had been, and by the time he reached them it had died away entirely.

"The ship was named *Inner Light*," he said, as if nothing untoward had happened. "She was a freetrader from

Mandeyn. I believe the interior is livable, or can be made so. But we have much to do if we are to lift tonight."

Mael Taleion's *Arrow-through-the-Doorway* was a smaller ship than any of those to which Klea was accustomed. Mael had shown a rather old-fashioned courtesy, insisting that she take the single cabin for her own use while he slept on the bridge. They took their meals together, though, in the *Arrow*'s galley, which had a table and benches large enough for two, and which doubled perforce as the common room. As the days of the transit to Khesat passed, she found herself often in conversation with Mael over cha'a or *uffa* and the plates of small fried breads that he made to supplement the usual space rations.

"Have you felt anything odd lately?" he asked her one ship's-morning.

Klea looked at him uneasily. "What do you mean, 'odd'?"

"What I said. Feelings, dreams, premonitions, ripples in the currents of time and space, unusual shadowings to the lines of life." He frowned. "Perhaps 'odd' is not the word. Do you Adepts even have a word for it—for the sense that something is amiss with the weaving of the universe?"

She thought about the question for a while. Mael did not press her for the answer. Like most of the Adepts she'd known in her life, the Magelord also had the ability to wait quietly, without impatience.

"Not all have the same gifts," she said. "But those Adepts who have an awareness of such things can feel it when the natural flow of the currents of Power has been disturbed." She picked up a scrap of fried bread and turned it over in her fingers. Mael had dusted the fritters with powdered sugar this morning, making her think for the first time in years of the sweet lacebreads her grandmother had made, back when Klea was very young. "The only problem is, to most of us Magework feels exactly the same way."

Mael's dark brows rose. "Can your people, then, not recognize intent?"

"How?"

"You, at least, were present at the end of the great working that closed the rift between the two sides of the Gap Between. You should be able to tell from that alone the difference between good Magery and ill."

"Hardly," said Klea. She gave a nervous half-laugh. "Most of what I remember about that day is tied up with what happened to Errec Ransome. And *that*—to the shame of the Guild, that wasn't Magework at all."

"Ransome was a powerful disturber of the true weaving," Mael agreed. "And strong in ill will. My First tells me he died that day, in the Void—which is bad, it leaves the *eiran* loose and confused."

Klea stood up from the galley table. The plate of fritters was empty now; she took it and slid it into an empty slot in the cleaning unit. Some *uffa* remained in the hotpot; she brought the pot over to the table and refilled both mugs. Then she carried the hotpot back to its niche and stood there looking at it.

"Your First doesn't know the half of it," she said without turning back around. "She wasn't there at the time. But I was."

Jens led the way back up the ramp into the ship. To him, the air inside smelled clean by comparison with what it had been like when the hatch first opened, but Miza made a face as they stepped inside, and Faral said, "Pfaugh!"

"You should have been in here before," Jens said. "This is nothing."

No one mentioned the thing that had attacked them. It was clear—to Jens, anyhow—that without Guislen's intervention they would have been dead, or something even worse than dead; and if Guislen said that they needed to lift before morning, he'd bought the right to have his words listened to. Faral seemed to have come grudgingly to the same conclusion, though his expression remained dark, and Miza was regarding both Guislen and Jens himself with frank mistrust.

"You're the one who's going to lift the ship," Jens said to

her. "If you don't think you can do it, we'll have to go back to the *Dusty*."

She shook her head hard enough that her tail of red hair whipped against her shoulders. "With that—that *thing* loose out there in the forest? I'll take my chances on board here with a Class B pleasure craft license, thank you."

That was a dirty move, foster-brother, growled Faral in Trade-talk.

I know that. Now shut up. Jens turned back to address Guislen. "Where are the switches for the light panels?"

"Let's get the power systems fully operational first," Guislen said. "Come."

Together the four of them made their way up the ladders to the engineering spaces. The blank monitor screens now glowed faintly, and the gauges and meters were in their low-powered standby mode. One by one, under Guislen's direction, Jens and Faral and Miza brought the systems all back on line. At the last, with a blaze that made Jens flinch and cover his eyes, the overhead light panels came on at full intensity.

"That's done," he said, taking his hand down again after a few seconds. "Let's finish checking out the ship."

They continued on up to the top of the craft, where the bulkheads were noticeably slanted as the hull tapered to an airframe point. A sliding airtight door opened at a touch of the actuator switch. The cockpit lay directly ahead. Small and cramped, its forward viewscreen a narrow slit, the compartment held only two seats with no room for a third. Guislen stepped inside and glanced back at Miza.

She hesitated in the doorway, looking from Faral to Jens as if expecting some kind of guidance.

This was all your idea, Faral said to Jens under his breath. *You set her up for it—you talk to her.*

Jens ignored him. "Miza," he said. "Now that you've seen what we've got, do you think you can handle it?"

"I don't know," she said. "Some of the instruments look familiar, but a lot more of them don't. I don't know if I can even lift without full instrumentation, and I sure don't see any of that here—at least not the kind I learned on. I can't even read the labels."

"I can," Guislen said. "Don't worry about the lift-off; I'll talk you through it."

"You're a pilot?" Faral asked.

"No, I'm a navigator," Guislen said. "But I cross-trained in piloting and engineering both, back when I worked the spacelanes. In dangerous times everyone in the crew has to be able to handle any position at a moment's notice."

Miza looked at him uneasily. "When was that?"

"A long time ago . . . but the *Light*'s navicomp was old even then. It's going to take us at least ten hours, Standard, to set up a valid course."

"You sound like we've got an alternative," said Jens.

"We do. There should be coursebooks on board for the common runs like Sapne-to-Khesat. Look in the drawer under the main console on the navigator's side."

"There should be what?" Jens said, but Miza had already crossed over to the drawer and pulled it open. Inside was a stack of thin, slablike objects—like text readers, but bulkier, with cords and plugs dangling from the ends.

"Coursebooks," Miza said. "We learned about them in class. But the only one I ever saw was an antique that Huool was selling to a museum." She lifted out first one slab and then another. " 'Suivi In-System' . . . 'Ilarna to Galcen South Polar' . . . I can't even recognize the alphabet on this one . . . here we go. 'Sapne and Khesatan Farspace.' "

Guislen looked pleased. "That should be good enough to get us within close visual range of Khesat's star," he said. "From there, even the *Light*'s navicomps will be capable of doing the rest."

Klea replaced the hotpot in its niche and came back to the table. She sat down opposite Mael and drew a long breath before she spoke.

"There were four of us," she said. "Owen Rosselin-Metadi, his brother, his sister, and me. We brought back the Domina

Perada from the Void. We ended a war. And we killed Errec Ransome."

Mael looked grave. "My old teacher," he said, "spoke of Ransome as one who should not be killed without breaking him first, lest he fail to notice that he was dead."

"I don't know how we could have broken him. Killing him was hard enough."

"Tell me how it happened," said Mael. "I begin to think that it may be more important than you know."

"We were all there," she began slowly. "In the Void. I was the odd one of the lot; Ransome wanted a hostage for his escape, or he wouldn't have bothered with me in the first place. As far as he was concerned, I was nothing—a Nammerinish tart with no training and a dubious past—and once he had me, he barely remembered I was there.

"But I was the one who struck him first."

Klea gazed into the crimson depths of her mug of *uffa* for a time, remembering. The blow had driven Errec Ransome down to his knees, there in the room his mind had constructed for a refuge in the trackless Void. Maybe combat in the Void was only symbol and metaphor, as the instructors at the Retreat would have it, but her staff had vibrated against the palms of her hands like a live thing when the wood smashed against Ransome's skull.

"He should have died when I hit him," she said finally. "And Owen's sister shot him twice before he hit the ground. All that happened, though, was that everything turned into fog. And Ransome was still there.

"So in the end Owen had to fight him. Master against student—'after the way of the Mages,' Ransome said."

"He spoke from ignorance," said Mael. "Such things are not done in anger, and never in the Void."

"I wouldn't know. But it doesn't matter, because Owen wasn't the one who killed him. It was the older brother, Ari— the one who married Mistress Hyfid. He was a big man—"

"I've met him," said Mael. "I know."

"—and he walked into the middle of the duel and picked

up Errec Ransome in both hands and snapped him across his knee like a stick."

Klea stopped talking. Mael sat waiting, patiently as always, until she drew another deep breath and went on.

"Ransome was dead then; I'm sure of it. What we saw next was an illusion, a memory given shape by the Void . . . Errec Ransome, as the Domina Perada knew him when they both were young."

"Did it speak?" Mael's eyes were dark with worry. "And did you answer it?"

"Oh, yes." Klea shivered, remembering how the phantom had stretched out a hand to the Domina—*"Have I wronged you, Perada? What can I do to make things right?"*—and then had let it fall. "It spoke. And the Domina answered. She called him a wanderer, and gave him leave to go."

Mael made an impatient noise. "Does no one in the Adeptworlds understand the Void at all? Not even an unranked Circle-Mage would think of saying a thing like that."

"What do you mean?"

"A wanderer she called him," said Mael. "And a wanderer he has become. He goes now to Khesat, and I . . . I am summoned to meet him there."

" 'Patience is all very well,' " said the young man in a servant's free-day livery. From the tone of his voice, he was quoting the words of another. " 'You have counseled patience. We have been more than patient. But time grows short, and the Worthy you promised us has not appeared.' "

"Whoa—they *were* getting into it," said the woman who sat beside him on the riverbank. "What did my lord of Redonti say to that?"

The young man shrugged. "What could he say? 'The Worthy will appear, I promise you'—but personally, I doubt it."

"That entire cabal is cutting things too fine," said the woman. "The Manches already have their worthy, and so do the Barbicans. And let's not forget the Roundels. They don't have just one Worthy—their public one—or even two Worthies—counting their secret candidate that they intend ev-

eryone to know about. They have three Worthies, if we include that pitiful creature living in their pockets whom they
actually hope to see ascend to the Jade Eminence."

"The upshot of the whole argument," said the young man,
"was that they're going to go find some other poor fool to
carry their banner. I was out of the room fetching a bottle of
the Erilani vintage when they named the man, but figuring
out who they lighted on shouldn't be a problem."

The woman narrowed her eyes. "There's something else
that you aren't telling me."

"I was saving the best for last. The Exalted of Tanavral
still backs his missing man. Which meant that the meeting
grew rancorous—as far as such dignified gentlemen lower
themselves to rancor."

The woman tore a small piece of bread from the roll she
held in her hand and tossed it to the wildlife which teemed on
the waterbank. On the river itself, winding through downtown
Ilsefret, colorful pleasure boats with scarlet and blue sails flitted before the light autumn breeze.

"With your position in the household of Caridal Fere," the
young man went on after the silence had stretched out too
long, "you'll be in a poor position if someone decides to cry
'treachery.' "

"We have to tell Master Pariken," she said.

"Important as this is, maybe we should bypass the
Guildmaster and send a notice all the way up to Master
Rosselin-Metadi."

The woman frowned. "Pariken says that he sent one messenger already."

"Maybe Master Pariken is playing his own game."

"If we're unable to trust one another at our level, we are
lost. Unlike the Guildmaster, you and I have seen enough of
the future to know that a crisis is drawing near, and one without favorable result. Unless some kind of action—"

"—is taken," finished the man. "Actions of the kind that
some people contemplate would make us worse than our enemies."

"Which is why"—the woman smiled sweetly—"*we* will

not take that action, but rather watch in outward horror while others perform tasks which are not far removed from our needs.

"Don't fret," she added. "You won't be called on to do anything more than your conscience can stand."

"Sometimes just carrying Kasander's slippers is more than my conscience can stand. What an immoral—"

"Don't even think it," the woman said. She stood up and brushed off her skirt. "I'll meet you again next LastDay at the usual place."

They parted beneath the bright spires of central Ilsefret, and the man went back to the servants' quarters beneath the house of the Exalted of Tanavral.

A ringing bell greeted him almost as soon as he had entered. He let his free-day livery fall to the floor, and pulled on his servitor's robe as he dashed for the stairs. One tread before the top he paused, took a breath, and stepped forward and out, standing like a carven thing until he saw where his master waited. There was Kasander, over by the balcony. The young man walked slowly over.

When he got to the customary distance of three paces, he paused and bowed his head.

"Fetch my slippers," the Exalted said. "We must go visiting."

"May one be so bold?" the man asked of the air beside the Exalted's head.

"To the residence of the Republic's negotiator," the Exalted said. "Bring two bottles of claret. Good, but not great, vintages. You may choose which ones."

A gift chosen by a servant, the young man thought. *The insult direct.* Maybe the timetable had moved up.

Faral didn't much care for the idea of leaving Miza alone in the *Light*'s cockpit with the enigmatic Guislen, but as long as his cousin was determined to leave Sapne in this ship and no other, he didn't seem to have a choice. Something strange was going on—something that went beyond even oracular old ladies and hooded Adepts with murderous intentions.

If Jens knew what the problem was, however, he wasn't telling. He accompanied Faral on his inspection of the rest of the starship, and never once mentioned either Guislen or the strange Adept. He and Faral worked their way through all the *Light*'s compartments one at a time—most of the spaces they found had obvious uses, but one or two proved utterly baffling. Faral supposed it took being brought up on shipboard to recognize them.

"What I'm worried about," he said, "is food and water. If the engines go we're dead in a second. But thirst—that's a nasty way to die."

"You're certainly cheerful tonight," said Jens. "Look over here. I think I've found the galley."

A closer inspection proved that he was right. The closet-sized nook held a washer and a cook-set, and dinnerware stacked for lift-off in secured trays. Not surprisingly, the fresh-provisions locker had failed to remain cold under standby power, and the meat and vegetables inside had first rotted and then dried into a foul-smelling powder. Jens wrinkled his nose.

"If we can't find an airlock to cycle this out of when we make high orbit," he said, "we'll need to toss it now."

"Right," said Faral. He opened another formerly-sealed cabinet. "Hey, look at this—space rations, in packets. Let's see if they're any good."

The foil packets had their seals intact, and pulling the tab on one of them revealed a dried bricklike substance. The pictorial instructions on the back of the packet showed a similar brick immersed in boiling water.

Faral put the opened rations back into the cabinet. "I guess we're supposed to boil these and trust to luck."

"I've got luck," Jens said. He fingered the necklace of bone and leather that the old woman had given him. "Our hostess back at the customs office gave me some. How are you doing for cleaning supplies to make this place tidy?"

"Not so good. Let's look below."

The next level down from the galley was crew berthing. There were no overhead light panels here; only red safety glows that would keep people's eyes from being blinded, and allow those crew members off watch to sleep during the ship's day. The air on this level was thicker than it had been up above.

Faral pushed on ahead into the berthing area. "We'll need more than soap and a plastic sponge for this one," he called back out to Jens.

"What do you have?"

"The crew," Faral said.

His cousin joined him in the berthing area. The small compartment had two bunks mounted to the bulkheads. One bunk held blankets collapsed over a thin, long lump. A brown skull lay with jaws wide above the top sheet. Faral noted that the skeleton's arms were crossed across its chest.

The occupant of the other bunk had never made it back there. He—or maybe she, Faral couldn't tell—lay facedown on the deck in a pair of stained, unisex coveralls. With no insects on board the *Light* to finish the work of decay, mold and bacteria had reduced the crew member's flesh to a film of greasy brown dirt. The skull had patches of skin and hair stretching over the partly dried and partly rotted cranium.

"That one died first," Jens said, pointing at the bunk. "His partner laid him out, and then took ill himself—too suddenly to reach the bed."

"Save the archeology. We have some cleaning to do."

"Respectful cleaning," Jens said. "We're borrowing their ship, after all."

Faral sighed. "After all." He nodded toward the bunk. "This one first, I think; he's already partway wrapped."

Working together, he and Jens bundled the sheets and blankets up and around the body, and carried it outside between them. They halted at the foot of the ramp, uncertain what to do next. The ground was too hard for digging, and didn't provide enough loose stone to raise a suitable cairn.

"We can't just leave them out here for the animals," Faral said. "Or for that—that whatever-it-was your friend Guislen chased away."

"On Entibor they used to cremate people," Jens replied after a moment's thought. "Lay the bodies down under the ship's jets. Let the fire purify them."

XIV. Sapne

FOLLOWING GUISLEN'S instructions, Miza took her place on the *Light*'s command couch and went to work. The couch was dirty, and the fabric of the seat coverings, no longer as flexible as it had once been, crackled under her as she sat.

I hope that doesn't mean that we're going to find a major problem later on, she thought, *a seal that's lost its airtight integrity or something.*

She put the thought aside and kept on going over the numbers and instructions. The annotations for the coursebook were in Galcenian, though they had been amended in some other script—not the Ilarnan of the engineering control panels but something that Guislen had identified as one of the Infabedan languages.

Miza frowned. Guislen was a strange one, with his Adepts' gifts and his spacer's ways, and she wasn't sure what to make of him. He could have come from almost anywhere. She'd never seen any members of the *Dust Devil*'s crew except for the captain, and there was no way of knowing what other ships might be using the Sapnean port. That Jens trusted the man was obvious, but as far as Miza was concerned that didn't necessarily count as a recommendation—she still wasn't altogether sure that she trusted Jens.

Faral had his own doubts about Guislen, she could tell that much from just watching him. Faral, unfortunately, *did* trust Jens. He'd accepted Guislen's offer of help on his cousin's word alone, and nothing Miza could say was likely to move him from that position.

Let's hear it for family loyalty, she thought. *I hope it doesn't end up being the death of all of us.*

When night fell, and after some hours Captain Amaro had still not returned from his courtesy visit to the Eraasian ship, Trav Esmet began to worry. Around local midnight, he left the bridge and went down to the common room. As he'd hoped, he found the *Dusty*'s owners still awake and playing kingnote—waiting up, he presumed, for the return of the three young people who'd ridden as smuggled cargo from Ophel.

They were talking, for some reason, about ghosts.

"All the Mageworlders believe in 'em," said Bindweed, scooping up the cards from the table and shuffling the deck again. "If you ask them, they'll tell you right to your face that Sapne is haunted."

"They've got plenty of good reasons to feel that way," Blossom said unsympathetically. "It was Mageworlds bio-chem that brought down Old Sapne in the first place. I'm surprised that they've got enough nerve to show up."

"There's money in it. And where there's money, folks will find the nerve." Bindweed paused in dealing out the cards, in order to look more closely at Trav. "You don't look like a happy man, Esmet. Is there a problem?"

"The captain's not back yet," Trav said. "And I'm concerned. Ghosts or no ghosts, Sapne isn't a healthy place to be, at night and on foot."

"Have we talked to the Mages yet?" Bindweed asked.

"No. If you could—"

Bindweed laid her cards facedown on the table and stood up. "All right, people. Let's go make a comm call."

The two owners followed Trav back up to the *Dusty*'s bridge. The pilot-apprentice opened up the ship's comm log and found the frequency that *Set-Them-Up-Again* had used before. Bindweed keyed on the link and waited until the squeal and crackle had stopped.

"This is Gentlelady Bindweed, half-owner of *Dust Devil*," she said. "I need to speak to your captain."

"I am Haereith, captain of *Set-Them-Up-Again*," a Mageworlds-accented voice replied over the link. "What is your pleasure, Gentlelady?"

"Our captain—may I speak with him?"

"He is not here."

"He isn't?" Bindweed glanced over at Trav, and her expression told the pilot-apprentice that he had been right to worry. "We expected him back here at the *Dusty* several hours ago. When did he leave?"

"He stayed to share supper with us," Haereith replied. "But he left afterward, not long past dark. Is there some emergency?"

"No, no emergency," Bindweed said. "But we're a bit concerned. Did he have time enough to walk back here?"

"In the dark . . . hard to say. But yes, I think that there was time."

"Thank you, Captain," she said. "Bindweed out."

She keyed off the link. "Well," she said to the others on the bridge, "now we know. I hope I haven't embarrassed Captain Amaro too badly in front of his counterparts from the other side of the Gap."

"Don't worry about it," said Blossom. "Ship's owners do so many stupid things that one more bit of dottiness on our parts isn't going to make a difference. Esmet, you were right to come and get us."

Trav felt relieved. "The captain's always been on time before, is all. And this is Sapne—I don't believe what the Mages say about the place being haunted, but the locals are a funny lot and you can't really trust any of them with your back turned."

"Dirtsiders are like that everywhere," Bindweed said. She looked thoughtful for a moment. "One thing we can do right now is set up a vertical light beam—something that'll show above the trees—for Amaro to guide home on."

"Shouldn't we assemble a search party?" Trav asked.

"I don't think so," Bindweed said. "In the dark, there's too much danger of someone else falling into a hole or getting lost, and we don't have enough people on board to mount an effective night search anyway. In the morning, if he hasn't returned—"

Blossom nodded agreement. "But your idea of rigging a light makes sense for now. It'll take more than three pairs of hands to do it, though. Trav, you go wake up Sarris down in Engineering, and let's get moving."

"I've never crewed a starship in my life," Faral complained. He and Guislen were in the *Light*'s engine room, going over the gauges and readouts one last time. "How am I supposed to do it now?"

"There's an acceleration couch in here," Guislen said. "All you have to do is strap down and wait. During planetary departure there's nothing you could do anyway if things went wrong."

"Maybe the ship's had all its bad luck already."

"We can only hope." Guislen checked the lighted gauges. "We seem to have reaction mass enough to get to the Central Worlds. Unless the gauge is frozen."

He laughed, and swung onto the ladder to take him up. Faral closed the vacuum-tight door behind him, and went over to the acceleration couch to strap down. There was a comm-link button on the arm of the couch. He keyed the link.

"You ready topside?"

"Ready as I'm going to get," Miza's voice came back. She sounded scared but resolute. "Waiting for my copilot."

"He's on his way."

Faral keyed off the link and settled back into the couch

padding to wait for lift-off. All things considered, this place in the brightly lit engineering compartment, surrounded by burnished metal and sharply angled machines, was better than the strapdown position Jens had found—the unused bunk in crew berthing. The ship had been designed for two, and two bunks were all there were. The padding and parts of the other bunk had been discarded entire, and now lay on the ground below with the bodies of the former crew, awaiting the cleansing flames of the Elevener's jets.

But first Miza needed Guislen forward, to instruct her in working the unfamiliar gear.

A nagging thought came to Faral that this was wrong, this was all too convenient. *The easy way leads to the ambush,* he kept thinking, recalling cliffdragons waiting above the worn game trails in the Gahlbelly Mountains of Maraghai. I hope we aren't doing something really stupid.

Jens lay back against the cushions of his bunk and tried to relax. He and Faral had cleaned out the berthing compartment as best they could with scant time and no proper equipment, but the odor of corruption—and the memory of the two dead crew members—still lingered. He envied Faral his proper acceleration couch down in the bright lights and relatively clean air of the engine room, even though the decision to take the unused bunk for a strapdown position had been his own.

All this was my idea; so if anybody has to sleep with the ghosts and skeletons, it's me.

Nevertheless, he reflected, he could have used some human company. Faral's, preferably; Jens's cousin had been his agemate and fellow-conspirator for a long time. Faral had been hurt, though, when he'd learned of the plan to abandon him and Chaka at the Sombrelír spaceport—he'd concealed his reaction well, but not well enough.

Jens grimaced, thinking that Faral was going to be hurt yet again when he found out what the other things were that his cousin hadn't yet bothered to mention.

I hope I haven't managed to mess up everything completely before I even start.

The intraship comm system clicked on, and Miza's voice came over the link to interrupt his thoughts.

"Copilot's in the cockpit. Let's go down the checklist, and see what happens when I press the Launch button."

Pleasure craft, limited, Jens said to himself. *Class B and up. Guislen . . . whoever you really are . . . make certain that she knows everything she needs to know.*

"Shut down exterior vents. Shut down nonessential internals. That's the blue switch. Seal for launch. Hatch reports positive lock."

Miza ran down the checklist as Guislen read it to her. When they reached "crew strapped down for lift-off," Faral answered up from engineering, though he added, "You have to understand that I don't have the slightest idea what to do back here."

"Not a problem," Guislen said. "The old Gyfferan Eleveners were pretty much automatic in this phase. The *Light*'s designed to run with a crew of two, both of them in the cockpit—pilot and navigator for the launch and the run-to-jump."

"And here we both are," said Miza. She was beginning to feel somewhat giddy with tension and uncertainty, and had to suppress the urge to laugh at the absurd mental picture of herself-as-starpilot. "Next step?"

"Exterior hazard lights on. The yellow toggle, above you. You'll have to stretch to get it."

She reached, flipped the toggle, subsided again onto the cushions. "Okay. Got it."

"Internal test, check fuel system, check engines."

"The board is green."

"Test airtight integrity. Overpressure on."

"Testing." She felt her ears pop, but the indicators on the board stayed green. "Test sat."

"When you come to launch," Guislen said, "you'll have to do a lot by feel. If there's excessive vibration, then you change attitude, or increase the power or decrease it until the vibration eases.

"Mostly, what we have to do here and now is get into space. We don't have to worry about reaching an assigned orbit, so half of your problems have gone away already. Keep her pointed more or less straight up and you'll get where you're going. The throttles are on the arms of your chair. You can do it any time."

Miza flexed her fingers and looked over at Guislen uncertainly. "Aren't we supposed to call Field Operations and Inspace, and tell them that we're launching?"

Guislen smiled faintly. "Under the circumstances, I don't believe that's necessary."

The pleasantry didn't reassure Miza as much as it could have. She clicked on the interior communications. "If you're ready back there, I'm ready up here. Departure as soon as I click off, if I haven't heard different from you by then."

Miza hoped that she sounded more confident than she felt. She knew that the real difficulty wasn't at this end—some astoundingly primitive systems could reach orbit. All it took was pumping out enough energy. Landing at the far end would be the tricky part. She had no confidence at all in her ability to maneuver antique computers through a fins-down pillar of fire landing. But if she thought about it too long she'd never get anything done.

"Gentlesir Huool had *better* give me an A for this course," she muttered to herself, and rammed the throttle levers full forward.

The acceleration answered a lot faster than she'd expected. This wasn't a slow and stately launch like the shuttle that had taken her to the liner for Ophel, or a smooth lift followed by a quick boost like the nullgrav-assisted short-hoppers she had learned on. It was more like getting kicked in the small of the back by a street fighter.

Outside the viewport, the *Light*'s drapery of jungle vines flashed into sudden fire. A weird howling came from all of the ship's metal parts shaking and singing at once. The vibration made Miza's jaws ache, and she reached for the throttles to ease back on the thrust.

"No," Guislen said. "This isn't excessive vibration."

She drew her hand back. "I'd hate to see what is."

The pressure squashed her. Her cheeks felt funny, and she thought she was going to sink right through the cushions of the pilot's couch and down into the deckplates.

The stars outside were bright, then brighter, and Guislen said, "Now cut them."

She cut power to the engines, and the pressure eased. "Are we where we need to be?"

"Off the surface—yes, and safe. We can let the orbit stabilize for a while, and discuss what comes next. Tell the crew to foregather in the common room."

"Where's that?"

"Next to the galley."

"Where's *that*?"

Guislen looked amused. "I'll show you."

Miza unstrapped—and promptly floated away from her chair. "Damn. I forgot to switch on artificial gravity."

"This class of ships never had it," Guislen said. "The shipbuilders put the resources into increasing the Eleveners' range and reliability instead. So we'll be floating for a while. In the meantime, let's head aft."

"Meet me in the galley," Miza said over the internal links. Then she clicked off, and gave a huge yawn.

"Lead the way," she said. "And if the galley has a cha'a maker, and you know how to use it, I'll bless your name."

"For that," Guislen promised, "I'll do my best."

The jungle felt oddly safe, in spite of the dark. He knew that his goal lay somewhere up ahead, and that when he found it he would need all his wits about him. The foe was clever, but he knew he was the more cunning. Hadn't enough people said that?

He wondered where the memory had come from. Every day another memory came into his head. Soon, he was sure of it, he would remember his name.

Plants brushed against his face, and vines whipped and tore around his legs. Under this planet's pale and single moon, the shadows under the broad leaves lay black as ink, concealing who knew what dangers.

Ahead, that was his goal. Someone he had to meet, someone he had to kill. Plans. They came maddeningly close to the surface sometimes, taunting him, teasing at his memory.

Parts of the past were clearer too: the long run to the Cracanthan spaceport, the contact with the ship's engineer, the taking of his body. And now, like a beacon ahead, the goal. It was near.

All at once, a glow burst above the tops of the trees, ahead in the same direction toward which he was half-running, half-walking. A streak of fire rose into the night.

He recognized the fire as a ship lifting. Why was a ship lifting from the jungle?

It left a cloud of smoke against the stars.

With a feeling of loss, of sadness, he watched it go. He had failed; his goal had departed.

But there was another goal. Somewhere else where he needed to be. Another ship. He would follow the one that had departed, and find the ones that he had to kill.

Ones.

For the first time he knew that there was more than one person he needed to find. Another memory tickled at the bottom of his conscious mind.

He turned sharply to his right, and once more set out loping through the dark.

From her hidden location in the woods, under the curve of a hydraulic landing cradle from which all the fluid had long since leaked through cracked seals, Chaka the Selvaur watched the outer door of the spacecraft spin closed. She waited, still in concealment, until bright lights blossomed around the trailing edges of the fins, pulsing in a danger array. A horn howled from the little ship.

Chaka stared. *Those mud-eggs are going to try to launch!*

A flickering glow appeared through the shrubbery under the craft. A blast of orange fire exploded outward, throwing sticks and branches into stark black silhouette. In the next instant the branches turned to dust and vanished before the thermal energy of the launch. The vessel's loading ramp upended, thrown clear of the jets by the blast.

Then the vines that covered the ship caught fire, surrounding it in a pall of smoke and red-orange flame. Only a moment had passed since the first light had flickered beneath the ship, but everything seemed to be moving slowly to Chaka's eyes. A roar like thunder filled her ears as the engines fired, their throttles opened wide. A moment longer and the ship lifted, with a tongue of fire burning beneath her, and more fire drifting down in sheets as the vegetable growth of nearly a hundred years sloughed away from her polished metal skin.

Bastards! Chaka howled at the sky. *What do you two mean, going off and leaving me *again*?*

The forest floor was adrift with acrid smoke. Tiny embers glowed amid the ash. The clearing was empty.

Chaka turned and headed back for the *Dusty*. Perhaps Bindweed and Blossom would know what the three humans had done, and why.

As she went, she became aware of someone else moving away from the trail—not one of the natives of this world. They were silent, they knew the trails. And even the locals hadn't come near the overgrown landing field since the sun had fallen from the sky.

A faint smell of sweat and commercial laundry soap told her that the stranger was a thin-skin, and civilized. Then she recognized him—Captain Amaro of the *Dusty*, a long way from his ship.

Lost and wandering? If so, she'd found him, and a Selvaur who couldn't find her way home wasn't fit to live under the Big Trees. She approached the captain and called out his name.

Ho! Captain Amaro! Going back to the ship?

To her surprise he answered her in Trade-talk. She hadn't realized that he knew it.

Yes, he replied. *Come on; we've been away too long.*

The exterior of *Dust Devil* was ablaze with lights. If anybody out there was trying to find the ship in the dark, they'd have plenty of help. The *Dusty*'s two owners stood at the top of the vessel's extended ramp, inside the security force field.

"We haven't heard yet from Chaka, either," Blossom said. She'd taken a blaster in a holster rig from the *Dusty*'s small-arms locker, and now she drummed her fingers restlessly on the weapon's grip. "I wonder what sort of trouble the boys have managed to get into."

"Maybe the folks at the passport office insisted on throwing them a party," said Bindweed. "You know, loud music, strong drink, vertical and horizontal dancing—"

She broke off as the sky to the south lit up without warning in a sheet of orange flame.

"Lords of Life!" Blossom exclaimed. "What in the name of everything holy was that?"

"You know as well as I do," said Bindweed tersely. "Small cargo craft launching without nullgravs."

"Do you think it was that Mage captain kidnapping Amaro?"

"Wrong direction for them."

Blossom tapped the grip of her blaster again. Her fingernails clicked against the hard plastic. "If this was the old days I'd launch right now, meet our mystery ship in high orbit, and ask what them what the hell they thought they were doing. And if the answers didn't come fast enough to suit me, I'd shoot out their engines and take their cargo by way of a lesson in manners."

"It's a tempting thought," conceded Bindweed. "But these aren't the old days. Besides, we're shorthanded without the skipper. And the purser and the supercargo still aren't up to standard on the guns."

"I suppose you're right."

Blossom and her partner went back to waiting in silence. They didn't have to wait much longer, however. Before another hour had passed, Captain Amaro and Chaka emerged from the forest and came into the circle of the *Dusty*'s exterior lights. Bindweed cut the force field to let them in.

"Stand by to launch," Captain Amaro said without pre-amble as he strode up to the foot of the ramp.

Chaka was right behind him. Bindweed held out a hand to slow the young Selvaur down.

"What about the boys?" she asked.

They're already away, Chaka answered. *I'll tell you about it later. I think you won your bet.*

Amaro looked from one of the ship's owners to the other. "Nannla—Tilly—what are you doing lounging around? Stand by your guns. We're lifting."

He continued toward the bridge at a fast walk, not looking back. Behind him, Bindweed stood still, with the color draining from her face. She turned to Blossom.

"Did you hear that?" she asked her partner.

"I did. But for now, I think that the captain wants us to stand by our guns."

Trav Esmet was already at work on the bridge when Amaro arrived. The captain strapped himself into the command seat without a word, and began running through the prelaunch routine. Trav glanced over at him curiously.

"Where're we heading, Captain?"

"Khesat," Amaro returned, not looking up from his checklist.

"I have the navicomp data ready for that transit," Trav said. "Will you be wanting me to take her up?"

"No," Amaro said sharply. "On my ship, I fly."

"Aye, aye, Captain," Trav said.

Disappointed, he turned back to the navigator's station. Maybe he'd been out of line, he told himself; maybe his request to handle the launch was putting himself forward and he'd earned the rebuke.

But that wasn't like the Captain, he thought. They'd been working together for a while now, and Trav knew that such curtness, for Amaro, was definitely out of character.

"Stand by to launch," Amaro said, breaking into his reflections. "We have places to be."

Almost on the word, he pushed the *Dusty*'s forward

nullgravs to max, tilted the ship to its launching attitude, and fired the jets.

Afterward, Trav had to admit that he'd been impressed by what he'd witnessed. It was the first time he'd ever seen a run-to-jump commence from the planet's surface rather than orbit: a military takeoff that hadn't been used by civilian spacecraft since the days of the Second Magewar.

XV. HYPERSPACE

NIGHT AND day were much the same aboard the tiny Gyfferan Elevener. Dark and light cycles, dim and bright, ran from automatic timers. The fathomless grey of hyperspace swirled outside the tiny viewscreen. Miza sat in her command chair and watched it sometimes, until it threatened to drive her mad with its endless, illusory motion. Then she would go back to her study of the *Light*'s logbooks, which had been kept in a bizarre patchwork of languages, and of the various technical manuals, which were mainly written in Galcenian with marginal notes in Gyfferan and in the Ilarnan script. When even those failed to distract her, she pushed her work aside and thought.

At the moment it was ship's-midnight. Miza was alone in the *Light*'s cockpit—her berth since the start of the hyperspace transit—when she decided that she didn't like the way her thoughts had been tending over the last few days.

I need to talk to somebody else before I start talking to myself, she thought. *Failing that, I need a cup of cha'a.*

The spacers who had crewed *Inner Light* in her working

days had kept the ship's hotpot in the same good order as everything else aboard. The cha'a itself tasted dreadful. The stored water had gone flat and metallic, and the leaves had lost most of their essential oils and complex flavors. Still, the drink was hot and it was there.

She unstrapped from the couch and headed for the *Light*'s galley, push-pulling herself awkwardly along in the zero-g environment. *I don't care how much power they saved,* she thought as she swung herself into the shadowed galley nook. *Failing to rig artificial gravity was a bad idea.*

As she'd half-hoped, Faral Hyfid-Metadi was also in the galley, nursing his own cup of cha'a.

"Couldn't sleep either?" he asked.

Miza nodded. "I got tired of watching hyperspace outside the window. So I decided to come down here instead."

She drew a fresh cup with its zero-g cover from the maker, then concentrated on getting the cup working and on orienting herself so that she was rightside-up with respect to her companion. She'd heard that even these days, real spacers prided themselves on being comfortable regardless of whether their personal "up" and "down" matched anybody else's, but she wasn't a spacer and didn't see any point in pretending.

Faral was another one who didn't care much for the absence of gravity—unlike his cousin, who appeared to find it enjoyable. Considering the things people said about Khesatans, Miza wasn't surprised.

"Do you think I'm going crazy?" she said at last.

Faral pulled a sip of cha'a before answering. "No more than the rest of us. Why?"

"I didn't used to believe in ghosts. Now I'm not so sure."

"The Adepts tell all kinds of strange stories," he said. "And the Mages tell even stranger ones. What's got you worried?"

"It's Guislen," she said. "I know your cousin trusts him and all that . . . but I've been wondering about him ever since before we left Sapne. And I think that he's a ghost."

She help up her hand to forestall a reply. "Listen. First, he shows up while we're inhaling that incense at the passport office, and he never does explain where he came from. Next, he just happens to know where this ship is—a ship that's almost a century out of date—and he also just happens to be an expert on flying it."

"Nothing so mysterious about that," Faral said. "There's a lot of antique ships still around and working. By the time we reach Khesat you'll be the same kind of expert that he is. And you sure aren't a ghost."

She gave a nervous laugh. "I don't think I am, anyhow. And I'm fairly sure about you and your cousin. But Guislen . . . the ship's lockplate recognized his hand."

"I saw that," Faral admitted. "But if he's an Adept, or even Adept-trained, the lockplate would open for him regardless. My mother can do the same thing, and I know that she isn't a ghost."

Miza reddened. She'd forgotten that Faral's mother was the Mistress Hyfid who'd abandoned her Adept's training to become First of all the Mage-Circles, and that his uncle was the Master of the Guild. For all his comforting matter-of-factness, he was probably accustomed to seeing marvels and apparitions every time he turned around.

Still, she felt compelled to keep on with her argument. "There were two crew members," she said. "Guislen and that thing in the clearing make two ghosts. And there's other stuff. I've counted the rations here in the galley. I know how many packets there were when we started, and how many packets there are now. I can account for the ones that you've eaten, and the ones I've eaten, and the ones that Jens has eaten. And that's it. Guislen hasn't eaten anything at all since we've been aboard."

"Are you sure?"

"I spent the past six months learning how to take inventory," she said. "And I know how to count. I'm sure."

"That *is* odd, then." Faral frowned at the lid of his zero-g cup. "Thing is, I saw Guislen twice before we ever got to Sapne. Once on board *Bright-Wind-Rising*, and once on Ophel."

"Did you touch him?"

He glanced up at her sharply. "Did I what?"

"Touch him." She tapped the back of Faral's hand by way of demonstration. His flesh was warm against hers in the chilly recirculated air. "I'll bet that you didn't."

"Well . . . no."

"You can't. I've tried. He's always someplace else by the time you get there—so smooth, you wouldn't notice he'd done it if you weren't already waiting for it to happen. I've never seen him asleep. I've never had to wait for him to get out of the 'fresher. And I've never seen him do anything mechanical, either. He always asks one of us to turn any knobs that need turning or push any buttons that need pushing. He's never touched any of them himself that I could see."

From Faral's expression, she gathered that he was going over his own experiences with Guislen and comparing them with hers. At last he said, "You may be right."

"I know I'm right," she said firmly.

"Suppose that he really is a ghost," Faral said. "The big question then is, why is he bothering to do all this?"

"Wrong," she said. "The *big* question is, how much does your cousin know?"

The number-one cargo bay aboard *Dust Devil* was chilly and full of echoes. Amaro had lifted from Ophel with only a partial load—intending, Blossom supposed, to make up the difference at the far end with exotic goods picked up cheap on Sapne. The captain had an eye for bits of primitive artwork that would appeal to the dilettanti on places like Khesat and Ovredis, and he'd made a profit from such things before.

But not any longer, Blossom thought. *Not if we're right about what happened on Sapne.*

She looked at the other two people in the cargo bay: her partner Bindweed and the *Dusty*'s navigator and pilot-apprentice Trav Esmet. Trav seemed uneasy. The cargo bay was a good place to have a conversation without being overheard, but there was no telling who might have snoop-buttons planted anywhere—and a late-night summons to a clandestine meeting with the ship's owners was enough to make any spacer nervous.

What they had to talk about wasn't going to make Trav any happier, either. But there wasn't any point in delay.

"We've been in hyper for a week now," she said. "And we've been watching Amaro the whole time. What do both of you think?"

"I'm concerned," Trav said. "We're talking about the captain. Isn't that mutiny?"

Bindweed gave him a pitying glance. "My dear boy, we *own* this ship. The captain serves at our pleasure. Whether we are pleased or not . . . you've known him on a day-to-day basis far longer than we have. Has he been in any way odd?"

"He hasn't been off the bridge since we left," Trav said. "Look, I'm very uncomfortable with this. Leave me out of the rest of it, all right?"

He turned and walked quickly from the cargo bay without saying anything more.

Blossom watched him go, then looked back at her partner. "That leaves us to make a determination."

Bindweed shrugged. "You knew that it would. Why you even bothered—"

"It never hurts to observe proper form," Blossom said. "Even in a crisis, which is what we've got. It's not just that Amaro knew our true names, it's that he sent us off to the guns as if this were the *'Hammer* from fifty years back. So if he isn't Amaro any longer—who is he?"

"Who was on *Warhammer* in those days?" Bindweed asked. "Jos, Errec, and Ferrda. You and me. 'Rada. A few others, on and off. Of the ones who flew, Jos and Errec."

"And Jos is still alive, or was the last time I heard."

"So," said Bindweed. "Errec."

Blossom nodded. She'd known in her heart what the answer had to be, but knowing the answer didn't make reaching a decision any easier. "He always was the one who could go right inside someone's mind. And being dead isn't likely to matter as much to him as it would to some people."

Bindweed started pacing, always a sign that she was thinking hard. "Let's go over the options. Suppose I walk up to Captain Amaro in the common room after breakfast and say, 'I believe that you're Errec Ransome.' Either the good captain says 'Yes' or he says 'No'—"

"Or else he says, 'Gentlelady, you must be joking,' and never answers you outright at all. Which is what Amaro would say if you asked him, and *exactly* what Errec would say if he didn't want to give you a straight answer. Do you really have any doubt about who's walking around inside that body?"

Bindweed didn't need to shake her head. Her expression was answer enough. "Do we stop him, then?"

"Stop him from what?" Blossom tapped the grip of her blaster—a nervous habit she thought she'd shed during the years on Ophel. *Hah. Bring back the old ways, and all the old twitches come back right along with them.* "We haven't got the faintest idea what he's planning to do."

"Then all we can do ourselves," said Bindweed finally, "is watch. And be ready to help out our shipmate if we can."

The *Light* continued its hyperspace transit to Khesat. Frustrated that her late-night conversation with Faral Hyfid-Metadi hadn't arrived at any useful conclusion, Miza kept on watching Jens and Guislen both. Neither one of them, however, did anything outside the already-established shipboard routine. Eventually Miza relaxed her scrutiny and went back to reading the ship's logbooks.

The old Gryffcran Elevener had plenty of them for her to choose from, kept mostly on pad-readable datachips and stored in the same drawer as the coursebooks. She'd found a working datapad in there as well, and she used it—as other crew members would have before her—to read and annotate the logs.

She took the entries in the order she found them, the most recent first—"*Today Winzie died. May his spirit find peace*"—and working backward. Some of them were in Ilarnan or other languages she couldn't read, but all the ones she could read had a sameness to them: cargoes, prices, ports of call, encounters with other ships. The condition of the engines. Costs for maintenance. Captain Veybesht of *Inner Light* had been particularly careful with that.

I wonder if our Gentlesir Guislen went by the name of Veybesht when he was alive, Miza thought. *Or was he Winzie?*

She kept on reading. The line of entries stretched backward in time. The last captain of *Inner Light* had taken over when the previous skipper had earned enough for a stake as a dirtside merchant—*"And the only time I'll see the stars is when I go to bed late, but at least in my own bed."* Crew members came and crew members went. Cargoes stayed more or less the same for run after run.

You're an analyst, Miza told herself. *You take facts and see the patterns in them that others can't. These are facts. Analyze them.*

She entered a note to herself in the margin of the data display, and read on.

The log was long on descriptions of gravity wells and short on descriptions of crew. Sometimes the *Light* had flown with two crew members aboard, sometimes with three—a relative luxury that allowed for one crew member on watch, one on non-flight-related duties, and one on free time. Normally, though, the Elevener's two crew members stood watch and watch, one on duty and one off. And the log entries went on and on.

"Entered hyperspace, bound for Ghan Jobai. All normal."

"Fueled. Costs higher on Pleyver since last visit."

"Navicomp upgrade completed, chipset serial number 151908 installed."

"Feguot of Andera has put out a call for crallach meat, bonus to fastest delivery."

"Engineer Wielk paid off, one share of mess fund reimbursed. Hired new engineer, Oredost. Bought into mess."

Line after line, Miza scrolled through the log. Then, without warning, she came to a name she recognized.

"Navigator Ransome paid off. Departs for the Guildhouse on Ilarna. We wish him well."

Miza closed her eyes.

Ransome the traitor. Errec Ransome, who was pointed out to schoolchildren from one side of the civilized galaxy to the other as the proximate cause of the Second Magewar. Ransome the Adept.

Guislen was an Adept too.

She continued on to the end of the log, and the day when the ship had first come into service. No other name struck her. She'd found the connection that she knew had to exist.

Letting the datapad drift aside, she floated free of her chair and stretched. *Now what should I do?* she wondered.

Tell Faral, of course. That was easy. And Jens. Let them know who had brought them this far—a man famous for villainy while he was alive. What would someone like that stick at now once he was dead?

She found Faral and Jens together in the engineering spaces. Like Miza, they were using their spare time and the ship's old manuals to learn the system. They had several plates removed from the overhead, and Jens was floating near the opening and checking the components while Faral read out the specs from a datapad down below. They looked in Miza's direction as she came gliding in.

"I think I know who our fourth companion is," she began, "and you aren't going to like it."

Jens went on tracing a wiring conduit in the overhead with his finger. "So—are you going to tell us?"

She drew a deep breath. "I think he's Errec Ransome. The traitor."

"Granda never would let us talk about Ransome like that," Faral said. "Whenever the subject came up, he always said, 'What's done is done, and Errec was my friend.' "

"Whatever," said Miza impatiently. "But he was also the navigator on *Inner Light* before he got paid off and went to join the Adepts."

"Maybe you're right and there's a connection," said Faral. "Or maybe there isn't. What's important is that Guislen is here now, and that he's helped us. Do you want to be the one who tells him, 'By the way, you're the most hated man in the known universe'?"

"No." She shook her head. The motion made her float away from Faral at a slight angle, and almost bump into Jens. "But I don't think I'll sleep again while he's here."

"The galaxy is full of dead bad men," Jens said, "and dead good ones too. Sooner or later everyone sleeps."

He twisted to look directly downward into Miza's eyes. "Whoever Guislen is, or whatever, he's my friend. To be frank, Gentlelady, I've known him longer than I've known you. I don't ask you to like it. But you are going to have to settle your mind to it."

He turned back to his tracing of the circuits.

Miza was silent, waiting for Faral to say something. When he didn't, only gave a helpless shrug, she felt her eyes begin to sting. She wiped her eyes with her shirtsleeve—on top of everything else, she didn't need the humiliation of seeing her tears float loose in free-fall—and fled for the sanctuary of the *Light*'s cockpit.

Once she got there, she dogged the door shut behind her, secured herself in the command chair, then pressed her face against the acceleration padding and wept. After a while, through her sobs, she heard a voice speaking her name.

"Mizady Lyftingil," it said quietly. "When you named me, I knew. You are right. I should go."

She opened her eyes again. She was alone in the cockpit, and the door behind her was still dogged down.

Several hours passed. Miza didn't much want to leave *Inner Light*'s cockpit. She knew in her heart that when she did, she'd find no trace of Guislen, or of Errec Ransome, anywhere on board the ship—and now that her naming of him had driven him away, she found the thought of finishing the transit without him almost as unsettling as she had found his presence earlier. Whatever else Ransome might have been and done, he'd made a good teacher in the basics of crewing an antique spacecraft.

Now there's just the three of us.

That, too, was a depressing thought. Jens Metadi-Jessan had called Guislen a friend, and he wasn't going to be happy when he found out that his friend was gone. It wouldn't take him long to decide that Miza was to blame, either, and then she could say good-bye to whatever traces of uneasy fellowship they might have had.

And Faral goes where Jens says to follow. That thought was even more depressing.

She sat up straighter—or would have, if she'd been actually sitting, and not just anchored to the *Light*'s command couch by the safety webbing. *It doesn't matter if neither one of them is speaking to you,* she told herself. *Once you've gotten them safely to Khesat, you've taken care of Huool's commission and can go back to Ophel.*

With that decision behind her, it was easier to unbuckle the webbing and open the door. She couldn't have stayed inside forever anyway—as a place to withstand a siege, the *Light*'s cockpit lacked some of the basic requirements, food and water being only two of them.

All the same, she was relieved to see that no one was waiting for her outside the cockpit door. She made her way aft to the 'fresher, then forward again toward the galley.

A cup of cha'a, she thought, *then to the cockpit to get some sleep. Maybe things will look better in the morning.*

The galley wasn't empty. Faral was there already, with a zero-g cha'a cup in either hand. He looked like he was about to leave; she pushed herself backward out of the door to clear the way for him. To her surprise, he didn't go on past her, but stayed where he was and held out one of the zero-g cups like a peace offering.

"I was going to bring one up to you," he said. "I thought you might want it."

"Thanks." Miza took the cup and sipped at it. Maybe she was getting used to the wretched quality of space rations in general, but the cha'a didn't taste half-bad. "Where's your cousin?"

"Down in the cargo hold. He said he was damned if he was going to sleep in crew berthing anymore."

"Oh." She took another sip of the cha'a. "Frankly, I can see his point. I'm surprised he held out this long."

"Me too." Faral didn't say anything for a while. Then he said, "We looked all over the ship for Guislen."

"And you didn't find any trace of him. Right?"

"Right. Jens isn't real happy right now."

"I don't blame him," she said. "Not really. I'm sorry I ever—"

"It isn't your fault. All you did was tell the truth." There was another awkward pause. Then Faral seemed to make up his mind about something. He gestured with his free hand at the door of the galley nook. "Sit out in the common room for a while?"

After the emotions of the past few hours, the friendly invitation almost undid her all over again. She kept herself from sniffling—she was *not* going to go all weepy at the slightest provocation!—and said, as lightly as she could manage, "Sure."

The bolted-down table in the common room wasn't any good without proper gravity. Miza suspected that its main use had been as a surface for doing dirtside paperwork with port officials the captain didn't want going any farther into the ship. However, the shipwrights who designed the old Gyfferan Elevener had provided the compartment with plenty of handholds and gripping bars. She and Faral found a couple near the table to wrap their legs around for anchors—as close to sitting anywhere as they were likely to get until the *Light* made planetfall on Khesat.

Neither one of them said anything for a while. Faral was a good person to sit and be quiet with, Miza decided. And having another person nearby made the *Light*'s chilly silences a great deal easier to bear. She decided that she felt sorry for Jens, down by himself in the cargo hold.

Her own cup of cha'a, unfortunately, wasn't going to last forever—and ship's-night had come while she and Faral were together. The lights in the common room had dimmed, and the companionway leading forward to the bridge was almost completely black. She pulled her jacket around her—it was too long in the sleeves and too tight in the chest, a chance discovery in the ship's storage locker, but it warmed her. She knew that the feeling of cold was an illusion caused by the dimming of the lights, but ship's-night always seemed to have a greater chill to it than the artificial day.

She wasn't eager to face the trip back through the dark, tunnel-like passage to the *Light*'s cockpit. Not while there was still someone to stay with here.

I'll wait until Faral leaves, she thought. *Then I'll go.*

She glanced over at Faral. He'd secured his empty cup in a bin by the table, and now his hand was floating—casually, as if his will had played no part in the decision—so close to hers that it would be a simple matter for her fingers to link with his.

She didn't precisely will it, but when her hand floated toward his, she didn't snatch it back. She felt the warmth of contact—casual, accidental—and then more warmth as he took her hand lightly in his, and held it as if it were a bird that would be killed by too tight a grasp.

Miza relaxed, enjoying the human contact. A ship on loan from the dead was no place to turn down the pulse of life. She leaned back into the zero gravity and closed her eyes. Soon enough she slept.

She awoke to the sound of relays clicking over in the gently brightening light of ship's-dawn, and found herself floating in the middle of the common room with her head against Faral's shoulder. Sometime during the night they must have moved closer together for warmth, then embraced to keep from drifting apart.

She opened her eyes and saw that Faral was awake also. Looking at him from this distance—it was no distance at all, really, with her arms wrapped around him and his around her—she noticed for the first time that he had almost absurdly beautiful eyelashes. They made a curious, touching contrast to the muscular body she was currently holding.

"Good morning," he said. He sounded somewhat tentative, as if none of the lessons in good manners he'd learned at home had covered what to say to the person you woke up with.

On Artha, fortunately, the lessons covered everything.

"Good morning," Miza replied, and hugged him briefly before letting go.

"You made supper last night," she added, feeling oddly cheerful. "I'll fix breakfast for us this morning."

XVI. Khesat

W E'RE ALMOST to dropout," Jens said to Miza. The two of them currently occupied the pilot's and copilot's positions in the *Light*'s cockpit, white Faral hung weightless in the cramped space behind them. "Do you have any idea how you're going to land this thing?"

Faral scowled at his cousin. *Take it easy, will you?*

Jens had been in a foul mood for some days now, ever since Guislen/Ransome's departure, but in Faral's opinion that was no reason to make their only pilot nervous. The navicomp alarm rang as he spoke.

"Stand by for dropout," said Miza.

She cut in the *Light*'s realspace engines and took down the hyperdrives. Faral held his breath and hoped for the best. A Gyfferan Elevener was a long way from a light touring craft with an idiotproof navigational interface.

Stars appeared in the narrow slit of the viewscreen ahead, shifting rapidly from red to their normal color as the grey dazzle of hyperspace departed. Faral saw Miza relax a little in the cradle of her safety webbing.

"Before we talk about landing," she said—speaking to him, he noted, and not to Jens—"let's talk about where we are. I'm no expert on these things, even if I have read most of the tech manuals. Most of the ones in Galcenian, anyway."

She glanced at the console in front of her, then up at the navicomp where it was welded to the bulkhead just abaft the viewport. "I think that I have to do *this*," she said, and flipped a switch that looked like it might have been labeled "locate" if it hadn't had a scrawl of Ilarnan beneath it instead.

"Now what?" said Faral.

"Now we wait until either the machine tells us that it has a fix, or it doesn't. I don't know about you, but I can't tell one part of the universe from another by eye."

Jens regarded the navicomp with disapprobation. "I suppose you've already considered that this thing is looking for aids to navigation that may not have been maintained, and that may or may not have been changed, and that may have been relocated or drifted off course during the last sixty years, or been blown up in either of two different wars?"

"The thought was never far from my mind the whole way," Miza said. "If I recall correctly, this part of the process could take several hours. I'm going to spend the time having lunch. When I come back, either the navicomp will have a posit waiting for us on the readout, or it won't."

She left the cockpit, swimming downward toward the galley and leaving Faral and Jens to watch over the console.

"You're certainly putting yourself out to be charming this morning," Faral told his cousin. "And you probably know even less about landing a spaceship than she does."

"Khesat had an in-system fleet eight years ago," Jens said. "I suppose it still has one. They kept watch for distress calls from ships in trouble."

"Are we in distress?"

"I'll tell you after lunch," Jens said, and followed in the direction Miza had gone.

Faral remained behind, gazing out moodily at the brilliant stars glittering just beyond the viewscreen. A light began to blink on the main console panel, immediately below a handset.

Comm link? thought Faral, and picked the handset up.

A voice speaking in what he supposed was Khesatan came from beyond a grille in the overhead. Faral waited for the voice to go silent and the carrier wave to drop before speaking into the handset.

"This is *Inner Light*, last port of call Sapne. Please wait while I call the captain."

Rhal Kasander hated leaving the planet's surface.

He disliked the undignified nature of a shuttle ride to orbit, with its couches and webbing and uncomfortable physical effects. Zero-g was not kind to a man with a delicate stomach and a precisely calibrated sense of balance. The presence of disposal bags for dealing with the results merely sufficed to make the Exalted of Tanavral feel condescended to by those with coarser natures than his own.

The artificial gravity of Khesat Orbital Reception provided only physical relief. The builders of the planet's main space station and manufacturing hub had followed their own governing aesthetic during its construction, and that aesthetic was not the one that ruled on the world below. Even the public and diplomatic areas were clean and spare, and stripped deliberately of ornament. They gave the eye nothing to delight in, only the gleam of polished metal and the dazzle of light on sheets of armor-glass.

Working areas like the salvage docks declined to make even those concessions. The lines in such places were those of function alone and not of art. Nevertheless, when the heavy blastproof and vacuum-tight doors of Salvage Dock Number One groaned open, Rhal Kasander—attended as always by his slipper-bearer—was there in person to greet the three young people who came out.

Politics, after all, was the art above all arts, and the Exalted of Tanavral was its most zealous practitioner. Let the others, Hafelsan and the rest, wait on the arrival of that freetrader from Sapne, even now grounding at Port of Diamond. Not there but here, Kasander was positive—based on faith and a comm call that had roused him from his bed the moment the ship entered system space—*here* was his Worthy.

He cast an appraising eye over the two young men and the young woman as they approached. The golden-haired youth . . . that would be the cadet-Jessani himself, a few years older than when Kasander had last seen him, and still more than sufficiently personable. His companions made a charming matched set in their own right—male and female, dark and fair—undoubtedly chosen for their good looks as well as for whatever practical skills they might possess.

But the clothes! Common Galcenian-style travelers' garb, at best, and that would have been before whatever misfortunes had added all the dirt and snags and wrinkles. Something would have to be done about that, the Exalted decided, as soon as the proper courtesies had been observed.

The cadet-Jessani and his companions were halfway across the distance from the open door of Dock Number One. Kasander hurried forward with both hands extended.

"My dear boy! My very dear boy!" He spoke in Galcenian, since who knew what languages the companions might speak, and it was unwise to alienate such people prematurely. "Forced to travel in circumstances I hesitate even to imagine. . . ."

The cadet-Jessani—Jens Metadi-Jessan D'Rosselin, Worthy scion of a Worthy lineage—answered him with a touch of amusement. "It was nothing, honored cousin-once-removed. I came as soon as I got word."

"You got—?" Kasander began before catching himself. "Oh, yes, of course. I've prepared a place for you in my own house, while we await the Day of Change."

The cadet-Jessani nodded as if he'd expected nothing less. He gestured toward his companions. "And my staff?"

"The same, of course."

"My thanks for your consideration," the young man said. "It's a pleasure to see you again after all these years. But now, shall we repair to the surface . . . perhaps, even, to the shops? As you can see, we were forced to abandon our luggage, and have become far too well acquainted with our present garments."

"My own tailors stand ready," Kasander said, turning to escort them back through the far locks and through the diplomatic sections to the yacht slips. The Exalted's slipper-bearer stood silent as they passed, then followed.

"I wonder what all this is in honor of?" Blossom said. She looked down onto the landing field at Port of Diamond from her position at the *Dusty*'s guns. "Flute players, flower girls, and a gentlesir in a morning-robe that I wouldn't have believed in even if you'd described it to me twice . . . I haven't seen a reception committee like this one since Jos took 'Rada home to Entibor."

"We'll probably find out about everything soon enough," Bindweed replied over intraship comms from the other gunnery station. "Amaro—Errec—has gone down with Trav to meet the natives."

"Trav knows he's supposed to keep an eye on the captain, right?"

"Right. I just hope he remembers."

Blossom heard the sound of the *Dusty*'s ramp sighing open, then the noise of footsteps on metal as Trav Esmet and the captain walked down. She could just see the two men at the edge of her gunnery station's viewscreen.

The gentlesir in the amazing morning-robe stepped forward to speak with the captain and the navigator. There was a brief colloquy at the foot of the ramp. Then the gentlesir turned aside and made a tiny hand gesture. The flower girls began to drift away with their baskets of white and lavender petals, and the flute players started putting their instruments back into their cases.

"Looks like trouble," Bindweed said.

"I guess we didn't have the right cargo," Blossom replied. "Since up until Sapne our cargo was just three young people that nobody was supposed to know were here—"

"—I'd say we need to look more closely at the situation."

Blossom leaned forward suddenly. She'd spotted an unexpected flurry of movement at the edge of her screen. "Wait a moment. The game's not over yet. The gent in the morning-robe is going off with our captain."

"Strange are the ways of Khesat," Bindweed said. "But unless I'm awfully mistaken, this isn't the sort of greeting every random merchant gets, even here."

Blossom switched the intraship comm to the engineering spaces. "Chaka? If you're not occupied, come up and meet us in the common room. It's time we had a serious talk."

The town house of Jens's cousin-once-removed was like nothing Faral had ever seen, except in holovids and in the illustrations of adventure books about the days before the Magewars. The private entrance hall into which the Exalted of Tanavral first escorted his guests had walls paneled in carved ebony inlaid with mother-of-pearl. Heavy brocade curtains with deep valances covered the windows. The ceiling had chandeliers and allegorical frescoes, and the floor had parquetry and Ilarnan millefleur carpets.

Miza, wide-eyed, had identified all those things to Faral, and had given him an estimate of their worth that made his breath catch in his throat. The two of them hadn't had long to talk—a few minutes only, while Rhal Kasander spoke urgently with his personal tailor at the other end of the long chamber. Then the tailor's attendants, both male and female, had descended upon Jens and his companions, and hurried them off separately for measurings and fittings and the presentation to each of them, in less time than Faral had believed possible, of an elegant new wardrobe.

Now the cousins were back together for the first time in several hours, in the upstairs reception room where they had been taken to await the return of Miza. Jens, newly resplendent in the High Khesatan mode, wore a full-sleeved day coat of black moiré spidersilk lined throughout in lapis lazuli, with a string of opals braided into his long yellow hair. Around his neck, plainly visible against the pure white of his shirtfront, he still wore the leather cord strung with bits of bone that the oracle on Sapne had given him for luck. Combined with the opals, the effect was one of perverse, and somehow entirely Khesatan, distinction.

Mercifully, the tailor had not attempted a similar transformation with Faral, contenting himself with providing a plain suit of well-fitted garments in the basic Galcenian style. Faral supposed that the difference in clothing implied all sorts of things about rank and status to the eyes of Khesatan observers, but he didn't care. What counted at the moment was that for the first time in some hours he had an opportunity to talk with Jens alone.

What are we really doing here, foster-brother? he asked urgently. *And when do we get something to eat?*

He spoke in Trade-talk for privacy's sake, and because the shared language was still a link between them. To his relief, Jens answered him in the same tongue.

If you're asking for a hearty serving of rare meat and blood sauce, you won't get it any time soon. Late afternoon is for small pale sandwiches with the crusts trimmed off.

I can hardly wait, said Faral. *And you didn't answer my first question.*

I'm here for reasons of my own, Jens said. *And you're here because you stuck to me like a wool-burr from the moment we left Maraghai—*

I stuck to . . . ! Faral's indignation left him briefly speechless.

—and I'm damned if I know why your friend Miza is still with us at all.

Faral regained his voice again with some difficulty. *That "reasons of my own" line is getting thin, foster-brother. Time for me to speak plainly, I think.*

If you must.

All right. It was important for you to get to Khesat, I could see that. So I went along. You mentioned danger and intrigue and backing the winning candidate. That didn't sound like your usual style, but I didn't argue with it because the other choice was calling you a liar. But things are happening now that I don't understand even a little, and I think you ought to tell me the truth.

Jens let out his breath and sat down abruptly on one of the carved wooden chairs. All of a sudden he looked much more like his usual self, in spite of the moiré spidersilk and the string of opals. *I got a message,* he said, *the night you were going to leave Maraghai with Chaka and go off wandering.*

What kind of message?

My father was with Space Force Intelligence for a long time, Jens said. *Maybe he still is, I don't know. Anyway, he arranged things so that if anything bad ever happened to my mother or to him, I'd be sure to get word of it whether he could make contact himself or not. *That* kind of message.*

Did it say what was going on? Faral tried to imagine how trouble that bad could possibly have befallen his aunt and uncle. He'd always thought of them as dazzling and somehow invincible, living an exciting life in some place very far away, like people in a holovid. *Did they ask you for help?*

Jens shook his head. The opals glittered. *Nothing that clear and obvious. But I'm worried that both Dadda and Mamma are being held incommunicado by someone on Khesat who wants to use them in setting up a new Highest. If I want to learn anything more, I'll have to play the game as if I intend to be a candidate for the office myself. Is everything clear enough for you now?*

Faral couldn't think of an answer that wouldn't sound either rude or stupid. Finally he gave up. *Shouldn't you call Public Security to report a kidnapping first?*

So far, nothing illegal has happened. But you can go a long way on Khesat and stay inside the boundaries of the law . . . especially if you're a Worthy and confine yourself to dealing with others of similar rank.

I can see why your father joined the Space Force and left the planet, said Faral after a moment.

Not yet you can't, Jens told him. *But you will.*

"Well," Blossom said. "That was certainly an unusual reception."

Along with Bindweed, Chaka, and Trav Esmet, she was sitting at the table in *Dust Devil*'s common room. She poured herself some cha'a, hot and bitter, and swirled it around in the cup before looking over at her partner. "Have you ever seen the like?"

"No," said Bindweed, "but I've never been to Khesat before, either."

"Granted. Trav, did you happen to catch who that gentlesir in the morning-robe might have been?"

"Hafelsan," the navigator replied. "Gerre somebody somebody Hafelsan."

"You must improve your memory for names," Bindweed told him. "Such things may be important someday when you've got a ship of your own."

Blossom ignored her partner's comment and concentrated on the navigator. "But do you recall what was said?"

"Yes," Trav replied. He laced his fingers around his cha'a cup—Blossom had poured it for him herself, so that he'd know he wasn't in trouble with the owners—and continued.

"The gentlefellow in the morning-robe inquired of the captain for his passengers. Captain Amaro said no, we carried none. The fellow with the morning-robe grew impatient, and asked if the captain was sure that no one named Jens Metadi-Jessan D'Rosselin had taken passage. 'None such,' the captain said, but from the way he looked when the fellow spoke the name 'Metadi' I could see that some memory was being jarred loose.

"The fellow in the morning-robe started to head off, but then he seemed to change his mind. He came back and put an arm around the captain's shoulders and said, real hearty-like, 'There are some things I want to show you.' Then they walked off together and neither one looked back."

Blossom turned to the Selvaur. "What do you think, Chaka?"

Weirder than anything I've ever heard.

"This whole trip has been strange, I'll grant you that. Now, my dears, here's what we will do. Bindweed and I will play the role of dotty old ladies on holiday."

"That sounds like grand fun!" Bindweed said. "We shall go shopping, yes we shall!"—delivered with a manic leer that made the others laugh in spite of themselves.

"Trav, you will remain on the ship, with Sarris and the rest of the crew," Blossom continued. "Carry out business as usual, the same way you would in any working port. The captain may return, and he may wish to set a course elsewhere. Follow his orders, of course.

"However," she went on, "unless I miss my guess, someone will approach you and ask you to hire on with them, or to sell them information, or something of that nature. Normally, I'm sure, your loyalty to the ship would preclude your accepting any such offer. This time, you will accept after holding out for the best price you can."

"We'll let you keep whatever you gain," Bindweed put in. "Don't sell yourself cheaply. No one will believe it."

Blossom nodded. "As I was saying, we as owners of this craft give you permission to sell out. Do what's asked. Take careful note of who, where, and what, as well as other details you may notice, and bring back a full report."

"It should be fascinating," Bindweed said. She rose and set aside her empty mug. "Now we'll have to dress for town."

And if fame beckons? Chaka asked.

"Then seize it with your fangs," Blossom replied, "and don't let go. Despite your misgivings, I believe that fame is to be had here."

She took a deep breath. "Yes, fame is in the air of Khesat today."

"Does no one in this room speak whatever beastly language those two boys are using?" asked the Exalted of Tanavral. He sat with Caridal Fere, Master of Nalensey, in the latter's study. The voices of the Worthy cadet-Jessani and his traveling companion issued from a desktop comm link molded in the shape of a black crystal lily. "What's the use of sewing ears into their robes if they're going to jabber to each other in some uncouth tongue?"

"I believe that they're speaking one of the Selvauran

dialects," said Fere. "Nearly impossible to learn unless you're brought up with it. Or so I'm told."

"Find me a translator," the Exalted said. "One without political affiliation, if possible."

"If such a thing exists on Khesat at a time like this," said Fere. "The scholars at the university have a Worthy of their own already, so we can't ask them. And the staff at the Maraghaite Embassy claims to refuse all such requests as a matter of principle." He paused. "If we look outside the usual channels . . . on that ship from Sapne, the one that Hafelsan made such a fool of himself over meeting, the engineer's apprentice is a Selvaur. Shall we hire it to listen to these two and bring us translations?"

Rhal Kasander began to smile. "An off-worlder," he said. "Excellent. No local ties to create . . . misperceptions. And no one will notice its absence after the events, when witnesses may no longer be necessary."

The Master of Nalensey clapped his hands twice. A young woman appeared. He did not address her, but instead spoke aloud with his back to her.

"There is a ship in port from Sapne," he said. "There is a Selvaur on that ship. Hire it. Bring it here."

The woman bowed, and left.

Kolpag Garbazon sat with his partner Ruhn at a sidewalk cafe in Ilsefret, sipping fruit juice and looking over the poetry section in the *Galactic Intelligencer.* Kolpag was finding the famed Khesatan decadence to be considerably less impressive than folklore made it out to be—for his money, you could find more of it, and better, in Freemarket Plaza on a LastDay night.

Ruhn was even less impressed. He cleared the screen on the *Intelligencer*'s text display and said, "More nonsense. We might as well have stayed home in Sombrelír."

"Patience," Kolpag said. "Everything is here, and all we need do is wait for it to present itself. Our analysis could not be wrong."

"Oh yes it could," Ruhn said. "And we're sitting a long

way out in the cold for my comfort, on a planet where they won't put booze in their fruit juices because they think it ruins the natural bouquet."

"They've got a point, you know."

"Of the *juice?*"

"Some people care about such things, I suppose." Kolpag nodded toward Ruhn's discarded newsreader. "And speaking of cold comfort, did you catch the word of a new plague out of Sapne? The opening of the Tremoncton Gallery—it's in that squib."

"There's nothing of interest in these papers written in Galcenian," Ruhn said. He picked up the newsreader again anyway. "Did you know that in Khesatan, the same word means stranger, foreigner, non-native-speaker, and mannerless boor?"

Kolpag grunted. "Not surprising. What's more surprising is the number of words that rhyme with it."

"I still don't see where you got that bit about the plague."

"Plague from Sapne, that's what they mean by the Miller's White. And when you combine that with the news of a merchant spacer found dead in an alley yesterday afternoon . . ."

"Where did you see that?" Ruhn demanded.

"In the off-planet message feed," said Kolpag. "It helps to pay attention. I put up a stop-and-hold on any mention of known members of the *Dust Devil*'s crew, and guess who didn't make it?"

"Bindweed and Blossom," said Ruhn, "if there's any justice in the universe."

"None that I know of. It was our friend Captain Amaro, the man in too much of a hurry to pick up the cargo he'd contracted for."

"Maybe one of the people he stiffed wasn't happy with him, and sent him a present."

"Maybe indeed," Kolpag said. "But when you combine that story with no news of anyone of importance arriving on that ship, it tells me that our package surely did arrive on it. Now watch the long knives appear."

"In what form?" Ruhn asked.

"A series of entertainments," said Kolpag, "to which we won't be invited. Followed by an entertainment to which everyone will be invited, and to which we'll invite ourselves."

"Don't be so cryptic. You're starting to go native."

"Not if I can help it," Kolpag told him. "I improved my mind during the transit by reading everything that was available on Ophel about Khesatan politics. Made me glad I'd been born in poverty before I was done."

He had arrived on Khesat. That was right, it was the proper place. More and more was coming to him. People he recognized. He was sure he had been a starpilot, the skills were there. Skill did not fail him.

In dreams he saw himself dressed in white, a white staff in his hand, striding across the worlds, finding the corruption and exposing it, cleansing the worlds, then binding them so that they could never escape from control again.

Then came the waking, and a delegation meeting him. A memory stirred, of the end of a war, of being happy, the awards and the honors. Coming down from the starship where Tilly and Nannla ran the guns, a Selvaur in the engineering spaces, and there he stood with the captain beside him—

And the man in the morning-robe said the word "Metadi."

Rosselin and Metadi.

The memories came in a rush. He was Ransome, Errec Ransome, the Breaker of Circles. The final chance had come, the final Circle waited to be broken. Now everything was within his grasp, along with the vengeance.

Vengeance on Rosselin and Metadi, the ones who had killed him before his time.

Ransome willed the man before him to approach.

"There are some things I want to show you," the man said.

Good, Ransome thought. *There are some things I want to see. And I shall see them through your eyes.*

XVII. KHESAT

JENS METADI-Jessan D'Rosselin, cadet-Jessani, Worthy scion of a Worthy Lineage, stood in the reception hall of Rhal Kasander's town house, sipping moon-flower wine from thimble-sized glasses while being sized up, it seemed, by every Worthy dowager on the planet.

Shopping for their great-granddaughters, he thought. *At least I* hope *it's for their great-granddaughters.*

The reception hall was high and airy. An early-autumn rain pattered against the windows, and the breeze through the clerestory brought blessed coolness to what might otherwise have been an overcrowded scene. Retrofitting the antique heating and cooling systems of the town house for proper climate control was well within the means of Jens's cousin-once-removed, but doing so would have spoiled the archi-tect's carefully planned patterns of natural air circulation.

Jens put aside his wineglass without looking—one of the Exalted's servitors slid a silver tray into place beneath it be-fore he released his fingers—and strolled over to the retiring-corner. There, low tables and piles of cushions awaited the pleasure of those who chose to recline and view the passing scene. Having chosen a cushion, he sank back, resting on his elbows, and surveyed the room.

His purpose here, at the party and on Khesat in general, was merely to exist, or so his cousin-once-removed had claimed. Apparently a rival faction within the current faction had pressed the advantage of another Worthy, one whom the Exalted of Tanavral found far less worthy than strictly necessary. As an off-world candidate of impeccable lineage—but somewhat disreputable upbringing—Jens was to be the lever to remove that fellow, and bring up another.

"An intelligent man, but not *too* intelligent," Rhal had said of that second Worthy, and everyone in the little prereception room had laughed. Jens thought that his being present for the witticism was indiscreet, to say the least, but who was he to say? His cousin-once-removed stood upon the pinnacle of fashion, and was far more aware of nuance than was Jens.

A maze of curtains and cushions led farther away from the main reception hall. Low murmurs and squeals of laughter came from back among the deeper shadows.

Jens glanced about the hall. As he had half expected, Faral was nowhere to be seen, and neither was Miza.

It was something, he supposed, that he should have seen coming. The way the two of them had carried on aboard *Inner Light*—holding hands, gazing deeply at one another, blocking the route from engineering to the galley so a man couldn't get himself a midnight cup of cha'a without having to duck under a pair of sleeping amorati floating fully clothed in the middle of the common room—it hadn't improved his outlook on life at all. Maybe they had finally . . . no, both of them were too straightlaced to avail themselves of the semi-private cushions at a reception. If they hadn't locked themselves in the pilothouse of the *Light* for a couple of hours during the transit, they weren't going to do anything now.

Holding hands, he thought. *And talking. I wish . . .*

Jens wasn't certain exactly what he wished, but he knew that he wasn't likely to get it. Not tonight.

He closed his eyes for a moment, then opened them again

and scanned the hall once more. Still no sign of his cousin or of Huool's courier, but not far from the retiring-corner a Worthy in a crimson evening-robe was in earnest speech with the Master of Nalensey. They had their heads practically on each others' shoulders, and from the expression on his face, the crimson-robed Worthy was deeply worried.

To make such a slip from studied indifference was a bad sign. The Worthy had certainly fallen a notch in the estimation of everyone present.

Jens studied his own indifference and found it excellent. He tried to look as if he were trying to stifle a yawn brought on not by fatigue but by boredom. The former was dishonorable—a true Worthy never slept before dawn, and then only enough to prepare himself for the next night's revelry.

Time to make Cousin-once-removed Rhal happy and circulate some more, Jens thought. He pushed himself to his feet. Before he could take more than a few steps in the direction of the wine fountain, he heard a whisper in his ear: "Come."

An invitation? Jens turned toward the speaker and found himself facing Heridand Agilot, Freeholder of Derizal. Though only of middling rank, the Agilots had been the leading family in Derizal for longer than most Worthy Lineages could claim existence. Nothing political happened in Ilsefret, it was said, without an Agilot working somewhere behind the scenes.

"Yes, Gentlesir?" Jens asked politely.

"Serious business," the Freeholder said. "You're wanted." With that he turned, without the common obeisance to one of higher grade that could be expected, and walked off.

The woodwind consortium was in the midst of Zaragini's Third Obsession, but to Jens the entire place seemed muted in an instant. A glance about the hall showed him that the number of guests, especially among the truly important, was noticeably lower now.

Jens trailed after the Freeholder's retreating back as Agilot went out through a pair of double doors onto the rear balcony. The light rain spattered Jens briefly before the nearby entry-servant draped a cloth-of-gold weather cloak over his head and shoulders.

A hovercar on high-step nullgravs waited on the far side of the balcony railing, its passenger-side door lifted up. A servant placed a set of polished ocherwood steps against the railing, and assisted the Freeholder up and across. Jens followed after him, and the door of the hovercar swung down.

The trip wasn't long—just to another spot on Rhal's estate. The hovercar settled to the ground in front of what appeared to be a caretaker's cottage, lifted up its side door long enough for Jens and the Freeholder to step out, then closed the door and sped off.

The cottage turned out to be almost empty of furniture, but full of people. Not that many, perhaps—his cousin-once-removed, the Master of Nalensey, the crimson-robed Worthy whose name he had never quite caught, a handful of others—but with enough accumulated rank and importance to crowd a much larger room. They were gathered around a large holovid tank, the first one that Jens had seen since his arrival on Khesat. He wondered if the cottage was where Cousin-once-removed Rhal betook himself to indulge in holodramas, cheap factory-made snacks, and other tasteless pleasures.

At the moment, though, the tank showed only a picture of a statue, with a fountain behind it. "I will speak plainly." Rhal's voice came to him above the steady plashing of the water in the holovid. "We had thought to spend some weeks, or months, in search of a Worthy fit to stand before the mobile party. That time is now no longer ours. I have been reliably informed that the Highest is brought low."

So that's the reason for the fountain, Jens thought. *The waters of weeping, all according to good form.*

Jens saw the Freeholder looking directly at him in an unprecedented display of rudeness. Tonight seemed to be the night for aberrant behavior, far beyond that expected of the well-bred. Perhaps it was the crisis that did it.

Rhal continued. "This sudden development renders all our intended stratagems unworkable. We—those of us gathered here—must put forward a plausible candidate at once."

* * *

The morning after Rhal Kasander's official introduction of his Worthy dawned clear and bright. The rain had come to a halt shortly after midnight, and the day bid fair to be unseasonably warm—or so said the weather section in the Galcenian-language *Galactic Intelligencer*, when Miza woke to find the newsfiles and a text-reader lying on her bedside table.

She hadn't thought much of the introductory festivities. The Khesatan Worthies had apparently placed both her and Faral somewhere between servants and poor relations on the social scale, at least until one of the genealogy-mad dowagers had worked it out that the young man from Maraghai was as much a member of the distinguished Rosselin lineage as the cadet-Jessani himself, and that his father's sister's husband was the senior Jessan. After that they hadn't ignored Faral at all, only Miza.

When three Worthy gentlesirs in a row had failed to acknowledge her presence even when she was standing directly in their line of sight, and a fourth—younger and more high-spirited than his fellows—had noticed her only to offer her an hour of light pleasure upon the retiring-cushions, Miza had slipped away and gone back to the private wing. Not long after, as she got into her bed and turned out the light, she'd heard footsteps pass by in the corridor outside as Faral made his way to his room.

Apparently, he hadn't found the party worth staying at without her. Now, in the morning, the thought made her smile. She picked up the *Intelligencer* and began scrolling idly through the sections. She knew, in general, what she was looking for: an address, of sorts, that those who knew the secret could find and use. Huool's training was admirably thorough; Miza knew all the secrets. Halfway down the Select Rental Advertisements page, she found the address she needed, and smiled again.

She finished her morning cha'a and biscuits, then allowed the maid to assist her in dressing—High Khesatan garments, even at the poor-relation level, were more complex affairs than she was used to—and went in search of Faral. She found him in the morning room, where a sideboard held platters of cold meat and warming-trays of poached eggs in case any of Rhal Kasander's guests should feel the need for more sustaining food.

"Where's Jens?" she asked.

"I don't know," Faral said. He added a serving of eggs to his plate. "He's not in his room—I don't think he ever came back to it. Kasander's not around anywhere, either."

She made a face. "More Worthy nonsense. That's all right . . . I've got plans of my own for today."

"What sort of plans?"

"I need to contact Huool back on Ophel," she said. "Let him know I got the two of you where you were going, like he said to do . . . find out what he wants me to do next . . . that sort of thing. But I don't particularly want to use the Exalted's comm set to do it, if you know what I mean."

"Makes sense to me," said Faral. "Whose comm set are you going to use instead?"

"No names," she said. "Let's just say that Huool has exchange agreements with all sorts of, well, entrepreneurial organizations. I've located the contact point for one of them, down in Riverside Park. Want to go sightseeing?"

Mael Taleion was in his newly rented apartment in the Castledown Acres Guesthome in suburban Ilsefret. From the balcony overlooking the river, he could see the Golden Tower rising in the distance deep within the city.

Twenty years ago, the delegation from the homeworlds had come to Khesat to negotiate with the Adept-worlders following the end of the Second War. That delegation had been deliberately free of any person with ties to the Circles. Mael himself had decreed it so.

He had been Second of the Prime Circle then—as he had been since the day Grand Admiral Theio syn-Ricte sus-Airaalin had first chosen him—and it had fallen to him to set the conditions of the treaty team. The new First was a latecomer to the ways of the Great Lords, and she was aware that there was much she did not know.

"I trust you, Mael," she had said. It was the way of Adepts to act alone, and Llannat Hyfid had been Adept-trained before she found her proper teacher; she thought nothing of putting the power to change everything into the hands of one man. *"Act for me in this. Do what is good for the Mageworlds, and do what is honorable."*

Mael had labored to fulfill that commission. Magery altered luck. Therefore Mael had thought it less than honorable to allow Mages to come to Khesat. So far as he knew, he was the only Masked One currently on-planet.

The time had come for him to violate his own rules. "If you will forgive me," he said aloud, addressing the far-distant Llannat. "But I must find the *eiran* and see how life and luck stand in this place."

Mael sat on the sun-dappled balcony and balanced his staff across his knees. Then, without his Circle to support him, without a friend to guide him back should he get lost in the visions, he donned the black mask that was a distinguishing mark of those who saw with more than their eyes.

As the cool breeze from the river fanned him, he closed his eyes and stretched himself forth. Before long, the vision came.

The city was overlaid with Adeptry, so that the silver lines here were tangled and untrimmed. He felt a certain distaste even in looking at it, and had to restrain himself from the temptation to make changes, just small ones, that would set a tiny bit of order amid the sloppiness of this world. It would be so easy to grasp one of the *eiran* and pull it a little more into accord with its neighbors, or set it at a pleasing angle against another behind it. But no—balances are delicate, and to commence a working without the intention of completing it would be immoral, as well as against the conditions he had set that nothing on this world was to be touched.

He allowed himself to wander amid the lines.

Then he saw that all was not random, that a pattern did exist. The lines tended to a point. He stretched out more, to know of this pattern. Was it the power of the universe, creating order from chaos, or was it the work of human hands? He had to know.

He approached it, and looked closer. Here, too, was the tarnish that he had noted on Eraasi, when it had sent him in haste to the First to ask for the guidance—for the permissions—that only she could give. How deep did the corruption run? In this place where the Circles had never held their workings, he dared not touch the line to find an answer. The slightest motion would ruin it all.

The world had gone still around him, in the inner place where he could see the lines. But here in his mind, he heard the sound of footsteps, and knew that they belonged to the *ekkannikh* he had fought against in the Void.

"Look for me on Khesat," it had said, and now it was here.

He turned toward the footsteps, and saw, then, the pattern. The *ekkannikh* stood in the midst of the visionary city, grasping the lines of silver light and twisting them, adding them to a cable made up of many strands—wire ropes like the mooring hawser of sea-ship or the cables of a hanging bridge. Huge it was, as thick through as a man was tall, and it looped out of sight, stretching up into the sky, long enough and strong enough to bind whole worlds. And it was tarnished black all the way through.

"This is what you came here to see, before you die," the *ekkannikh* said. "This is my victory, and my vengeance."

"I will prevent it," Mael said.

"Will you indeed? But you have already lost."

Then, in the way of visions and dreams, the silver lines melted before Mael's eyes. The breeze from the river, so steady that he had taken its permanence for granted, was suddenly gone, sucked into the creature before him and replaced by a debilitating heat. Mael strove to trace the lines before they vanished completely, and to mark in his mind the pathways between them that would lead him home.

Though he sought the paths, he could not find them. He exerted all of his will, but the vision that had always come to him before was gone. He could not see the cords of life. And all around him, the city of his mind had become a desolation of stone.

He turned to leave, to return to the world of waking men and normal vision, but found that he could not remember the way.

Panic rose in him. *Remember,* he commanded himself. *You know this. It's second nature to you—more than that, it's first nature, your true existence. Find the way.*

It was useless. He collapsed with his head in his hands. How much power was it possible for an *ekkannikh* to have?

He already knew the answer. Killed improperly, in the Void, where all time and space are one—its power could have no limits. Did he really seek to fight such a creature?

I have no choice.

That decision made, he felt at once a cool, refreshing breeze spring up. He opened his eyes, and found himself lying on a pad in a dim room, with Klea sitting beside him. The cool breeze was her hand, laid against his forehead.

"Where have you been, Mael?" she asked. "I looked for you, but I couldn't see you anywhere."

"I was searching for something," he replied tiredly. "And finding more than I sought. There is more wrong on this world than politics alone. Someone is working with power in ways that corrupt everything they touch—and there are no Mages on Khesat, except for me, to put it right."

Kolpag and Ruhn sat eating fruit-ices beside the wheeling-path that ran along the eastern waterbank. The morning sun threw sharp white sparkles across the river's blue. A waveskimmer sped by them on its way downstream, throwing up a wake of white froth as it went. The wavelets from its passage spread outward, lapping at the pilings of the rustic boating pier.

Two young people, obviously more interested in each other than in the view of the river, sat on the bench at the end of the pier.

Ruhn looked at them sourly. "I wish those two would get out of here, if we're going to meet our contact."

"Maybe," Kolpag said, between spoonfuls of honeymint ice, "the message we got wasn't really a message. Or maybe it wasn't meant for us."

"You mean that finding the hidden meanings in newspaper advertisements isn't as easy as you made out?"

"Not an exact science, no . . . wait a minute." Kolpag set his paper cup aside on the grass and shaded his eyes with one hand for a closer look. "I think we've seen those two before. Isn't that one of our packages, plus Huool's courier?"

"Son of a bitch," said Ruhn. "All tricked out like nobs, but that's them. You were right."

Kolpag returned to eating his honeymint ice—he'd found that he liked honeymint, and he didn't want to abandon the cup half-finished if the situation should change in a hurry. "The question is, do we snatch them now, and try to pick up the other package later, or do we follow them, see if the other package shows up, and get 'em both at once?"

"Hang on. Someone's going out to meet them now."

"That's not the other package," Kolpag said, as the woman in shop-keeper's garments reached the end of the pier and conferred with the two young people. "Package two is a male and fair-haired."

Package number one and the redheaded female got up from the bench.

"There they go," said Ruhn. "Now what?"

"Follow them, for now." Kolpag stood up and tossed his now-empty ice cup into a recycling basket. "We have to assume that we'll need the hovercar near the Plaza of Hope, another stashed near the Fishcomber's Market, and one more in the Regent's Masqueing-Park. Once we've got a firm posit on those slippery little bastards, we can refine the plan."

Kolpag and Ruhn drifted on foot along the waterbank, doing their best to look like a pair of data clerks on their half-holiday. They kept the two young people and their companion in sight without difficulty until the three of them reached a wheeler-rental establishment on the border of the park and went inside.

"Make a note of this one," Kolpag said, after some time

had passed without any of the three reappearing. "I think we'll need the snatch ship sooner rather than later."

Klea sat back on her heels and regarded Mael Taleion anxiously. She was not familiar enough with the ways of Mages to know whether his collapse was a normal thing or not—but he still looked unwell. And his words had been unsettling.

"There may be no Mages except yourself on Khesat," she said. "But Adepts—yes, there are Adepts."

"I recall the Adepts of Ophel," Mael said. He pushed himself up into a sitting position. "They were . . . interesting."

Klea tightened her lips briefly. "They were that," she said. "Master Owen will be interested indeed, I assure you. That is one planet, and this another. Shall I attempt to see what it is the Adepts of Khesat are doing?"

"If you feel it will do any good," Mael said. "But tell me: when you Adepts look for such things, do you follow the lines of life and luck?"

"Luck doesn't exist," Klea said. "Which makes following it difficult."

"We will not debate the details," Mael said. "Do you see with other eyes, and go to other places, when you meditate?"

"I go there in fact," Klea said, "and the things that I see are real."

Mael nodded wearily. "As you say." He stood, swayed, and walked toward the door. "Shall we go?"

"I'll go," Klea said. "You stay here and rest." She hefted her staff, then slung it across her back on its leather cord. "Wait for me here. If I don't return in a reasonable amount of time . . . well, perhaps I was detained."

She opened the door, and stepped through before Mael could say anything more. Outside, she found the morning streets oddly subdued. A thrill was in the air, as of thousands of voices whispering a long way away. What the news was, she had no idea.

Sooner or later, she knew she would find out. First she had to discover what the Adepts were doing on Khesat, and where—if not in their own Guildhouse—they were doing it.

She had seen no one who carried the staff so far during her time on-planet. That was not unexpected. By all accounts Adepts were not numerous here on Khesat, or highly placed. And Owen had said he'd not heard much from them in a long time.

Only Mages changed the course of events by altering the universe. Adepts found the way the universe was going and went with it. Klea opened herself to the universe, trusting that the same forces which had put her on the liner to Ophel would direct her now in the way that she needed to go. She wandered idly, as the fit took her or the flow of pedestrians moved her, until she found herself at the foot of the Golden Tower.

"Ho, m'lady," said a child—one not out with a nanny or keeper, and therefore of a different order than the tidily dressed tots who rode their cabriolets through the district. "Be here tomorrow?"

He spoke in Galcenian, she thought; or perhaps he spoke in Khesatan and she understood him, even though she didn't have the language. A tingling sensation spread up her back: *This is significant. I must mark it, and learn its meaning.*

"I believe I will be here," she said. "Why?"

"This is yours," the child replied, reaching into a basket and withdrawing a pale-blue envelope. "Cry 'huzzah' and there's more to come, to them's got the seal."

An elaborate red-wax seal did indeed grace the envelope, when Klea accepted it. She walked on, and turned the corner before deciding to open the billet. When she did so, her eyes got large. The envelope held a sizable amount of nontraceable hard-asset credit, payable to "bearer," non-rescindable.

"Lords of Life," Klea said. "I'd be tempted to shout 'huzzah' for that, if I knew what I was applauding for."

The road she followed was taking her close to the Palace of the Jade Eminence, within the center of downtown Ilsefret. She placed the envelope in an inner pocket of her tunic, then stood briefly against a wall and effaced herself. Now that no one would see her, for when she passed by them they would all choose to look away, Klea felt safer. She would find out what was happening.

The guards of the Jade Eminence were not lax, but they did not happen to see when she walked between them. Nor were the silent alarms within the palace less than cunningly hidden, but Klea saw their location as if they glowed, and avoided them.

She walked on until she came to a central courtyard, and found there a casket placed on a heap of aromatic woods, and a man lying in it. She stepped up and laid a hand on his forehead, in order to know him after the Adepts' fashion, and found that the traces of poison tingled on her skin like a dusting of red pepper. It was so subtle that it would be invisible to a toxicological examination—she could sense it only through her extended feelings.

The palace was empty, only one dead man within all its silver and ivory corridors. That was wrong, Klea knew, except in the logic of vision and dream. She continued on, past crystal and carved plaster, past lapis and carnelian. Nothing. No one.

Ahead she saw an object out of place, fallen on the polished marble floor like a thing discarded: an Adept's staff. She picked it up. It, too, tingled with the trace of poison.

"Adepts?" she asked. "No."

But then came a memory of what Owen had told her about times long ago, when Adepts had garnered to themselves the enmity of many worlds by their love of power, and by the means through which they gained it.

She dropped the staff. It clattered to the floor, and the sound melded in her ears with the noise of a passing wheelcart bumping over cobblestones, and the corridor of the palace was instead the sun shining on the white walls of a building she recognized, without surprise, as the Khesatan Guildhouse.

"If luck existed," she told herself, "I'd surely need some now."

She stood debating whether she should enter the building immediately or not. *My only ally a Mage,* she thought, and turned to retrace her path, this time through the real world to where Mael Taleion awaited her return.

" 'O down by the river I met with my love, a-washing white linen on the rocks where it flowed,' " Gentlelady Bindweed sang softly under her breath, as she and her partner exited the Golden Lily Pleasantry Shop, each of them bearing several large, gift-wrapped boxes. "Blossom, we should have visited Khesat long ago."

"An oversight we've mended," Blossom said. "Shall we go back to the hotel?"

"I suppose; then we can find out if there's any news since last night. The whispers this morning were fierce."

Blossom nodded. "Just like the old days, when Jos would come roaring into town and turn everything topsy-turvy."

"So it is," agreed Bindweed. She looked about her at the tree-shaded streets of the riverside shopping district. "It really is a lovely day. Shall we walk?"

"Why not? I didn't pass through fire and the shadow of death to look at the inside of a taxi. I think there's a park on the way. Maybe tiffin from a pushcart?"

"I don't know if they serve tiffin this early around here," Bindweed said. "But something nice might present itself. They said the weather would continue unseasonably warm, but to my old bones, the sun feels nice today. . . ."

They crossed the street and passed through the arched gateway of the park, then continued along the waterbank toward their hotel. The gravel path crunched under their feet; the leaves rustled pleasantly on the quilfer trees; all was serene. A few other pedestrians strolled along the paths, also taking their pleasure in the warm autumn day. Through a gap in the trees appeared a glittering bend of the Leeden River that ran through the heart of downtown Ilsefret.

All at once Bindweed stopped, stuffed her recent purchases into a recycling bin, and said, "Lords of Life."

"What's wrong?" Blossom demanded.

"That pair who just passed us. I don't know who the short

guy is, but the other one I know. The last time I saw him I had him in my sights back at our shop."

"And you missed?"

"He ducked very fast."

Blossom ditched her purchases as well. "Think they recognized you?"

"No—their attention was on something else."

"Not very *talented* talent, indeed," Blossom said. "They may not recognize me at all. I'll stay on them. You go back to the ship and get our blasters. Meet you at the hotel."

XVIII. Khesat

CHAKA HAD been sitting for three days now in the small room in the house of Caridal Fere. When she got tired, which was seldom, she rested, but always there were recordings for her to translate if she could, of what had been said by and around the two boys.

Faral and Jens spoke together very little these days—and not much, when they did, in the Trade-talk of Maraghai—but Chaka was nevertheless learning many interesting things. And she kept written logs of the translations.

Perhaps she was being checked. The servant who had hired her spoke enough Trade-talk to be understood, and to understand in turn if Chaka spoke slowly and simply enough. That one might read the first page, or perhaps the first line, of any translation, and if it matched the recordings well enough, the servant would pass the rest.

At least Chaka hoped the rest would pass without a full reading. When the boys talked, it wasn't always of food or home or old friends. They also spoke of their secret plans and their private opinions of the people around them. Chaka left those parts out. Time enough later to put them down, once she was convinced that it did her friends no harm.

The next question was, did she trust Fere? The automatic answer was no—he had never walked under the Big Trees. And no Forest Lord, to make only the obvious comparison, would stoop to eavesdropping on an honored guest.

The comm link hummed and clicked, and a sound of conversation started up—Jens and Faral, in the house of the Exalted of Tanavral. Chaka reached for her datapad, and began to write:

J: *Where have you been all day?*

F: *Out with Miza, looking for something besides pale sandwiches to eat. They've got tiffin carts down by the river, you know.*

J: *There was haunch of something-or-other in frillfruit puree at dinner. And the chef made something else that Cousinonce-removed Rhal said were authentic Maraghai-style groundgrubs. But they weren't really.*

Then the tone of Faral's voice changed, as if he'd only then noticed something. He said, *They've come up with a plan for your future, haven't they? That's where you were, all last night,* and Chaka decided not to write that down for right now, since she couldn't tell which way it was going.

And Jens said, *The Highest is dead. And the Exalted Rhal Kasander has grown disillusioned with the Worthy whom he first intended to see elevated. He's picked out someone else instead.*

There was a pause. *You?*

That's right.

We can get to a ship tonight, and be long gone by dawn, Faral said at once. *Unless you want to risk getting spattered all over the plaza?*

I can't refuse the public Acclamation until I'm sure Mamma and Dadda are safe, Jens said. *If I refuse, and they're being held prisoner . . .*

Now Chaka was glad she wasn't writing things down.

Caridal Fere's friend Rhal Kasander—Jens's cousin-once-removed, who went by the absurd thin-skin title of the

Exalted of Tanavral—entered the room just as the conversation switched back to grilled grubworms. Chaka kept on writing. Kasander came and went almost as often as Caridal Fere himself; the two men were close as blood-brothers.

"Well?" Kasander demanded. The Exalted's slipper-bearer came over to Chaka's desk and retrieved the datapad. Kasander viewed the private conversation, then threw down the datapad onto the floor, cracking the screen beyond hope of repair.

"Do those two think of nothing but their stomachs?" he demanded. "If they aren't eating, then they're arranging to be eating, or else they're discussing great meals from the past. Groundgrubs! Pfah! The cook couldn't even palm off the leftovers on the underservants!"

The Exalted strode from the room, gone before Chaka could react to the loss of her datapad. Well, there were still scraps of paper around. She'd use those.

And what the Exalted didn't know was not Chaka's problem. She had enough problems without that.

By nightfall in Ilsefret the whole city lay quiet with anticipation of the coming morning. The funeral of a Highest brought down by time and circumstance would keep until a later day; tomorrow's Acclamation, though, would see whether Khesat would be holding the rites for one Highest, or for two. On a few past occasions—or so Faral had learned from the historical-background section of the *Intelligencer*— the populace of Ilsefret had run through as many as five or six Highests before settling the issue.

The *Intelligencer* had not identified the candidate for Acclamation; such premature revelation would go against Khesatan custom and tradition. Faral had no doubt that the people in Ilsefret knew, through gossip and rumor and the same kind of veiled hints in the public newsfiles that had shown Miza how to find her contact with Huool. But nobody off-planet would have a suspicion of the truth until it was too late.

Faral had tried to make contact with Maraghai anyway—

surely there was something that the First of All the Mage-Circles could do about what was going on—but he had discovered that the comm setup in Kasander's guest wing had no access to the hyperspace links. Neither did the public kiosks.

If I'd known about the problem when I woke this morning, he thought, *I could have asked Miza to pass on a message through her contact with Huool. Now it's too late.*

Then a thought came to him. Rhal Kasander was an important man on Khesat, hip-deep in politics and intrigue. There was no way that he would not allow himself, at least, the use of the hyperspace links.

All I have to do is find the Exalted's personal comm setup. After that . . . if I could cheat the console for the force fields back home, I can get through whatever Kasander's got. And I'll bet I know where he keeps it, too.

Having something concrete to do gave Faral new optimism. He didn't wait any longer, but left his room in the guest wing and made his way through the halls to the private study of the Exalted of Tanavral.

The study was empty. To Faral's chagrin, a quick but efficient search didn't uncover anything like a full comm setup. Kasander had one somewhere, that much was obvious. He had a transfer link resting in plain sight on his desktop—but the link had an ID scanner built into the grip, and the master control console was nowhere that Faral could see.

I could find it if I had a day or two. But I don't. If only I'd started looking sooner . . .

A stack of folded cards lay on the desktop beside the useless transfer link—party invitations, Faral supposed, awaiting formal signature. If the Exalted of Tanavral turned out in the morning to have backed an acclaimed Highest, he would certainly be holding another party tomorrow night. And after the amount of money Jens claimed that the Exalted and his faction had already laid out in bribes, the Acclamation was only a formality.

I wish I really believed that, thought Faral. He picked up the topmost invitation.

It was written in Khesatan, of course, but Faral had expected that. He hadn't expected *not* to see the one scrap of the language that he did recognize in its written form—his foster-brother's name.

Is Kasander abandoning his own candidate? Or is calling an acclaimed Highest by his old name an insult or something?

Jens would know. Faral tucked the invitation into his jacket pocket.

Footsteps sounded in the hall outside the study. He looked around in a panic—Jens could smooth-talk himself out of being caught snooping, but Jens wasn't here—and saw the heavy velvet curtains that hung across the office window. He ducked behind them just as the door of the study opened.

As a place of concealment, his position was traditional but effective. An eavesdropper not trained in hunting by the Selvaurs of Maraghai might have ruined everything by fidgeting, or by breathing too loudly, but Faral had lain in wait for a passing fanghorn while the bloodflies crawled across his bare shoulders. Standing motionless behind a curtain was easy.

With his eye pressed against the hairline opening between the folds of velvet, he could see most of the room. The man who entered was one he recognized from the entertainment of the night before: Gerre Hafelsan, a gentlesir of respectable lineage with a taste for flamboyant tailoring, but not, or so Faral had gathered, one of the Exalted's intimates or a member of his faction. But here he was, unannounced.

Strange stuff is going on, Faral thought. *If the Exalted turns up and Hafelsan wants to hide behind a curtain, I'm in big trouble.*

But Rhal Kasander entered almost in Hafelsan's shadow, carrying a tray of jellied grass-mallow in his own hands.

No servants in sight. Even stranger.

For the next three-quarters of an hour, the two men conversed in light and bantering Khesatan, and tried a flute duet which Faral found pretty but sinister. Then, after bowing to one another, they left.

Faral wished he knew what the two of them had really been talking about. He still had the invitation in his pocket—Jens would be able to read the Khesatan script, and maybe even explain what the Exalted of Tanavral was up to, playing flute duets in private with a political adversary.

After counting two hundred heartbeats, Faral left the concealment of the curtains and stepped silently to the door. He waited again, but no sound telling of a watcher came from outside.

He stepped briskly into the corridor, and headed for the wing in which he and Jens were housed.

Miza couldn't sleep. She tried more covers and fewer; she piled the pillows into a stack and spread them out again; she tried leaving the light on and turning it off. Nothing worked. She looked at the clock on her bedside table. It didn't help; it was an antique, and told only the local hours.

No way of telling how many Standard hours we have left until dawn.

After a while she got up. Jens Metadi-Jessan's cousin-once-removed the Exalted of Tanavral had supplied her with an ample wardrobe, including a white silk sleeping-gown and a night-robe of deep green velvet. She put on the night-robe, tied its sash around her waist, and ventured out cautiously into the upper corridors of Rhal Kasander's town house.

No servants were in sight, which was good. Miza wasn't used to servants at all—on Artha, people did for themselves what needed to be done, or else programmed robots to do it. Nor had Huool been the kind to hire others for menial tasks. For that he had student interns, who themselves paid good money for the privilege.

Moving quietly, Miza went on down the hall to the extensive suite of rooms that Kasander had assigned to Jens. The door wasn't locked; locks would be impractical in a house where servants came and went with full hands at all hours.

She opened the door no farther than necessary, and slipped in through the gap. There was nobody in the darkened outer chamber, nor in the changing room.

As she had half-expected, light showed around the edges of the bedroom door. She knocked, tentatively, and waited for an answer.

"Come on in." It was Jen's voice.

She entered and let the door close itself behind her. Jens's room was twice as large as the one she'd been given, and even more exquisitely decorated. The bed alone, with its tapestry hangings and high, arched canopy, was almost as big as the cabin the three of them had shared back on the *Dusty*; the padded crate in which they'd made their escape from Ophel would have covered no more than a corner of the mattress. The light she'd seen came from a shaded reading-glow on the bedside table. It cast a pool of stark white light onto the pillows at the head of the bed and threw the far corners of the room into darkness.

Jens wasn't reading, though. As far as she could tell, he never had been. No text reader stood on the bedside table, and no print-on-paper material either. He lay gazing up at the underside of the canopy, and Miza saw at once that he was at least as wakeful as she had been. He turned as she came in and propped himself up on one elbow to look at her.

"Gentlelady Lyftingil," he said. "What brings you in here at this hour?"

He's only got the light on because he doesn't want to lie there by himself in the dark, Miza thought. The realization strengthened her resolve.

"I couldn't sleep," she said.

"Faral's room is down at the other end of the hall."

She felt herself reddening—the curse of a fair complexion. "It's not *that!*"

"Ever my misfortune," he sighed, and lay back again on the pillows. The leather-and-bone necklace he'd gotten from the oracle on Sapne lay against the golden-tanned skin of his chest. "What, then?"

"It's . . . tomorrow morning they do the Golden Tower thing—"

"I am not precisely ignorant of the fact. Believe me."

"—and I couldn't get to sleep for thinking that I ought to apologize to you tonight, just in case—"

"Right. Just in case I hit the pavement with a resounding splat and render the question of apologies completely moot."

"Stop that!" she said. "You haven't even asked me what I came in here to apologize to you *for*."

He closed his eyes. "All right. What was it?"

"A bad idea, I think." She turned to go.

"No—wait!" He sat up abruptly and held out a hand. "I'm the one who ought to be saying I'm sorry, for talking to you this way. It's no way for anyone to act, the night before they—"

"Everything is going to be all right," she said. "The Exalted said so. He's spent piles of money making sure."

"So has everybody else. And there's never been any way of making sure that the bribed stay bribed." Jens laughed without mirth. "And if they do . . . then I'm stuck with being the Highest of Khesat for the next fifty or a hundred years, which probably isn't as painful as diving headfirst onto a marble pavement, but it lasts a whole lot longer."

He sounded unhappy, which wasn't surprising. She sat down on the edge of the bed next to him—all the chairs were off in the dark corners of the room—and said, "What will Faral do if they make you the Highest?"

"Go home to Maraghai," he said. "If helping a friend ascend to the Jade Eminence counts as gaining enough fame for an allowable return."

"It certainly ought to," she said. "But that's one of the things I wanted to say I was sorry about."

"Faral?"

She nodded. "Things haven't been easy between the two of you ever since we left Sapne, and I'm afraid that it's all my fault."

"No, it isn't." She could see a faint flush of embarrassment spreading along his cheekbones and down his neck to his bare chest. "It's mine, for being jealous."

"The next Highest of Khesat, jealous?"

He gave her a crooked smile. "Gauche, isn't it? If the

Council knew about it, do you think they'd find somebody else to haul up to the top of the Golden Tower?"

"You could always ask them," Miza said.

"If I thought it would do any good ... but no friends of mine are on the Council, just allies of Kasander's."

She looked down at her hands. "That's the other thing I meant to say I was sorry about."

"That I don't have any allies on the Council?"

"No. I'm sorry I was the one who made your friend Guislen go away. I didn't mean to do it. Will you forgive me?"

"If you'll forgive me," he said. He smiled and reached out a hand to take hers, free-spacer fashion, as he had with Captain Amaro back in the *Dusty*'s hold. "Done?"

She smiled back at him and met his grip. "Done."

The more Faral thought about what he had witnessed in Kasander's study, the less he liked it. By the time he entered the guest wing, he was almost running, with the invitation out of his pocket and ready in his hand. He ran through the darkened outer rooms of Jens's suite and up to the bedroom door, knocked perfunctorily once to warn of his approach, and pushed the door open.

The room was lighted, and Jens was lying in the bed.

"Jens," Faral began, "there's something ..."

Then he faltered. Someone else was on the bed beside Jens—Miza, with her red hair down and loose over the shoulders of her robe. Their hands were clasped, and she was smiling.

"Oh," Faral said, turned, and shut the door behind him.

He walked down the carpeted passageway to his own quarters, unable to see clearly for the dark cloud hanging in front of his eyes. He felt like he'd been kicked in the guts, and all his assorted viscera removed and replaced by cold swamp water with bugs in it. He held the cream-colored invitation from Rhal's study in his hand, crumpling it into a tiny ball as his hand worked without his direct control.

A patter of light footsteps, running, came from behind him.

He stopped and turned as a hand touched his arm. It was Miza.

"Faral," she said. "It isn't what you think—"

"Then what would it be?" Faral asked and turned away, pulling himself from her grasp. He resumed walking.

"Faral, please!"

Faral ignored her and continued walking. He went on to the darkened library all the way at the end of the hall. He sat at a polished table, not bothering to turn on the light, and watched out the window as the vornatch trees blew in the dark winds of the estate.

A while later, Jens knocked on the door and entered, wearing a formal robe of black silk and silverthread, patterned with lilies. Without speaking, he laid a long, handwritten letter on the table beside Faral, then turned and left. Faral took the letter, and tore it into tiny pieces, unread, without looking away from the vornatch trees.

And that was where the servants of the Exalted of Tanavral found Faral in the predawn hours, when it came his time to rise and enter the City, there to view from the windows of Caridal Fere his cousin's enlargement.

Mistress Klea Santreny and Mael Taleion left the Castledown Acres Guesthome in the predawn light.

"I need to go to the Khesatan Guildhouse," Klea said, "to see if any messages are waiting for me—and to send some messages of my own."

Mael looked at her curiously. "And for this you require my presence?"

"At the moment," Klea said, "I only trust one person on this world other than myself. If that person is a Mage ... well, Master Rosselin-Metadi had misgivings about the Khesatan Adepts, and if what I saw yesterday has any value, I think I share them."

"I have, in my own way, seen things which give me pause," Mael said. "It is not your Guild that causes the harm, but a vengeful ghost."

"Maybe. But I don't think that we've got helpless innocents

in the Guildhouse of Ilsefret, either. If the Adepts on Khesat have betrayed their vows—to seek always the common good, to do no ill—then they will answer for it."

Together they set out for the Guildhouse—listed in all the guidebooks and street maps as standing in Higedon Street, not far from the Clockmakers' Tower. Before long Klea and Mael stood on the sidewalk in front of the gates, in a chill morning fog that seemed to come from the very stones of the plaza.

"To enter such a place," said Mael, "still grieves me."

"You survived the experience once before. Being an Adept isn't catching."

"Very well." Mael settled his mask over his face, then stepped up to the door and struck the heavy ring-shaped knocker three times against the solid brass plate beneath.

The door did not open, nor did some sleepy-eyed apprentice come tardily to answer it.

"Perhaps the Adepts of Khesat sleep late," Mael said.

"All of them?" Klea laid her hand upon the door knocker, then let the ring drop from her hand with a boom that echoed clear across the street. She grimaced. "They believe in serious door knockers in this town. Where do you suppose everyone is?"

"This morning they elevate the Highest," Mael said. "I heard it on the early news at the Guesthome."

Klea's skin prickled. "Did you hear a name?"

"If they gave one," Mael said, "it was not in the news that they make files of for outworlders."

Klea shrugged. "What a curious place," she said. "Well, Master Owen has entrusted to me the charge of keeping his nephews safe, and it is my opinion that they were planning to come to this world. To keep them safe requires the help of the Guild. Messages may have come for me from Master Owen, and they would have come here. . . ."

"What are you nerving yourself up to do?"

"This," Klea said. She unshipped her staff from its thong along her back and held it up in both hands.

"I am the representative of Owen Rosselin-Metadi," she said, "and in my place, he would do *this*!"

The staff blazed up blue-green in her hands, and she struck the lockplate with the end of it, driving forward with her shoulders. The doors bowed inward for an instant, then rebounded out, springing open in the process. Klea grabbed the knocker by its ring and pulled, opening the door a bit wider for her to enter.

"Somehow," Mael said, "I think Master Rosselin-Metadi would have been more subtle."

"I know him better than that," Klea said, stepping in through the gap. "Are you coming?"

Mael followed Klea into the antechamber, then paused while she closed and re-locked the door. "The Adepts here may consider this to have been an unfriendly act."

"My motives are pure," Klea said. "Come on."

The antechamber could have been located nowhere else except on Khesat: the tastefully understated furniture; the tiny glowing gems set into the walls at unexpected angles to form patterns of subtlety and grace; the faintest hint of perfume on the air.

"This way, I think," Klea said.

She went up a short flight of marble steps, and turned left down a corridor. The corridor opened onto a stone cloister that surrounded a severe rock garden open to the sky.

"No one here," she said. "Something is very wrong."

"I agree," Mael said, and unclipped his short staff. "This place is dead."

In the small plain room at the base of the Golden Tower, Jens Metadi-Jessan D'Rosselin stood in the midst of the members of the Court of Raising, with the Presenter of the Highest before him. Jens had already removed his sable and silver morning-robe, and wore only the plain white and black of an Unacclaimed. The leather and bone necklace from the Sapnean oracle lay against his skin underneath the loose cambric of his shirt.

"Your pardon," said the Presenter, as two burly fellows in

the mauve livery of the Council of Worthies approached Jens and confined his wrists behind him in stout metal binders.

Jens raised an eyebrow. "Are those truly necessary?"

"After the unfortunate circumstances surrounding the Raising of Finuale the Sixth," the Presenter said, his expression sad under his shaven brows, "they have been customary. They will be removed on the platform, if the cry is 'huzzah.'

"As I have no doubt it will be," he added, with a twitch that might have been a smile.

"Suppose I wished to flap my arms the whole way down?"

"Waferan Elderos already did that. You wouldn't want to appear a mere imitator, would you?"

"I suppose not," Jens said. He turned to the spiral stairway. "Let's get going. Dawn isn't going to wait."

"One matter more." The Presenter ran his hands rapidly over Jens's body. "Once, not too long ago, someone brought along a parachute."

Jens suppressed the nervous laugh that would otherwise have become a hysterical giggle before he could make himself stop. He drew a deep breath.

"I understand," he said. "Shall we?"

He nodded to the stairway. The Presenter nodded back. Jens led, with the guards a step farther behind, and the Presenter following the entire procession.

It wouldn't be so hard, Jens thought, *if I didn't have to lead the way. This is probably another one of those hidden tests of character. Rhal Kasander has promised that the crowd is well bribed. Everything's in order. He says.*

Each time they completed a circuit of the spiral they passed another fretwork window. The sky outside was growing light.

Dawn soon. When the sun touches the golden dome, then . . . well, no choice now. One way or another, I'm the Highest of Khesat. I wonder if the wrinkleskins on Maraghai will count that as fame?

There was the platform, surrounded by a waist-high stone railing, the arch above it wrought with cunningly carved leaves to look like a garden bower. Jens stepped through, and walked directly to the edge and looked out over Ilsefret. The streets were crowded as far as he could see, the Plaza of Hope obscured by close-set, upturned faces. Only the square of marble paving at the very base of the tower remained clear. There were stains on the marble from other Raisings, stains that had soaked into the stone and never washed out.

The fronts of the buildings around the plaza were still shadowed. He tried to make out the windows of Caridal Fere. Two figures, dark in silhouette against the lights within, stood in an embrasure. It was too far and too dark for him to see clearly. Faral and Miza, though, they had to be.

"Well, coz," Jens said quietly, "now we come to the final parting."

The two fellows in livery walked forward. They were pleasant-enough-looking lads, although they both seemed nervous.

Probably never threw a Highest from a golden tower before, Jens thought.

"Whatever happens," he said, still quietly, "I have no grudge against you for this."

The two nodded, showing that they heard, but they wouldn't meet his eyes. The Presenter leaped up onto a stone platform at the right of the archway and turned to view the top of the Tower.

"Watching for the light?" Jens asked.

"Yes," the Presenter said.

Jens craned his neck around to look at the Tower. The golden tip of the spire was brightening, catching the rising sun and throwing it forth again in a dazzle of reflected light.

"Are you ready?" the Presenter asked.

Jens considered. "I suppose I am."

"Then it's time."

The Presenter turned to the crowd below, and in a voice of iron, so loud that Jens could scarcely believe it came from so small a man, he called, "Behold the Highest!"

And from below came a sound, a growl at first, unintelligible. But it grew louder, and the voices began to chant in chorus, so that the words were plain.

"Bring him low! Bring him low!"

XIX. KHESAT

FARAL STOOD at the window of Caridal Fere's apartment overlooking the Plaza of Hope, his shoulder braced against the embrasure. The sky was dark in the west, behind the Golden Tower. The plaza below was filled with a mass of humanity, shoulder to shoulder, jammed together. A low muttering rose from them, the combined sound of hundreds—thousands—of whispered conversations.

Miza stood at the other side of the window, looking miserable. She wore a long white gown that Faral would otherwise have thought was becoming. He was still angry with her, and there was a cold feeling in the pit of his stomach whenever he looked in her direction.

"I was apologizing to him," she said into the silence. It was the first thing she'd said to Faral since the servants of Caridal Fere had left them alone at the window.

It wasn't what Faral had expected to hear. "You were . . ."

"I didn't think I'd get another chance." She drew a shaky breath, and he realized that she had been crying not long before. "So I went to say I was sorry for naming Errec Ransome's ghost and sending it away, and for . . . well, for me and you."

Faral shook his head, not understanding. "For me and you?"

"Because I'd come between him and one friend already." Faral glanced at her. She gave a wavery half-smile. "And he said he was sorry for being jealous, and we agreed to forgive each other. And we shook hands on it."

"Oh," said Faral, feeling numb. Now it was too late.

He turned back to the window. The sky had grown noticeably lighter in the last few minutes. He could see, a long way off at the other side of the plaza and hundreds of feet above him, some motion amid the shadows under the golden dome.

The people below saw it too. The crowd quieted. Faral could feel the tension as they looked up at the little group standing so high above.

Then the spire at the top of the Golden Tower blazed with the reflected light of the rising sun. At the same moment, a voice cried out, echoing off the housefronts, ringing out in spite of the distance:

"Behold the Highest!"

"Huzzah!" Faral shouted in reply. The servants of Caridal Fere had explained the ritual to him—the words of the Presenter and the words that the crowd would shout in reply. "Huzzah!"

He shouted as loud as he could. He could hear Miza shouting huzzah as well. But then it came to him, the people in the crowd weren't shouting huzzah at all. They were crying out, in rhythmic chorus, "Bring him low!"

Miza drew a sharp breath and turned to Faral. She took a step toward him, holding out her arms. At that same moment, a figure fell from the tower, four hundred feet down, and landed with a sodden crack on the stones below.

Faral was already moving, leaving Miza to follow after him. He strode back through the private apartments, to the inner rooms, then across to the other windows.

He stepped through the door. There was Rhal Kasander,

there was Caridal Fere, there was Gerre Hafelsan in another of his highly colored morning-robes.

"You!" Faral said, seeing Gerre.

"Yes," Hafelsan replied. "That *was* well done, wasn't it?"

The voices from the Plaza of Hope sounded in Jens's ears like the roar of the sea.

"Bring him low! Bring him low!"

The two men in the livery of the Council of Worthies stepped forward. Jens waited, expecting at any instant to feel the grip of their hands on his body, and then the lifting and the sudden descent. . . . *I wonder if Cousin-once-removed Rhal was lying all the time about the bribes? . . .*

Then, like an arrow of fire, a blaster bolt came sizzling out of the archway at the top of the stairs. It struck the nearer of the two men in livery, dropping him with his hand only an inch away from Jens's shoulder. Before the body hit the floor of the tower, another bolt took out his fellow.

The shooter stepped forward. "I have my orders," he said to Jens, "and they're to bring you back."

Jens stared. If this was a reprieve, it was like nothing he could have imagined. "And who the hell are *you*?"

The man stepped forward and grabbed Jens's shoulder. "I'm Kolpag. My partner's Ruhn. And we've got orders."

Before he had finished speaking, the Presenter leapt from his platform out of sight beyond the stone archway, and came down with all his weight on Kolpag's back. Kolpag twisted under the smaller man and heaved him outward, over the railing, to fall into the crowd below.

Then Kolpag turned back to Jens. "You're coming with us to Ophel," he said, and shoved him through the archway.

Jens fell awkwardly onto the landing at the top of the spiral stairs, where another man was waiting— *This one must be Ruhn,* he thought. *But why do they want me on Ophel?*

"Everything arranged below?" Kolpag asked.

"I sure hope so," Ruhn replied. "Let's get this little bastard out of here. The longer I stay on this planet the more it makes my teeth hurt."

Kolpag turned to Jens. "Stand up. I'm going to take those leg irons off of you, so you can move quicker. But if you do anything at all besides what we tell you, I'll stun you and carry you. It's all the same to me. Ready to go?"

Jens pulled himself to his feet, encumbered by the wrist binders and the hobble chain. Kolpag worked on the locks of the hobble briefly, and took it off.

As soon as Jens felt the links fall away from him, he turned and sprinted for the stairway. If he could only get out of sight around the first curve ... A stinging blast took him in the spine and he fell limp to the stone floor.

"That's a quarter stun," Kolpag said. "Higher power hurts more. Don't do anything stupid again."

No one is going to believe that I didn't arrange for this myself, Jens thought as he was dragged backward down the stairs, the heels of his slippers bouncing on each tread as they went.

"I think we've lost them," Bindweed said.

She and Blossom stood at the edge of Ilsefret's main plaza, beneath the historic Golden Tower. They had been waiting there, blasters fully charged and discreetly concealed, ever since watching the two men from the Green Sun enter the Tower some hours earlier. That had happened while the streets were still dark, before the plaza had started to fill with pedestrians, and neither of the two operatives had come out again later—though there was no telling, Bindweed had to admit, about things like back doors and underground passageways.

"Maybe," said Blossom. "But whatever's going to happen here looks like it might be interesting—I think this is the Acclamation of the Highest that we saw mentioned." She broke off and pointed. "Look there."

"Where?"

"Behind us—see that window, third from the right, past the arch? Who does that look like?"

Bindweed looked. "Hard to see with the light behind them,

but from the shoulders on him I think it's Faral Hyfid-Metadi."

"And the other one is Miza from Huool's," said Blossom. "But no Jens. I don't like *that* at all. Not when our friends from the Green Sun were trying their clumsy best to snatch him and his cousin both out of our shop."

"No," said Bindweed. "It isn't good."

She and her partner remained silent, watching. After a few minutes she glimpsed what might have been movement up at the top of the Golden Tower. A figure in white and black, his fair hair showing plainly in the predawn light, stepped into view above the tower railing.

"Blossom," said Bindweed quietly. "I think I've got a fix on Jens."

The crowd fell silent in anticipation. The sun rose, the first spear of light passing high above and striking the tip of the Tower. A voice lifted above the plaza, calling out a phrase in Khesatan.

A low grumble rose from the crowd, a steady, rhythmic chanting, growing louder and louder. Then there came another sound, in a language that Bindweed knew very well indeed.

"Karpov '75 blaster," she shouted at Blossom over the noise of the crowd. "Open-bell model, firing full-power bursts!"

"That's what I thought," her partner shouted back. "It's coming from the Tower. Let's go."

They started forward. The crowd slowed them—nobody was moving out of the way of a pair of elderly tourists, not today. Before they could reach the foot of the tower the crowd roared out, and a white-clad figure came hurtling from the balcony. Then, in spite of themselves, Bindweed and Blossom were surging forward with the rest of the crowd toward the point of impact.

Soon enough they came in view of the body. The white robes it had worn were crimson now. Members of the crowd were lining up to dip their handkerchiefs in the rivulets of blood that flowed from the broken body. The partners looked at each other.

"That's not Jens," Bindweed said.

"Right. Which means that he needs a backup."

"No." Bindweed put her hand on her partner's arm. "We can't go inside the Tower. We'd be trapped, and in no position to help anyone."

Blossom's cheeks were bright red with frustration. "Where then?"

"The Green Sun men spent most of yesterday stashing hovercars near this plaza," said Bindweed. "You cover one, I'll cover another, and we'll see what comes of it."

The underground parking area near the Golden Tower was large and echoing, its roof supported by stout pillars and lit with overhead tubes. The walls were made of stone, intricately carved in arabesques and patterns of stylized fish and worms. When Jens had seen them for the first time that morning, arriving by hovercar from the town house of the Exalted of Tanavral, he'd thought the carvings a gruesome conceit. Now, as he was dragged past them with the effect of the quarter stun barely starting to wear off, he found them even less appealing.

He had no illusions about his future. He might have been saved from a collision at high speed with the plaza's historic bloodstained marble, but his time was limited none the less. His captors had made no attempt to hide their faces, or to conceal their names—they knew, then, that he would not be living long enough to identify them. Whatever fate awaited him on Ophel would not be pleasant.

They were dragging him to a parked hovercar. One of them—Kolpag, the blaster man—slid into the driver's position and switched the machine on. It rose, humming, on its nullgravs, and hung there vibrating gently.

The other man shoved Jens into onto the front seat beside the driver. Jens fell heavily backward onto his bound wrists, and the man who had dumped him—Ruhn, if the driver was

Kolpag—started to walk back to the rear passenger compartment, where he would sit behind Jens.

Time to go out with style, Jens thought; *now or never*—and smashed his left foot sideways into the driver's ribs.

Kolpag lost his breath in an explosive whuff and fell partway out of his still-open door—twisting the hovercar's control yoke to the left and dragging it all the way out to reverse as he went down. The car spun backward and to the right with startling speed, increasing its angular velocity as it pivoted. The side of the hovercar took Ruhn in mid-body, crushing him between the vehicle's mass and the unyielding granite of the wall. An explosion of blood flew from the man's mouth and spattered the window above Jens's head.

Jens drew back his legs and kicked again. This time he knocked Kolpag entirely out of the vehicle. Jens kicked the control yoke with the right side of his foot to put the hovercar back into forward motion.

His hands were bound behind him, which wasn't going to make controlling the vehicle any easier. At least the car was powered up and hovering, or he'd never be able to make it.

He squirmed and twisted to get himself up and sitting in the driver's position. He raised his knees. By hitting the bottom edge of the control yoke he could steer the hovercar to right and left.

A blaster shot took out the rear windscreen, and a second shot plowed up a furrow along the roof.

So his captor was up and moving—and, more important, shooting. Jens snapped his left knee up to hit the bottom left side of the control yoke. The vehicle twisted right, but with plenty of forward momentum still on it. A pillar loomed up— the hovercar slipped by, but the pillar clipped the open door, ripping it off with a loud bang. The car shuddered but continued on.

Wind whipped through Jen's unbound hair. He'd lost the ribbon that held it somewhere on the stairway going down, at about the same time as he'd acquired a cut on his face that stung and dripped salty fluid past his mouth. He wanted to slow the hovercar—or at least to have that option—but without the use of his hands he lacked the leverage needed to pull back the yoke and decrease speed. He could lean forward, perhaps, and increase his velocity, but other than that his choices were limited.

He was coming out of the underground parking area now. Daylight showed ahead and to the left. He smashed his right knee up to put the car into a screaming left turn. It broadsided a parked duo-van before it came straight again.

I think I'm starting to get the knack of this.

The exit from the garage was just ahead. He steered smaller, lining up his departure. It was up a ramp—Jens could see buildings beyond the sunny gap. A right turn, he figured, on the way out.

The hovercar scraped pavement all along its bottom when it hit the foot of the ramp, and went completely airborne at the top. Jens lost sight of the ground—he couldn't see anything but the onrushing building ahead. He pushed up on the yoke with his left knee, and leaned his right shoulder down against the other of the yoke to press it down farther.

When the car hit the ground again the impact jolted through him—from the seat, from the yoke, from every point of his body that was in contact with a solid part of the car. Then the side vector took effect and he felt the car slew to the right. He was almost thrown out through the missing door by the centrifugal force of his turn.

He braced himself and rode it out, allowing his head to come up at the finish to see where he was and where he was going. He saw a broad boulevard—not much traffic, not many pedestrians. *Everybody must still be over in the plaza,* he thought, *trying to soak the hems of their garments in the spattered Highest.*

Then he glanced behind him. Another hovercar was exiting the garage, coming up behind him fast. Capture or worse had been delayed—but not, perhaps, for long.

Chaka was again on duty in the listening room, though it was barely dawn and none of her employers had seen fit to order her attention. On this day, at least, she had reasons of her own for listening.

So far, she had heard nothing of interest. It seemed that no one had been able to, or had thought it necessary to, put a listening device in Jens's new clothing—when he changed garments in preparation for his Acclamation, the ambient noise became that of a clothes hamper, and his voice was heard no more.

Faral, however, was in one of the front rooms here in the house of Caridal Fere, speaking in Galcenian to the redheaded female. They had quarreled, it seemed, and now were restoring their friendship. Without Jens present a word in Trade-talk would be unlikely.

Chaka let herself relax a little, thinking of Jens and his current situation. He had certainly found fame, though of a kind which was unlikely to let him return to the high ridges and the Big Trees. Or maybe not. Both his mother and his grandmother had renounced a crown, and had gained considerable fame thereby. Jens could do something equally unlikely.

A change in air pressure told Chaka that the door at the end of the hall had opened. A smell of perfume mixed with anxiety floated in. The Selvaur remained seated. Someone was approaching, and that someone was trying to be stealthy. It occurred to her, not for the first time since the start of her employment, that persons who hired an unlicensed translator from a transient ship might well have reason for disposing of that translator afterward.

Faral's voice came through the speaker of the listening device. "Huzzah! Huzzah!"

At the same time, a woman stepped into the doorway. She wore plain livery—somebody's servant, then. Chaka observed her without turning, following her reflection in the sheet of glass fronting an ornate arrangement of pressed dried flowers.

The woman in the glass raised a blaster, aiming it at Chaka.

The Selvaur rose, sidestepped, and as part of the same motion picked up her chair and hurled it across the room. The item of furniture struck the woman just as she shot, knocking the blaster aside. She fell, and the bolt went wide.

Chaka leapt across the room and, with one taloned hand, grasped the woman's right hand, the one that held the blaster, and pulled. The arm came off.

Find another translator, Chaka said, straightening as she extracted the blaster from the limp fingers. *Your old one just quit.*

Holding the weapon awkwardly—it had not been designed for a Selvaur's grasp at all—the young saurian loped down the hallway, dodged through the door, and made her way toward the front windows of the house of Caridal Fere.

Klea and Mael walked the through silent, polished halls of the Adepts' Guildhouse in Ilsefret. Nothing but echoes responded to their voices, and their feet made the only other sounds within the walls.

"Mistress," Mael said, "I fear that this place has been long deserted."

"Never inhabited, you mean," Klea said. "Come here and look at this." She was standing in the doorway of a library. "Books, scrolls, readers, and pads. What do you see?"

"Records, I suppose. The secrets of the order?"

"Nothing," Klea said. "Look!" She pulled one of the books at random from the shelf at her left hand. She opened it and riffled the pages. "Blank. Empty."

"All of them?"

"Every single one I looked at. From the oldest to the newest. This is a stage set. A sham."

"Where, then, are the Adepts of Khesat?"

"Hidden. I'm sure that hundreds of witnesses see Adepts entering and leaving this building every day. They don't stay here. So where do they go?"

"Are you proposing that we tap on the walls, Mistress, to seek the hidden door?"

"Something like that," Klea said. "It won't be a path that many can find. But in here, somewhere, is an answer to all our questions."

"If you can find it."

"I think that I can." Klea shut her eyes and relaxed. Such mental wandering had been her gift ever since Owen had found her years ago—untrained, and afraid she was going mad. The past and the future were locked to her. But the present she could see. And this time, when she looked, she found a trail, and the signs that marked out a pathway between the smallest particles of matter that made up the measurable world.

"There are markers," Klea said. "Like the pebbles beneath the surface of a pool. Like stones that can be grasped. They will lead us through."

This part of the hall was dead. The passages that continued had none of the vibrancy that went with passing life. Klea turned back down the passage in the direction they had come.

"Under the stones of the rock garden?" Mael asked, hastening to catch up.

"No, no," Klea said. "That one's a trap. The right place is somewhere else. . . ."

She came to the passage leading to the foyer and the street. With the coming day, the sky was growing light beyond the high stained-glass windows above the door. Deep red splashes fell onto the floor of the lobby, making it look more like an abattoir than like the reception room of a powerful and respected Guild.

The gems set in the entry wall twinkled at her.

"Those aren't stones," Klea said. "They're the marks. They tell those trained in power the way to go."

"Mistress, what are you talking about?"

"Those," she said, and pointed at the glowing patterns.

Mael shook his head. "That's the sunlight coming in through the window."

"Don't you see? Here!"

Klea pushed her hands forward against the cold strength of the wall, the painted plaster over stone of which the building was made. She stretched more, and her hands sank into the solid material.

"Klea!" Mael shouted. "Mistress Santreny! This way you are going—I cannot go that way!"

"Yes you can," Klea said. "Just as a Mage can take an Adept into the Void. Take hold of me, and let me take you where you cannot pass."

"Meaning no disrespect," Mael said, and stepped behind her, putting his arms gently around her, trying not to touch her more than necessary.

"You'll have to hold me tighter than that," Klea said. "You won't be the first, or the rudest."

His arms tightened around her waist, and she stepped through.

Jens looked back. His lead would never be greater than it was right now. If he could just find a soft place on the left-hand side near a cross street, he might be able to make a clean getaway. Then find a ship, and get off planet. Faral could help with that, if he could just get to Faral.

I've done what I was supposed to do—been presented as the Highest of Khesat. What I do next is my problem.

He nudged the control yoke with his right knee in order to drift left and stay in the street. No good crashing, not unstrapped as he was. Having avoided an official sudden impact already this morning, he had no desire to try an impromptu one against a building.

A little park was coming up on his left. The wind through the opening where the door had been torn off howled and whipped at his hair. Jens spotted a connecting road leading off to the right. Opposite that point, in the park, he didn't see any trees, just some shrubs and a grassy slope. He counted to himself, checking his speed, trying to figure out where he'd have to turn, and where he was most likely to land.

The gap between where he was and where he wanted to be decreased. He knocked the vehicle a little to the left, so that it was halfway out of the roadway and skimming by the springy bushes.

Here. This is the place.

He smashed up with his left knee and down with his right shoulder, whipping the hovercar over to the right.

It started to go, skidding sideways on its frictionless nullgravs while the side and rear thrusters labored to straighten and start the vehicle on its new path. This time, when centrifugal force hit him, Jens went limp and allowed himself to be thrown clear.

The thin stalks of the bushes caught and slowed him—though they hurt, hitting at this speed. Then he was through them and rolling down the hill, burning off more of his momentum as he went. He slowed, then stopped. His arms and wrists, caught in the binders, pained him exquisitely. He hadn't had time to think about them until now.

He lurched and scrambled to his feet, and found he was standing before a little group of schoolchildren, together with their teacher, sitting around a cloth spread with delicacies. They all had telescopes and binoculars—it seemed that he'd stumbled into a breakfast picnic to observe the events at the Golden Tower from afar. The children were all gazing at him with large eyes.

Jens smiled at them and bowed.

One little girl began to applaud, then all the others joined in.

"Thank you, thank you," Jens said. "Performance art is my life. You're too kind. Now, alas, I must go."

With another bow, he set out across the springy turf, the applause of his little audience following him.

"I'd hate to have to do that every day, twice a day, and three times on matinee days," Jens muttered as soon as he was out of earshot.

"No," said a voice to his right. "But the time comes when I need your help."

Jens looked toward the voice. His new companion was the man in black with whom he'd been conversing all his life, and who had manifested himself so thoroughly on Sapne . . . and who had left without farewell when Miza named him.

"Guislen," Jens said. "Or do I call you Master Ransome?"

"Either, I suppose," Guislen said. "But I prefer the former.

There is another who bears the name of Ransome—I must meet him today and carry out my last commission."

"And what is that?"

Guislen looked sorrowful. "To put to right the evil that I have done. Most of that I have accomplished, but part still remains unfinished. And that requires . . . but I have no right to ask."

"You have that right," Jens said. "You've earned it, as far as I'm concerned. Where shall we go?"

"To the Khesatan Guildhouse," Guislen said. "For I am already there, and I fear that I am up to no good."

XX. Khesat

Y OU!" FARAL said to Gerre Hafelsan. "You arranged all this."

Before Hafelsan could reply, the door of the room sprang open, kicked wide by a green-scaled, shoeless foot.

Faral stared. *Chaka! What are you doing on Khesat?*

Saving your life, I think, Chaka said. *These people are all double-crossers, every one of them.*

"What did the absurd creature say?" asked Caridal Fere.

"It doesn't matter," said Hafelsan. "When the next Highest is proclaimed, I will be here to rejoice in his elevation—and you will not. Caridal Fere, I challenge you for this house and all that it contains."

Faral expected the Master of Nalensey to laugh aloud at the unexpected and tasteless witticism—but he did not. He held up his hands, and something appeared between them that had not been visible a moment before.

An Adept's staff.

"This is the Guildhouse of the Adepts of Khesat, as it has

been since time immemorial," Fere said. "And I am their Master."

"No," Hafelsan said. A glowing rod of light appeared in his hand as the sky outside the window darkened. "You were."

Mael experienced a feeling of motion without moving, then the sound and sensation of rain striking against the hard plastic of his mask.

He opened his eyes and looked around. He stood with Mistress Klea Santreny on a wide plain, the ground made of jumbled rock, tossed and broken. It was night, and pale moonlight glowed past the edges of hurrying clouds. A wind, sharp and chill, swept past, whipping his robes about him.

"What is this place?" he asked.

"The other side of the wall," Klea said. "Where that is, I don't know."

"Is it a vision?"

"Oh, no," Klea said. "The ways of Adepts are not yours. What you see is real."

"Perhaps," Mael said, "some of my reality is here, too." He looked about him with his inner sight, trying to find the cords of life. *No wonder Adepts speak of riding the winds and currents of power,* he thought. *Is this how they see everything, as nothing but chaos?*

The cords of life were there, dim in the darkness. More than the night obscured them—they were all tarnished and black.

"I think we're close to the source of the evil," he said.

"The source, or the cause?" Klea asked. "It's cold here. Let's get walking, and see where we come to."

"If we come to anywhere."

"We must," Klea said. "The universe won't allow it to happen otherwise."

"I'd like to summon a light," Mael said, "but I'm worried about what might notice us."

"Don't concern yourself about that," Klea said. "I see a city's glow up ahead. If the Adepts of Khesat are here at all, that's where we'll find them."

"I don't like the looks of this place," Mael said. "The lines of life and luck are the worst I've ever seen. There is no pattern. . . ."

As he spoke, a mighty rumbling sounded from under the ground, and a tremblor moved the rock beneath their feet.

Klea cried out and fell against Mael as the ground shifted. She tried to straighten, using her staff for balance, but the ground shifted again and she went down, striking her head against the jagged rock as she fell.

Mael bent over her. Dark against her pale face, blood trickled across her forehead, and she did not move.

The earth shifted again, and there, at last, Mael saw the pattern he had sought: the cable of *eiran* rising out of the earth, a few strands still showing bright amid the tarnish.

Klea moaned and tried to move.

"Lie still" Mael said. "I think we have found what we came to find."

Kolpag kept the speeding hovercar in view ahead of him. He'd have to be careful of this one. The young man had proved to be far more capable than Kolpag had given him credit for.

Now that his first flash of anger was over, Kolpag felt only a grim determination. He drove, pushing the hovercar as fast as he considered safe, while at the same time thumbing his blaster down from kill to stun. The boy was coming along to Ophel whether he wanted to or not, and Kolpag would worry about Ruhn later. The silly bastard hadn't been worth much anyway.

The hovercar up ahead was steering erratically, and starting to veer off the road. That wasn't surprising; given that the boy had his hands locked in binders behind his back, it was a wonder he'd been driving at all. Kolpag dropped back a bit to stay clear of the inevitable crash. Then the car ahead swung rapidly to the right, and flashed up out of sight between a pair of buildings.

Side street, thought Kolpag. He'd been swinging wide left so he could make a high-speed turn to the right. *Damn. Well, I know a few tricks too.*

He pushed the yoke in for speed, then twisted it hard right, and at the same time pulled back on the yoke for braking. The vehicle slewed around until it was sliding with its left side forward. When the nose of the hovercar was pointed straight up the side street, Kolpag shoved the yoke all the way in, and scooted forward. It was as close to a square turn at speed as anyone could do and maintain even tenuous control.

He'd gained on the boy, too. The lead hovercar was up ahead, going down the street but tending to the right. Kolpag saw it drift over until it hit a tree growing from a cutout in the sidewalk. Then it spun to its left and skidded all the way across the street to smash into a building.

The careering hovercar spun again and went forward the way it had been going, but even more erratically. Finally it came to rest half on, half off the pedestrian walkway as its nullgravs cut out in response to the impacts. The thrusters were still going, making the vehicle tremble and try to inch along the pavement.

Kolpag got from his car and walked over to the wreck. He looked in. No one was inside.

"The bastard," he said. "The bastard!" He pounded both fists on the front of the hovercar, still holding his blaster in one hand.

Then he straightened. Where could the boy have gone?

Kolpag turned and walked back down the street. At the moment the boy's car had made the turn he'd still been aboard, controlling. By the time the car came to rest, he was gone. So somewhere between the one point and the other, he had to be located.

Kolpag came to a thicket of bushes. The bruised leaves from where the car had sideswiped showed white from their exposed undersides. And there—a broken gap. Big enough for a body to have gone past. Kolpag pushed his way through the broken foliage. A steep hill on the other side, covered with wiry grass, led to a valley. The package wasn't there.

This snatch was botched. Kolpag returned to his hovercar, pushing through the crowd of onlookers at the scene of the wreck, got into his vehicle, and drove away.

* * *

Mael Taleion made Klea as comfortable as he could, wrapping his outer robe about her and settling her staff into her hands.

"Wait here," he said. "I'll be back."

Then he stood, the black mask on his face, the silver-bound staff in his hand, and opened himself to the universe.

The *eiran* came to him, glowing silver against the dark sky. Wind whipped his hair, but Mael did not notice. Skyglow from the city lit the bottoms of the clouds. The rain fell harder.

Mael grasped the lines and pulled them, trying to reach the center of the great cable. A cord there would be corroded, decayed to nothingness, its shape defined only by the other cords which lay so tight about it. A negative space, the lack of something rather than its presence, like the hollow where a clinging vine had choked the tree it climbed. He pulled harder.

The light grew along the horizon, splitting the sky from the ground. Mael knew that he had to find the rotted cord. It tarnished everything that touched it, and it passed the corruption on. Already the tarnish had spread farther than he had imagined it could, out to the limits of his sight.

"I've found you! I know you're somewhere close!" Mael cried aloud as he dragged on first one cord then another. But instead of loosening the knot his actions only drew it tighter.

The frustration was grinding on his soul. He searched back and forth along the great looping cable of lines, trying to find a more open place. Everywhere the tarnished silver cords opposed him. Still he pulled and prodded, seeking a weak place among the cords that guarded the decayed center.

Then he became aware of another figure approaching him through the dark and the rain.

"Klea?" he called.

"No," came back a mocking voice. "The wench was mine, and I have made her mine."

"No!"

"Then see!" The newcomer held aloft a staff such as Klea had carried. "Do you recognize this?"

The staff glowed at once in blue-green, Klea's color. The light washed down from the staff across the face of the newcomer. In its lurid glare, Mael saw that this was his *ekkannikh*, not robed and hooded as before, but in plain shirt and trousers like an ordinary man. Ordinary—but the face was a sink of corruption, ruined cartilage and quivering jellies of rotten flesh hanging in tatters from the skull.

"When does an Adept part with her staff?" the *ekkannikh* asked. "When she is dead!"

And with that word he broke the staff between his hands. The fire of the universe glowed brighter in its center, then flowed away in rags and tatters, while some of it ran down the *ekkannikh*'s arms to pool around its feet.

"Who speaks of death? The dead?" Mael raised his staff and let light pour into it. "Speak to me of death, you who are already gone?"

The solidified mass of tarnished cords beside Mael began to sway, as if the wind had taken them and made them vibrate.

"I died unbroken, my will prevailing," the *ekkannikh* said. "Such a fate will escape you; you will break before you die."

Beside the *ekkannikh* a rod sprang from the ground. When the rod had grown as high as a man's head, the creature seized it, and it became a staff, blazing up white and dazzling. Mael had to turn his face aside to protect his eyes from the glare. The tarnished silver of the *eiran* glowed in reflected light as if they were once more pure.

At that moment the *ekkannikh* attacked.

Mael sensed the blow aimed for him more than he saw it. He punched the side of his staff up and to the left, diverting the lashing blow and making it slide harmlessly past him. The staves shivered under the impact—this was no insubstantial illusion that he faced, nor a mere phantom of ill-will. This was a physical presence bent on his destruction.

"I have gained strength in my travels," the *ekkannikh* said. "And allies."

From out of the dark came a large man, dressed as a Khesatan noble. He walked up to the *ekkannikh* and grasped hold of it. The two bodies merged, flowing into one another, the form of one and the substance of the other, until they became a man of middle years, a slight, dark-haired man dressed in dusty black. The decay was gone from his face.

"I grow, I am one," the spirit said. "I am the greater."

"You fight like an Adept," Mael said. "Come with me to the Void."

He turned the peculiar corner which always before had brought him to the land of no-space and no-time, where he might be able to take the *ekkannikh* to the time and place of its first death. If he could kill it properly there . . .

"That way is blocked to you," the *ekkannikh* said, and Mael found that he was unable to move, that the road was truly closed.

The staff of the *ekkannikh* crashed onto his back across his shoulder blades, lacing him with a burning agony. He stumbled and fell forward against the tarnished silver lines.

Jens and Guislen had almost reached the edge of the park. Up a rise, across the roofs of some buildings, they could see the Golden Tower sparkling in the sun.

"I hadn't thought to meet you again," Jens said. "I thought that once named, you were gone forever."

"Not yet," Guislen said. "There is still work for me to do. Shall I take those binders off of you?"

"I'd been under the impression that you couldn't do . . . well . . . physical things."

"Nor can I," said Guislen with a smile. "But you can. Are you aware of the binders?"

Jens grimaced. Now that he was free to think about the restraints that clipped his wrists tightly behind him, he seemed to feel every molecule as a separate source of pain. "Only too aware."

"Good. Try to touch their nature. Know how they hold you. Find the mechanism. Follow the circuits, watch the electrons flow within them. When you understand them, you will be free of them."

Jens concentrated for a moment as they walked, but nothing out of the ordinary occurred.

"Let me help," Guislen said. "Concentrate again. Or, if concentration doesn't bring results, relax and let your mind be empty of all preconceptions about the nature of locks."

Then, as with the hatch of the *Inner Light* on Sapne, Jens became aware of the inner nature of the lock's materials. He knew the bolt, the catch, the magnet that held them in place, and the lines of flux that wrapped around them.

He touched the lock with that awareness, and the binders clicked open and fell away. Jens brought his hands in front of him and looked down. Angry red lines circled his wrists. He massaged them while he spoke to Guislen.

"Did you do that, or did I?"

"You did it. With some help."

"Am I an Adept, then?"

"You have the talent. But I told you a long while ago that you were meant to be neither Adept nor Mage. Come—we are almost at the Guildhouse, and time grows short."

They came out of the park and crossed a street. Around the corner and under a pointed arch, an alley led up to a set of wide stone steps between two buildings.

"I recall this," Jens said. "It's not the Guildhouse. It's the way to the house of Caridal Fere, the Master of Nalensey."

"The Guildhouse and the house of Caridal Fere are the same place," Guislen told him. "Master Fere has decided to seek temporal power for the Adepts of this world, and to rule its rulers. From here our ways part for the last time. Your task is great, but mine is urgent. Farewell."

"Farewell," Jens said, but he was speaking to no one. Guislen was gone.

Jens turned, and walked up the stairs toward the upper entrance of the house of Caridal Fere.

"Freeze right there," came a man's voice behind him. Jens recognized the Ophelan slur to the words. "Don't turn around. Very slowly, walk back this way."

"Why, that sounds like my good friend Kolpag," Jens said. "What brings you here?"

"Shut up. You've cost me too much time and trouble. Keep walking back."

From the sound, Jens could tell that Kolpag was keeping well out of range of a kick. And if Jens turned, he'd only buy himself a stun, or worse.

He reached up to touch the amulet he had worn since Sapne. In spite of the morning's adventures, it still lay against his chest. Perhaps it worked, perhaps not, but he'd had a great deal of luck lately. He grasped the amulet.

Luck, he thought. *She gave me luck for a reason.*

If he could get some of that luck now . . . the amulet broke from its cord and fell to the pavement in a tinkle of tiny shards. Without thinking, Jens bent forward to pick it up. A blaster bolt sizzled above his back, inches above his spine.

He really is shooting at me, Jens thought. *So why am I still alive?*

On the heels of the thought came the sound of a body falling to the pavement behind him. Jens straightened and looked around. Kolpag lay on his back partway up the marble stairway. Then Jens turned again and looked forward.

An elderly woman stood there, dressed like a midclass Khesatan matron on a holiday. She held a blaster in both hands. To Jen's surprise, he knew her.

"You're Tillijen—Gentlelady Blossom from the tea shop!"

The woman nodded. "And Armsmaster to House Rosselin. Took you long enough to move out of my way so I could get a clear shot."

Jens went over to where Kolpag lay on the shallow steps with his head lower than his heels. The blaster-man was dead, his forehead marked with an ugly hole surrounded by seared flesh. Jens reached down and pulled the weapon from the man's hand.

"Looks like I'm going to make a career of stealing blasters off of dead bodies," he said. He straightened and spoke to Blossom. "Do you know where my cousin is?"

"Somewhere inside, I presume," she said.

"Is your partner here too?"

"Bindweed's gone around to the front."

"Well, I'm going in myself. Please tell her not to shoot me on the way out. I don't want to ruin a perfect day."

Then Jens looked down. The luck amulet lay on the pavement, cracked and broken, shattered by its fall.

"Good thing the Adepts say that luck isn't real," he said. "Otherwise, I'd have to start worrying."

With that he walked forward, past Blossom and into the house of Caridal Fere.

Mael had lost his staff when he fell. He pulled himself to his feet, grabbing the woven cable of silver cord and using it to pull himself away from the blows of the *ekkannikh*.

Ahead of him Mael could see the strands flying out from the end of the cable, like a rope unlaying. At the cable's end stood another figure like the one who still pursued him. Its staff was also a glowing white—and by that glow, Mael saw that its face was a younger twin to that of the creature who followed him.

Mael felt himself begin to despair. He was trapped between the two phantoms, the cords of life all around him tangled, their right order gone, with the tarnish spreading in all directions and shooting off into the night.

The wind sang among the wires.

Mael stopped, and leaned his forehead against the cable. This was the end-point of his vision. No time now to arrange the cords into the pleasing pattern that he knew was required. No place to run.

He lifted his head to look at his approaching foes with pain-dimmed eyes, then turned to the mass of jumbled cords. With bare hands he grabbed them, seeking the rot at the center to pull it forth and expose it.

"I will be found doing my duty," he repeated to himself. "I will be found doing my duty."

The light approached him from either side. In the combined glow of the staves, he could see the *eiran* cords, his hands small and weak beside the great cable. To what arrogance did he owe his belief that he could change this and make it right? All was lost.

Then the phantom that had awaited him spoke—not to him, but to its elder double.

"We met once before, on Sapne. You did not face me then—but now you must."

"Have it as you will," said *ekkannikh*, and struck the first blow, not at Mael but at the newcomer.

Mael watched them for a while as they fought. The glowing staves wove and plunged, while the crack of wood on wood was like a drumroll, rhythmic and steady.

Then Mael turned away and began struggling once again to find the place where the great cable unlaid, sending its tarnished strands out into the universe, flying up beyond sight into the dark sky. A gap in the cords appeared, and he could see almost to the cable's inner core.

He pushed on farther, though he was torn and scratched by the contact. Daring to grasp the essence of life and luck, that was what wounded men. . . . There was the inmost, the final strand. Mael could hardly see it. It was lost in its own darkness, as if it sucked in the light.

He reached out and grasped the deepest strand. It felt hot to his touch, hot and burning. The pain spread up his arm to his shoulder. He would not let go. He pulled harder. Two of the inner cords shifted slightly. Behind him, as he worked, he still heard the noises of combat—the clash of staves and the thud of wood against flesh.

"I must break you," said one voice; and—"You shall not," said the other.

Mael pulled again. Some of the inner, flexible, rotten cord broke free and slithered toward him. He fell backward, but kept his grip on the burning silver wire. The cord followed him. He seized it with both hands and pulled again. The pain was excruciating, but more of the cords came free. Perhaps it was a trick of the unsteady light from the moving staves behind him, but the *eiran* seemed to be less tarnished than before.

Faster and faster the cords unwound. The rotted cord piled

up at Mael's feet, and still he pulled. His wounded back throbbed with every effort, but he didn't dare let go.

"They're both insane," said Rhal Kasander, drifting toward where Faral and Miza stood. Miza moved closer to Faral, and without needing to think about it, Faral put an arm around her. "You're off-worlders," Kasander added, "but at least I know what you are."

Chaka growled under her breath.

I wouldn't, Faral said. To Kasander he said, "My friend tells me that she took the weapon she's holding from the cold dead fingers of the person you sent to kill her. She wants to know if you prefer the blaster shoved down your throat or up your ass."

"This creature is your friend?"

"Friend, agemate, neighbor, all that. We grew up together. Never expected her to show up here, though."

"Please be so good as to inform your agemate that any attempt to kill her was not by my command."

Chaka replied, and again Faral translated, "You're still a mannerless thin-skin who spies on his guests."

"All that, I do confess," Kasander said. "Now can we please take this opportunity to decamp?"

"No," said Faral. "If it wasn't you that screwed up bribing the crowd—"

Kasander shook his head. "No, no . . . I was as shocked as you."

"—then either Fere or Hafelsan set up Jens to get thrown off the Golden Tower. Now I want to watch the two of them try to kill each other."

In the center of the room, the combat had already begun. Even to Faral's eyes, it was clear from the very beginning that the Master of Nalensey was overmatched. Fere's every move was anticipated and blocked, while Hafelsan—moving lightly in spite of his greater bulk—toyed with him, touching him here and there, light taps, as if to say, "I could kill you at any time, but I choose not to."

Caridal Fere was getting pushed back, away from the window, toward the center of the room. His arms brought his staff up more and more slowly with every block and strike. A predatory smile came to the face of his opponent.

Then Hafelsan paused and looked aside—at what, no one could tell. In that instant, Caridal Fere seized the opportunity and struck, spearing his staff into the other's midsection. But Hafelsan did not collapse. Instead, he split in two. For a moment Faral saw a dreadful vision of a skeletal figure covered in a black cloak and scraps of rotten flesh, standing between two layers of skin covered with morning-robes.

Then the revenant vanished, taking his staff with him. On the floor, in a puddle of disgusting fluid, lay only an empty skin.

The cords were unlaying faster and faster from the woven cable. And faster and faster, Mael pulled in the flawed cord that he held in his hands.

And still, behind him, the Adepts fought, in a blaze of light and a clash of staves. When Mael looked in the direction of the combat, he saw that one of the two phantoms now had a clear advantage—he was driving the other one back, attacking while his counterpart was forced to defend.

In the distance beyond the combatants, Mael saw another figure approaching.

Who now? he thought. *What chance is this?*

Then he saw: it was Mistress Santreny, and she had her staff. Another of the walking dead? He feared it. These Adepts were a cursed race.

But while he had gazed even that briefly into the distance, the fight closer to hand had ended. The Adept who had waited for Mael's approach was the victor, and the *ekkannikh* was beaten to the ground. It knelt there, head hanging, its breath coming in ragged gasps.

"Yield," the Adept said. "We are one; we must be together."

"I yield," said the *ekkannikh*, and lifted its empty hand.

They made contact, flesh to unliving flesh—and the one began to melt into the other.

Still Klea approached, not seeing the drama before her. The light of the staves flickered out, and the sole illumination came from the lights of the distant city, reflecting from bent grass and hewn stone.

The silver cords were untangling themselves now, pulling away from one another, springing up into the sky or sinking into the earth.

The two phantoms, victor and vanquished, merged fully and became one, looking the same as before—a slight, dark-haired man in black, leaning on an Adept's staff. He raised his face to the sky, and to Mael's eyes his substance seemed to waver and fade.

Then Klea walked unseeing through him, and the vapor that had been his being ascended.

Mael felt very tired. The black cord that had piled around his legs nearly calf-deep was gone, dissolved into mist. He fell to the ground as the last of the *eiran* faded from his sight.

Klea came up to him and helped him to rise up from the dirt.

"Mistress Santrony," he said. "I feared that you were dead."

"No," she said. "Hurt, but no more. Come—let me take us home."

"The revenant has gone," said Caridal Fere, "and I remain. I rule those who rule the world of Khesat."

"I don't think so," said a voice that Faral knew—and his cousin Jens stepped over the threshold with a blaster in his hand.

"Another ghost," Miza said. Her voice trembled. "Jens, I didn't want this to happen."

"It hasn't happened," Jens said. He turned to the Master of Nalensey. "There's only one ghost here, and that's you."

He raised his blaster and shot Caridal Fere, there in his study with the windows overlooking the Plaza of Hope.

"If you're real, let me touch you," Faral said to Jens.

"Oh, I'm real," Jens said. He reached out his hand, the one that didn't hold the blaster, and Faral gripped it hard. Miza was hugging Jens and Faral both, and laughing and sobbing at the same time.

Rhal Kasander came forward, delicately sidestepping the body of Caridal Fere. "Highest," he said to Jens, "command me!"

"I'm not the Highest," Jens said. "They didn't shout 'huz-zah!,' remember?"

"Shouting 'huzzah!' is a minor thing," Kasander said. "The requirement is only that you be presented. You are already Highest at that moment, and—unless you choose to retire—you reign as long as you live thereafter."

"Oh, I may choose to retire," Jens said, "but not just yet. If I *am* the Highest, I have things I need to attend to."

Kasander paled slightly. "What do you mean?"

"I came in response to a message," said Jens, "saying that my parents were in danger here. Everything—the Presentation, the Tower, all of it—comes from that. And I will find out what happened to them if it takes the land, the sea, and the sky to do it."

"You don't need to go that far." If Kasander had gone pale before, he was pink with embarrassment now. "I sent the message to secure your presence here, as a Worthy, for the changing of the rule—it cost me a pretty sum to get the codes, I'll have you know. I wouldn't have dared to do it at all if your mother and father had actually been within a sector of Khesat."

"Do you mean," said Jens, "that I went through all of this for nothing?"

"Not exactly," said Kasander. "You *are* the Highest now, after all—that should count for quite a bit."

Jens stared at him for a moment longer, then laughed and shook his head. "I suppose it does," he said. "If I'm the Highest, then where do we go next?"

"To my town house," Rhal said. "I've got dozens of invitations to your Acclamatory ball all written out. I promise you, the celebrations will go on for days."

Epilogue
Maraghai

THE HIGHEST of Khesat had come to Maraghai. His security guards, his personal staff, and even the elderly nobleman of exceedingly Worthy Lineage who claimed the courtesy title of Hereditary Slipper-Bearer, discovered—too late for effective protest—that the Selvauran rulers of the planet would allow none of them closer to the surface than the nearspace docking station.

They protested, vigorously, but the Highest merely looked amused. He divested himself of his jewel-encrusted travel coat, purchased with his own hands a cheap quilted jacket from a station-based clothes vendor, and borrowed a knife from one of the security guards "in case of rufstaffas on the way." Then he presented his passport—not the Khesatan one, which was written in purple ink on tablets of gold and ivory, but a common plastic affair with lettering in the local script—to the Selvauran immigration clerk.

With much chortling and hooting, the clerk accepted the passport and fed it through the reader. The Highest accepted the stamped and returned passport with a laughing comment in one of the local dialects. Tucking it into his pocket, he bowed a smiling farewell to his entourage.

"Entertain yourselves until I get back," he told them, and disappeared through the blastproof door to the shuttle bay.

In the South Continent High Ridges the season was midwinter, the time of the Year's Turn. The quilted jacket that Jens had bought on the docking station was of local make and designed for the weather. What it lacked in elegance it made up for in padding and interlining that kept him warm in spite of the falling snow.

He had chosen to walk from the last stop on the hoverbus line, rather than renting an aircar in Ernalghan, in order to spend as much of his stolen time as possible among familiar landscapes. When at last he reached the final uphill trail, the sky had long since grown dark. A cover of thick snow lay over everything, bending down the lower branches of the great trees and muffling all sound except the sighing wind. No rufstaffas or other predators stalked the home woods tonight, and the borrowed knife he wore at his belt remained unused.

Drifted snow obscured the path, and the snow on the trees hid many of the marks and blazes that pointed out the trail. But his feet still remembered the way; and ahead, at last, he saw the lighted windows of the house in the woods, all bright yellow and welcoming.

He walked up to the house and mounted the steps. He hadn't yet reached the door when a giant burst outward onto the veranda, swept him into his arms, and whirled him into the air.

"Jens! It's good to see you," said Ari Rosselin-Metadi, his voice a deep rumble. "We were afraid you wouldn't be able to come."

"Let me breathe a minute," Jens said, laughing, as he regained his feet. "I told Aunt Llann that I'd be here if I could arrange it. As it happens, the Highest of Khesat can arrange quite a bit if he feels like it—and I did."

"Come inside, then, and be welcome," said Ari, kicking

open the door and pulling him into the immense, high-raftered reception room. "We're in the small room, in back.... Llannat! Faral! Jens is home!"

They hurried through the great room, which was as tall and echoing as Jens remembered it, and large enough to entertain most of Ari's Selvauran relatives at once. From there they went into the informal family hall behind it.

The family hall was a cozier place altogether, a big room with one wall made of glass and another wall mostly fireplace. Chairs and benches and piles of cushions were scattered here and there across the floor. A warm light came from candles and from low-power amber glows, and from the orange-yellow flames on the hearth. Jens's nostrils prickled with the familiar Year's Turn smells of mulled wine and hot berry-cider and aromatic wood.

As soon as he entered, he was clasped in more embraces, first from his Aunt Llann and then from Beka Rosselin-Metadi, and from her husband.

"Mamma!" Jens said, still somewhat breathless, as he returned the hugs. "It's high time you and Dadda decided to reappear ... where *were* you, anyway, while I was racketing all over the galaxy thinking you were locked up in a cell somewhere?"

His parents looked at each other. "Hiding," his mother said. "People started to sidle up to your father at parties and say things like, 'trifling questions of eligibility can be ... dealt with'; so we decided that it was time to go check out some urgent security breaches in the Accardi Sector."

"And left me holding the bag," said Jens, taking a seat on one of the piles of cushions near the fire. "I like that, I do."

"You can always quit the job," said his mother. "I did. And threw the Iron Crown of Entibor out of the airlock into deep space afterward."

"An inspiration to all of us," murmured Jens, "but I think I'm getting accustomed to the work."

The conversation turned to other things as the evening wore on—in between wine and cider, and roasted fruit, and other traditional Year's Turn delicacies. The family gathering this year was made even larger by the added presence of Owen Rosselin-Metadi, who in the past had only sent Aunt Llann the traditional greetings and his apologies, and of Owen's trusted right hand, Mistress Klea Santreny. Another unexpected guest was Mael Taleion. The Second of the Prime Circle had recovered by now from his struggle to put right the life and luck of Khesat—and his newfound closeness to Klea Santreny appeared to be puzzling the Master of the Adepts' Guild considerably.

An interesting set of relationships, thought Jens. *Even money which one wins, I think. But it should be amusing to watch.*

All the Hyfid-Metadi siblings were there—Kei and Dortan and 'Rada-the-brat, and Faral home from studying with Gentlesir Huool on Ophel. He had Mizady Lyftingil with him; the pair of them were sitting close together on one of the high-backed benches.

"How's life treating all of you in Sombrelír, coz?" Jens asked.

"Well enough," Faral said. "Chaka's apprenticed on board the *Dusty*—she liked the taste of free-spacing she got there, and I think she plans to own a ship of her own some day. And Huool gets enough work out of me, one way and another, to keep me from getting bored. I'm not as famous as the Highest of Khesat yet, but give me and Miza time."

"Any more trouble from the Green Sun?"

Miza looked amused. "They're very quiet and well behaved whenever the subject comes up. But they aren't taking political commissions much these days at all. I think our friends Bindweed and Blossom had a few words with the boss-man after they got back from Khesat."

"Good," said Jens. "We've been asking questions on Khesat along those same lines, trying to figure out who paid whom for what. My cousin-once-removed the Exalted of Tanavral admits to sending me the false message as a lure—he doesn't say anything about hiring the Green Sun, but all the trails lead that way, so I expect that he's guilty."

"No," said Faral. "That was Gerre Hafelsan, before

Ransome got to him. He wanted to deprive the Exalted of Tanavral of his prize Worthy. Then the Adepts on Khesat got word of what was going on—not hard to do, since Caridal Fere was the Exalted's fellow-conspirator—and removed a lot of the background data from the Green Sun's intelligence files in the hopes that they'd fumble the snatch, and maybe even get the two of us killed in the crossfire."

"Huool gave Faral a B-plus for that analysis," Miza said proudly.

Jens raised an eyebrow. "Only a B-plus?"

"I skimped on the footnotes," Faral admitted. "Sorry."

"Kasander would have wanted one of the Jessani for a Worthy," said Jens's father. "Ideally, one whom nobody would actually pick as a candidate for presentation—just so that his faction could derive prestige from convincing one of us to make the attempt. And our branch of the family, I greatly fear, is thought of on Khesat as sadly unstable."

"You worked hard on that impression for years," Beka Rosselin-Metadi said. "It had to convince someone eventually."

"*I* want to know what the Khesatan Adepts thought they were doing," said Llannat. "Staying out of local politics has been a Guild rule for as long as I can remember."

"And I," said Owen. "Which was part of the problem, I think. Errec Ransome—whatever else he did—put a stop to that sort of thing most places. It was the Guild for the Guild alone, with him. Those of us who grew up under his rules forgot that things had ever been otherwise."

"Khesat was one of the places where they were otherwise," Jens told him. "Very much otherwise, apparently; I've read my predecessors' journals. The Khesatan Adepts gave up local politics when Errec Ransome reformed the Guild after the First Magewar—or at least they said that they did. What we're finding out now is that they merely changed their act on the surface and kept all their old bad habits underneath.

"So Caridal Fere—acting as the Master of the local Guild—made certain that the Green Sun on Ophel was hindered in its kidnapping attempts, and bribed the crowd in

Ilsefret to reject me at the Acclamation. And it was Caridal Fere and the Khesatan Adepts who killed my predecessor, instead of letting the poor man retire in good time."

"They were afraid he'd support your candidacy if they let him live," said Miza. "You *were* related to him, after all— even if your branch of the family isn't respectable. So he had to die, and you had to be put out of the running, as soon as possible."

"And letting the Council of Worthies regretfully decide that I wouldn't be suitable wasn't good enough for them." Jens shook his head. "I don't know why—I certainly never had any quarrel with the Khesatan Guild. Not before now."

"I think," said Miza, "that the Khesatan Adepts were afraid of you, even as a candidate not seriously intended for presentation. They didn't want you or any other member of your family coming anywhere near the contest. You're too well known and well connected outside of Khesat's own sphere of influence, you're far too close to the Guild Master and the First—and face it, exciting times follow your family around like a stray pet looking for a home."

"Enough talk of troubles past," said Mael Taleion. "On Eraasi, this would be the season to speak of new beginnings, and to offer peace to those who are gone."

He poured mulled wine and berry-cider for all present, even the young ones, and raised his cup to his lips. A moment before drinking, he poured a splash onto the floor.

"For all the spirits who still seek rest," he said, like a benediction. "An old age is ending; a new age begins. May it bring good fortune to the Republic and the Homeworlds both."

"Good fortune," Jens echoed him—and the Highest of Khesat spilled a drop of wine, and drank.